Stormfront

Stormfront

BOOK ONE OF THE STORMSONG TRILOGY

STEPHEN A. REGER

outskirts press

For Mrs. Midolo and Mr. Bohardt, who taught me how to write,
And for my beautiful wife, Amy, who taught me how to live.

Author's Note

Legend is often truer than history and always more interesting.

-anonymous

Everything you've ever been told about history is a lie. All of the history that you *learned* from kindergarten to college has been a carefully crafted series of falsehoods and fabrications designed to keep you from knowing the truth. I should know. For more than three decades, I was a teacher of history (American, European, World), and during that time I was an accomplice (before and during the fact) to a vast conspiracy to shield you from the truth – and the truth is far different from what you thought you knew. In fact, the role of the spiritual, supernatural, and (dare I say) magical, has always been far more prevalent in and pivotal to history than you've ever been taught.

But I am retired now, and I intend to use whatever time I have left on this mortal coil we call Earth, destroying the intricately woven web of deceit that I helped build. I'm going to peel back the curtain, as it were, and reveal to you the far more interesting, infinitely more complex and chaotic, and (at times) terrifying truth about who we are and how we got here.

I begin in the Holy Roman Empire, during the seventeenth century, with the strange but true tale of what really happened during the so-called Thirty Years' War. Prepare to be illuminated and incensed that this was all kept from you for so long.

Prologue

Between 1154 and 1184, eager to restore the Holy Roman Empire to the position it had once occupied under Charlemagne, Frederick Barbarossa (also known as Frederick I) launched six different campaigns into Italy. History has recorded that those campaigns, combined with his participation in the Third Crusade (1189-1192), were Barbarossa's attempts to expand the size and influence of the Holy Roman Empire, reconquer the Holy Land following Sultan Saladin's capture of Jerusalem in 1187, and restore law and order to the various and disorganised German states. In reality, however, it was neither land nor riches nor holy relics that Barbarossa was after. In reality, he had come to the conclusion that, hidden within Europe and the Middle East, were scores of "devils and deviants" – practitioners of the dark arts.

Shortly after he was crowned Holy Roman Emperor by Pope Adrian IV on June 18, 1155, Barbarossa, while still in Rome for the coronation, summoned to Saint Peter's Basilica all of the patriarchs of an incredibly powerful (and incredibly secretive) German family – the Stormsongs. At that place and time, Barbarossa granted the Stormsongs hereditary title to an extremely powerful order that would serve as his personal army. The Stormsongs would be rich beyond the dreams of avarice, but they would also be indebted to serve as Barbarossa's "truest protectors of the faith and empire."

And so, it began. For more than 460 years, the Stormsongs faithfully, and quite violently, defended the Catholic Church, the Holy Roman Empire, and the German monarchy against all enemies (real and perceived). But little did Barbarossa know that the same practitioners of the dark arts the Stormsongs were meant to shield his empire from were, in fact, alive and well within the Stormsong family. And by the dawn of the seventeenth century, the order of Stormsongs grew both darker and more powerful, while the Holy Roman Empire they allegedly still served found itself surrounded by powerful enemies – and on the brink of collapse.

Once more we are wholly/ still more than
wholly, laid waste.
The invaders' brazen rabble/ the braying
trumpets' fury,
Swords greasy with gore/ the siege cannons'
thunderous roar
Have all our sweat/ and labour/ and reserves
consumed away.
The towers stand in flame / the church has
keeled over.
The town hall lies in rubble/ the steadfast
are hacked to pieces,
The virgin girls are raped/ and no matter
where we look, we see
Fire, pestilence and death / that pierces heart
and spirit.
Here, through the ramparts and the town/
blood runs, ever fresh.
Three times six years already/ since our
river's waters flow
All but choked in corpses/ ooze on, and slow.
And even then, I am silent still on that/
which bitter more than death,
Harsher than the plague/ and the burning
and starvation:
That even the soul's wealth / from so many
too was forced.

-*Tears of the Homeland,*
1636, Andreas Greif

Part One:

Storm Clouds Gather

Chapter One

Judgement was close at hand.

She could practically smell it – she always could.

Or, perhaps, this time she was confusing it with the odour emanating from the wildlife near the Řeka *Lužnice* (Lainsitz River). Then again, perhaps it was a different form of wildlife – the three men she'd been tracking for the past three days – that she smelled. The hunt for these three had begun just outside of *Hradčany* (Hradschin Castle) in Prague, and it would end here, nearly eighty miles southeast of where it had begun. And God willing, it would end today.

Her name was Vanessa Stormsong, and she was the only child of Archduke Johann Albrecht von Stormsong. Due to her father's peculiar (and geographically nonsensical) obsession with all things nautical, she had been christened twenty-two years earlier as Lady *Atlantis* Vanessa von Stormsong, but she'd never taken to the name Atlantis, and for reasons she had long-since forgotten, had only ever answered to Vanessa. Three days earlier, during an unusually hot May (made even hotter by the political climate of the time), the men she was about to bring to justice had committed an unpardonable sin – and their judgement, as ordered by her father, was now close at hand.

The year was 1618, and for the past six years, ever since the death of Rudolph II (the eldest son of Maximillian II, an emperor who was thought by most, including Archduke von Storm-song, to have been ineffective and obsessed with the occult), *das Heiliges Römisches Reich* (the Holy Roman Empire) had been ruled by Maximillian

II's even less capable second son – Matthias. However, as had been the case for more than eight-hundred years, the true seat of power in Germany, Bohemia, Hungary, Croatia, and Austria had been Vanessa's family, and as so often seemed to be the case, her beloved homeland was surrounded by enemies both within and without. Within, the cancer of Protestantism continued to grow throughout many dark corners of the empire. Without, the increasingly volatile empire was surrounded by enemies in Denmark, Sweden, and, of course, France – where the Bourbons (like the Valois before them) remained a perpetual, and potentially lethal, threat.

But, as Vanessa knew all too well, the true enemy of both her family and the Hapsburg dynasty they so faithfully served was not this so-called reformed religion unleashed upon Europe by that heretic and degenerate Martin Luther; nor was it the growing list of countries which would seek to do the Hapsburgs harm. The real enemy of the Holy Roman Empire, and of the one true, Catholic, and apostolic Church, could best be described as "Satan's servants."

Since the twelfth century, the Stormsongs had been aware of, sought out, and attempted to eliminate what Vanessa's father called "God's mistakes." Vanessa and her father both knew that God was infallible, but they also knew that since the fall of Adam, the children of God had lived in a broken world, and that brokenness had allowed Satan to produce frailty, fragmentation, monstrosity, and followers devoted to his "dark arts." As someone once told her – she could no longer remember who – the garden of Eden was now hopelessly overgrown with weeds and thorns, and it was the duty, honour and obligation of the Stormsongs to eradicate that evil from the garden.

That duty is what had brought Vanessa to *Bechyně* (or *Bechin*, in her native German), a small Bohemian town located on the Řeka *Lužnice*. Whether or not the men currently making camp just outside of the town were "Satan's servants" was irrelevant to Vanessa. Their actions at the recent meeting from which they had fled had revealed their nature – and sealed their fate.

4

The meeting in question had been assembled by Ferdinand of Styria (a cousin to the ageing and childless Emperor Matthias) in an attempt to quell the recent violence that Bohemian Protestants had unleashed in and around the city of Prague. Ferdinand had invited, among others, Heinrich Matthias, *Graf von Thurn* (a Protestant noble and leader of the Bohemian revolt against Emperor Matthias) to the Bohemian Chancellery within *Hradčany*. However, early on the third day of the meeting, any sense of diplomacy and decorum was shattered when von Thurn's servants hurled Counts Vilém Slavata von Chlum and Jaroslav Borita von Martinitz (both devout Catholics and faithful servants to the emperor) and their scribe, Philipp Fabricius, out of a third-floor window.

Vanessa had offered several prayers of thanksgiving to the blessed Virgin Mary when she heard that all three men had survived the seventy-foot fall; and despite the fact that the extraordinary luck which saved their lives was simply a comic accident to some, she knew it was a holy miracle and wondered how anyone could doubt the intercession of the saints upon hearing of this miraculous event. But, regardless of the cause of this fortunate outcome, the infamy of the crime had to be atoned for, and that was why Archduke von Stormsong (whose representatives had been present to witness the infamous affair) had sent Vanessa, who in addition to being his daughter was also his most trusted and capable soldier, on this quest to track down Count von Thurn and his men – a quest which had now arrived at its conclusion.

It was early evening when Vanessa slipped from a copse of trees and silently approached the campsite of the three brigands. She was able to determine almost immediately that von Thurn was not with his men, but that in no way deterred her from what had to come next.

The light was dim and an eerie green as Vanessa approached, and the largest of the three men glanced up, looking past the fire where the three were cooking what looked to be a small rabbit. After making eye contact with Vanessa, the tall man nodded to alert his two companions that they had an unexpected dinner guest, and they all stood slowly to the sound of low thunder in the distance.

The shortest and hairiest of the three took the largest one's cue and, upon standing, instantly unsheathed his sword and turned Vanessa's way. One look at her long, inky black hair, impossibly high cheekbones, full lips which were a shock of red against her pale skin, and piercing blue eyes was all that was needed to arouse his interest, and he was quickly turning his thoughts towards unsheathing a sword of a different kind.

As all three men were fully engaged in imagining what Vanessa might look like beneath her clothing, they were totally oblivious to what she was actually wearing. Her armour was white (both in colour and style), which meant that she came from money. The shimmering blue, mother of pearl inlay on the breastplate, in the shape of a cruciform sword – *das Familienwappen* (family coat of arms) of the Stormsongs – was a second important sign they missed. But, most importantly, the expensive, midnight blue cloak which completely concealed Vanessa's arms and hands also went unnoticed by all three.

"Was ist das?" the short, hairy one asked, ogling her from head to toe. "Are you some kind of woodland fairy? Come from the forest to keep us company, have you?" As the other two laughed, Vanessa quietly knelt. On one knee, she made the sign of the cross and began to whisper.

"Deus meus, ex toto corde paenitet me omnium meorum peccatorum, eaque detestor, quia peccando...."

"She's no fairy," the fat one observed. "She's too tall for that." And he wasn't wrong. At five feet, ten inches, Vanessa was as tall as most men in the Empire, and the two-inch heels of her boots made her taller still.

As if not having heard either man, Vanessa continued *".... non solum poenas a Te iuste statutas promeritus sum, sed praesertim quia offendi Te,......"*

"What the hell is she going on about?" the tall one asked. "Is she touched in the head, you think?"

"She'll be touched in a lot more than her head in a minute," the short, hairy one joked as he ran his grubby hand over his greasy lips.

"And she's already on her knees for us. She's an obliging girl, isn't she?" As the other two laughed, Vanessa continued.

"......*summum bonum, ac dignum qui super omnia diligaris.*"

The fat one pushed past his hairier and shorter companion and withdrew a small dagger. "Come here. Let's get a better look at you. Maybe we'll have two rabbits tonight," he chuckled. As he approached, Vanessa kept her head bowed, but her voice began to rise and take on an edge.

"*Ideo firmiter propono, adiuvante gratia Tua, de cetero me non peccatorum peccandique occasiones proximas fugiturum.*" Finally, as all three men began to slowly make their way towards her, Vanessa's head snapped up, and her piercing eyes seemed to flash with blue lightning. Before any of the three brigands could respond to the pale, raven haired beauty before them, she uttered one final word.

"Amen." With that, she stood, and in one lighting fast motion produced a small, white crossbow from the belt around her slim hips. Having first gained notoriety at the Battle of Hastings in 1066, the crossbow had become a common battlefield weapon and had superseded longbows in many European armies during the twelfth century. However, because of their weight, the cost required to pro-duce them, and the arduously slow process required to reload them, by the late fifteenth century, crossbows had fallen out of favour and had begun to be replaced by gunpowder weapons like the arquebus.

For Vanessa, however, cost was no object, and her bow was as unusual as it was expensive. It was a repeating crossbow that fed from a top mounted magazine, which allowed gravity to help push the bolts towards the barrel. In addition to being able to fire mul-tiple bolts before having to be reloaded, her bow was unique in that it had been made from blond ash, making it much lighter in both colour and weight than a traditional arbalest. As a result, she was able to wield it with tremendous speed, and the three men scarcely had time to blink as she aimed and discharged the weapon multiple times.

With a force that belied the size of the small weapons, three six-teen-inch metal bolts leapt from the bow, the first catching the short, hairy man directly in the left eye, the second and third striking the fat one and cutting through the shoulder plate of his iron corselet, knocking him to the ground.

As the two wounded men fell, convulsing in agony, the large, un-harmed one produced a massive, two-handed sword (appropriately called a *Zweihänder)* and growled at Vanessa. As he did, she calmly but quickly produced her own sword – a Tuck with a long, slim, but sturdy blade. The blade and the hilt were both forged from steel and had a hand-rubbed finish that gave it a satin lustre. Impossibly, the entire sword appeared to be snow white, and it appeared to flash like lightning as Vanessa raised it into a defensive posture.

Stunned by the beauty of the blade, and of the swordswoman wielding it, and further taken aback by the nimble grace with which Vanessa brandished the weapon, the growling giant took an uncer-tain step backwards. By now, the screams of the short man had faded into a sort of wet gurgling sound, but the fat one was slowly regaining his composure and attempting to make it back to his feet.

"What are you?" the large one demanded. "And what does you want?" he added, while dancing back and forth from one foot to the other in a nervous fashion that gave away his total lack of confi-dence in dealing with the situation before him.

"I am a simple messenger from God," replied Vanessa. "And I am here to see that His will be done." With that Vanessa confidently strode toward the large man and began, once again, to whisper.

"Pater noster qui es in coelis, sanctificetur nomen tuum, adve-niat regnum tuum, fiat voluntas tua......"

With that, as she anticipated he would, the large man lunged forward and struck a blow that, had it landed, would have cleaved Vanessa in two, from head to toe. But it did not land. Instead, Vanessa gracefully avoided the clumsy strike by sidestepping to her left, and, as she did, she used her right hand to slip her sword into the stomach of the awkward, lunging attacker. With practised skill, she managed to avoid striking her opponent's ribs; however, the same could not be said for the man's vital organs, pieces of which were pushed through to the exit wound on his back.

As she stared into the wide-open eyes of the shocked brute, she whispered in his left ear. *"Sicut in caelo et in terra. Panem nostrum quotidianum da nobis hodie, et dimitte nobis debita nostra, sicut et nos dimittimus debitoribus nostris."*

Slowly easing her blade back out of the man, she barely acknowledged either his weight or his moan as he leaned against her shoulder and slipped to the ground.

By now, the third man had completely regained his feet and started to back away from Vanessa. "Who are you?" he demanded again. "Why are you doing this?" As he backpedalled, he struck up against a nearby tree and attempted to raise his weapon. Vanessa, however, was too fast. She was on him as quickly as she had struck the other blows and, switching from Latin to her native tongue, said *"Und führe uns nicht in Versuchung, sondern erlöse uns vom Bösen."* (And lead us not into temptation, but deliver us from evil.) With that, she quickly and neatly drew her blade across the throat of the bewildered third man.

As the fat one collapsed, blood bubbling from the clean slit in his throat, Vanessa turned to survey the damage she had wrought. All three men were dead, and her hands were drenched, literally and figuratively, in their blood. Then, knowing what needed to happen next, she sheathed her sword, and removed a small dagger from her belt.

As a light rain began to fall over the ruined and bloody campsite, Vanessa knelt over one of her victims, shook her head in disgust and whispered, "Bless me Father, for I have sinned." Then, without another word, she made the sign of the cross and sliced open his chest.

Chapter Two

Justice was close at hand.

She could practically taste it – she always could.

Or, perhaps, this time she was just tasting the bread and sausage she'd had for breakfast. Probably not, because that breakfast, her most recent meal, had been two days ago. Since then, she had been tirelessly following a small party of travellers as they moved through *der Kunratice Wald* (the Kunratice Forest) on the southeastern corner of Prague, and she would spring her trap today.

She had no idea what her name was. She seemed to remember her mother calling her Marina, but that was a long time ago, and not only had she forgotten her name, she had all but forgotten her mother. For as long as she could remember, she had been an orphan and the only family she knew was the band of thieves with which she had taken up at the age of twelve. And after fourteen years with them, the only name she answered to was the one they had given her – *Šarlatová* (Scarlet).

Known throughout the Empire as *die Grüne Gauner* (the Green Thieves) due to the signature green-hooded cloaks they wore to blend into the forested regions of Bohemia where they worked, this band of outlaws was the only family Šarlatová had ever known or needed. While most in the Empire feared, avoided, and reviled them as rogues and mercenaries, the Green Thieves preferred to think of themselves as part of a larger extended family called *die Volks Knechte* (servants of the people), and they operated on a simple, altruistic philosophy: "What happens to one of us happens to all of us." And in service to that philosophy, they often had to operate well outside of the law.

And operating well outside of the law was what Šarlatová did best. She had no idea that the party she'd been tracking these past two days included the wife of Count Jaroslav Borita von Martinitz – travelling, ostensibly, to *Hradčany* to care for her husband and not knowing that he had already fled, in disguise, to Bavaria – nor did she care. It was clear from the company of armed guards and the carriage in which they were riding, that whoever these people were, they had money. And equally clear to Šarlatová was her obligation to relieve them of it.

As the carriage approached, escorted by two mounted soldiers both in front of and in back of the impressive vehicle, Šarlatová stepped from the trees and stood silently alongside its path. With her head bowed down and her hand out, she was easily mistaken for a beggar – something that was, sadly, all too common in Bohemia these days.

The 1552 Peace of Passau had ended the Schmalkaldic War between the Protestants and Catholics in *das Heiliges Römisches Reich*, and the 1555 Peace of Augsburg had tried to prevent future conflicts by adopting the principle of *cuius region, eius religio*, (whose realm, his religion), which allowed some parts of the Empire to be Lutheran while others remained staunchly Catholic. However, these agreements were increasingly undermined by the continued expansion of Protestantism (even in strongly Catholic areas ruled by the Habsburgs) and by the repeated attempts of the ruling family to reclaim and restore areas lost to the Lutherans since the 1550s. The birth and growth of Calvinism and Anabaptism, theologies viewed with equal hostility by the warring Lutherans and Catholics, further complicated the issue and resulted in a fragmentation of the empire into nearly two-thousand separate fiefdoms spread throughout the German states, the Low Countries, northern Italy, and southeastern France.

Disputes occasionally resulted in full-scale conflicts like the Cologne War of the 1580s and smaller skirmishes such as the 1606

Battle of the Flags in the town of *Donauwörth* in Bavaria. As a result of these continued conflicts, all sides began to strengthen their armies and increase their fortifications, so much so that by July of 1609, the empire had divided into two warring camps – the Catholic League set up by Emperor Maximillian II and the Protestant Union led by Frederick IV, Elector Palatine. And an unfortunate but natural consequence of this militarised, dirty scramble for power was that authority figures throughout the Empire were too busy trying to convert or kill each other to properly tend to "less vital" needs – such as feeding the people. As Šarlatová often noted, the faith was flourishing in the empire, but so was poverty, and it was clear to all that the "powers that be" (Pope Paul V, Emperor Matthias, and the Stormsongs) would much rather build a *Schuldturm* (debtor's prison) or another cathedral than build a school or a hostel for poor relief.

While she had not been properly educated, Šarlatová knew this history all too well, because she had been living it for the past eighteen years, and she also knew that the orgy of violence and depravity that the so-called "Wars of Religion" had created in Europe was worthy of someone as debased as Gaius Caesar Augustus Germanicus (more commonly known by his sobriquet, Caligula).

As the carriage passed Šarlatová, Countess Maria Eusebie von Sternberg (the first of what would be Count Jaroslav Borita von Martinitz's four wives and the mother of all ten of his children) reached her hand out of the carriage's window and, in a rare display of *noblesse oblige*, dropped a coin in Šarlatová's gloved hand. As the carriage continued to pass, heading south towards *Hradčany*, Šarlatová called out angrily, "Is that it?"

Either having not heard her properly, or perhaps simply so shocked that a filthy beggar would have the temerity to speak to her, Countess von Sternberg ordered the carriage to stop. As it did, she glanced out of one of its two windows and, looking back Šarlatová's way, said "I beg your pardon."

As Šarlatová lifted her head, the forest green hood of her cloak fell back, revealing a copper-skinned, green-eyed beauty with a wild and lustrous shock of red hair. In fact, aside from the red hair, she looked far more Mediterranean (Spanish or Italian, perhaps even Greek) than Bohemian or German. Despite how strikingly beautiful she was, Šarlatová gave the impression to most that she was humble, carefree, and blasé about most things, including her looks. But this was a disguise born out of careful practice. In reality, as those who knew her best were well aware, Šarlatová was a cobra, ready to hiss and strike out in a flash – and the slight compression of her full lips and the fixedness in her sparkling green eyes often served as the only warning before she did.

Šarlatová spoke even louder and more confidently the second time. "You heard me. Is. That. It?"

The guards, sensing the possibility of an altercation, reined their horses around so that they were all facing the audacious beggar, while Countess von Sternberg unwisely attempted to step down from the carriage to get a better look at Šarlatová. Although she was prevented from doing so by the three ladies-in-waiting who were sharing the carriage with her, the countess was still able to shout in Šarlatová's direction. "How dare you?" she demanded.

Countess Maria Eusebie von Sternberg, like most "proper ladies" of the seventeenth century, was a firm believer in two things, the first being Catholicism. The second being the equally important religion of social order. In other words, the "lower classes" should know their place, and speaking out of turn to a lady of her position was, to her thinking, wholly inappropriate, and tantamount to a crime.

"How dare I?" Šarlatová responded with a snide laugh. Gesturing with the coin to the lavish purple gown the noblewoman was wearing, Šarlatová added "What you paid for that little frock there could feed me and my friends for the rest of the year. So, I was wondering….is this it?"

By this time, despite the attempts by two of her servants to prevent her from doing so, Countess von Sternberg had stepped out of the carriage, helped down by a third servant who had exited ahead of her so as to assist her. The countess couldn't decide whether to order one of her men to properly punish this impudent wretch or to approach her so as to personally slap her across the face. As she weighed these options, more than two dozen arrows rained down from the trees above, imbedding themselves in the wood panelling of her carriage and making it look much like an extremely large and equally expensive porcupine. Remarkably, however, not a single arrow struck either a person or a horse.

Immediately the guards went to draw their swords, but the emergence from the trees of an enormous red-headed Moravian named Roan, who was wielding an equally enormous broadsword, stayed their hands. At nearly seven-feet-tall, and weighing more than three-hundred and fifty pounds, Roan was an incredibly impressive figure, but he was also a terrible thief. Because of his size, he lacked the ability to do anything silently or quickly, and he was as inconspicuous as a bear in church. But he was the recognized leader of *die Grüne Gauner*, and he made up for his deficiencies in stealth with his sheer size and strength. Over the years, many a Green Thief had been saved from impending danger by a swing of his mighty blade – a massive and deadly weapon he simply called *Schwert*.

"No, no," he cautioned, practically tsk-tsking the four armed guards. "Let's not make a mess of things in front of the little lady, now." At this, all four soldiers glanced towards Countess von Sternberg. "*Nein*, not that pretentious little bitch," Roan corrected them. "*That* little lady." He gestured with his sword towards Šarlatová, who was openly smiling now.

Uncertain what to do, and unwilling to tangle with the red-headed giant, not one of the four men unsheathed his sword, further enraging Countess von Sternberg. "In my entire life, I have never…." she stammered.

"And you probably never will," finished Šarlatová as she approached the noblewoman and eyed the large quantity of jewels adorning her hands and neck, almost as if examining wares in a store. With her rudimentary inspection complete, Šarlatová made a clicking sound with her teeth and said, "I think we'll take it all." With that, a score of green cloaked archers poured from the woods, keeping their individual and collective aim trained on the four soldiers.

The archers appeared more like refugees than soldiers to Countess von Sternberg. They were not in uniform, and they all sported hollow cheekbones, layers of clothing, and heavy green coats or cloaks – garments that were far too heavy for May, leaving her with the impression that they were afraid to take off any of their belongings. Their faces were gaunt, their clothing careworn, and they reeked of an odour that made the countess wrinkle her nose in disgust. Fortunately for *die Grüne Gauner*, they were all equally grubby and rank so that they were not put off by the stench of their comrades.

"You filthy vermin will not lay a single shabby finger on me!" protested the enraged and humiliated noblewoman as she spun around, intent upon reentering her carriage.

"That's one thing we can agree upon," replied Šarlatová. "I wouldn't soil my hands touching the likes of you." With that, Šarlatová produced a small dagger and quickly and skillfully used it to snare and remove a trio of necklaces from the wealthy woman's lovely neck.

As the irate countess spun to confront Šarlatová once again, she noticed that several of the green cloaked archers now had arrows nocked and trained on her. Fuming, all she could muster was "You'll pay for this, you little bitch!"

Šarlatová's smile grew even wider. "A bitch I may be, but *you* are the one who's going to pay for it."

Failing to comprehend Šarlatová's meaning, Countess von Sternberg pivoted to see that some of *die Grüne Gauner* had removed her four would-be-protectors from their horses and were in the process of relieving them of their arms and armour, while still others were pillaging anything of value – of which there was a great deal – from inside the carriage and from the clutches of her three terrified ladies-in-waiting.

"And we'll take the frock, too." Šarlatová used her dagger to gesture up and down the length of Countess von Sternberg's gown. Summoning what little pride she could muster, the imperious noblewoman crossed her arms, attempting to stare Šarlatová down in one final act of stubborn defiance.

Šarlatová shrugged her shoulders. "Have it your way," she said as she expertly sliced down the front of the gown with her dagger, allowing the lush material to neatly and evenly divide into two pieces and fall to the ground. While a woman of her station should have been practically mummified by yards of perfectly pleated and lapped fabric beneath her dress, the countess – shocking to all but her servants – was wearing surprisingly little by way of undergarments. As the exposed noblewoman shrieked and attempted to dart back into her carriage to hide her shame, she managed to slip and fall, twice, thus adding a layer of dirt to her already intense humiliation.

Roan glanced disapprovingly towards Šarlatová who shrugged her shoulders and mouthed "I didn't know she wasn't wearing anything under there. Who does that?" Šarlatová paused for just a second before adding, "Or that she was so damn clumsy." Both then smiled and went about their business.

In seconds, the now nearly naked woman began alternately sobbing and cursing, surrounded inside her carriage by a huddle of frightened servants – who, unlike her, had been allowed to escape with the clothes on their backs and who were now slipping rings off of their lady's fingers and surrendering them to Šarlatová. And just as the countess was left with no jewels, no money, and practically no clothes, her would-be-protectors – who were smart enough not to engage with *die Grüne Gauner* – were left with no weapons, no armour, and only two of eight horses – just enough to drag the humiliated noble woman's carriage to its destination, albeit ever so slowly.

Just before the carriage resumed its journey, Šarlatová stepped up onto one of its running boards and peeked in the window. "Actually, I'm really doing you a favour," she said to the irate and humiliated noblewoman. "Matthew's gospel tells us that Jesus said *It is easier for a camel to go through the eye of a needle than for a rich man to enter the kingdom of God.* So, if you think on it that way, I've just saved your soul." Just before hopping back down off the running board, Šarlatová leaned in one more time to add, "You're welcome," and punctuated her final comment with an impish smile. The glare she received in return from the countess was far from impish.

Having just taken the noblewoman's money, pride, and dignity (all crucial parts of Countess von Sternberg's carefully crafted identity), Šarlatová and the others quickly stole back into the woods with four new horses and a trove of new treasure, including a torn gown and complete set of jewels, which Šarlatová was certain she could use as part of a disguise for a future undertaking.

As they worked their way back into the safety of *der Kunratice Wald* (or *Kunratický Les*, as it was known by the local Bohemians), Roan shook his massive and shaggy head. "Stealing from spoiled rich Catholics is one thing, *dívka*. But you keep on treatin' 'em this way, and they're likely to lock you in a dungeon somewhere in the Vatican," he warned.

Šarlatová loved Roan like a father; in fact, he was the only father she'd ever really known. And with the same forest-green eyes, and shockingly wild, red hair as Šarlatová, he could have easily passed for her father – except that he didn't share her beautiful copper complexion. Having lived deep inside the forests of Bohemia and Moravia for most of his life, his complexion was so light that, depending on the temperature and the time of year, it alternated between undertones of blue or pink.

Šarlatová loved this pale, red-headed giant unconditionally – which was why he was the one person on the planet she would permit to call her *dívka* (girl); however, she had always felt that, like any father-figure, he was much too overprotective of her. And as skilled as she had become with both bow and blade, she didn't really need anyone to protect her – that, however, didn't stop Roan from trying.

She grinned and patted him lovingly, but more than a little condescendingly, on one of his bearded cheeks. "You know me," she teased. "I'm always as careful as a church mouse."

Roan laughed deeply. "*Ja*, careful as a church mouse and as poor as one, too."

"Not anymore," Šarlatová corrected, holding the newly procured gown and jewels up in front of the red giant and allowing him to survey the impressive new haul. "Besides, with you watching out for me, who could ever do me harm?"

With that, Roan's face quickly darkened, and his jovial mood passed. "I'm just tryin' to tell you, *dívka*, that there's a storm a comin', and it's a comin' fast. With Catholics, Calvinists, and Lutherans all thinkin' they know what's best for everyone else and tryin' to kill each other over it. As if God gives two shits which pew our asses grace on Sunday." To properly punctuate his point, Roan spat in the ground in front of them and then turned to look Šarlatová directly in the eyes. "And I wouldn't want to see you get caught out in the storm, is all." Just then, as if to emphasise his ominous warning, a low rumble of thunder built in the distance.

This time Šarlatová's smile was much less playful than before, and her green eyes flashed as she said menacingly, "But, Roan, you've forgotten – I *am* the storm." As if on cue, the low rumble of thunder grew instantly and noticeably louder.

Chapter Three

———✦———

Less than a week after successfully completing her latest "mission," Vanessa returned home to *Schloß Stormsong*, something that was always a bittersweet proposition for her. It was the only home she'd ever known and, as such, was a source of many fond memories. However, most of those most fond memories belonged to the first few years of her life – when her mother was still alive, and when her father was still….himself. Increasingly though, as the years had passed, it had become a source of pain and sorrow for her, and a constant reminder of all that she had lost and been forced to endure these past eighteen years.

Occupying an area of nearly 750,000 square feet, *Schloß Stormsong* was one of the most impressive structures within *das Heiliges Römisches Reich*. Situated within walking distance of *Hradčany* on the western banks of the *Vltava* (*die Moldau* in German), it dated back to the ninth century when it had been gifted to the Stormsong family by Charlemagne himself. Its first walled building, *die Kirche der seligen Jungfrau* (the Church of the Blessed Virgin), was completed in 870, and subsequent basilicas to St. George and St. Wenceslas had been added in the first half of the tenth century.

A Romanesque palace – which now contained, among other things, Vanessa's absurdly large and ornate bed chamber – was added during the twelfth century, as was the first Catholic convent in Bohemia. In the fourteenth century, the palace was rebuilt in Gothic style, and the castle's already impressive fortifications were significantly strengthened, including new defence towers on the north and south faces of the castle.

In 1541, a large and unexplained fire destroyed much of the castle, leaving intact only the great Summer Palace, where the Stormsongs vast and invaluable art collection had been on display. In the decades following the destruction, Vanessa's Grandfather, the young Count Rudolph von Stormsong who was only fifteen-years-old at the time of the fire, oversaw a Renaissance inspired reconstruction and renovation of the entire complex. In all, the massive and ornate fortress now boasted two cathedrals, six smaller churches and chapels, four palaces, five great halls, and dozens of gardens and other structures. Like something from a fairy tale and imbued with all of the trappings of royalty, it was, as Vanessa well knew, every bit as impressive as either *Schloß Schönbrunn* or *Schloß Hofburg*, both located in Vienna and both belonging to the Hapsburg royal family.

In fact, it was virtually impossible to overstate the awesome magnificence that was *Schloß Stormsong*. It was, like all things that belonged to the Stormsongs, an ostentatious symbol of the wealth, military might, and artistic sophistication of Europe's leading family.

Vanessa knew every bit the entire architectural history of the historic compound, because she had been forced to learn it through rote repetition administered by her father and, more recently, by her father's personal priest, a vile little acolyte known to most as Monsignor Mučitel, but known to Vanessa and a select few others as *der schwarze Beichtvater* (the Black Confessor). Vanessa knew that she would be meeting with both men today, and she couldn't decide which visit terrified her most.

Terrified wasn't the right word, because Vanessa had been forged to be fearless – a hard, pitiless, and remorseless warrior who knew no fear. So, it wasn't so much fear that chilled her heart as she returned home this morning as it was dread for meeting her father – and loathing for meeting his dark priest.

Expertly circumventing *Schloß Stormsong's* impressive and, at least supposedly, impregnable defences, Vanessa located a passage towards the east wall, known only to her, that was entirely obscured by the dense foliage of *der Böhmerwald* (the Bohemian Forest).

Stealing quickly and silently through the woods, she ultimately approached a door on the east wall that was long forgotten by all but her. This hidden door was a holdover from the original construction of the fortress and had never been replaced or walled off during the post fire reconstruction. While it was almost certainly an architectural oversight, a much younger Vanessa had often fantasised that it had been intentionally left for her by her grandfather, Count Rudolph von Stormsong. As a child, she had used this same "secret passage" to slip out of the fortress to gain some precious time away from her parents and tutors – and there had been a lot of tutors. But those carefree days were long gone, and there was no play or amusement in store today – at least not for her.

Using the door to slip into the kitchens on the east side of the castle, Vanessa returned home. The kitchens, as they often were these days, were virtually empty, and the few servants who were present had been trained well enough to know not to look up from their work as Vanessa quietly made her way through.

Pausing just long enough to grab a small piece of *Hutzelbrot* (a traditional German fruit and nut bread) from a cutting table, Vanessa promptly made her way to the one place she knew her father would be – the library. Although it took her nearly fifteen minutes to reach the elaborate French doors that signalled the entry into that room (one of the largest in the castle), Vanessa had still not finished the small piece of *Hutzelbrot* that she carried with her. The closer she got to this room, the less her hunger seemed to matter.

As she stepped inside and offered a prayer to the blessed Virgin Mary, Vanessa took in her surroundings – which had changed very little the past few years. The library, or *Bibliotheca Stormsong* as her father preferred to call it, was furnished elaborately but strangely – strange in the sense that the sofas, chairs, and tapestries were all modelled after the look of Louis XIII's personal library. That her father should mimic someone else's choice of style was one thing, but the fact that he modelled his design after a *French* King – well, that was almost inconceivable and, as far as Vanessa was concerned, inexcusable. Although the intellectual and social life of the German states was an amalgamation of all things European (with fashion heavily influenced by the Spanish; music, dancing, and poetry guided by the Italians, and artwork shaped by the Dutch masters), the ruling German families had long considered the French capable of producing only love-letters and occasionally fine cuisine, which made the archduke's fascination with Louis XIII that much more bizarre.

However, despite the unsettling influence of French design, the layout of the space was distinctly German. Its shelves were systematically divided into six distinct sections: Art, History, Law, Literature, Science and Mathematics, and Philosophy and Theology, with each item having been hand chosen for its cultural and intellectual significance by the archduke himself. It was one of the most impressive collections of printed books and manuscripts anywhere in the world, and both the size of the collection and the rarity of the items in it made it the envy of all of Europe.

However, as she could soon hear the repetitive mumbling of her father from within, Vanessa wondered why her father had collected so many books, when he seemed to only ever read from one. While she wasn't quite certain what it was that he routinely chanted while in this room (some odd combination of Greek, Latin, and gibberish – but certainly not German), she did know what he was reading. It was always the same. The book of Genesis, chapters fifteen through seventeen. Never anything else. For reasons Vanessa could only guess at, there were times when the archduke was reduced to a babbling madman who would sit for hours on end reading the same three chapters of the Old Testament. These strange days – the ones on which her usually proud and vital father was reduced to a fraction of his former self – used to occur only once or twice a year, but of late they seemed to be occurring once or twice a month.

Knowing better than to interrupt this bizarre but, at least to her father, most sacred ritual, Vanessa approached silently and knelt, with head bowed, next to her father's chair, just out of reach of his left hand. She never knew how long his "spells" would last, nor how long he would leave her like this. Sometimes it was a matter of minutes, other times it could take hours. But, for better or for worse, today was an exception. He noticed and acknowledged her presence almost immediately.

"Welcome home, Atlantis. I would hear you say the words now," he commanded.

As her father resumed his quiet mumbling, Vanessa responded reflexively with the oath that she had taken countless times over the past two decades. She could recite it the same way many Catholics might recite the Nicene Creed – without thought as to the meaning of the words being professed. "I am Lady Atlantis Vanessa von Stormsong, child of Archduke von Stormsong. I am now, and will remain until *your* death, your obedient and faithful subject. But above and beyond that, I am now, and will remain until *my* death, a loyal servant to my Heavenly Father, to His son, Jesus Christ, and to his divinely appointed Emperor."

With that, Vanessa's father extended his left hand (always the left, and never the right), allowing Vanessa to kiss the Stormsong family ring. As she did so, she noticed that her father's hand was paler and colder than it had been just a few days ago when she had been sent out on her latest "mission."

"And what have you brought *us*?" he prompted.

"Three this time, father. From three of the heretics who brought dishonour and disgrace to themselves and to their rightful God and Emperor." Vanessa kept her head bowed, wondering, not for the first time, who constituted the *us* that her father always referred to, and praying that he would somehow forget what came next in this bizarre and gruesome ritual.

"I would see them now, daughter," he whispered, still not even looking in her direction. And with that, Vanessa removed the leather satchel that had been riding on her hip the past few days. She opened it and removed a smaller, wet bag from within. Rising only long enough to place the contents of the second bag on the table in front of her father, she immediately returned to a kneeling position at his side.

On the table before the Archduke lay the wet and sticky hearts that had recently belonged to the three heretics who had perpetrated what was already being called the "Defenestration of Prague." Because she was well-schooled in the history of *das Heiliges Römisches Reich*, Vanessa knew all too well that this latest crime was, at minimum, the third such "Defenestration" within the past two-hundred years in Prague – but for the life of her, she couldn't figure out why the Bohemian people were so obsessed with throwing each other out of windows.

For what seemed to her like an eternity, Vanessa's father toyed with the three cold and sticky organs. Moaning almost erotically as he examined them, he then asked her, "Is Count von Thurn's among them?"

"I'm afraid not, father. He was not with his men."

Grunting with displeasure, the archduke then mumbled to himself, "Nevertheless, we are very pleased with these. Very pleased indeed." But there was no disguising the disappointment in his voice – a disappointment that Vanessa knew stemmed from the fact that she was his daughter, rather than his son.

Vanessa had heard that bizarre statement before, and she still had no idea what it meant. She had read somewhere of ancient cultures that used to eat the hearts of people they killed in battle. Apparently, they had believed that if they ate the hearts of their victims, the souls of the dead would somehow be subsumed into their own, thus giving them the spirit and the power of two. But Vanessa could not imagine, even for a moment, that her father (despite how bizarre he had become) was regularly engaging in this pagan ritual. Regardless, at least for the moment, it couldn't have mattered less, because her father was about to continue the bizarre inquiry. "And why did you do this, Lady von Stormsong?"

Knowing full well that her father knew the answer to this and to the next two questions, Vanessa tiredly but dutifully played along. The consequences of not doing so were too gruesome to contemplate. Only once had Vanessa failed to play her part in this macabre ritual, and she would never forget the punishment that came with that rare act of insubordination. After all, how could one forget being force fed the entire heart of a dead man? Especially when it had been two full weeks after she herself had plucked that heart from the man's chest. And rather than gaining any additional power or spirit, all she had gained was a violent (and, quite nearly, lethal) bout of dysentery.

"Because you commanded me to do so, father. And because I am your true and obedient daughter."

Vanessa thought she heard some sound rattle in her father's throat at her use of the word *daughter*, but she couldn't be certain. And it didn't matter anyway, because the play in which she was engaged had not yet reached its second and third acts.

"And *how* did you do this, Lady von Stormsong?"

"Through sin, father. And for this, I humbly beg your forgiveness."

The slight pause before the third and final question gave Vanessa just a momentary pause – a vain hope that she might be granted a respite from what was to come next.

Leaning his head back and closing his eyes, as if in some form of meditative contemplation, her father continued. "And how is forgiveness achieved, my child?"

Choking back her disgust, Vanessa dutifully responded. "Through reconciliation and…. atonement, father."

Archduke von Stormsong sighed heavily before releasing her. "Then you are free to go visit Monsignor Mučitel, so that you may be forgiven these latest transgressions, *daughter*." And with that, he returned to his reading and his incoherent babbling.

"Thank you, father," Vanessa managed to utter before rising slowly and leaving the library. She was, once again, on her way to the chapel of Saint Augustine of Hippo, and waiting there for her would be her father's personal priest – the "Black Confessor" himself.

Chapter Four

Šarlatová laughed so deeply that the taut muscles in her flat stomach hurt – Günther's jokes always had that effect on her. The one-time blacksmith from Oldenburg was now a member of *die Grüne Gauner,* and while Šarlatová didn't know how good he was at smithing, she knew he had no equal when it came to telling bawdy jokes. And this latest one – which involved Pope Paul V, a bosomy tavern wench, and a donkey – was his magnum opus.

Two dozen of the Green Thieves were seated around a fire they had built within one of the sandstone tablelands that formed a series of rock cities within *Hruboskalsko*, a forest on the northeastern outskirts of Prague. They were finishing the last of the food that had been provided to them by the Count and Countess von Ottweiler, German nobles from whom they had stolen two horses; several baskets of bread, cheese, and fruit; two casks of wine, and a small chest of jewels earlier that day. This "recovery" (and that's how Šarlatová viewed it – a recovery from people who had too much to begin with) from Count and Countess *Rottweiler*, as Roan had referred to the stout and homely Ottweilers, had completely replenished their stores and given them cause to celebrate.

Herman Jobst, an out of work potter who had been forced to resort to thievery to feed his family, was Günther Oldenburg's oldest and best friend. When he finished choking back the wine that had come out of his nose at the climax of Günther's joke, he shook his head and observed to the merriment of all, "God bless you, Günther, you are living proof that brothers and sisters shouldn't fuck." This, of course, produced more roaring rounds of laughter, particularly when Günther leaped from his position around the fire and pounced on Jobst, setting off a wrestling match worthy of a pair of adolescent monkeys.

When the impromptu wrestling match threatened to spill some of the much-treasured wine, Roan ordered it to come to a quick end, and a collective sigh of relief escaped the group. In the silence that followed, Roan, who was seated next to Šarlatová, leaned back against a sturdy larch tree and belched. "What a glorious day, boys. On a night like tonight, with warm food in our bellies, plenty of good wine to go 'round, and a perfect, cloudless sky up above, who could deny that God's in his Heaven? At least for tonight, all's right with the world."

Disagreeing with Roan, but also not wanting to upset the generally cheerful mood of all of those present, Šarlatová simply leaned her head on the giant's left shoulder, patted his arm, and closed her eyes.

"Speaking of God in His heaven," began Simon Berger, arguably the smartest and most obnoxious of the bunch, "What are we to make of these latest offences made upon us by the Catholics?"

A collective groan answered his question and was followed up by a rather loud fart from Theodore Berger, Simon's less intelligent, less pompous, but better-liked older brother. "There, that's what I make of them, little brother."

Simon and Theodore couldn't be less alike. Whereas Simon was well-read, pompous, and fastidious about his appearance (keeping his dark hair and even darker beard neatly trimmed at all times and wearing clothes that would look more appropriate on a prince than a thief), Theodore was cheerful and friendly, possessing a good-natured energy that radiated from his light blue eyes. Like most of *die Grüne Gauner*, he was also illiterate, and he made friends rather easily.

Simon, on the other hand, had very few friends. Instead, he had sources. And despite his disdain for those less educated than himself (including, sometimes, his own brother), he made a point of carrying on lively conversations with every cook, farmer, smith, thatcher, tailor, butcher, and fishmonger he encountered. Not because he particularly cared for those people, but because he found that forging relationships with them provided him with numerous and valuable sources of information.

A nervous and uneasy laugh rippled through the small crowd, but Simon Berger was not satisfied. "I'm perfectly serious, Theo. You know as well as I do that, for weeks now, Catholics throughout Bohemia have been pillaging and plundering our towns and villages. They've been forcing conversions, torturing and murdering anyone who refuses to convert. And just last month….." Simon's voice was both higher and louder now. "Last month they publicly executed a dozen of us, impaled their heads on iron hooks and hung them from the fucking bridge tower at *Schloß Schönbrunn*." Allowing that thought to fester for a moment, Simon then lowered his voice to an almost pleasant, conversational tone. "And, as a Protestant, I simply refuse to believe that I am the only one who is shocked by that."

"I'm a Protestant, Simon. And I'm not shocked by any of that," retorted Šarlatová without even opening her eyes.

"Same goes for me," added Hester Neuss, a widow who had joined the group two years earlier when her husband and two sons had all died of scrofula (a common form of tuberculosis that occurs *outside* of the lungs). Mysteriously, she had not died. In fact, she hadn't even gotten sick. "I'm a Protestant, and I…."

"You're a Protestant, Hester?" challenged Simon Berger. "You….you haven't even been to church in….years!"

"I didn't say I was good at it," added Hester to the amusement of all, even Simon.

Eager to lay the issue to rest before it became an even livelier argument, which she felt was far too late in the day to begin, Šarlatová opened her eyes and sat up right. "Are you surprised by any of that, Simon? Torture? Murder? Forced conversions? Have you not been paying attention? That's what Catholics do. When they're not trying to figure out whether to stand, sit, kneel, or shit, they kill anyone who doesn't agree with them. Since when is that news? It's like getting all worked up about the fact that a pig took a roll in his slop – it's in their nature."

"I'm not disagreeing with you, Šarlatová," Simon countered, pleased to have started what he hoped would be a lively theological debate. "But they're disseminating handbills everywhere with the false claim that angels saved Counts von Chlum and von Martinitz when they were defenestrated at Prague, and I think people are going to start to believe them. We have to find a way to counter that message!"

Theodore Berger leaned in towards his younger brother and asked in a whisper "What's *deep-penetrated* mean?"

With a look of mild amusement on his lean and angular face, Simon Berger sighed and corrected his brother. "DE-FEN-ES-TRA-TED," he enunciated loudly and slowly. "It means thrown out of a window."

"Oh. Then why didn't you just say that? I thought it had something to do with…."

"Please don't finish that thought, Theo," Šarlatová interrupted, to everyone's laughter and amusement. Then, turning towards Simon Berger, she said, "Of course that's what they're claiming. Since when has the Catholic Church been in the truth telling business? Everyone knows that those two weren't saved by angels. They were saved by a conveniently placed pile of horse shit. I know it, you know it, and I'm pretty sure that the ones who landed in the shit know it too."

"But…." interjected Simon.

"No – there are no buts, Simon. Unless, of course, we're talking about your brother's rather large and melodious butt. We're not fighting a war of religion." As she continued, she began to address the whole group. "Let Luther or Bucer or Phillip *der Großmütige* fight the religious civil war. Or let God do it Himself, if He's so damned worried about it. We're not in the religion business. We are in the business of feeding our people and keeping them, and ourselves, alive. That's it, and that's all of it." She punctuated her point by tossing a half-eaten chicken leg in Simon's lap.

Using the chicken leg to point back towards Šarlatová, Simon – who, like most of the men in *die Grüne Gauner*, had long held an intense but unrequited attraction to Šarlatová – responded by saying "May I remind you, my large-breasted, red-haired friend, that all of those men you just named are dead?"

Before Šarlatová could respond, acting as if someone had called his name, Roan jumped to his feet and placed both of his hands on his tree-trunk-like chest. "Large-breasted red-head? Is he talkin' about my tits again? I'm startin' to worry about you, Simon." Roan's joke set off the largest wave of laughter yet, and it seemed to serve as a signal that the debate was over. Roan had stood and spoken, so there was nothing left to be said or done – at least for now.

With the issue temporarily settled, and with everyone laughing once again, Šarlatová smiled and left the group in search of a place to relieve herself and to settle down for a few much- needed hours of sleep.

However, rest and relief would have to wait, because a suddenly serious Roan gave Simon a friendly punch on the shoulder, bade good night to the rest of the group and followed after her.

They still had much to discuss.

It's happening again, Šarlatová observed silently, once she had removed herself from the group. And it's a little worse each time.

Šarlatová wiped away the milky discharge coming from her left eye. Fortunately, she'd felt it coming on this time and had managed to escape the perceptive and prying eyes of her comrades before anyone noticed. The problem with keeping company with a bunch of thieves was that they were trained to miss nothing. The bigger problem was that this was happening again and again, and each time it did, it left the sight in her left eye just a touch weaker than it had been before. While that might make for a relatively minor inconvenience for most, for a woman whose livelihood, and often life, depended upon her vision and her aim with a longbow, it was a *very* big deal.

Worse yet, Šarlatová had a pretty good idea as to what was causing this recurring malady; unfortunately, however, stopping it was not an option – at least not so long as she was Roan's second in command over *die Grüne Gauner*.

Speaking of Roan, Šarlatová had been so intently focused on cleaning her cloudy left eye and removing any of the white, milky residue from her cheek that she hadn't heard him approach from behind her.

"You alright there, *dívka?*" he asked softly, immediately snapping her out of a cloud of distraction.

Acting purely on instinct, Šarlatová spun, produced a yew wood self-bow (a narrowed limbed long bow with a rounded cross-section) and nocked an arrow, all in less time than it took for Roan to put up his hands in a display of mock surrender. "Easy now, *dívka*. It's just me," he assured her.

Exhaling silently, Šarlatová lowered her bow. "Jesus, Roan. You scared the shit out of me!"

"I scared the shit out of you? Then why am I the one with the soiled trousers?" he asked, causing them both to laugh. Pausing a second after they both stopped laughing, he asked, "Is it the eye again?"

Even though she shouldn't have been, Šarlatová was still taken aback by Roan's question. Knowing him as long as she had, and knowing that nothing escaped his keen eyes, she should have suspected that he knew. Instead, because his question caught her off guard, she stood in front of him, saying nothing, and trying hard not to blink as a little more of the milky white substance gathered in the corner of her left eye.

With a gentleness that belied his massive size, Roan produced a clean cloth from a leather pouch at his belt and used it to gently wipe the mucus from Šarlatová's eye and cheek. With her lower lip quivering and teetering on the edge of tears (she did *not* want to cry in front of anyone, least of all Roan), she whispered, "How long have you known?"

Pressing the cloth into Šarlatová's hands, he whispered back, "For a long time now, *dívka*."

Šarlatová took the cloth from Roan and used it to wipe away several greasy bits of meat that remained flecked in his unruly red beard from his earlier meal. Then she lowered her head and sighed heavily. Tears of two different types were now streaming down her cheeks. Roan used his massive paw to reraise her chin and smiled at her, which produced the laugh he was aiming for. Roan knew that she couldn't resist his foolish looking, gap-toothed grin.

"Do you think it's because of the....?" He left the last part of his question unspoken, as Šarlatová would have wanted.

"Shit! You know about that, too?"

"Listen, *dívka*. Just 'cause I move slow, doesn't mean I think slow."

Šarlatová nodded slowly as she took in this new and unsettling piece of information. "Does everyone know?" she asked softly.

"I don't know. But if they do, who cares? Or if they don't, who cares? They're your family, *dívka*," he reassured her. "But that's not what I wanted to talk to you about." With that, Roan sat down and gestured to Šarlatová in a way that indicated that she was to lay down and curl up on him as if he was part bed, part blanket, and part bear.

Gladly obliging him, she folded herself into his embrace and felt instantly at ease when his tree-trunk arms closed around her.

"What is it, then?" she asked softly.

"It's this business that Simon Berger was talkin' about. He is a stubborn and annoying son of a bitch, to be sure. But he may also be right."

"About what?" Šarlatová replied, her voice even softer now than before.

"About the whole bloody business. After that nonsense in Prague, both sides are going to be preparing for war. As if they ever really needed a reason to try to kill each other. Christ, it may have already started, for all we know. And our *fine* Emperor Matthias, God rot the bastard, isn't gettin' any younger. He's got no kids, thanks be to Jesus, so your guess is as good as mine as to who's going to replace the bastard when he dies."

"Maybe it will be you," Šarlatová jested, snuggling even deeper into Roan's warm embrace.

Ignoring her joke, Roan continued. "To be sure it's goin' to be some new bloodthirsty zealot who'll want to restore everything that we've taken from the Catholics – and just as sure he's goin' to want to wipe out anythin' what doesn't conform with the pointy hats in Rome. He'll brook no dissent, mark my words. And that means war, *dívka*. War. Devastation. Entire towns and villages left in ruin. And if it comes to all that…." he trailed off for a moment. "Well, it'll be years….maybe decades….before everything's made right again."

Roan paused for effect, wanting his next words to really sink in. "And with the chances you take, *dívka*. Even with your….you know….your business, I'm just afraid that…." But Roan never got to finish the thought. Šarlatová's soft snoring alerted him to the fact that she probably hadn't heard a word he'd been saying – not that she would have paid it any heed even if she had heard it.

Stubborn girl, he thought to himself. *You'll be the death of me yet.* And then he, too, nodded off to sleep.

Chapter Five

Monsignor Mučitel wasn't ready for her yet, and while the delay only increased her anxiety about what was to come, it also allowed Vanessa some much-needed time to pray. Kneeling in a pew just outside of Monsignor Mučitel's "confessional," which was really a torture chamber, she was so focused on her prayers that she was completely oblivious to the beauty around her.

The Chapel of Saint Augustine of Hippo had been designed by her great grandfather in the mid-sixteenth century, and it had all of the beauty of the Renaissance combined with the defined, symmetrical proportions of classical Rome. The ceiling was a flattened barrel vault, cut transversely by six smaller vaults over each of the stained-glass windows adorning either side of the chamber. The barrel vault was painted such a brilliant sky blue and dotted with such realistic looking clouds that, upon first looking up, one had the impression that the chapel had no ceiling at all. Six stained glass windows on the east wall depicted scenes from the Old Testament, while six others on the west wall depicted scenes from the New Testament. The east wall scene of Moses parting the Red Sea and the west wall scene of Jesus' resurrection of Lazarus had always been Vanessa's favourites. Not only had the rendering of these two iconic scenes, which had allegedly been produced by *Lucas Cranach der Jüngere* (Lucas Cranach the Younger), been done realistically and beautifully, but both of these images revealed the awesome power of God – something that had always fascinated and, at alternating times, terrified and empowered Vanessa.

While kneeling before the altar didn't allow her to view either of the scenes at the moment, those displays of God's power were never far from Vanessa's mind, and it was that power that she was beseeching of Him now as she fumbled with the rosary that she had just removed from around her neck.

The rosary had been a Christmas present from her father, back before he became....whatever he was now. As an infant, it had served as a teething ring and a sort of security blanket for her, and as she grew older, it was never far from her reach. It now served as a constant, dual reminder that she once had a gentle and loving father here on Earth, and that she still had, and would always have, one in Heaven. One who loved her unconditionally. One who would never change and would never abandon her.

While she tried hard to stay focused on the Father, the Son, and the Holy Ghost, she couldn't keep thoughts of her biological father from intruding upon her prayers. She knew that he'd always been strict and firm, but underneath his hard and uncompromising exterior had once run a streak of curious gentleness. To those in need, he had once been instantly helpful, and to his family, he had at one time been a source of never-ending patience and grace. Vanessa supposed it was that gentle and genial nature that had made both his marriage and his relationship with his daughter such a success – at least at first. But all of that had ended when Vanessa was just four.

Now, eighteen years later, as she prayed for the strength to endure what was to come next, she kept whispering again and again, "As we sin, so must we suffer. As we sin, so must we suffer."

So lost in prayer was she that it took her several moments to realise that she was no longer alone. A black robed priest had approached silently and was now standing directly behind her. As her senses finally alerted her to his presence, Vanessa slowly raised her head, breathed in deeply, and with her eyes still closed said "Bless you, Father Joseph. I knew you would be here."

Vanessa stood and turned, fixing her gaze on the short man in front of her. His halo of white hair, his double-chin and gentle brown eyes all combined to instantly, albeit only temporarily, ease her anxiety. As he smiled and opened his arms, she rushed into his embrace and buried her head in his chest.

"Of course, I'm here, my Raven. But how did you know it was me? Have you been blessed with omnipotence along with your beauty and grace?" Vanessa had known Father Joseph her entire life. He was a fixture that had simply always been present for her, much in the same way that God was. In fact, it wasn't until she was thirteen or fourteen years old that she finally came to the realisation that Father Joseph wasn't God Himself. And for as long as she could recall, he had always referred to her as Raven….his little, blue-eyed Raven. While her thick, sable hair and dark eyebrows had certainly invited the comparison, as a child Vanessa had mistakenly believed that the likeness was more than just a passing one. She had envied, and attempted to replicate, the ability of her namesake to simply fly away whenever and wherever she wished. In fact, it was Father Joseph who had rescued her at the age of eleven when she had made her way to *der Weißer Turm* (the White Tower), the tallest of three towers within *Schloß Stormsong's* Winter Palace, intent on either taking to the skies, or ending her suffering – equally appealing options for her at that time.

"It's no special talent, Father Joseph. Who else in *Schloß Stormsong* is known to carry the odour of goat-cheese and Benedictine *Weihenstephan* everywhere he goes?" Apart from his weakness for German cheese and beer, Father Joseph was, in Vanessa's opinion, the perfect father-figure. Wise, gentle, trustworthy, and completely incapable of anger or hatred, he strove constantly and conscientiously to fulfil his responsibilities to God, his emperor, his archduke and his archduke's only child, Vanessa. While he was not strong of body, he was strong of spirit and character, and he had helped to provide Vanessa with an education unsurpassed anywhere in Europe.

"Why do you torment me, Raven?" he asked, pretending to be hurt. "Good cheese and good beer offer so much, and yet they ask so little in return. And you know how I struggle mightily with my two great weaknesses of the flesh."

Smiling mischievously, Vanessa patted Father Joseph's large, round, and expanding stomach, noting as she did, "Well, the struggle doesn't seem to be going your way, father." She held her hand in place until they both burst out laughing and embraced a second time.

"So, what brings you home, my child? And how long will you be with us this time? We are so infrequently blessed with the presence of your grace and beauty in these halls that it is indeed a rare treat to find you at home."

Vanessa thought to herself, *There's that word again....home.* Then, blushing politely at the priest's compliment, Vanessa responded, "Now who is tormenting whom, Father Joseph? You know precisely why I am here. I came to see my father."

"I do not mean to torment you, Raven. I am simply asking questions."

"Yes, but you only ever ask questions to which you already know the answers," Vanessa replied playfully.

"I am a priest, my child. That's what we do best."

Vanessa smiled and nodded in agreement, while Father Joseph glanced around to ensure they were alone. Then he took Vanessa by the arm into the chapel's apse, a semicircular recession covered by a hemi-spherical vault known as an exedra. The apse was on the eastern side of the chapel and contained a very plain altar – something that seemed out of place given the rather ornate surroundings that constituted the rest of the place of worship.

Behind the altar was a simple crimson curtain that Father Joseph pushed aside, allowing both he and Vanessa to gain access to his private chambers. If the altar was plain, then Father Joseph's quarters were positively spartan. In what could best be described as a monastic cell, he had only a bed, a small dresser, and an even smaller desk with a very uncomfortable looking chair.

Looking out past the altar to ensure that they had not been followed, Father Joseph let the curtain fall back into place, realising he probably had less than five minutes, and that they had much to discuss.

"Tell me your troubles, child," Father Joseph began.

"If you want to hear my confession, father, you'll have to stand in line. Monsignor Mučitel already has a place in front of you."

Watching how Vanessa's face darkened at the mere mention of *der schwarze Beichtvater* broke Father Joseph's heart – and not for the first time.

"Why does my father order me to do such terrible things, and then prescribe such painful punishments for faithfully following his orders?"

Father Joseph sighed heavily and sat down on his bed, motioning for Vanessa to sit next to him. When she did, he put his arm around her. "Your father is an incredibly complicated man, Raven. He was even before…." What went unspoken weighed heavily and ominously over the conversation.

"What exactly did happen, father? I remember everything changing, almost overnight, when….when my mother died. Was it losing her or losing the child that she was trying to bear him that caused him to change so much? Could having a son possibly mean that much to a man?"

"There's so much more to it than that, Raven."

"Then tell me, father. I want to know. I *deserve* to know."

"Yes….yes you do, but not just now. Later. For now, just know that your father does still love you, and that he thinks he's doing what's in your best interests."

Vanessa practically tsk-tsked the old priest. "You need to practice your lying, father. Even for a priest, you're terrible at it. My father cares now for one thing and one thing only. He wants to make the emperor supreme in Germany…."

"Yes, and to make Germany supreme in Europe," Father Joseph finished for her. "He's too much like his idol, in that regard. And you know who he idolises, don't you?"

"Tomás de Torquemada?" Vanessa guessed, referring to the infamous fifteenth century Dominican friar whose widespread use of torture to extract confessions during the Spanish Inquisition had made his name synonymous with cruelty, intolerance, and religious fanaticism.

"I think that is an unfair comparison, Raven."

"Unfair to whom, Father Joseph? To my father? Or to Torquemada?"

"Vanessa!" The fact that Father Joseph actually used her name, something he had done only one other time, combined with the way he said it was like a slap to Vanessa's face. "Torquemada was a monster! Your father is not."

"As we sin, so must we suffer, Father Joseph." Vanessa's deliberate use of that oft repeated phrase was a verbal slap of her own, and it stung Father Joseph a little harder than she intended.

"That's not what First Peter, chapter four, verse one says, and you know it." Vanessa could tell that Father Joseph was growing angry now.

"I know that, Father Joseph. Of course, the Bible doesn't say that – but my *father* does." With that, Vanessa stood and resignedly faced Monsignor Mučitel who had entered the room silently and was standing like some sort of gollum waiting for her.

"I'm ready for you now, *little Raven*," he hissed in a cold voice that was more reptilian than human.

As Vanessa followed Monsignor Mučitel out of the cell, she turned back to look at Father Joseph who was choking back tears. "Remember, my child, that your penance is for *your* benefit – to remind you that your Father's will comes first and that yours comes last."

Despite the fact that she knew Father Joseph was referring to her Heavenly Father, not Archduke von Stormsong, Vanessa couldn't resist the temptation to offer one last barb. "Believe me, Father Joseph, I am the *last* person in this entire empire to whom that needs to be told."

With that, she and Monsignor Mučitel disappeared beyond the other side of the curtain.

Chapter Six

The screaming was intense.

But screaming was nothing new to her.

Living with a band of outlaws in the time and place in which she did meant that violence and corresponding shouts and screams were an ordinary part of Šarlatová's life. However, she and *die Grüne Gauner* were thieves who were practised at using silence and cover as two of their primary weapons. That, taken together with the fact that she'd never heard Simon Berger raise his voice in all the time she had known him, made the shouts were beyond alarming.

It had been less than two weeks since *die Grüne Gauner* had left *Hruboskalsko*, and less than two hours since Šarlatová had closed her eyes to get some much-needed sleep when the Berger brothers returned from their mission. Earlier that day, Roan had sent them, and a dozen others, in search of food, supplies and, possibly, even some new recruits, but they were returning less than one full day later – without the others, and in a very different state.

Both men were riding on the same one horse, with Simon holding the reins and Theodore slumped across the mare's back. Simon was screaming frantically for help, while his brother appeared to be unconscious – or, given the fact that both men were covered in blood, dead.

Alerted by the commotion, Šarlatová, Roan, and several others leapt to their feet in a small clearing in *der Thüringerwald* (the Thuringian Forest) where *die Grüne Gauner* were currently encamped. The *Thüringerwald* was a range of forested hills and mountains in Germany, approximately one hundred and seventy miles north-west of Prague, extending in an irregular line from Eisenach in west-central Thüringen southeastward to the frontier of Bavaria, where it merged with *der Frankenwald* (the Franconian Forest).

Much of the landscape of the area was characterised by picturesque hills, but *die Grüne Gauner* hadn't chosen the area as their base camp for aesthetic reasons. They chose it because it was a fertile agricultural region which gave them access to a number of eastward-flowing streams. Additionally, the climate of the area was relatively temperate, and the dense woods provided a high degree of secrecy – something that Šarlatová was very happy to have, especially given how loudly and violently Simon was yelling.

"What happened?" Šarlatová asked desperately, as Simon leapt from his saddle and helped his older brother slide down to the ground.

"We were ambushed!" Simon shouted, still feverishly animated as he lowered Theodore to the ground.

"Where?" Roan demanded as he pushed Simon aside so that he could examine Theo's wounds.

"Wartburg."

"Wartburg? But....that is friendly territory," Šarlatová noted, still confused as to what was happening.

The castle in Wartburg, a model of late Romanesque architecture, was built sometime during the eleventh century and was situated on a precipice overlooking the town of Eisenach, approximately forty miles northwest of *die Grüne Gauner's* camp in *der Thüringerwald*. From 1172 to 1211, it had been one of the most important courts in the Holy Roman Empire, and during the thirteenth century it had even served as home to *Heilige Elisabeth von Thüringen* (Saint Elizabeth of Hungary). But, starting around 1485, the castle and the surrounding lands came under the control of the Ernestine Dukes of Saxony. In fact, it was the elector Frederick III of Saxony who sheltered Martin Luther, under the name *Junker Jorg* (the Knight George), in

Wartburg while he was translating the New Testament from Greek into German. That meant that it was friendly territory and a "safe zone" for *die Grüne Gauner*, which was why Šarlatová and Roan were so confused.

"We never made it to Wartburg," Simon clarified, just now beginning to calm down. "We were ambushed before we even got there – by Jesuits. Or Stormsong men. I don't know. It all happened so fast....I couldn't really tell."

"That's impossible," Šarlatová observed. "Stormsong men don't operate that far north....or that far west. And the Jesuits would have no reason to be anywhere near Wartburg."

"Well, somebody was there today!" Simon protested. "And in huge numbers, too. They had at least a dozen arquebusiers and maybe two dozen archers. And the attack came....well, as if they knew we would be there. Everyone scattered as soon as the first shots were fired, so I have no idea how many of us were killed or captured. I managed to avoid injury, but Theo was hit."

Roan knew that an arquebusier was an infantryman armed with a gunpowder weapon like a Dutch "hook gun" or a caliver (a forerunner to the flintlock musket), and Theo's wound clearly indicated that it was from a gunpowder weapon.

"He wasn't hit by a long gun," he noted as he examined the wound in Theo's right shoulder. "This wound is too small, and it isn't even that deep."

"Then why is there so much blood, and why does he look like he's half-dead?" Šarlatová asked excitedly. As she did, Hester Neuss and several others gathered around.

Examining his own blood-soaked clothing, Simon explained. "The blood isn't his. Or mine. It's from the Stormsongs....or Jesuits....or whoever the hell they were. Even though he was wounded, Theo still managed to kill four of the bastards." Simon seemed to want to say more, but he hesitated.

"And how many did *you* get?" Roan wondered, causing Simon to lower his head in shame.

Šarlatová placed a reassuring hand on his arm. "It doesn't matter. All that matters is that you're both alive – for now. But that still doesn't explain what's wrong with Theo. I've seen him suffer much deeper wounds than this without so much as blinking an eye."

"He's been poisoned," Hester Neuss interjected. As everyone turned their attention her way, she approached and knelt down next to Theodore. "It's obvious. Look at his colour." Hester was right. Theo's face simultaneously looked both swollen and skeletal, and the bulging pockets beneath his eyes and around his mouth were black, while the rest of his skin was clammy and stone grey.

"He wasn't poisoned," Simon barked. "He was shot!"

Hester knelt next to Theo and placed a hand on his forehead and cheeks. "He's burning up." Then, as she examined the wound, she added, "I can feel the ball in his shoulder. Something on it has gotten into his blood, and it's poisoning him. That's what's killing him."

Before she was a Green Thief, Hester Neuss had been a midwife, and an efficient healer. She had lived in *Dormagen* and had married a miller named Peter. During that marriage, despite the fact that she was healthy enough to present Peter with two fine, healthy sons, Hester began to suffer from severe "episodes." Those episodes, which were characterised by periods of violent shaking, varied from brief and nearly undetectable ones to others that were so long that they even resulted in physical injuries to herself or those around her. To treat her own "condition," Hester had begun to study herbalism, and found great success with a plant native to the Mediterranean known as the Autumn Mandrake. However, when mere herbalism was not enough to cure her family of scrofula, she turned her time and attention to the study of spellcraft. While her initial foray into the field of white magic did not save either her husband or her sons, she had continued to study it. However, she had never become skilled in either its use or application.

"You mean to say that the Stormsongs have taken to poisoning their ammunition?" Roan asked, incredulous. It was widely known that the Stormsongs were adept at using devilish weapons against their foes, including some form of poison gas produced by throwing chemicals onto bonfires and allowing the winds to carry the fumes to their enemies. But, as far as Roan knew, this would mark the first time that they had poisoned their shots before firing them.

"Perhaps. Or perhaps it's just the lead of the ball itself that has infected his blood stream. There's simply no good way to tell. But even if we cut the ball free from his shoulder, it may already be too late."

At Simon's request, Hester continued to examine Theo. At the same time, Roan gently took Šarlatová by the arm and led her away from the commotion.

"What do you think, *dívka*?" Roan asked.

"About what? About the ambush, or about the poison?"

"Neither. About the…." Roan indicated his meaning by gesturing first towards Šarlatová's left eye and then to her throat. "Do you think *it*….that is, do you think *you* could help Theo?"

Šarlatová sighed. "I don't know. I don't think….I mean, I don't know if it is that powerful. I've certainly never tried anything like that before. And if it doesn't work…."

Unsure if Šarlatová was more concerned about revealing her secret or about increasing the danger to Theo, Roan stepped forward and put his hands on her shoulders. Looking down at her, he maintained eye-contact for several long seconds. "If it was me over there dyin,' there's no one on God's green Earth I would rather trust with my life than you, *dívka*." He paused for effect before adding, "Now before we go out there and kill the bastards what done this to him, why don't you give it a go?"

Šarlatová was terrified. Terrified of going public with her secret. Terrified of hurting Theo. And, above all, terrified of disappointing Roan. Roan could sense that anxiety. "What happens to one of us…." he began.

Summoning every ounce of courage within her, she looked up at the giant, took a very deep breath and nodded. "Happens to all of us," she finished. Smiling now, she asked, "So why didn't you just put it that way in the first place?"

With that, she and Roan turned back towards the large and growing group that had encircled Theo, having no idea just how irrevocably the next few minutes would change both of their lives.

Šarlatová knelt at Theo's left side and asked for absolute silence. As the others quieted, they unconsciously widened the circle around both patient and healer to give Šarlatová space to do….whatever it was she was going to do. As he was the only one who suspected what was about to happen, Roan grabbed the hands of Simon Berger and Hester Neuss who were standing on either side of him. Soon, the entire group was standing hand in hand, not quite knowing why, nor what else they should be doing.

Placing her right hand on Theo's heart and the left on her own, Šarlatová breathed in and out in a way that at first seemed rhythmic. As her breathing started to evolve into something almost lyrical, she began to hum. At first, the humming was simply a pleasant, sweet stringing together of notes. But it soon swelled into something greater. The sounds coming from Šarlatová's slender throat remained beautiful and lyrical, but they also began to slowly strengthen…. rolling like the sound of building thunder.

As the group around her became enthralled by the sounds coming from Šarlatová (or were they emanating from the space *around* her?), it seemed as if they could actually hear musical instruments coming from within her. While each person heard something slightly different – some a flute, others a lyre, and still others a harp – it was now clear that the sound was no longer coming from within her throat. It was more elemental than that, and it seemed to be originating from everywhere at once, including from Theo's injured shoulder.

When she began to add lyrics to whatever it was she was singing, the wind began to pick up slightly and the colour of the air

45

slowly changed from pitch black to a muted slate grey. *"φιλόθεος, προσεύχομαι, δώσε μου δύναμη, δίνω δεξιότητα στα χέρια μου, δώσε μου δύναμη...."* she sang. Not one person in the group, not even Šarlatová herself, had any idea what the words meant, or even what language they were – but it didn't matter. The music now seemed to be coming from within each person. It was no longer simply something Šarlatová was doing; rather, the notes and lyrics were swelling in a way that was uniting everyone in the circle, warming each, and altering each one's heartbeat until they were all striking in cadence with one another. The audience and the singer had briefly become one.

"βάζω όλη μου την εμπιστοσύνη σε σένα, μπορεί να είναι τυλιγμένος στη χάρη σου, Αφήστε το δηλητήριο να φύγει, ας τον ανανεώσει...." she continued, and now even Theo seemed to be part of the melody. Afterwards, no one could be sure, but several of those gathered around thought they saw Theo's body rise slightly from the ground, supported by nothing other than Šarlatová's voice. But that was impossible, they would all agree later. A song couldn't do that. Could it?

"ὑμᾶς πᾶν αἷμα δίκαιον ἐκχυννόμενον. Ἀμήν" As the crescendo built, the music and the words grew louder and louder. Then, as the music reached a climax, Šarlatová's final words – *"ὑμᾶς πᾶν αἷμα δίκαιον ἐκχυννόμενον. Ἀμήν"* – were punctuated by a tremendous roar of thunder and a flash of lightning, from what had earlier been a cloudless, moonlit sky.

Then, just like that, it was over. The wind began to settle, the sky returned to its previous cast and colour, and the sounds of thunder and music were replaced by brief gasps from all of the spectators. Then – silence. No sounds of any kind. No movement from anyone or anything, until....

As Theo opened his eyes and cleared his throat, a thick stream of dark pus oozed from his shoulder, pushing the leather ball and all sorts of putrid filth completely clean from his body. As the wound seemed to be healing itself, several of *die Grüne Gauner* fell to their knees in thanks and praise. Still others backed slowly away from

Šarlatová, uncertain of and terrified by what they had just witnessed. But Roan did neither. He simply looked at Theo and asked, "How do you feel?"

Theo cleared his throat and sat up a little before saying, "Embarrassed, more than anything else, I suppose."

Roan chuckled and asked, "Embarrassed? Why?"

"Because I forgot one of the cardinal rules of being part of *die Grüne Gauner.*"

Smiling, his brother Simon asked, "Which rule is that, Theo?"

"Never get shot unless you're near a priest."

As an uncomfortable laughter rippled through the assembled crowd, Theo fixed his gaze intently on Šarlatová, who was still kneeling at his side. She smiled, wiped some milky discharge from her left eye, and then quite simply toppled over like a marionette who had just had its strings cut.

It was quite clear to everyone assembled that Šarlatová had just saved Theo's life, but that, in so doing, she had given up her own.

In short, it was clear to all that Šarlatová was dead.

Chapter Seven

"She's not dead," Hester assured everyone. "She's just recovering. It seems that….healing Theo took much from her."

The predawn air was biting, and the morning fog remained low and foreboding as *die Grüne Gauner* gathered around Hester.

"You sound like you speak from experience," Simon noted, still stunned by what had transpired mere moments earlier.

Glancing around at the expectant faces of her compatriots, Hester hesitated at first. Then, glancing over at Šarlatová and Theodore, both exhausted and asleep, she summoned the nerve to continue. "Yes, I do speak from experience." The gasp from the others was part shock and part accusation.

"Then you're a witch," someone challenged, earning a disapproving scowl from Roan.

"Nein! I am not a witch. I *was* a midwife; I am a healer – but I was never a witch!" Hester retorted. "I can see that several of you would be content to burn me at the stake right now, but may I remind you first that I have faithfully served *die Grüne Gauner* for two years now, and that I have used my skill to heal more than a few of you. I ask now that you grant me a few moments to explain how I acquired those skills."

At first, no one moved. Then, sensing that they were waiting on a cue from him, Roan sat down somewhat ceremoniously, extended his hands to indicate that the others should do likewise, and said to Hester, "Witch or no witch, you are our true friend. Take as much time as you need, *sister* Neuss." Roan emphasised the word sister as a way of reminding everyone of the creed by which they lived.

One by one, the others each took a seat, and Hester exhaled as a sign of relief. She, too, then sat and folded herself into a position in front of the group as if she were a shaman or a mystic.

"There is magic in the world. This we all know. But not all magic is dark magic. Yes.... many who have been arrested, tortured, and executed by the church – and not just the Catholic Church, mind you – have been witches, sorcerers, necromancers, and the like. But just as many, like me, have been students of white magic – very different from the dark arts."

Seeing that her initial explanation had not satisfied the assembled group, Hester decided to continue. "When magic or supernatural powers are used for selfish purposes, such as cursing one's neighbour, or placing a hex on a competitor's crops, that is black magic – the dark arts. Some have even been known to use these gifts to leave their earthly bodies and travel great distances in spirit so as to commune with devils or to have sexual congress with demons."

By the shocked faces in the crowd, Hester could see that she was actually scaring the group far worse than Šarlatová's powerful display had. "But not all magic is selfish or malicious. Much of it, in fact, is benevolent. That's white magic; some call it high magic or natural magic. It's only understood by a small number of people, and it can only be used for unselfish and healthy purposes. Some say that Christ's miracles were white magic."

"That's heresy!" shouted one of the assembled, a man named Thomas.

"According to the church, so's Protestantism," noted Simon.

"But she's blaspheming the Lord. It's a sin to...." Thomas stammered.

Roan turned to face Thomas and put the dispute to rest. "It's a sin to fuck little boys in the ass, too, isn't it, Thomas? But you've never let that stop you now, have you?"

Thomas skulked off to a round of uncomfortable laughter as Roan continued. "Every single bitch and bastard here is a sinner. Let's be clear about that. If'n we weren't, then Christ Jesus wouldn't have had to come to pay the price for us now, would He? So, save the sermons for Sunday, all of you. I'll brook no further argument on that point. Understood?"

What was understood was that Roan's full-throated defence of the use of magic had nothing at all to do with Hester. It was entirely to do with Šarlatová, and how the group might respond to her now that they all knew what she had kept secret from them for some time.

Sensing that it was now okay to continue, Hester resumed her lesson. "One man's miracle is another man's magic. If I were to walk on water right now, or to turn water into wine, would you call it magic or a miracle?"

"I'd call it a waste, Hester. Now if'n you was to turn water into beer, then I'd be ready to proclaim you the Messiah m'self." Roan's blasphemous joke was meant to settle the anxiety that remained palpable with the group, but it only served to unsettle the congregation even more.

"The entire Bible is full of black magic. The devil disguising himself as a serpent., as just one example. But it's also full of white magic. Like Jesus raising people from the dead. Miracles, magic, what's the difference?" Hester asked.

"There's a world of difference, Hester, and you know it," challenged someone from near the back of the assembly.

Undaunted at not having made her point, Hester continued. "If I was to tell you that I was born of a fourteen-year-old virgin. That I could walk on water and feed thousands with five loaves of bread and two fish. That I rose from the dead, but only after instructing my followers to consume my flesh and drink my blood once a week, what would you call me? A witch? Or the messiah?"

Hester's point hung heavy over the assembled crowd. Not another word was spoken for several long seconds.

Hester finally broke the silence. "My point is that, whatever term you use to describe it, the supernatural is everywhere. It's as prevalent as the air we breathe. There's no more a debate about that than there is a debate about what colour the sky is. To deny the existence of spirits or magic is to deny half of the Bible."

"Are you a pagan then?" asked Simon. "A devil worshipper?"

It was clear to Hester that she was not getting her point across. "No. I'm a Christian – just like you. But just because I believe in the Father, the Son, and the Holy Ghost doesn't mean I can't believe anything else, does it? Since when does the Bible say to stop reading other books and to stick your head in the sand? The "good book" isn't the only book that's good."

She paused for effect and then directed her next question to the doubters and challengers. "What would you call it if I asked a supernatural power to provide me with some kind of supernatural intercession?"

"I'd call it a spell!" shouted one.

"Witchcraft is what it is!" called another.

"Exactly!" responded Hester, confident that she was now going to be able to make her point. "Do you know what the Church calls it?" When no one offered an answer, she stunned them with her own. "They call it *prayer*! To Christians, appealing for help to a supernatural being is prayer. It's only when it's someone other than a Christian who's doing it that the Church calls it dark magic or witchcraft!"

By way of response all Hester got was a bunch of blank stares and shoulder shrugs.

"What do you know of Horus, Osiris, Mithra, Hercules, Dionysus, Tammuz, Ra and Adonis? They're all pagan gods, right? But what if I told you that, according to *their* followers, they were all born on or around December twenty-fifth, hundreds or even thousands of years before Christ, to virgin mothers who had been impregnated by a deity, and whose births were heralded by stars or meteors or heavenly lights, and whose arrivals were then celebrated by three kings bearing gifts? The Greek word for magician, by the way, is *magos*. In Persian, it's *magoi*. We call them *magi*. But it's all the same thing."

"How do you know all of this?" Roan wondered aloud.

Flashing him a deprecating smile, Hester whispered "Because I can read, my giant friend. And because I think with what's inside my head and not with what's inside my pants like most of the lot of you." The slight ruffle of laughter gave Hester a much-needed signal to continue the lesson. "Each one of those so-called *gods* allegedly died and was reborn, with his blood redeeming the Earth as it fell from his body. And each one's worshipers then celebrated the salvation from death offered to them by the death and resurrection of their saviour with a celebration held in the spring – on or around March twenty-fifth – when we celebrate Easter. Christians may condemn magic when it's someone else doing it, but they're all for it when it's their God performing the acts."

A long and awkward silence ensued while the assembled crowd took in the weight of what Hester had just taught them.

When someone finally broke the silence, it was to ask "So what's Šarlatová then? Is she a sorcerer or a saint?" It was clear now to both Hester and Roan that everyone assembled was thinking the same thing.

"I don't know," Hester admitted. "I've never before seen anything like what she just did. As to whether she's a 'sorcerer or a saint,' I fear that maybe she's a little of both. But whatever she is, she has power beyond anything I've ever seen or heard of."

Chapter Eight

"I've never seen anything like it before," admitted Sister Roberta to Sister Theresa. "She's not dead, but she should be."

Vanessa was awake, nude, and lying face down on a bed within *das Gott Haus* (God's House) located deep within *Schloß Stormsong*. Modelled after a hospital built in Jerusalem after the first Crusade in the twelfth century, *das Gott Haus* was a large hall with dozens of rows of beds against the walls; in fact, it had room for nearly a thousand visitors (or patients). The massive chamber enabled the Stormsongs to provide hospitality for the many servants who inevitably accompanied visiting dignitaries, and it also served as a hospital to provide care for the sick or wounded within Archduke von Stormsong's own army of servants and soldiers. But like virtually everything else in *Schloß Stormsong*, it was steeped in religious overtones.

It contained a small chapel for prayers, a larger chapel for mass, and a fully functioning convent for the hundred-or-more Augustinian nuns who staffed the hall, often serving as nurses. Unlike most seventeenth century hospitals, where the sick might have to share a bed with someone and risk catching something other than what sent him or her there in the first place, this Gott Haus always had a fire going; the floors and sheets were washed regularly, and the guests received the best care available. Patients in most hospitals of the time weren't expected to live long, and certainly weren't expected to actually leave under their own power. That was not the case here, a place where the Bridgettine Sisters took great pride in their work; and unless the patient was suffering from lupus, leprosy, or the Black Death, visitors to this Gott Haus were expected to leave in better condition than that in which they had arrived. `

This was the first time that Sisters Roberta and Theresa had tended to Vanessa, and much to their amazement, she was well on her way to recovery. As Vanessa lay there silently, the sisters gently applied a salve to the fresh wounds left on her back by Monsignor Mučitel's "cat," a multi-tailed leather flail that he had invented and used to extract confessions from or administer punishments to whomever Archduke von Stormsong sent his way. Monsignor Mučitel had perfected the art of punishment in much the same way that Michelangelo had perfected sculpting marble, and his "work" with Vanessa was his own personal *Pieta*. For reasons the sisters never understood, Monsignor Mučitel's punishments of Vanessa went well beyond anything he doled out to anyone else, and this most recent penance (thirty or more bites from "the cat") should have killed a man twice Vanessa's size.

But, as always, Vanessa had endured it. In fact, just minutes after her "session" with the deranged priest had concluded, she had regained consciousness and had walked into *das Gott Haus* under her own power. Now, as the sisters worked, it seemed that Vanessa's wounds were almost healing themselves. The muscles in her arms, back, and legs were long and lean, and looked to the sisters like cable or corded rope beneath her skin. But mere musculature couldn't explain how Vanessa was able to endure her gruelling sessions with *der schwarze Beichtvater*. Some other factor had to be at play.

Conscious, but choosing to remain silent while the nuns worked, Vanessa heard them wonder at her miraculous healing ability. "How does she do it?" and "Why does her father put her through it?" they took turns wondering out loud.

"That is not your concern," barked Mother Ludmilla, as she approached the bloodstained bed upon which Vanessa was recovering. "Tend to her wounds, and mind your mouths," she instructed.

"Yes, Mother Superior!" both nuns responded robotically. They proceeded to go about their work in silence as Mother Superior Ludmilla stood watch over them.

Mother Superior Ludmilla was the abbess of the convent, and her authority within *das Gott Haus* was absolute. No other nun, priest, lord, or lady dared challenge her position as the spiritual leader of the convent; in fact, not even Monsignor Mučitel or Archduke von Stormsong himself would dare enter *das Gott Haus* (or her house, as she referred to it) uninvited, for fear of invoking the wrath of the Bridgettine Bear (as the sisters had taken to calling her – behind her back, of course).

The Bridgettine nuns, officially known as *Ordo Sanctissimi Salvatoris* (the Order of the Most Holy Saviour), were part of a religious order founded within the Catholic Church in 1344 by Sister Bridget of Sweden. Formally approved by Pope Urban V in 1370, the Bridgettines strictly followed the rule of Saint Augustine, which meant that they were governed by vows of chastity, poverty, obedience, detachment from the world, silence during meals, and care for the sick. A running joke within the convent was that Mother Superior Ludmilla had little trouble taking her vows, because she had no money, no friends, nothing interesting to say, and (due to her rather unfortunate and hairy countenance) no prospects of over engaging in physical intimacy with a man.

That joke, however, became decidedly less funny when the nuns discovered Ludmillas' religious fervour for obedience.

The most distinctive feature of the Bridgettine habit, *die Krone auf des fünf heilige Wunden* (the Crown of the Five Holy Wounds), was a metal crown they wore that had five red stones, one at each joint, to commemorate the five wounds Christ had suffered on the Cross. Over the years, Mother Superior Ludmilla had demonstrated that she was not above using her crown on the backsides of her sisters when she determined they were talking too much or working too little. In fact, sister Roberta had just recently received a "lesson" that left her unable to sit down for three days.

However, as tough as she was on her nuns (and everyone else, for that matter), Ludmilla had always held an unspoken soft spot in her heart for Vanessa. She knew all too well that, while the Stormsongs had once reproduced in almost biblical proportions, the current Archduke had no siblings, only one child (Vanessa), and a wife who had died giving birth to a stillborn son – the last and best chance at preserving the Stormsong line. While he had once doted on Vanessa, at least until she was four, the fact that she now represented the end of a centuries old dynasty had irrevocably changed the Archduke's relationship with his daughter. Consequently, lacking any siblings of her own, or a mother, or a fully functioning father, Vanessa had been virtually raised by Father Joseph and Mother Superior Ludmilla.

Examining Vanessa's wounds after having dismissed the other two nuns with a mere flick of her wrist, Ludmilla produced a rosary. However, instead of beginning with a profession of faith like the Apostle's Creed, she began to recite passages from chapter six of the book of Ephesians. Praying *die Rüstung Gottes* (the armour of God) over Vanessa's newly broken body, the old nun marvelled, once again, at the near miraculous recovery powers of the strong and beautiful young woman before her.

"Rest, my child. I place upon thee the whole armour of God that you might be able to stand against all evil. I place upon you the helmet of salvation, the breastplate of righteousness – *and Lord knows you'll need a big enough one of those* – the belt of truth, and the shoes of peace. I beseech thee to take up the shield of faith and the sword of the spirit, which is the word of God."

"Thank you, mother superior," Vanessa said when the prayer was complete, choosing to ignore the jab at the size of the breastplate she required. Ludmilla had always expressed a peculiar but disapproving interest in Vanessa's large, perfectly shaped breasts. "But, perhaps, it would have been better if I had been cloaked in the armour of God *before* I visited with Monsignor Mučitel."

"Or, *perhaps*, you could simply not visit with him at all," noted the nun.

"As we sin, so must we suffer," responded Vanessa reflexively.

"Quatsch! Where in scripture does it say anything remotely close to that? For that matter, where in scripture does it say that you must continue to carry out these "assignments" for your father?"

"It says it right there in Ephesians, mother superior. Chapter six, verse sixteen. We wear the armour of God so that we might 'extinguish all the flaming arrows of the evil one.' And that's what I'm doing."

"Quatsch!" she said again. But this time, when she offered the curse meaning nonsense or rubbish, Mother superior Ludmilla uncharacteristically spat upon the ground – uncharacteristic not because Ludmilla suffered from lady-like tendencies, but because her spit marred the floor that she suffered to keep immaculately clean.

"Verse thirteen says 'when the day of evil comes.' Am I meant to believe then, my child, that judgement day is upon us? How could I have missed such an important revelation?"

"That's naive thinking, mother superior. Perhaps you need to leave this convent every so often. 'The day of evil' is upon us. I see it almost every day. And the 'flaming arrows of the evil one,' – well, they're falling are all around us, too."

"Hush, child!" Ludmilla chastised Vanessa, giving her a disciplinary smack on her exposed bottom for emphasis. "I'm going to allow that you're still delirious from your ordeal, because if you were in your right mind, I'm certain you wouldn't attempt to correct *me* on the proper interpretation of scripture. Nor would you call me *naive.*"

Sufficiently but playfully, chastised, Vanessa smiled and said, "Yes, *mother* superior. I meant no disrespect. But the rulers and authorities and the powers of the dark world that the book of Ephesians directs us to fight are very real and very alive."

With this, Ludmilla came around to the front of the bed on which Vanessa was lying and bent down so that she could look her in the face.

"No, they are not, child. You need to reread Ephesians. It says, 'For we wrestle not against flesh and blood, but against principalities, against powers, against the rulers of the darkness of this world, and against spiritual forces of evil wickedness in the heavenly realms.' Do you understand what that means, my child? We are called to engage in a struggle against powers that are *not* of flesh and blood, but against *spiritual* forces of evil. And can you honestly tell me that everything you have done for your father, and everything you have suffered at the hands of Monsignor Mučitel, has been a part of the *spiritual* war we are commanded to wage?" Ludmilla paused for effect. "Or are you simply being used by your father – to dispatch his *temporal* enemies?"

As per usual, Ludmilla had no time for nuance or pretence. As she had always done with Vanessa, she cut straight to the heart of the matter. And this last question struck Vanessa especially deeply.

Despite everything, Vanessa loved her father very much. She hated the fact that he had gone away and left her – not physically, of course, but in every other way possible. But she still loved him, at least the memory of him, and she could easily recall how, after the death of her mother and stillborn brother, he had grieved endlessly. How, despite being surrounded by the trappings of wealth in the massive castle that bore his name, he could only be comforted by the odds and ends of Vanessa's mother – her dresses, combs, and jewels. But that period of mourning had never ended, and in his grief, he seemed to have relegated Vanessa to the list of the dead.

She tried to defend her father now – to offer Mother Superior Ludmilla some answer that would justify what her father had forced her to do, and to endure. She desperately wanted to explain how she hoped that fulfilling his commands would somehow, someday return him to what he had once been, but she couldn't. No words would come – only a quivering of her lower lip and a solitary tear streaming down her right cheek.

"I do not mean to bring you more suffering, my child. Lord knows that *Drecksau* Monsignor Mučitel has done enough of that. I am concerned only for your salvation, little one."

Before Vanessa could respond, Mother Superior Ludmilla wiped the tear from her cheek and placed a hard and calloused finger to her lips. "Hush now, and simply think upon this. Do you remember the parable of the weeds?"

"From Matthew, chapter thirteen?" Vanessa whispered weakly.

"Yes, my child. You do listen well, don't you?" The way that Ludmilla brightened up at her recall of Matthew's Gospel brought a faint, but fleeting smile to Vanessa's face.

"Now – tell me what you remember, *Atlantis*."

At first, Vanessa was somewhat taken aback by the fact that Ludmilla had actually called her by her given name. She couldn't recall a single occasion in which the nun had even called her Vanessa – much less Atlantis. However, unlike the way in which Father Joseph had invoked her Christian name, there was no judgement or condemnation in Ludmilla's use of it – only a gentleness, tinged with a sorrowful affection. Surprised by that, especially coming from the "Bridgettine Bear," Vanessa hesitated just a moment, but then began to recite the gospel from memory. "Jesus put forth a parable in which he likened the kingdom of Heaven to a man who sowed good seed in his field. But while the man slept, his enemy came and sowed weeds among the wheat, and then went on his way. So, when the garden yielded fruit, then the weeds also appeared."

Excited now, Ludmilla presseed Vanessa further. "And what did the man say to his servants when they asked him if they should go and gather up the weeds?"

"He told his servants not to. He feared that, in gathering the weeds, they would also uproot the wheat along with them. So, he instructed them to let the weeds and the wheat grow together until the harvest, when he would collect the weeds first and bind them into bundles to be burned, but *he* would gather the wheat into his barn."

Ludmilla was smiling so brightly now that Vanessa feared she might actually attempt to hug or kiss her. Instead, the nun rose, as if to walk away, and simply said "I think then that our lesson is complete, my child."

Confused, Vanessa sat straight up, totally oblivious to the fact that she was still completely naked. "That's it? But....I don't understand. What....?"

Taking a clean sheet from an adjoining bed and wrapping it around Vanessa, Ludmilla sighed. "The point is this, child. Your father has you out there pulling weeds. Why?"

"Because….*because the garden of Eden is hopelessly overgrown with weeds and thorns*, Mother Superior." Vanessa's response was a phrase that had been deeply ingrained in her as well as any of Ludmilla's Bible lessons. "And….*and it is the duty, honour, and obligation of the Stormsongs to remove the weeds.* Isn't it?"

"But when you're 'pulling the weeds,' how do you know that you aren't uprooting the wheat along with them? And, if you are, then you're usurping God's providence. It is for Him and Him alone to decide when to collect and burn *His* weeds, and when to gather *His* wheat into *His* barn."

Vanessa could not have been more dumbstruck if Ludmilla had hit her upside the head with a cooking pot – something she was not averse to doing, when necessary. As she stared at the nun, mouth agape, she unconsciously let the sheet Ludmilla had given her drop. Vanessa was, once again, naked – and, perhaps for the first time in her life, utterly speechless. No snappy retort came to mind, and Ludmilla, revelling in her ability to strike Vanessa dumb, simply stood there, for several long seconds.

After what felt like an eternity to Vanessa, Ludmilla broke the silence. "Now, close your mouth, child. And for Heaven's sake, put on some clothes. You're liable to hurt someone with those things," she said, glancing disapprovingly again at Vanessa's exposed breasts. "Besides, *you* have another visitor, and *I* have work to do."

Just like that, the old, familiar Mother Superior Ludmilla that Vanessa knew so well and had grown to love was instantly back. She simply turned and walked away from Vanessa, immediately beginning to bark orders at any nun (or any priest, for that matter) within earshot, and leaving Vanessa completely exposed – in every way imaginable.

Chapter Nine

Vanessa began to dress unusually slowly, and not just because it was incredibly painful to move after her most recent visit with Monsignor Mučitel. She was also postponing the inevitable – a visit from Stephen Stallknecht. Desperate as he was to see and hold her, Stephen was a proper gentleman who wouldn't dream of entering *das Gott Haus* without Mother Superior Ludmilla's permission and her acknowledgement that Vanessa was properly attired to receive guests.

Before she had left, Ludmilla had laid out for Vanessa a gorgeous blue gown with a high waistline and narrow sleeves, open at the front seam, both of which were considered quite fashionable. While the dress lacked either a drum-farthingale or a starched fan collar, two things Ludmilla knew that Vanessa would never wear, the exquisite blackwork embroidery, which worked in a continuous pattern throughout the body of the garment, and the white linen bobbin lace at the back of each sleeve were both clear indications that this dress was extremely expensive and fit for a lady of Vanessa Stormsong's station.

Next to it lay a loose, filmy-white, muslin cover that was short, thin, and intended to serve as a chemise. While it was clearly designed to be an undergarment, Vanessa knew that the cover would leave her arms and legs (and much of her ample bosom) bare, and it was so sheer that, any parts of her body it did actually cover, would be only partially veiled by material that was practically transparent.

Vanessa tended to be extremely modest in her choice of attire, especially when she was required to wear a dress or a gown, which (fortunately) was not very often. Additionally, she was not one to try to manipulate men by displaying her flesh. However, she was well aware of the effect that a typical woman's body had on the average male, and her body was by no means typical, nor was Stephen Stallknecht's attraction to that body average, and it was that very fact that she intended to use to her advantage now.

So, while Stephen waited just outside *das Gott Haus*, Vanessa slipped on the chemise, but nothing else. She did so not out of any flirtatious attempt to increase Stephen's desire, nor out of any malicious motive; rather, she did so out of a calculated and well-intentioned effort to dismiss Stephen before she could further hurt his feelings – something she was sorry to have done more than once before. But while she had no intention of hurting him again, she was not quite ready to see Stephen just yet, and she knew, gentleman that he was, that he would be chagrined – mortified might be a better word – by seeing her in what amounted to a flesh-colored body stocking. In fact, she expected that he would last no more than two minutes before he either politely excused himself from her presence or quite simply burst into flame.

Stephen Stallknecht was four years older than Vanessa, and he had been a part of life for her entire twenty-two years. When she was a child, he was a simple servant boy who always seemed to be conveniently present in any part of the castle where Vanessa could be found, and their "relationship" was one of her playing princess – ordering him around – and him playing the dutiful servant – doing his level best to fulfil her every wish and command, no matter how absurd those wishes and commands might be. For example, when Vanessa was a very spoiled and precocious four-year-old and had demanded a unicorn for Christmas, it was Stephen who had happily fulfilled her wish. Vanessa had been delighted; Archduke von Stormsong appalled, and the "unicorn" (a pony which Stephen had creatively outfitted with a horn made from the tusk of a boar) far from amused. In fact, it wasn't long before Vanessa's Christmas "unicorn" retaliated against Stephen by goring him and breaking off a significant piece of its "horn" in his backside. While she was saddened by the fact that her "unicorn" had reverted back to a simple pony, Vanessa was oddly overjoyed by the tapestry of profanity woven by Stephen when Mother Superior Ludmilla tended, rather harshly, to his wounded rear end.

As the years passed, and as Stephen's size, power, and military acumen grew, so did his interest in Vanessa. For the past six years, he had proposed to her almost as often as he bid her hello or good-bye. While there was no denying the boy was sweet, well-mannered, honest, and loyal, Vanessa could only see him as the little boy she knew as a child – despite the fact that he was both older and taller than her and had grown increasingly (and inconveniently) handsome.

Until recently, it had been easy to resist his advances, because Stephen came from the servant class and Vanessa was a Stormsong. And while those social class distinctions were antiquated and meaningless to Vanessa, they meant everything to her father. So that enabled Vanessa to refuse his proposals in a way that didn't require her to reject him. She could easily assuage the situation with a simple, "Now, Stephen, you know what my father would say."

Things had grown increasingly difficult, however, in recent years. When Vanessa had turned eighteen, and Stephen twenty-two, Archduke von Stormsong had chosen to supplement Vanessa's already extensive education (which previously included comprehensive courses in mathematics, science, literature, art, history, philosophy, theology and language) by adding a course of training in the physical arts – and he had placed Stephen, an expert marksman and swordsman, in charge of that training.

Student and teacher had met daily, training for hours on end. While her training required a level of proximity, and a corresponding level of physical intimacy, that Vanessa found uncomfortable (and in which Stephen delightedly reveled), it was something Vanessa actually looked forward to. She took to the training immediately and, in no time at all (despite how gifted of a warrior Stephen had become in his own right), had surpassed her teacher's skills and had become the preeminent weapon in Archduke von Stormsong's arsenal.

Despite his inferiority to her in social class, education, and even fighting skills, Stephen was undaunted in his pursuit of Vanessa's affections. And it had recently become even harder for Vanessa to sidestep those advances – not because her feelings for Stephen had changed, rather because Stephen's status had.

Less than a year ago, as a result of successfully carrying out several of the Archduke's "assignments," Stephen had been promoted to the position of Captain of the Castle Guard – a title that automatically inferred a degree of nobility upon him. In an elaborate ceremony (that Vanessa had been fortunate to miss), Archduke Johann Albrecht von Stormsong had named Stephen Stallknecht as *Sir* Stephen. Whether or not this promotion was a calculated act on the part of Archduke von Stormsong to ease the path of marriage between the two or was simply a proper reward for Stephen with no ulterior motive attached, was totally irrelevant to Vanessa. Either way it posed a serious problem, because gone now was the convenient barrier that social class norms and traditions had provided.

It wasn't just that Vanessa objected to marriage with Stephen, even though she couldn't seriously imagine being betrothed to (and, thus, the de facto property of) the only childhood playmate she had ever had. She also objected to marriage in general, because it implied some faith in a theoretical future with someone else, and her recent experiences had caused her to seriously doubt the existence of any future for herself – either coupled or alone.

Soon the barrier provided by the privacy of *das Gott Haus* would be gone, too. Mother Superior Ludmilla, who often mistook her role for that of a *Shadchanit* (a Jewish matchmaker), had always gone out of her way to make it easy for Stephen – now Sir Stephen – to find Vanessa, whether she wanted to be found or not. And she did so again now. In fact, as soon as she was finished barking orders to her army of nurses and nuns, and once it was clear that Vanessa was as fully dressed as she intended to get, Ludmilla ceremoniously opened the doors to the hall and, with a simple nod of her head, granted Stephen the permission he needed to enter.

"Praise God you're alright, Vanessa," Stephen said as he rushed towards her. He desperately wanted to throw his arms around her; however, given that she was still recovering from the wounds inflicted by Monsignor Mučitel, not to mention the fact that she was, for all intents and purposes, quite naked, he just couldn't bring himself to do it.

"Thank you, Stephen," Vanessa responded coquettishly. "It's lovely to see you, too. As always." Then, standing on the tips of her toes so that her breasts practically jumped from her chest and into Stephen's face, she kissed him on the cheek and added, "You wanted to see me about something?" She couldn't have been more flirtatious if she had actually batted her eyelashes at him.

Stephen was suddenly very aware of both his hands and his lips, and simply had no idea what to do with either of them. "Yes…. well….of course. I….er….that is….I mean to say…." Stephen's stammering could have continued indefinitely, if Vanessa had not intervened.

"Out with it, Stephen," she said, as she stepped even closer to him – so close, in fact, that he could actually feel the exquisitely tantalising texture of her nipples as they pressed up against his chest and hardened. "If you're attempting to *arouse* my curiosity, you've certainly already done that. So, what is it?"

Breasts are such a silly thing Vanessa thought to herself. In fact, the only thing sillier than breasts are men. After all, every other person on the planet is born with a pair – so they're perfectly ordinary. Yet, as common as they are, men – all men – seem to be obsessed by them. Vanessa's observation was not incorrect. In fact, experience had taught her that, if the pair of breasts in question was, like her's, truly spectacular, well then…. And while she was far from lewd in her behaviour around men (in fact, she was still a virgin and intended to remain one until the day she married), she found that her breasts were an extremely effective weapon in her arsenal – and one that she used judiciously. Truth be told, they were often, like now, more powerful than either her bow or her sword.

"Yes....well." Stephen paused just long enough to clear his throat. "Perhaps this is a.... conversation that we *breast*....I mean *BEST*....have somewhere else."

"Oh? And why is that, *Sir* Stephen?" she asked in an almost breathless whisper.

"Well....it's....well....this setting is just....so public. And.... yes, well....I think that....um ....I think your privates....I mean your *privacy* would be, well...."

"You think my privates....?" she interrupted teasingly, knowing full well what he had meant to say. Then, adding a salacious smile for effect, she asked, "Just how often *do* you think about my.... *privates*, Stephen?" Finally, placing her small left hand on his thick right thigh, she practically moaned, "And for how long?"

With that, a red-faced, completely flummoxed Captain of the Guard was rendered utterly speechless, and Vanessa was fairly certain that he was about to faint, or possibly melt into a puddle right in front of her.

Having had some much-needed fun, and having clearly achieved her goal, Vanessa decided to release Stephen from his prison of awkwardness and embarrassment. "Yes, well, we'll talk again later.... somewhere *private*. You may go now, Stephen."

"Yes, my lady," was all he could manage before retreating. Striding far faster, but much less confidently, than he ever had in battle, Stephen cleared the hall in less time than it took Mother Superior Ludmilla, who had been monitoring the whole affair from a distance, to roll her eyes and shake her head.

"*Spottdrossel*," Ludmilla snarled in feigned disapproval of Vanessa's naughty performance. In response, Lady Stormsong simply shrugged her shoulders, issued a light but lecherous laugh, and practically pranced as she left the cavernous hall – suddenly feeling much better and more alive than she had mere minutes before.

In fact, the whole childish episode with Stephen left her with an unusually sweet feeling of nostalgia. It was as if she were four years old again, and Stephen still eight – as always, desperately trying to gain her approval. Vanessa was pleasantly surprised how that feeling both warmed and lightened her heart, and she said a silent prayer that this feeling would be able to stay with her a little while longer.

Chapter Ten

"*Gott im Himmel*, I pray that You send Your Son back to Earth this very second, and I pray that He would make every one of these bitches and bastards *shut their fucking mouths* for all of two fucking seconds!" The silence, which ensued shortly after the bellowed reproach finished echoing off of the dungeon walls, allowed the massive and angry speaker to continue. "Christ, you all sound like a lot of women with the bleeding pots the way you're at it."

The colourful and irreverent admonition had come from Gustav Adelbern, a man whose last name derived from ancient Germanic words for noble and bear. In all of creation, never had there been a man born who was more capable of being heard from one side of a room to the other than Gustav Adelbern; and as one of the few men in the entire empire both larger and harrier (not to mention louder) than Roan, the term bear was an apt one. But a noble he definitely was not. According to legend, Gustav Adelbern could out eat, out fight, out drink, out curse, out fart, and (at least according to Gustav himself) out fuck any man in Europe. In fact, according to just one of the fables surrounding his exploits – a story he, no doubt, perpetuated himself – he had "broken his lance" no fewer than nine times on his wedding night, with only two of those instances having occurred with his new bride. And for the past several years, this giant man of giant appetites had served as the unofficial and unelected head of a hierarchy of nearly thirty different bands of *Volks Knechte* who had all decided that the Protestant calls for religious reform in Europe were meaningless unless they were accompanied by some direct action, including some much-needed socio-economic reform.

These gangs were but a handful of the various groups of bandits and outlaws populating the empire at the time. Because the 1555 Peace of Augsburg had fragmented the Holy Roman Empire into dozens, maybe even hundreds, of smaller territories and principalities – each with its own independent jurisdiction and set of laws – criminals and outlaws of all different stripes could now do their work quickly and then easily cross a border to find refuge in what amounted to a secure foreign domain, thus escaping the ability of their pursuers to bring them to justice. And this ease of operation had, over the course of the past sixty-three years, led to a proliferation of groups which operated outside the constraints of the law.

Officially *das Heiliges Römisches Reich* was ruled by Emperor Matthias of the House Hapsburg, but in practice virtual anarchy prevailed. The aristocratic families of the empire lived in their fortress-palaces, guarded by their own liveried soldiers, while the streets became breeding grounds for disease and banditry. Pilgrims were liable to be robbed, or worse, by the thieves, pirates, cutpurses and bandits who frequented the taverns and bordellos. In fact, this chaotic state of the Empire, combined with the presence of so many different religious, ethnic, political, and socio-economic groups within the Empire, had created a situation that would have perplexed Solomon.

However, while many of these groups were simply mercenaries out to serve nothing more than their own self-interests, as many as thirty others were dedicated to serving the common people of the German states by attempting to relieve the rich and the powerful of their excess....well, riches and power. And the assembly over which Gustav now presided constituted one or two representatives from each of those nearly thirty groups. Each was commonly known by the title it was given by the wealthy, the power elite, and the Catholic clergy (quite often the same people) in its respective area of operation within the empire. And these groups all took great pride in how disparaging their monikers were in relation to the others. Most notable among these were Roan's own *Grüne Gauner; die Roten Teufeln* (the Red Devils); *die Bösen Libellen* (the Wicked Dragonflies); *die Brechende Räder* (the Breaking Wheels); *die Dreketen Huren* (the Dirty Whores), and the name that was most envied of all – *die Schwarzen Schurken* (the Black Bastards).

Ironically, this meeting, which had been called within just a few days of Roan's men having been ambushed while making their way to Wartburg, was being held in the castle at Wartburg itself – specifically the dungeon within the South tower of the massive compound.

There were certainly much larger and much more hospitable locations within the castle to hold such a meeting. The castle's *Palas* (Great Hall), for example, which had been built sometime during the latter half of the twelfth century, contained rooms like *der Rittersaal* (the Knight's Hall) and the *der Speisesaal* (the Dining Hall), either one of which would have been far more suitable than the South tower dungeon for a large gathering such as this one. However, only the dungeon afforded *die Volks Knechte* the absolute secrecy that was required for this unusual and hastily assembled conclave.

After allowing the awkward silence that followed his initial outburst to continue for what he deemed to be an appropriately long time, Gustav continued. "Jesus knows that there aren't any bleeding geniuses in this room. But it doesn't take a damn genius to count to five. And by my count, we've been ambushed by Stormsongs, Jesuits, and all other kinds of papists at least five times in the past three weeks. Six if you count the most recent one against Roan's *Grüne Gauner.* Right in the very shadow of this castle, which is supposed to be a fucking sanctuary for *die Volks Knechte.*"

Gustav was referring to the fact that, for the past twenty years or more, Wartburg had been under the control of Duke Johann Ernst von Sachsen-Eisenach, a Lutheran of *Haus Wettin,* one of the oldest noble families in Europe. *Haus Wettin's* origins could be traced back to the eleventh   century. When the Treaty of Leipzig split the family into two ruling branches in the fifteenth century, the Ernestine branch became ardent Lutherans and played a considerable role in the Protestant Reformation, including appointing Martin Luther to the University of Wittenberg in 1512 (which they had established just ten years earlier). More recently, the Ernestine branch of *Haus Wettin* had also provided considerable aid and comfort to Protestants throughout the empire, including *die Volks Knechte.*

Therefore, a successful, surprise attack on *die Grüne Gauner* launched from Wartburg was considered virtually impossible. Nevertheless, that's precisely what had happened – which is why said attack was such a source of consternation and dismay for all of the assembled leaders of *die Volks Knechte.*

"How many men did you say you lost, Roan?" Adelbern asked.

"There's no tellin' for sure," Roan answered. "One who made his way back to us was wounded pretty badly, but....he....well.... he....just got better." Roan hadn't yet come to terms himself with Šarlatová's display of....whatever it was she had done to heal Theodore Berger, and he certainly wasn't ready to discuss it with the other men and women assembled here. "But a dozen or so are missin'. I suppose they've either gone to hidin' or been taken prisoner. Maybe killed."

"I'll be going into hiding, too, if things keep on the way they are," noted Sebastian Mauer, the leader of *die Roten Teufeln* (the Red Devils). Commonly referred to as *der Oberst* (the Colonel), Sebastian had, before joining *die Roten Teufeln*, been a senior and high-ranking field officer in the army of former Emperor Rudolph II and was widely regarded as the most brilliant military tactician within *die Volks Knechte.* "Old Uncle Matthias' Red Letter boys have really been hounding my lads of late."

"Consider yourself lucky, Roan. Not two weeks ago, I lost more than twenty of mine." This came from Eardwulf Hankel, the leader of around three-hundred members of *die Brechende Räder,* a gang of bandits within the hierarchy of *die Volks Knechte* that operated in the northern *Schwarzwald* (Black Forest). Known for assaulting and robbing parish priests as well as wealthy nobles, the actions of

71

this group had become increasingly violent of late and, as a direct result, the punishments for those who were caught became increasingly brutal – and public. In fact, the name of Hankel's group, the Breaking Wheels, stemmed from a punishment that many of his men (and even some of the women in his gang) had suffered.

The breaking wheel, also known as the Catherine wheel (because it was originally associated with Catherine of Alexandria, a Christian saint who was martyred in the fourth century at the hands of Emperor Maxentius) was a sadistic instrument of torture often used to perform lengthy public executions by ever so slowly breaking the bones of the accused and eventually bludgeoning him or her to death.

The sadistic procedure customarily began by dragging the accused to the place of his or her execution, where the wheel would be slammed twice into each arm – once above the elbow and once below. After a period of waiting, four more blows, one above and one below each knee, would then be delivered. Then the ninth, and ostensibly final, blow would be directed at the middle of the spine, so that the victim's back would be broken. Next, the shattered body, which was quite pliable now that all of the major bones had been broken, would be woven onto the breaking wheel – literally between the spokes. At last, the wheel would be mounted onto a pole and raised up like a cross in a crucifixion, leaving the accused "floating" on the wheel, possibly for as long as two or even three days, while carrion birds picked away at whatever was left.

Because of the brutality involved, the breaking wheel was a punishment that was supposed to be reserved only for men convicted of the most serious crimes within the Empire. But, some forty years ago, at the direction of then Emperor Maximilian II, the Stormsongs and many other "favoured families" in Germany had begun to employ it fairly regularly, which only served to make Hankel and his group wear their moniker as a sort of badge of honour.

"Twenty?! I've had at least twice that number killed or captured just this month," declared *Einäugige Agata* (One-eyed Agatha), the leader of *die Dreketen Huren* (the Dirty Whores). *Die Dreketen Huren* were not prostitutes, but because they operated primarily in and around *die Elbmarsch*, an extensive area of polderland along the lower reaches of the Elbe River, they often looked filthy, were filthy, and smelled....like dirty whores.

As the others in attendance nodded sorrowfully, indicating that each had similar tales to tell, *Einäugige Agata* continued. "So how come these nobles and Catholics and whatnot seem to be every-where we are? Until recently, they seemed to me to be nothing but a lousy bunch of shitting shepherds. How is it they've gotten so cunning all of a sudden?"

"Well, that's why we're here, isn't it?" reminded Gustav Adelbern. "To figure that out. But so far, I haven't heard a single thought or suggestion."

"I think it's quite obvious," responded Sebastian Mauer. "From where I sit, there's only one answer. It seems to me that we must have a Goddamned Judas amongst us – for someone's for sure been tellin' tales of what's what and who's where!"

Clearly, he hadn't been there, but it occurred to Roan that the shock and confusion displayed by the disciples at the Last Supper when Jesus had predicted his betrayal and execution could not have been much greater than the anger and outrage displayed by the as-sembled leaders of *die Volks Knechte* when *der Oberst* suggested that a traitor lay within their midst. With every leader except Roan and *Oberst* Mauer leaping to his or her feet to protest this outrageous claim and to argue whose gang was most likely to have spawned such a traitor, Gustav had to shout them down once again.

"Ach, for the love of the blessed Virgin Mary, could you cunts shut up and listen for two fucking minutes?" Despite his savant-like ability to blend the foulest curse words with his holy statements of faith, the "noble bear's" request was not met with silence a second time. On the contrary, the arguments and accusations continued unabated.

As they did, Roan, who was one of only two members still seated, took in his surroundings, and he was far from comfortable.

He'd always been a touch claustrophobic, and the cool, damp surroundings of Wartburg's dungeon felt much too close for his comfort. Additionally, he knew far too much about the history of this particular dungeon for his own good.

Virtually everyone, Protestant or Catholic, within the German states knew that this was the place where Fritz Erbe, an Anabaptist farmer from the town of *Herda*, had been held captive for nearly a decade, simply for professing his belief that baptising children was pointless and useless. His faith in what many called "believer baptism," a core tenet of the Reformation's Anabaptist movement, was antithetical to Catholic theology and considered a crime. Thus, it had resulted in Erbe's imprisonment in a thirty-foot-deep chamber within the castle's south tower. Since the only access to his cell had been the so-called *Angstloch* (the Fear Hole), a hole in the floor of the room directly above him, Erbe, who stoically refused to abjure his faith, had languished in the cold and darkness *for eight long years* before finally being released from his confinement by a merciful, but long overdue, death.

As Roan considered this story, he could practically feel the walls of the dungeon closing in around him, and he prayed that this gathering would soon end – sooner than the eight years Erbe had spent here, anyway. But once it was clear that the meeting, which had now degenerated into a storm of internecine bickering and fighting, would not conclude anytime soon, Roan, the only leader who had not stood to protest his group's innocence, rose and silently slipped away from the ruckus.

Feeling like he could finally breathe, Roan sighed heavily and headed towards a spiral stone staircase that wound its way up three levels and would soon take him to warmer and cleaner air. But before he even made it up three steps, he was intercepted by Franz Hohenleiter, the newly appointed leader of *die Schwarzen Schurken* (the Black Bastards). Franz had only recently acquired the position when the previous leader, Franz's older brother Ulrich, had inexplicably been captured, tortured, broken on the wheel, and publicly beheaded at *Schloß Schönbrunn* in Vienna. So he, more than most, had reason to believe in the existence of a traitor among *die Volks Knechte*, and yet even he could not bring himself to believe such an outrageous claim.

"You were unusually quiet just then, old friend," he observed, following Roan as the two slowly made their way up the narrow stairs that would eventually take them out of the south tower.

Roan nodded and growled. "*Ja*. That's because I'm afraid Gustav and *Einäugige Agata* are right. We've never run into problems like this before. How is it that, all of a sudden, every time we make a move, there's an army there just waitin' for us?"

"I don't know," Franz admitted. "But I do know the mettle of our men. There's not a one of us what wouldn't rather be drawn and quartered than give up one of his brothers. And if'n one of us did – well, I wouldn't waste any time saying novenas. I'd just take the bastard's head off – and not cleanly, either."

Roan stopped in his tracks, causing Franz to bump into him from behind. "You're assumin' we could catch the bastard," he pointed out as he turned to face his friend. "If'n we don't, then what? At the rate we're goin', by the end of the year the whole lot of us'll be in a place like this....or worse....in the ground."

"Possibly. Maybe even probably. But you and I both know that's going to happen whether we've got a traitor among us or not. We've gone out of our way to stay out of these damn wars of religion, and rightfully so. You know as well as I do that those wars have devastated the French....the Dutch....the Spanish. And none of us wants what happened to them to happen here, as well. But if and when one does come, we both know what side we're going to be on, and we both also know that a lot of us aren't going to live to see the end of it."

Franz's premonition hung heavily in the cool, damp air of the stairwell, until Roan responded to it with, "*Ja....Ich weiße das*. And that's what scares me to death. I think you're right, as always. And I think that war's goin' to be here sooner rather than later."

"You're wrong!"

Roan and Franz both looked down a few steps to see the massive Gustav Adelbern who, despite completely filling the narrow corridor of the staircase, had somehow managed to creep up on the two without making a sound.

"You're both wrong," he repeated. "The war's not coming. It's already here!"

Chapter Eleven

"Begging your pardon, Your Highness, but what do you mean by 'It's already here,'?" Sir Stephen asked the archduke.

"I meant precisely what I said, *Sir* Stephen," Archduke Stormsong answered snidely. "Now, did you not hear me, or have your powers of attention been compromised by the amount of time you spend obsessing over the thought of fondling my only child's tits?"

Stephen lowered his head in embarrassment. It was bad enough that Vanessa had just toyed with his feelings for her, and it would have been made worse had the Archduke reprimanded him in this way in private – but to publicly humiliate his own Captain of the Guard in front of the assembly of lords, military officers, and clergy that had gathered in the great hall of *Schloß Stormsong's* Winter Palace was a severe and irreparable blow to Stephen's pride. Almost as bad was the sniggering that rippled through the throng of the assembled men, at least half of whom had also entertained at least occasional carnal thoughts about Archduke von Stormsong's voluptuous daughter, and almost all of whom had felt the sting of his legendary wrath at one time or another.

So often had the patriarch of the Stormsong family publicly chastised his own men, and in this very room, that this part of the Winter Palace had become widely known as *der Wimmern Palast* (the Whimper Palace). The entirety of this infamous and foreboding part of the castle had, along with the less ignominious Spring and Autumn Palaces, been built in the second half of the sixteenth century, when the majority of *Schloß Stormsong* was reconstructed after the great fire of 1541. The great hall of the Winter Palace was ornately decorated with military and hunting paraphernalia, original manuscripts and early prints that had been donated by composers like Hans Neusidler and Arnold von Bruck (as well as some musical instruments that had been forcibly taken from Michael Praetorius), and Renaissance style art by Lucas Cranach *der Jüngere* (the Younger) and Pieter Bruegel *der Ältere* (the Elder).

Despite how impressive it was, the great hall of the Winter Palace was seldom this heavily occupied. Today, however, it was full to brimming with Germanic Catholic authority figures – most in the service of either Archduke von Stormsong or Emperor Matthias, but a few in the employ of Pope Paul V himself. It was to this prestigious assembly that the Archduke directed his next comments.

"In case anyone else is as hard of hearing or as preoccupied as Sir Stephen, let me make myself perfectly clear. War is no longer imminent. War is here! At the direction of Emperor Matthias and Pope Paul, I have already begun to organise our defence of Bohemia. That defence began three weeks ago with a series of sudden and decisive attacks against the various gangs of bandits that have been roaming freely throughout the empire these past few years. With the help of my various, ubiquitous, clandestine informants, I have already managed to root out dozens of these vagabonds. So successful have these attacks been, that I am now prepared to proceed with the second phase of the defence of our Bohemia."

"And what would that entail, Your Highness?" asked Theodor Riphaen, a Catholic prelate who had served as Auxiliary Bishop of Cologne and Titular Bishop of Cyrene since being appointed to both positions by Pope Paul V in 1606. Having allegedly died in January of 1616, Bishop Riphaen had actually been secreted to Germany by Archbishop Attilio Amalteo to serve as an Apostolic Nuncio to Archduke von Stormsong; as such, he was one of the few men in the assembly, perhaps one of the few in the entire Empire, who even the Archduke would not dare chastise or reprimand.

"Within the fortnight, we will launch a sudden and decisive attack on the heretic rebels who are promoting their so-called "reformed religion" within our very homeland; and, in so doing, we will send a memorable and valuable message throughout the empire. It is my sincere hope and expectation that, by the time we have replaced Emperor Matthias with his successor, the military campaign in Bohemia will be complete."

Taking his cue from the Archduke, Bishop Riphaen addressed the assembly. "As we all know, our dear Emperor is not well, and he shall soon perish without leaving an heir. Once he has departed this mortal coil, his cousin, Ferdinand of Styria, will serve as our new emperor, and he has already endorsed the coming campaign against the Lutheran and Calvinist heretics in our midst."

His curiosity overpowering his earlier shame, Sir Stephen looked inquisitively at the bishop. "Begging your pardon, Your Excellency, but how do you know that Emperor Mathias will 'soon perish,' and, for that matter, how do you know that Ferdinand will be his successor?"

Looking at Stephen as a parent might look at a child who had just asked a question so imbecilic as to be laughable, Bishop Riphaen responded, "Because both issues have already been decided, my boy."

Stephen couldn't help himself. "Decided? Decided by whom, Your Excellency?"

"By me!" thundered Archduke Stormsong. "Regardless of what you may think of me, Sir Stephen, I am a servant of God, first and foremost. I am the keeper of this castle, your lord and master, and loyal servant to the *empire* – not the *emperor* – and to the One, Holy, Roman, Catholic, and Apostolic Church. And long before your sole focus on this Earth was wriggling your wet way between my daughter's thighs, I was defending both the church and this empire from Protestants, witches, thieves, and....worse. Far worse. With both demands and criticism coming from every possible avenue, I have had to make one impossible decision after another, all the while experiencing losses far beyond...."

Hoping that the pregnant pause didn't reveal too much, the Archduke assumed that everyone assembled knew what he meant by serving the empire – not the emperor. Perhaps the only one who didn't was Sir Stephen. The boy was either too pure or too young or too dense to understand the complexities and intricacies of power politics. That, more than anything else, was why the archduke chastised him so much. There was no doubt that Stephen was capable and unquestionably loyal, but he was just too damn simple for what was to come, and he was no match for his daughter – not in any sense of the word.

However, as he glanced Stephen's way, the Archduke caught the look of utter shame burning on the young man's face. Suspecting that he might have gone too far in publicly disgracing his own Captain of the Guard this time, and fearing that the boy might very well burst into tears in front of the assembled dignitaries, Archduke von Stormsong chose to direct the remainder of his reprimand to everyone assembled – not just to Stephen.

"I know all too well what the lot of you think. Don't think that I don't hear how you whisper to each other about my 'declining mental faculties.' Like a sad lot of washerwomen, you all slink about the castle....*my* castle....which provides you with food, shelter, and all manner of amenities. You cast aspersions about me, about my dead...., and about my...." Sensing correctly that this second pregnant pause was even more dramatic than the first one, Archduke von Stormsong decided to stop his diatribe.

Instead of continuing, he covered his face with his hand, he shook his head as if to dismiss the rest of what he was about to say. "Never mind. It doesn't matter now. All that matters is what is to come. Bishop Riphaen, where do things stand?"

Unsure of just where the archduke had been heading with his rant, Bishop Riphaen was all too happy to redirect the conversation to more important matters – both the tactical and the strategic ones.

"Yes, Your Highness. Well....as you all know too well, the Protestants in Bohemia have enjoyed a far too generous level of religious *toleration* ever since Emperor Rudolph II issued his dreadful *Majestätsbrief* (Letter of Majesty)." This document, which granted full toleration to the Protestants, and which created a standing committee of Estates to ensure that said toleration would be respected and defended, was an on-going source of contention among German Catholics, as evidenced by the fact that this part of the bishop's lesson was met by a collective groan from the assembled commanders and dignitaries.

"I've never truly understood why he did that," one of the Archduke's commanders admitted.

"That was all von Schlick's doing," another noted, referring to Count Joachim Andreas von Schlick, a wealthy and well-credentialed Lutheran who had, at one time, been a close advisor to the late Emperor Rudolph II.

"*Trotzdem*, I wouldn't wipe my ass with his *Majestätsbrief*," added a third commander, to both the verbal and nonverbal agreement of most of the other men.

Bishop Riphaen looked to the archduke to see if he wanted to address the issue himself. When he passed on the question with a simple, dismissive wave of his hand, the bishop took that as a cue to continue.

"Yes, well....Emperor Rudolph II was many things. While he was known to be a generous patron of the arts, he was also quite weak and ineffectual and, sadly, a devotee of the occult arts and.... dark magic." Archduke von Stormsong seemed unsettled by the bishop's reference to the dark arts, but he chose not to interrupt. "And whether it was his weakness of mind or his weakness of spirit that led him to take such a vile and disgusting action, it matters not. He was simply unfit to rule."

"But our current predicament isn't entirely his fault," pointed out Ernst Gundrham, one of Archduke von Stormsong's most capable and trusted commanders, in a voice that sounded like he had eaten a steady diet of gravel for the past two decades.

"Quite right, Lord Gundrham," conceded Bishop Riphaen. "Sadly, it is true that, for nearly a century, the Hapsburgs have governed the Kingdom of Bohemia in a way that....well, just did not impose the true faith upon them. But rest assured, shortly upon being named as Matthias' successor, Ferdinand will do his duty and rectify this lamentable condition. He understands his duty to the church and the empire, and he has made a vow to eradicate heresy from the German states – which, based on what I know of the man, I imagine will come as naturally to him as breathing."

"And the Protestants in Bohemia know this, of course," Lord Gundrham pointed out to the entire assembly, his voice still heavy with a granite timbre.

"Correct again, my lord," responded the bishop. "They don't know that Ferdinand will be the new emperor. But they are understandably wary that, whomever the next emperor might be, he will reverse the permissive policies with which we have been forced to contend ever since the Peace of Augsburg. Which, of course, the new emperor will do when he revokes that hateful *Majestätsbrief.* And this has led to deep consternation among many Bohemian Protestants. They fear not only the loss of their properties, but also of their traditional autonomy."

"What do they intend to do?" asked Lanzo Oddvar, another one of the archduke's seasoned commanders.

"Since the recent unpleasant events in Prague, the heretics have been sowing the seeds of discord and spreading lies throughout Bohemia, Silesia, Moravia, and Upper and Lower Lusatia," responded the bishop.

Having regained a modicum of his composure, Sir Stephen weighed in. "Certainly, they will find no allies in any of those parts of the empire, Your Excellency." While it was meant to sound authoritative, it came out sounding like a question.

Archduke von Stormsong took over from here. "You may be right, Sir Stephen. The Bohemians are desperate for allies and, as such, they have applied to be admitted into the Protestant Union. To increase their chances of acceptance, they have chosen to support Frederick V in his false claim for the Bohemian throne."

Friedrich V, Elector of the Palatinate, was a prominent Calvinist, the leader of the Protestant Union, and, at least as far as the emperor and the Catholic Church were concerned, a pretender to the Bohemian throne. But he was also the son-in-law to James VI, King of Scotland – who was now also James I, King of England and Ireland – which meant that any alliance between the Protestant Union and the Bohemian rebels could result in an even greater alliance with England, Scotland, and Ireland.

While everyone in attendance understood the implications of the entrance of Bohemia into the Protestant Union, they were less prepared for what was to come next.

"Not only could we be fighting Bohemians, English, Scots, and Irish, but I expect that Upper Austria's largely Lutheran and Calvinist nobility may choose to throw their support behind the rebels," predicted Bishop Riphaen. "And if Upper Austria sides with the rebels…."

"Then Lower Austria may as well," finished Archduke von Stormsong. "Which, of course, brings in the possibility of that detestable Count von Thurn entering the fray."

Count Heinrich Matthias von Thurn was a Bohemian nobleman who had played a key role in the most recent defenestration of Prague. Despite the fact that both of his parents were Protestants, as a young man Count von Thurn served in the Imperial Hapsburg embassy and later served in the Imperial army during a series of ongoing wars between the Hapsburgs and the Ottoman Empire for control of Hungary. During his distinguished military service, Count von Thurn rose to the ranks of colonel and, like Count von Schlick, became a trusted counsellor to then Emperor Rudolph II. As a reward for his accomplishments in the war against the Turks, Emperor Rudolph granted him the *Burgrave* (the military governorship of a German town or castle) of *Karlštejn* in central Bohemia. Committed to honouring the freedom of religion granted to Bohemian Protestants by Rudolph II's *Majestätsbrief*, von Thurn became one of the most recognized leaders of the Protestant uprising against

Catholic Hapsburg control of Bohemia. Most recently, Thurn had been elected as one of the thirty Defenders of the Protestant Faith elected by the Estates of Bohemia and was now in position to take command of the Bohemian national army against the Hapsburgs.

While Count von Thurn had, for some time, been widely regarded by Catholics as a criminal and a traitor to the royal family, even more so now due to the prominent role he had just played in the Defenestration of Prague, his past military accomplishments and acumen made him a respected and feared opponent, and the silence that followed the Bishop's assessment revealed to Archduke von Stormsong that even his best men were reticent to engage with Count von Thurn. Hoping to ease the tension and raise the confidence of his troops, the archduke broke the awkward silence.

"And what allies can we count on, Bishop Riphaen?"

"Of course, Your Highness. As you know, the Spanish crown still maintains an interest in keeping us as a stable ally, which is why they have invested heavily in helping us protect *die Spanische Straße*"

Die Spanische Straße (the Spanish Road) was a military and trade route linking the Duchy of Milan in the Mediterranean to Luxembourg and Belgium in the north. Because sailing north towards their remaining colonies in the Netherlands meant running a deadly gauntlet of attacks by French, English, and Dutch navies, it was much safer for the Spanish Hapsburgs to transport their armies to their holdings in the Netherlands by marching them overland along the Spanish Road. And, given that the vast majority of the six-hundred-plus mile long road ran through the Holy Roman Empire, the Hapsburgs in Spain had come to rely heavily on their Austrian relatives to maintain the safety and security of that critical route.

"Additionally," Bishop Riphaen continued, "King Philip III is a Hapsburg and a cousin to both our current Emperor and to our future Emperor Ferdinand. Therefore, I think it is reasonable to count on Spain for....*assistance*."

Not at all impressed by the notion of aid from a country whose military reputation had been severely and permanently damaged by the disastrous defeat of the Spanish Armada thirty years earlier, Archduke von Stormsong's men seemed reticent, at best. "And what sort of *assistance* can we expect?" asked Lanzo Oddvar.

Taking a subtle nod from the Archduke as his cue to answer Lord Oddvar, Bishop Riphaen cleared his throat and said, "Well.... an enormous sum of treasure for sure. And the hiring of free companies and mercenaries to counteract the assistance that the Bohemians are sure to gain from the so-called *Volks Knechte*. Anything beyond that, well....remains to be seen."

"Lord Gundrham, you will be in charge of the campaign. How do you intend to proceed?" asked the archduke.

"Yes, Your Highness. And thank you for giving me the opportunity to serve you by routing these rebels and traitors." Stepping forward and turning to face the rest of the assembled men, Lord Gundrham outlined his strategy. "We intend to tease the heretics in a series of battles that will appear to be victories for their so-called Bohemian national army. Then, relying on Count von Thorn's massive ego and legendary overconfidence, we shall goad them into engaging in one decisive battle, one they will incorrectly assume that they will win, at a time and place of our choosing. Then, as soon as we have routed the bastards once and for all, we will be able to reclaim the vast lands and church properties which the heretics have seized since the beginning of this so-called Reformation. Once we have, the new emperor will dispose of the Estates, impose absolute rule on Bohemia, and launch a campaign to....*encourage* conversions to the true faith." The last part was said with a wry smile that was joined by nearly every man present.

Ironically, while for centuries following the crucifixion of Christ, Christianity had been a minority religion whose members were brutally persecuted, during the reign of Roman Emperor Constantine the Great, Christianity had begun to transform into the dominant religion within the Roman Empire; and in no time at all, the Christian Church began to persecute and suppress practitioners of the ancient pagan religions and other so-called heretics. After having made the conversion from being members of a persecuted faith to being capable of and, all too often, eager to engage in persecution themselves, Christians throughout Europe began to engage in a strategy of *forced* (not just encouraged) conversions that included the use of formal decrees, attacks on traditional polytheistic religions, open warfare and conquest, riots, massacres, torture, and every other imaginable form of intimidation. Consequently, everyone assembled within *Schloß Stormsong* knew precisely what Lord Gundrham meant by *encouraging* conversions of Bohemian Protestants, and all were more than willing to participate in the process.

"Very well, Lord Gundrham," said Archduke von Stormsong. Then he directed his attention to everyone else and began to quote from chapter five of the Gospel according to Mark: *"And they came over unto the other side of the sea, into the country of the Gadarenes. And when He was come out of the ship, immediately there met Him out of the tombs a man with an unclean spirit, who had his dwelling among the tombs; and no man could bind him, no, not with chains: Because that he had been often bound with fetters and chains, and the chains had been plucked asunder by him, and the fetters broken in pieces: neither could any man tame him. And always, night and day, he was in the mountains, and in the tombs, crying, and cutting himself with stones. But when he saw Jesus afar off, he ran and worshipped him, and cried with a loud voice, and said, 'What have I to do with thee, Jesus, thou Son of the most high God? I adjure thee by God, that thou torment me not.' For He said unto him, 'Come out of the man, thou unclean spirit.' And He asked him, 'What is thy name?' And he answered, saying, 'My name is Legion: for we are many.'* So, it seems, my lords, that precious little has changed since the time of Christ. The barbarians are within the gates again, and their name is legion….for they are many."

This third pregnant pause went almost completely unnoticed. "Now let's do our Christian duty and return them all to the fiery pits of Hell from whence they came!"

Chapter Twelve

"Everything is different now, Roan. Everyone looks at me differently anyway." Šarlatová wasn't even looking at Roan. Instead, she was staring into the fire that had earlier cooked their sparse meal. She'd taken to doing this a lot lately, because it was in the fire that could see faces that weren't either judging her or fearful of her. Indeed, she could see rivers and castles, places she'd never been but longed to visit; occasionally, the flames even produced animals which leapt and played for her amusement. Perhaps it was just the declining eyesight in her left eye, which still hadn't returned to where it was before she had healed Theo, that accounted for these visions, but she didn't much care. The images Šarlatová saw dancing and whirling in the flames provided some solace to her, and solace was something she'd been lacking of late.

"What do you mean?" Roan asked, watching her watch the flames. He knew full well what she meant, but he was trying to buy himself some time to come up with a decent response. He'd had the entire trip back from Wartburg to formulate one, but still….he had nothing.

"I mean exactly that. Ever since….ever since I saved Theo….the whole time you were away in Wartburg, everyone has looked at me differently. It's like they're afraid of me now."

"They're not afraid of you, *divka*. They just don't know what they saw, so they don't know what to think. But no one thinks any different from before."

"Yes, they do! And don't do that, Roan. Not to me. Not ever."

"Do what, *divka*?"

"Patronise me like that. You've never done that before. Don't do it now. Don't talk to me like I'm someone else. They know exactly what they saw, and I know exactly what they think. They think I'm a witch." Šarlatová was on the verge of crying as she made her final statement, but no tears would come – only the milky white substance that continued to seep out of her left eye ever since she had sung Theo back to health.

"Come here, *dívka*. It'll be alright," Roan promised as he wiped the opaque liquid from her cheek and embraced her with his massive arms. "And to hell with anyone what thinks that. And to anyone what says anythin' crossways to you....well, they'll be answerin' to me, to be sure. And to *Schwert*!" Roan punctuated his point by using his right hand to pat the pommel of his massive sword.

Šarlatová laughed lightly, in part because Roan's beard was tickling the top of her ears as he embraced her, and in part because it always came down to violence with Roan. He had not met a problem yet that he couldn't handle with violence – or at least so he thought. Born more from the Code of Hammurabi than the New Testament, Roan's rules for civil conduct were quite simple. Some asshole steals from you – cut off the *Arschloch's* hand. Some bastard bears false witness against you – rip out the *Schlingel's* tongue with your bare hands. Some fucker rapes your wife or your daughter – then take a sword and lop off the *Saftsack's....Lebkuchen*.

One of the many things Šarlatová loved about Roan was his simple, almost child-like sense of right and wrong, which was centred almost entirely on righting wrongs. Perhaps the only thing about him she loved more than his severe sense of justice was his ingenious ability to weave together his two great loves – food and violence – to form magical forms of expression, such as lopping off someone's *Lebkuchen* or kicking the *Potthast* out of someone.

"That's sweet, Roan. Brutal and barbaric, but sweet nonetheless." Šarlatová laughed and pushed herself out of the massive Moravian's bear-like embrace. "Remind me to never make you mad."

"You never have before, *dívka*. And I don't expect you ever will. That aside, what exactly did they....I mean I....we....see? I....we all know you're no witch, but....what was that exactly that you did to Theo? When I asked you to have a go at helpin' him out....well, I've caught glimpses of you doing things before, but I had no idea that you could actually do anything like what you did. How did you do it?"

"I don't know, Roan. I really don't. I just know that, when I need to, I can....summon my surroundings, or summon something within me. I'm not sure which it is. It's....it's like a.... quickening. I don't know any other way to describe it. And when I sing....it's like there's nothing I can't do. I don't even know where the words or music come from. It's like....like someone else is singing and it's my body she's using. Or *he*. I don't know....maybe it's the devil himself."

"As if the devil would waste the steam of his piss fiddlin' with a baseborn outlaw like Theodore Berger....or you or me, for that matter. It's not the devil, and to Hell with anyone what says so. You're no witch, either....so you can just put an end to that nonsense. You and me both know that all of that talk about witches is just a bunch of rot made up by the Catholics to scare people into goin' to church and prayin' to every saint in the book. And that's all it is."

Unfortunately, Šarlatová knew all too well that Roan was both right and wrong. The history of witches and witchcraft in Europe was as full of nonsense and hypocrisy as it was with irony and tragedy.

The accusations made *by* Christians over the years *against* so-called witches were virtually identical to those levelled against the early Christians by pagans in the third and fourth centuries, causing many to wonder if subsequent generations of Christians had learned the art of witchcraft accusal and persecution from the first-hand experience of their ancestors.

Whatever the case, as early as the fifth century, Saint Augustine had taught that witchcraft did not exist and that the belief in it was heretical. The consequence was that from the fifth century forward, while the penalty for witchcraft remained death, the ecclesiastical and civil authorities slackened considerably in their efforts to find and punish witches. However, after four centuries of dormancy, the popularity of witch-hunting was revived by the inhabitants of many European countries who began to believe that some unconstrained women (perverted by Satan, of course) could be seduced by illusions and phantasms of demons, and would, under the cover of darkness, engage in midnight rides upon certain beasts, or even unsuspecting humans, to covens where they would engage in lesbian orgies and cannibalistic sacrifices. And it was no surprise to Šarlatová that occult power was almost always ascribed to women; after all, the accusers were customarily male, and those male accusers had traditionally shared a common understanding that women, believed to be the weaker sex, were more susceptible to the influence of devils and demons than men.

While these claims revealed far less about witches and the supernatural than they did about the effects that the Christian suppression of sexuality had on stoking the pornographic fantasies of countless European males (fantasies in which Šarlatová was, unfortunately, far too well-versed), the result was no less deadly. From the tenth century on, civilian populations throughout Europe began to take the law into their own hands – with far more deadly and fearful results than ever before.

Then, starting in the fifteenth century, partly (and again, ironically) as a result of the new learning and discovery by Renaissance Humanists, the European male's obsession with witches was actually strengthened, not lessened. In fact, as society became more literate, due largely to the invention of the printing press, the witch-craze was refuelled by an increasing number of books, pamphlets, and musical tracts which outlined the witches' alleged sordid (and, of course, always hypersexual) activities. Additionally, during the sixteenth century, the initial discoveries of the Scientific Revolution, far from dispelling these notions, seemed to actually exacerbate them once again. The hysteria and lunacy seemed to reach its apex during the four decades between 1578 and 1618, when Jesuits took up the mantle of being the Catholic church's primary witch-hunters, and when Emperor Rudolph II initiated a long persecution of alleged witches throughout the Holy Roman Empire – a persecution that had outlived him, and that was still very active.

"It is and it isn't, Roan. The fact that witches aren't real doesn't mean anything to all of the women who were accused of being them. They're still just as dead. Have you ever noticed that there are no grey-haired women in *die Volks Knechte*?"

"No, I suppose not. But when I look at a woman, any woman, the colour of her hair is the last thing I'm looking at," Roan confessed unashamedly.

"My God, you really are a *Drecksau*, aren't you?" Šarlatová's observation only served to make the giant smile....and then scratch himself for effect.

Rolling her eyes and shaking her head, but smiling nonetheless, Šarlatová continued. "The reason there are no grey-haired women in *die Volks Knechte* is because the grey hairs are all in the graveyard....dead. And that's where I'm going to end up if...."

"If what?"

The unexpected question caused both Roan and Šarlatová to leap to their feet and produce weapons. Almost as fast as Šarlatová had wielded her bow and nocked an arrow, Roan had withdrawn *Schwert* out of its scabbard.

"Jesus! I'm sorry," stammered a terrified Simon Berger, throwing his hands into the air.

"Shit, Simon!" exclaimed Šarlatová. "The lot of you need to stop spying on me like that, or one of you is going to end up just as dead as Julius Caesar."

"I wasn't spying on you, Šarlatová. I wasn't spying on anyone. I was just....I'm sorry. I didn't mean to....that is, I heard Roan was back, and I....I just wanted to find out for myself how things went in Wartburg."

Having almost just been a victim of Šarlatová's jittery trigger-finger himself, Roan should have been at least somewhat sympathetic to the younger Berger's predicament. But he wasn't. Instead, he flashed a look at Simon that communicated just how unwelcome his presence was at this particular place and time. But before he could send Simon away, Šarlatová intervened.

"It's okay, Simon. It really is," she said, lowering her bow and gently placing the unfired arrow back in its quiver. "I need to go see your brother anyway. He prays to me in thanks five times a day now, and we're only up to three so far today. Maybe he's becoming a Muslim."

When neither Roan nor Simon laughed at her attempt at a joke, Šarlatová gave a half-hearted wave, faked a smile, and walked away.

"I'm really sorry, Roan," Simon apologised, watching Šarlatová walk away. "What has her so on edge anyway?"

"Shit, Simon! For someone who claims to be as smart as Cardinal Fuckin' Wolsey, you are awfully simple sometimes." Roan checked to make sure that Šarlatová was out of earshot before continuing. "Have a seat anyway. Let's talk."

"So how *did* things go in Wartburg?"

After first double-checking to make sure no one else had encroached upon the area around the fire where he now sat with Simon instead of Šarlatová, Roan began to answer the question. "Not well. Not well at all. It's nothin' but bad news, as usual. And now Gustav Adelbern thinks that we've got a Judas in *die Volks Knechte*. Seems someone's been passin' on secrets to the Stormsongs, the Emperor, the Pope and God knows who else."

Simon looked almost as shocked as he had been minutes earlier, when Šarlatová had nearly let an arrow fly at him. "Why does he think that? Is it because of the surprise attacks?"

"That, and the fact that he's always been convinced that every time us Bohemians are about to demolish them Austrian Catholics in a fair fight, a filthy informer betrays us to them."

Assessing the situation, Simon noted, "Those two things alone don't exactly make a very convincing case for there being a traitor amongst us, Roan."

"No. No, they don't. But there's more to it than that, Simon. Adelbern's convinced we have an informer among us because.... well, because we have one within the Stormsongs."

"An informer?" Simon whispered.

Roan couldn't quite gauge Simon's reaction. Not knowing whether Simon was encouraged by this news, shocked by it, or simply upset that he'd been left out of such an important development, Roan decided to proceed cautiously.

"Apparently. He told me so himself when we was alone. Just him and me....and Franz Hohenleiter."

"Well, who is it? Is it the Stormsong daughter with the perfect tits?"

"Christ almighty, Simon. Are tits all you ever think about? You ought to think about gettin' a pair of your own. Think about how much extra time you'd have to think if...."

Simon interrupted him by repeating the question. "Who is it?"

Roan lied. "That he wouldn't tell me. But he did promise to give me advance notice if somethin' was a comin' up....and so it is. The blessed archduke, the one what's got the 'daughter with the perfect tits,' is preparin' to launch a new, all-out offensive somewhere near Prague. It looks as if he means to wipe out the whole lot of us this time. That's why he's been attackin' us all over the empire. To soften us up before he strikes the final blow."

"So, I take it then that we'll be heading back in that direction to....to help out?" Simon wondered out loud.

Roan hesitated to reveal much more. "Maybe. Or maybe we should put as much distance between us and *Schloß Stormsong* as is humanly possible." At this, Roan decided to test Simon. "You're smart, eh? What would you do?"

Simon paused for a moment and rubbed his neatly trimmed chin as he pondered the options. "Hmmm....I don't know."

"That's all you've got? 'I don't know.' Christ, maybe I ought to be gettin' advice from your ass instead of your head, Berger."

"Well, in my defence, I wasn't really focusing on it that hard."

"And why is that, Simon? Have you got somethin' more pressin' to occupy that vast space between your ugly ears?"

"As a matter of fact, I was thinking about Šarlatová."

"Simon, you're a good soldier. And you're twice as smart as anyone I've ever called friend. But as God is my witness, if you tell me once more about how much time you've spent thinkin' about that girl's tits, or her ass, I swear I'm goin' to...."

Simon waved him off. "Stop. While I must confess, there are few things on God's green Earth that I find more wondrous than Šarlatová's tits....or her ass, for that matter, that's not what's been keeping me awake at night....not lately anyway."

An awkward silence ensued that lasted for several long seconds as Simon and Roan stared at each other knowingly. "What is it then?" Roan asked. "Is it her....gift that's been keepin' you up?"

"Is it a gift then, Roan? Or is it a curse?"

"That girl is many things, Simon. But cursed is not one of them, and I'll have words with anyone what says otherwise....including you!"

Simon put his hands up again, this time in mock surrender. "I meant no offence, Roan. And you know that I love her as much as you do. I did even before she saved my brother's life."

"But....?"

"But that....*ability* of hers...." Simon paused for effect and sighed deeply. "Whatever it is, I have a feeling that we've only seen a glimpse of what it....what *she* can really do."

"And?" prompted Roan.

"*And*....it's one thing for her to use it to save lives. But what would happen if she ever decided to use it to *take* lives instead?"

"She wouldn't!" Roan assured him.

Nodding in agreement, Simon replied, "But *if* she did, who among us....who anywhere could stop her?"

His face suddenly sombre, Roan shook his massive head. "Now we have somethin' in common, Simon. Because it is that very thought what has been keepin' me up at night, too."

"So where do we go from here?" Simon asked sincerely.

"I don't have the first clue, Simon. But, for now anyway, I just thank Jesus that she's on our side. Because if'n she weren't….there's not a damn thing we could do about it."

Chapter Thirteen

———⚜———

Vanessa was in heaven.

Being a voracious reader and an unrepentant introvert, there was no place she'd rather be than in a library. Since she was a child, she had always found truth in prayer, meaning in poetry, and joy in music, but her greatest peace had always come from books. And she knew that her father was off somewhere, probably planning a re-conquest of the Holy Land or something similar, which meant *Schloß Stormsong's* vast and impressive library was all hers, at least for the moment.

She sat in her father's favourite chair, a beautifully upholstered Louis XIII style chaire à bras, and held a volume of *The Lives of the Saints from the Old and New Testaments* open in front of her. The massive hagiography, more than one thousand total pages, had been written by a Polish Jesuit, Piotr Skarga, in 1577 as a way of combating the popularity of Protestant writings of the late-sixteenth century. While the Catholic Church actively and ironically discouraged reading of the Bible (for fear that Catholics might actually come to know what was and, more importantly, what was not in the "Good Book"), it did encourage reading of Skarga's two-volume "masterpiece," and viewed it as a means of refuting the heretical writings of men like Martin Luther and John Calvin.

While the work was popular primarily for its poetic descriptions of exotic locations, frequent forays into eclesiastical and royal politics, and graphic descriptions of the torture and suffering endured by saints (many of them being young virgin girls), it was the focus on the lives of Catholic saints that attracted Vanessa to it. While German translations had recently become available, Vanessa preferred to read it in the original Polish – just one of the eight languages she could read, write, and speak fluently.

She had always been fascinated by the lives of the various Catholic saints. While paintings always seemed to depict them in serene settings with bland expressions, Vanessa knew them to be anything but serene or bland. To her, they were superhuman, possessing the ability to heal the sick, or calm a storm, or even bring the dead back to life. That sort of power, used in the service of the Heavenly Father, had become something of an obsession of hers.

In fact, at the moment, Vanessa was so engrossed in reading about the life of Saint Christina the Astonishing that she did not hear the gentle rapping at the doors leading into the library.

"Vanessa, are you in there?" Sir Stephen asked quietly. "Mother Superior Ludmilla said that you were. May I come in? Vanessa? I need to see you. Please."

In the late-twelfth century, before she was "Astonishing," Christina Mirabilis was born into a religious family in the town of Brustem in French controlled Flanders (Belgium). The youngest of three daughters, she was orphaned at fifteen and was forced to take work taking herds of cows, pigs, and sheep to pasture. For the next five or six years afterwards, her life was fairly unremarkable – until her early twenties when she suffered a massive seizure of some kind and was believed to be dead.

During the *Agnus Dei* of her own funeral mass, and to the amazement and terror of the townspeople of *Saint Trond*, she awoke suddenly and sat straight up within her own, open coffin. The stupefied witnesses later claimed that she then levitated up to the rafters of the church, purportedly because she could not stand the smell of the assembled sinners at the service.

Later, ostensibly after having descended from the rafters, Christina claimed that her soul had been separated from her body and that angels had granted her glimpses of Purgatory, Heaven, and

Hell. She further claimed that the angels had offered her a choice of either remaining in Heaven or returning to Earth to convert sinners and prevent their souls from descending into a lake of fire. Allegedly, once she had agreed to return to her life on Earth, she simply woke up.

"Vanessa, please. I really need to speak with you!" Stephen implored, no longer quietly.

From the time of her purported resurrection on, Christina voluntarily lived in homeless poverty and avoided human contact to the greatest degree possible. According to witnesses, she also went to great lengths to increase her temporal suffering, doing things like intentionally throwing herself into fires and remaining there for extended periods of time, allowing herself to be attacked by dogs, intentionally running virtually naked through thickets of thorn bushes, and immersing herself in the freezing waters of local rivers for hours or even days at a time.

"Astonishingly," while each of these self-imposed tortures produced terrifying screams, both from Christina herself and from the witnesses to these bizarre scenes, she always emerged unscathed and alive, reportedly living to the unusually long age of seventy-four and ultimately dying of natural causes.

While many sceptics seemed willing to explain Christina's behaviour as a manifestation of madness or some other form of masochistic insanity, and while still others believed she was possessed by demons (which would explain why she was imprisoned so often), Vanessa knew in her heart that Christina was a holy woman who was sent as a messenger from God. And she felt a great kinship with this woman. While Bohemia could be heaven on Earth for men (Catholic ones, anyway), it was a veritable Hell on Earth for women and children. And for this woman, who was but a child herself, to suffer death, experience divine resurrection, and then put herself through a greater penance than even Vanessa had ever known, all the while maintaining the strictest chastity, just so that she could perform the will of God, gave

Vanessa hope that her own sufferings in service of her Heavenly Father might someday....

"LADY ATLANTIS VANESSA STORMSONG!"

This time she couldn't ignore the voice or the pounding on the door. In fact, at first, Vanessa was so startled and convinced that the voice belonged to her father that she literally jumped from her chair and dropped the heavy tome to the floor with a resounding thud. Then, before the voice could shout again, she realised that her father wouldn't knock. Possessing a key to every room in the castle and suffering no pretence as to whom the building belonged, he would have simply entered without either knocking or announcing himself.

"Stephen?" she asked softly at the door. "Is that you?'

"Well of course it's me, I've been out here for....May I please come in?"

Vanessa waited just a fraction of a second too long to construct a convincing lie. "But....I'm not decent, Stephen."

"You are in the library, Vanessa. If you are truly naked in there, then by almighty God we have much to talk about. And you couldn't be much more naked than when I saw you two days ago in *das Gott Haus*. That was a very nasty trick you played on me by the way. You know quite well that I had only the breast intentions....damn it all....best intentions when....Christ almighty, would you please let me in already?"

Stifling a laugh, Vanessa acquiesced. "Alright. Just be quiet about it." With that, she unlocked the door and allowed Stephen to enter. "What is it? I was trying to read."

"This is more important than Marlowe, Machiavelli, or Shakespeare. It's urgent!" Stephen protested in frustration.

"Marlowe, Machiavelli, and Shakespeare? My goodness, Stephen. You have actually been reading the books I lent you, haven't you?"

"Yes....well....I," Stephen stammered. The unexpected compliment from Vanessa had temporarily thwarted his steadfast resolve to engage her in meaningful conversation.

"And how have you had time to do so when you have so obviously been spending countless hours in vigorous *exercise*?" Vanessa practically moaned the last word as she placed both of her hands on his massive biceps.

"Enough of that. I'm not going to fall for that again. I love you to death Vanessa, but I have a good mind to…."

"To what?" Vanessa whispered breathlessly.

"Damn it, woman! We need to speak, and we need to do so *now*."

Simultaneously surprised, impressed, and somewhat disappointed that her recent attempts at flirtation did not yield the expected results, Vanessa relented. "Okay, Stephen. Fine. But not here. The walls of this castle have eyes and ears – especially in this room."

Relieved that he had finally gotten through to her, Stephen asked, "Where then?"

"Where else? *Der Orangengarten.*"

Der Orangengarten (the Orange Garden) was the largest and grandest of the many Italian Renaissance gardens within the grounds of *Schloß Stormsong*. Created in 1555, it was filled with dozens of fountains, statues, and artificial grottoes, and its symmetry – which was inspired by the Renaissance ideals of harmony, balance, and order – was designed to maximise the enjoyment of the sights, sounds, and smells of the area that had been a vineyard until it was destroyed by fire in 1541.

Prominent within the garden was a massive "orangery" (hence *der Orangengarten*), a French style greenhouse designed to protect Archduke von Stormsong's beloved orange trees from the relatively harsh and cold German climate – a climate that made it impossible to grow oranges anywhere other than within the walls of his castle, providing yet another status symbol indicating the wealth of grandeur of the empire's leading family.

The nearly four-hundred-foot-long structure was built from a sturdy white oak frame, with stone walls and a solid roof, and it provided the greatest degree of privacy to be found within the walls of *Schloß Stormsong*. It was that privacy that made this garden one of Vanessa's favourite places within the castle, despite – and not because of – the opulence of the surroundings.

Within the safety and privacy of the orangery's confines, Stephen and Vanessa could speak freely. But after several long and awkward minutes of silence inside, neither of them seemed to want to go first.

It was Stephen who finally broke the silence. "The emperor is going to start a war. More precisely, your father is going to start a war, and in the process replace the emperor with one of his cousins."

"My father doesn't have any cousins," Vanessa reminded him.

"No....not one of *his* cousins, one of the emperor's. Not that it matters much. The point is that civil war is breaking out in Bohemia, and it threatens to rip the entire empire apart – with or without your father's effort to supplant Emperor Matthias."

"I already know all of that, Stephen. Even if I hadn't already heard it from Father Joseph, Mother Superior Ludmilla told me just yesterday."

Stephen chuckled. "Mother Superior Ludmilla. Once that woman gets wind of something, and she gets wind of everything, you might as well post it on the church door and shout it out the windows yourself, because everyone else will know by the end of the day anyway."

Vanessa laughed, too. "God love that woman; she does know how to spread the word. Not just God's word – any word."

At this they both laughed and stopped walking long enough for Stephen to turn and face Vanessa. "War means that I'll likely be sent by your father to fight and kill Protestants in Bohemia. You, too, I suppose. After all, you're a better soldier than I'll ever be."

"You should know, you trained me," Vanessa reminded him and offered a faint smile. "So, is that what's troubling you?"

"Yes. No. I don't know. It just seems that….well, that the whole world is on fire right now. God made the world, and God is good. So the world is supposed to be good. But we look around and see that…. that it just isn't. Famine, followed by a hundred years of war, followed by plague. Then comes Martin Luther and his heretics, provoking wars of religion in France and in the Spanish Netherlands, even here now. With all of this rot and decay, can God still be in His Heaven?"

"That's blasphemy, Stephen. Of course, God is still in His Heaven, and He's still here on Earth with us – nothing can ever change that. And if you're looking for sympathy, you've come to the wrong place. Think for a minute of the Lord and of His sufferings on the cross. For you, Stephen. For you….for me….for all of us. He did all of that out of love for us. Think how His heart must break seeing what His children are doing to each other after what He's done for us."

"It's not sympathy I seek, Vanessa."

"What then? What would you have of him? The Garden of Eden? Paradise here on Earth?"

"The only paradise on Earth I have ever longed for is right here in front of me." Stephen's cheeks burned bright red as he looked hard into Vanessa's piercing blue eyes.

"Stephen," Vanessa responded softly, taking his hand in hers. "How many times must we have this conversation? We've had it so many times before, and it always ends the same way. What's changed?"

Stephen took a seat on a stone bench, keeping hold of Vanessa's hands. "We might die, Vanessa. Either of us – both of us. With this war we're about to wage, there are no guarantees that either one of us will survive. That's what's changed."

Fearing that Stephen might next take a knee and propose to her (yet again), Vanessa retracted her hands and reminded him that, "There are never any guarantees in life, Stephen. Outside of God's whole-hearted promise of a better life through His Son, nothing is for certain."

"You're wrong, Vanessa. My love for you. That's certain. It always has been, and it always will be."

"Stephen, you're a wonderful man, a hopeless romantic, and for as long as I can remember, the truest friend I've ever had. But as much as you might wish them to, my feelings don't extend beyond friendship. You've always been the big brother I never wanted," she said and then paused to ruffle his chestnut brown hair. "But that I always needed." She punctuated her point by leaning forward to kiss the top of his head, and she was amazed by how wonderful his hair smelled – some odd but intoxicating combination of oranges, wood ash soap, and something else she couldn't quite identify. Equally unidentifiable to her was the strange sensation she felt in the pit of her stomach when she breathed in this unusual but delightful aroma.

Suddenly uncomfortable with that feeling, Vanessa began to slowly back away, only to have Stephen stand and cup her face with his large and rough hands. As he stared intently at her, it seemed to Vanessa that his eyes were suddenly a remarkable shade of green, causing her to wonder if they had always been that colour. And if they had, why hadn't she ever noticed that before? His voice, too, was somehow different. It had always been pleasant enough before, but now it had an almost lyrical lament to it.

"I'll never stop asking, Vanessa. Never. Perhaps all I am to you is a friend or a brother. So be it. But you have always been much more than that to me, and you always will be. You. Are. My. Reason," he said with a deliciously rich timbre to his voice she had never heard before.

Swallowing hard before speaking she asked, "Reason for what, Stephen?"

"My reason for everything." With that he embraced her and, in a gesture that was both too intimate and yet not intimate enough, he kissed her lightly on the forehead, and took his leave, leaving Vanessa short of breath and wondering when, or even if, she would see him again.

Chapter Fourteen

The decisions made in Wartburg by Gustav Adelbern and in *Schloß Stormsong* by the Archduke combined to set the stage for yet another confrontation between members of die Volks Knechte and the Stormsong's (ostensibly also the emperor's) troops. The pieces were in place for that next skirmish to take place in *der Böhmerwald* (the Bohemian Forest, known as *Šumava* to the local Bohemians), a heavily forested mountain range one-hundred miles southwest of Prague which created a natural border between Bohemia on the eastern side and Bavaria on the western side.

While the low mountain range had been a source of contention between Serbs, Bavarians, Bohemians, and Ottoman Turks for nearly four centuries, it remained largely uninhabited. However, that was not to say that *der Böhmerwald* was unpopulated. On the contrary, because much of *der Donau Fluss* (the Danube River), a vital trade route through central Europe dating all the way back to ancient Greece, flowed through *der Böhmerwald*, it was frequently travelled, with goods being moved by boat or barge on the river itself, or by cart and horse along either of the river's banks.

In fact, it was precisely that kind of transport of goods that had, on this particular afternoon, attracted the attention of *die Grüne Gauner*, and a handful of *Roten Teufeln* and *Schwarzen Schurken*. Numbering approximately fifty men and women, the collection of *Volks Knechte* were hidden within the spruce, beech and fir trees just off the eastern bank of the Danube (known to Bohemians as *řeka Dunaj*), and from their cover, they could easily see the caravan of heavily laden carts and wagons that was slowly inching its way along the eastern shore.

"What do you think?" Roan whispered to Šarlatová. "Looks maybe like Jesuits to me."

Šarlatová squinted through her unimpaired right eye so that she could properly appraise the situation. "I don't know. But if it is Jesuits, then they're sure to have some fancy books and expensive bottles of wine."

Officially known as the Society of Jesus, the order of the Jesuits had been founded by Pope Paul III in 1540 with the mission to root out and eliminate the "cancer of Protestantism." Their harsh and militant tactics, combined with their radical political motives, aroused hostility even among fellow Catholics, and the vast wealth they amassed under the leadership of the brilliant Spanish priest and theologian Ignatius Loyola made them a source of envy throughout the world of Christendom and beyond.

"*Ja,*" Roan concurred, practically licking his lips at the thought of what treasure might be awaiting them. "Probably some silver candlestick holders and golden chalices, too. I say we give it a go."

"What would the son of a carpenter who said, 'Blessed are the poor' think of the church's tapestries, gold candlestick holders, paintings and sculptures?" Šarlatová wondered aloud. "I swear, if Christ returned today, the Vatican wouldn't let him get past the front gate."

"Leastways, not without a little somethin' for the offerin' plate," joked Roan. But neither Šarlatová nor the new leader of *die Schwarzen Schurken*, Franz Hohenleiter, laughed. They were both far too focused on the task at hand.

"I don't see a lot by way of weapons," Šarlatová observed. "But I don't like the fact that we can't see what's under the tarps in the carts."

"Why?" asked Franz. "You think the bloody Pope himself is hiding in one of them? As if he'd ever actually leave his fancy palace in Rome."

"I don't know. I just don't like the fact that there are so many wagons travelling out in the open like this. No guards. No use of the cover of darkness. And if those carts do have anything of value on them, why not put it all on a barge instead? That'd be faster, cheaper, and safer." Šarlatová squinted again to see if she'd missed anything the first time. "I say we pass on this one, Roan."

Franz interjected before Roan could respond. "I'll be pissing from my eyes and crying from my *Schwanz* before I let a haul like that just walk away. Not today, and certainly not in my own damn forest."

Roan's eyes narrowed. "It's not *your* forest, Franz. And it's not your call. If Šarlatová says no, then I'm inclined to agree with her."

"Christ, Roan. If you don't want to have a go at it, so be it. But don't presume to be tellin' me what I ought to do with my own men. I have a dozen Black Bastards here with me, and that's more than enough to get the job done – with or without you."

Šarlatová and Roan shared a knowing look with each other. If it was, in fact, a trap, and Franz's men assaulted the caravan on their own, they would be slaughtered without the help of Roan's Green Thieves or the Red Devils. On the other hand, if the Black Bastards went in alone and discovered a tidy haul of unprotected food, supplies, weapons, and gold, then they would be under no obligation to share the find with the other two tribes of *die Volks Knechte*.

After several long seconds, Šarlatová finally shrugged her shoulders. "If we go, I insist that you let me, Herman, and Simon provide cover from *der Schutzengel* (the Guardian Angel) spot back here. If anything should go wrong, you'll want your best archers watching your asses."

"You insist?" mocked Franz. "Do my ears deceive me, Roan? Or did a girl, all of twenty- years-old, just tell you what to do?"

Roan flashed Šarlatová a conspiratorial grin before responding. "First of all, she's only eighteen," he lied, knowing full well that Šarlatová was twenty-six. "Second of all, she's a better thief and archer than you or I will ever be. And third of all, I will break my massive foot off inside your tiny little ass if you ever disrespect that *girl* again. Do I make myself quite clear?"

With his face hot with anger, Franz asked, "Was there a 'fourth of all,' Roan?"

"Aye. Go fuck a pregnant goat, Franz!" Then Roan smiled. "But not until after we get this job done. Now let's go."

As the various outlaws took their positions in preparation for launching the attack, Šarlatová wanted to know, "Why a *pregnant* goat, Roan?"

"What?"

"When you told Franz to go fuck a goat. Why a pregnant goat? Why not just a goat?"

Roan's brow furrowed in concentration as he paused for a second to ponder this delicate but important question. "I don't know, *dívka*. In the moment, it just felt right."

"That's good enough for me." Šarlatová smiled and patted the mighty Moravian on the shoulder before taking her leave of him to find a spot that would allow her, Herman Jobst, and Simon Berger to provide a triangulation of crossfire with which to cover the soon to be launched operation.

With Šarlatová serving as one of the three guardian angels, this time it would be up to Hester Neuss to serve as *der Hase* (the rabbit), a role usually reserved for Šarlatová. As Hester assumed her position directly in the path of the caravan, just a few hundred yards down the eastern bank, and as she prepared to start crying and begging for *Geld für die Kleine* (money for the little one), nearly fifty other members of *die Volks Knechte* prepared to descend upon the caravan.

Cradling a loosely wrapped bundle in her arms that was meant to look like a baby, Hester dropped to her knees as the caravan ever so slowly approached. From inside the cover of her green cloak and cowl, no one could see that Hester was cradling a crossbow, not an infant. Nor could anyone see her eyes, which darted back and forth from the caravan to the tree line.

With practised skill, she watched and waited. While an untrained eye would see nothing but foliage, Hester could make out dozens of shapes moving within the forest. And where a casual observer might only see merchants making their way to market, Hester saw opportunity.

Just a little closer now, she thought to herself. *Almost there.* Then, just as she was about to make her staged plea for alms, a shot rang out. Someone from behind Hester, no more than four- hundred feet further down river, had stepped out from the tree line and fired a shot from a matchlock rifle. As the ball tore into the back of Hester's left shoulder, she dropped her crossbow and fell to the ground.

That's when all Hell broke loose.

As she lay face down on the bank of the Danube, Hester could hear a volley of additional shots from gunpowder weapons tearing into the forest around her. That sound was followed by a few grunts and the familiar zing of arrows as Šarlatová, Simon, and Herman fired into the caravan.

As the caravan came to a sudden and complete stop, it was immediately defended by dozens of armed and armoured men pouring from the trees just a few hundred yards further down shore from where *die Volks Knechte* had taken their positions. The caravan itself produced a second set of armed men. Dozens of swordsmen, archers, and arquebusiers carrying an assortment of different types of calivers came out from underneath the tarps that had concealed them in the wagons.

All told, more than a hundred Stormsong men, both in and around the caravan, now covered the shoreline and fired repeated volleys of arrows and bullets into the woods.

"Shit!" Šarlatová cursed, raining arrows down on the Stormsongs. She was tempted to rush from her position of concealment to lend aid to the men from *die Volks Knechte* who were engaged in close quarters combat on the shoreline. However, she could no longer see or hear either Simon or Herman, which meant that she might very well be the last *Schutzengel* left.

Refusing to leave Roan and the others without adequate cover, she fired arrow after arrow, each and every one finding its mark. As her deadly accurate fire continued, she could see that Roan and Franz were also giving as good as they got. Between Roan's massive sword and Franz's equally impressive axe, soldier after soldier fell with his face, head, arm or legs mangled beyond all recognition or repair.

Putting an arrow into the back of a Stormsong man who had approached Roan from behind, Šarlatová yelled to him to be careful. But he could no more hear her than she could hear what he was shouting at his attackers. Unable to resist any longer, and seeing that a number of men had gathered around Hester, Šarlatová leapt from her cover and rushed to the shore.

"Get up, you bitch!" a Stormsong swordsman commanded Hester. "When we're done taking turns with you, your thieving days will be done." As the man yanked her to her feet, Hester produced a dagger from within her cloak and, using her remaining good arm, slashed the throat of the soldier holding her. As he fell back with a wet spurting sound, Hester spun to face four other armed men.

She hissed and spit at them while sweeping her bloody dagger in vicious circles around her. Confident that she could at least hold the four at bay until help arrived, Hester suddenly saw a bright flash from the corner of her eye and felt a second piece of metal tear through her body. This time it was her right knee that was smashed, and as she fell to the ground a second time, she knew she could not get back up.

However, no sooner had she dropped her dagger than Šarlatová was with her, or more precisely, all round her. A blur of dark skin and green cloth flashed in every part of Hester's field of vision, and each of these sudden, seemingly impossible movements produced a wet slashing sound, followed by an inevitable cry or scream. It was as if the wild redhead was both everywhere and nowhere all at the same time.

As Šarlatová knelt, barely even breathing hard, to lend aid to Hester, another Stormsong man approached. This one was larger, faster, and better looking than any of the others, and he had nothing foul to utter as he rushed into the fray. In fact, Šarlatová barely had time to lift her sword to block the large man's first savage strike, and she was sent crashing to the shore by the force of the blow. As the boyishly handsome man prepared a second strike, Roan appeared from nowhere, and split the knight's shield in half with a massive blow from *Schwert*, nearly breaking the knight's left arm in the process.

The two men proceeded to circle each other, each one taking measure of the other's size and speed. Meanwhile, all around them. chaos continued to reign. While two Stormsong men lay wounded or dead for every one of *die Volks Knechte* who had fallen, the outlaws were rapidly running out of both time and troops.

Wanting to have another go at helping Hester to her feet, Šarlatová circled around the battle between Roan and the knight and took two more steps in Hester's direction before a metal bolt ripped into her right thigh. Screaming in pain, she looked to the other side of the river where the most unbelievably gorgeous woman Šarlatová had ever seen was reloading a gleaming white crossbow.

The woman moved as fast or faster than Šarlatová thought was possible and proceeded to score hit after hit as she fired on *die Volks Knechte* from across the river. Cursing both the speed and the accuracy of this beautiful but deadly warrior, and unable to stand on her own power, Šarlatová began to crawl to where Hester had fallen. While she was no longer moving, it was obvious from her tortured screams that Hester was still breathing.

As she crawled to within a few feet of her fallen friend, Šarlatová felt herself being hoisted unceremoniously into the air by massive arms. At first, thinking that the boyish knight had bested Roan and was now taking her captive, Šarlatová shrieked, only to realise a second or two later that it was Roan himself who had taken hold of her.

"We have to go, *dívka*!" he shouted, bits of blood, skin, and froth spewing from his mouth as he did. As she screamed in protest, Šarlatová could still see Hester, as well as the knight who had fallen near her. She was no longer certain that Hester was breathing, but the wounded knight clearly was; in fact, he was breathing quite heavily as he applied pressure to his neck which was spurting a fountain of blood from where Roan had just bitten him

"Roan, stop! Get Hester! We can't just leave her!" Šarlatová continued to scream. But by the time Roan yelled at her to shut up and that Hester was probably dead, Šarlatová was already growing lightheaded from loss of blood.

As the white-hot pain in her leg continued to throb like a heartbeat, and as she was jostled painfully up and down on Roan's massive and unforgiving shoulders, Šarlatová was being pulled further away from Hester by the second. Delirious with a cocktail of emotions ranging from anger and confusion to pain and betrayal, Šarlatová was completely overwrought. Feeling a feverish rush come over her, she resorted to the only weapon still available to her. She began to sing.

But this time no words and no sound would come. Instead – only blackness.

Chapter Fifteen

Šarlatová could hear before she could see. "The bolt is out, and the wound is clean and wrapped. But if it was poisoned like the round that hit Theo....I just don't know what else to do. Only Hester would, and she's...."

"She's what?" Šarlatová moaned. She still couldn't see out of either eye, but she could hear quite well, and the voices around her belonged to Roan, Simon Berger, Günther from Oldenburg, Theodore Berger, and Franz Hohenleiter.

The fact that her question went unanswered agitated her more than the screaming pain in her sinewy right thigh or the cold numbness she felt everywhere else. Clearing her throat to make her voice stronger, Šarlatová again asked, "Where. Is. Hester?"

Šarlatová couldn't see that Roan looked worriedly at the other men gathered around her, but she could instantly hear it in his voice. "She's gone, *dívka*. They've taken her. We don't know where, but as I was carryin' you out, Franz saw a couple of Stormsong men draggin' her towards the river."

"And I don't suspect they were taking her there to baptise her," added Franz, which earned him a look from the other four that told him it was best to keep quiet.

Šarlatová's voice softened some now. "Why did you leave her, Roan. Why didn't you go back for her? Why didn't any of you? I did! What happens to one of us happens to all of us, right? Or are those just some words that we say to make ourselves feel better?"

The five men who were gathered around the soft bed of leaves that was Šarlatová's makeshift hospital ward exchanged looks with each other, but it was abundantly clear that it was Roan's responsibility to answer her.

"We all thought she was dead, *dívka*. So many of us were.... *are*. Herman Jobst, almost all of Franz's men. More'n half of all of us is dead or missin.' If'n I hadn't got you out when I did, you'd be dead, too."

The look on Šarlatová's face, which had nothing to do with her own perilous situation, nearly broke Roan's heart – Simon's, too. The younger of the two Berger brothers approached her and took Šarlatová's hand in his own. "As God is my witness, Šarlatová, we'll get her back."

Before Šarlatová could respond, Franz interjected again. "But God isn't your witness, Simon. He isn't beholden to any of us." As he scanned the disapproving looks from the others and the blank expression on Šarlatová's face, he continued. "Look, I understand that I'm not the most likeable person here. And comin' from the Black Bastards instead of the Green Thieves, well....I know what you all think of me. But if she's alive at all, and I hope for her sake that she isn't, then she's already rotting somewhere in a dungeon cell that we'll never find. And if we all go rompin' around the whole of Bohemia trying to find her, then that's exactly where we're going to end up, too. In a dungeon cell....or in the fuckin' cemetery."

As an awkward silence descended on the group, Šarlatová's vision began to slowly clear, just enough to allow her to stare hard at the faces of each of the men assembled around her.

"You're a fine commander, Franz. And a good friend. But you're wrong. We don't dislike you because you're not a Green Thief. In fact, we don't dislike you at all. There's not much wrong with you except for perspective. If it was your brother Ulrich that the Stormsongs had hold of, you'd be singing quite a different tune."

"That's different, Šarlatová, and you know it. Ulrich was family."

Šarlatová shifted position painfully but gave up for the moment the notion of trying to stand. "Hester is a widow. All of her children are dead. So there's no one to look after her. No one but us. We're all she's got. We're her family. What happens to one of us happens to all of us, and as *God* is my witness, we *will* go looking for her – all of us!"

Roan realised at that moment that Šarlatová had – without intending to – just usurped his position as commander of *die Grüne Gauner.* As Šarlatová's now de facto second in command, he asked, "And what of the Stormsongs, *dívka?*"

"I feel a great swell of pity in my heart for any Stormsong dumb enough to stand in between me and my friend. And if I ever again see that bitch with the blue cloak who shot me, I'm going to cut her fucking heart out and serve it to her with a side of *Kirschen.*"

"It's settled then," Roan announced. "We'll need to get the word out to all *Volks Knechte* we can find, 'cause we'll need to pool our resources on this one. And we'll need to move quickly. You four look to it. In the meantime, *dívka*, you and I need to speak….in private."

There wasn't much of Hester Neuss left for Monsignor Mučitel to work with. But he made do as best he could.

She was brought to his "confessional," deep within *Schloß Stormsong*, completely naked, her hair shorn as if she were a sheep, her right knee shattered, and her left shoulder continuously bleeding from the small hole in it. Upset that she had slipped into a state of semi-consciousness, and fearing that she would bleed out before he could interrogate her, Monsignor Mučitel "tended" to Hester's bleeding shoulder by filling a small cauldron with water, oil, and tar. He then brought the mixture to a boil and poured it slowly over Hester's seeping wound. Not only did the molten mixture cauterise her wound, but it revived her from her delirious state, bringing her sharply back into a world of pain, and ensuring that she was fully alert and screaming for what was to come next – *der schwarze Beichtvater's* chair.

The chair was outfitted with sharp and rusty iron spikes over the back, armrests, seat and legrests. To prevent any unnecessary movement after he had placed her limp body into the chair, Monsignor Mučitel set two heavy iron bars across Hester's arms to push them against the spiked arm-rests and two more across her thighs, allowing the spikes to further penetrate her flesh. He then left her sitting in the chair for almost three hours, but because none of the spikes had penetrated any of her vital organs, and because the wounds were closed by the spikes themselves, Hester's additional blood loss was minimal – meaning that she could remain in the chair for several more hours, if not days, before finally expiring.

During the time in which the sadistic priest had left her in the chair, Hester had gone through three predictable stages of agony. During the first hour, the pain had been such that she had lost control of her bowels, urinating and defecating all over herself, the chair, and the floor. By the second hour, she had become so delirious that she had wavered in and out of consciousness and had lost the ability to speak or formulate a conscious thought. The third hour had brought relief. After vomiting several times, she had finally passed out. Despite the fact that the stench of piss, shit, blood, and vomit permeated the air, she likely would have remained that way for hours if Monsignor Mučitel had not intervened again.

Upon reentering the dark and rank chamber, he took one look at Hester and gave a sort of tsk-tsk. "This will not do, heretic. Your time in Hell is not yet."

Hester neither heard nor saw him retrieve a serrated kitchen knife and a pair of rusty stable pincers that were intended to handle horseshoes. Taking those two crude instruments, Monsignor Mučitel approached Hester, seized her left nipple in the jaws of the pincers and used the jagged knife to saw away at her flesh. While Hester's violent spasms prevented him from completing the procedure, it had the desired effect. The white-hot pain shocked the poor woman out of her delirium and back into the painful purgatory of Monsignor Mučitel's confessional.

Allowing a few seconds for her tortured screams to abate, the priest replaced his instruments and proceeded with Hester's interrogation.

"Do you know where you are?" the Monsignor asked her. Sobbing and breathing heavily, Hester surveyed her surroundings, but said nothing.

"Do you know where you are?" he repeated tersely.

This time Hester hesitated but did manage to summon what little strength she had left. "Yes."

"Very good. And do you know *why* you are here?"

Hester hesitated again before answering. The delay gave her just enough time to catch her breath. "Yes," she sobbed. And before Monsignor Mučitel could ask her anything else, she added, "I'm here to amuse you, you sick bastard!"

"No. no. You are not here to amuse me. You are here because you are a heretic and a witch, and it is time to confess your sins." Monsignor Mučitel corrected her in much the same way that a professor at *die Universität Heidelberg* might correct a student who had offered the wrong answer to a question of theology. His tone was surprisingly calm and conversational and belied the awful and bizarre circumstances at hand.

"You are a witch, are you not?" he asked. Knowing full well what that accusation meant, all that Hester could produce by way of reply was a tortured sound that might have come from an animal caught in a steel trap.

Shaking his head disapprovingly, Monsignor Mučitel rephrased the question. "For how long have you been a witch?"

When the second iteration of the question yielded only a series of tortured sobs, he shook his head again, took Hester's partially severed nipple in his gloved left hand and ripped it completely away from her breast, producing a new cacophony of tortured screams.

The look in Monsignor Mučitel's eyes was strange, almost hungry, as if he was being fed by Hester's pain. "Tell me what you know of lycanthropy, witch," he commanded in a cool, almost detached manner. All that Hester could offer by way of response was a gurgled wheeze that caused a combination of blood and saliva to ooze down her chin. In response, the priest seized a small hammer and brought it crashing down upon her already mangled knee. With a sickening crunch, the entire joint popped and caved in on itself, causing Hester's eyes to roll back into her head while her body shivered with uncontrollable spasms – each one causing the flesh of her legs, back, and arms to work down even deeper onto the spikes of the chair's seat.

Sighing in frustration, Mučitel continued. "Tell me what you know of the witches' Sabbath." Then, sensing that Hester was about to slip back into oblivion, he produced a small bottle, which contained an odd concoction of vinegar and iodine, and poured it slowly over her many open wounds, into her mouth, and around her nose and eyes. The utterly inhuman sounds that this produced caused the demented confessor to smile ever so slightly.

"Tell me what you know of deliriant nightshades," he asked calmly.

Hester's screams were replaced by guttural whimpers that were part sob and part moan. Between tortured breaths, she managed to wheeze out a few words. "Just….tell….me….tell me….what….to say."

Exhaling with satisfaction, the Monsignor cradled her shaved, bloody, and sweat soaked head in his arms. Having broken her, something he could never quite do to Lady von Stormsong, Hester was his now, and he held and stroked her head in much the same way a parent would hold a child who needed comforting.

"Say that you have committed fornication with dark men and devils of all kinds. Say that you have damaged humans and animals and crops with your black magic. Say that you have cast spells to cause disease, raise storms, cause infants to be stillborn, and conjure the dead. And above all, say that you have renounced the one true God, have betrayed your Lord and Saviour Jesus Christ, and have worshipped at the altar of Beelzebub, regularly servicing him in the most vile and carnal ways."

Unable to produce any intelligible sounds, Hester simply nodded her head ever so slightly, but even that small effort seemed to exhaust her, and her breath began to come in a series of short and quick gasps. As she struggled for air, Monsignor Mučitel stroked Hester's bare head in a surprisingly gentle manner. He then proceeded with the rest of her confession.

"You have renounced the one, true, holy, Catholic faith, witch. You have devoted your body, when you still had one, and your soul to Satan. You have engaged in orgies with the Devil. You have engaged in shapeshifting, flying through the air, abusing the Christian sacraments, and concocting all sorts of magical ointments." At this point, the priest was simply reciting from rote memorization passages from within the *Malleus Maleficarum* (the Hammer of Witches.)

First published in Germany in the late-fifteenth century, the work by a German Catholic clergyman and inquisitor named Heinrich Kramer was the most trusted and utilised compendium of knowledge on witchcraft, demonology, and the occult through the fifteenth, sixteenth, and seventeenth centuries. While the work was officially condemned by the Church as being inconsistent with Catholic doctrine and theology, it underwent twenty-eight different revisions between 1486 and 1600, and the immoral and illegal procedures it recommended were still commonly practised well into the seventeenth century.

"You have confessed all of this to me in the sight and presence of our Heavenly Father, and His mercy and His grace are unsurpassed. In His holy name, I now accept your confession and grant you His forgiveness. I shall now retire and go pray to Him until such time as He decides an appropriate penance."

Hester never heard her "absolution," nor did she hear the door shut behind her confessor after he walked silently out of the chamber, leaving her corpse in the clutches of his iron chair.

Like all of the other wounded Stormsong men, Stephen lay on a bed with clean white sheets inside the warm confines of *Schloß Stormsong's Gott Haus*. His injuries were relatively minor compared to the dozen other men with whom he shared the spacious hall. Most of the others had suffered severed arms or legs, or severe head wounds. Surprisingly, however, their numbers were very few. In fact, as a testament to the deadly accuracy of the archers within *die Grüne Gauner*, only a handful of the Stormsongs had been injured. For the most part, the Archduke's men were either perfectly fine, or they were dead. Additionally, of the dozen men who, like Stephen, had been wounded but not killed, at least half of them would also be dead before the day was out.

The pain Stephen felt in his neck was nothing compared to the agony he felt listening to the wails and cries coming from other beds in *das Gott Haus*. Stephen was desperate to leave the hall, but Mother Superior Ludmilla simply would not allow it – and Stephen wanted to face her wrath about as much as he wanted to face off again with the wild, red-haired giant who had shattered his shield with just one blow and had taken an enormous bite out of his neck. He did, however, convince Mother Superior Ludmilla to at least move him to the opposite end of the hall from the rest of the wounded.

Bored and restless, he did just about the only thing that the Bridgettine nuns would allow – he read the Bible and he prayed the rosary. Both usually made him feel much better – calmer, more centred, and much more connected with the Lord. This time, however, probably due to a mixture of pain and exhaustion, reading and praying just made him sleepy. He was just about to doze off again when a familiar and pleasant voice said, "So....you're quite a mess."

Smiling even before he opened his eyes, he responded, "If I knew that this is what it took to get you to come visit me in bed...."

"What? You would have let a seven-foot-tall barbarian eat your neck earlier?" Vanessa asked.

At this both of them laughed, causing Stephen to wince in pain and place a hand over the thick dressing that the Mother Superior herself had applied to his wound.

"I'm sorry," Vaneesa apologised. "I didn't mean to cause you any more pain." She paused meaningfully before adding, "I mean that in a lot of ways, Stephen."

"It's perfectly alright," he assured her. "I don't mind the pain. It's manageable. But you're about the only sunlight that has entered this place in two days, and I'm happy to have the company. Although, I'd be even happier if you had brought a mug or two of your father's ale with you."

Vanessa smiled again. "And risk the ire of Mother Superior Ludmilla. I'd sooner travel to the dark continent and feed raw meat to one of those giant, toothy lizards they have there. What are they called again? Crocodiles?"

"Actually, I think they're called nuns," Stephen responded with a smile.

"I heard that, you two. And the dark continent is no place for a proper lady or a Captain of the Guard, no matter how much of a *Klugscheißer* either one is."

"Yes, Mother Superior," Vanessa answered. Then she and Stephen shared another laugh. "How are you, Stephen? I mean really."

"Well, enough I suppose," he surmised while glancing to the end of the hall where a soldier whose name he did not know was being prepared for a crude amputation of his left leg. "Not so well as during our last meeting here though."

"And why is that, Stephen?" Vanessa asked with a playful smirk on her face. "Could that be because you were not injured then or could it be because I was...."

120

"Half naked?" Stephen finished. "That? No. Truth be told, I hardly even noticed. I just thought that our conversation that day was...."

"Was what?" Vanessa asked, fearing that Stephen might reveal even more about his deep feelings for her.

"It was quite....*titillating*."

Pretending to be shocked, Vanessa asked, "Stephen Stallknecht, did you just make a joke? And one at my expense, no less?"

"I did," he answered, flashing her that boyish grin that she had been thinking about far too much the past few days. "Granted, it was my first one, but I thought it went quite well. What did you think?"

Exhaling deeply and giving him a sultry smile, she said, "Well. It wasn't bad. But it wasn't the *breast* joke I've ever heard."

Stephen started to laugh so hard that he couldn't catch his breath. Soon his laughs began to devolve into a coughing fit that he couldn't stop. As he placed his hand over his wound to keep the dressing from coming undone, new blood began to seep through the silk gauze and over his fingers, prompting Vanessa to turn and yell for help. However, before she could get a single word out, Mother Superior Ludmilla was already there.

"Blessed Mother, just look at what you two have done." She immediately began reapplying the dressing and shot Vanessa a knowing look, indicating that her visit with Stephen was over – right now!

"Excuse me, Stephen....I mean, Sir Knight. Excuse me, too, Mother Superior Ludmilla. I have things to tend to just now, but I'll be back later."

Still coughing and fussing with the Bridgettine nun as she tried to help him, Stephen could only get out a few words to Vanessa as she started to walk away. "Soon....come....back.... soon."

"I will, Stephen. I promise."

Chapter Sixteen

Šarlatová waited for the others to depart before apologising to Roan. "Look, I know what you want to talk to me about, and I'm sorry. In fact, I'm *really* sorry. I didn't mean to challenge your authority like that. It's just that...."

"Hush now, *dívka*. Don't waste the steam of your piss about all that. Everything you said was right, and I agreed with the lot of it. Anyway, it'll be nice not havin' to make all the damn decisions anymore. I haven't got the head for it."

"Yes, you do!" Šarlatová insisted. "And no one is taking anything away from you, Roan. You are now and will forever remain our leader."

"*Dívka*, you've been leading this bunch in all but name for quite some time now, so let's just put an end to that, okay? That's not what I wanted to talk to you about."

"Okay. But we're coming back to that later. What *did* you want to talk about?" Šarlatová asked.

"Hester. You know what they're going to....do with her....I mean, to her, don't you?"

Šarlatová closed her eyes, as if doing so could shut away the horrific images of what might be happening to Hester at that very moment. "Yes, I do. They'll put her on the wheel until she reveals everythin' she knows about *die Volks Knechte*. She'll try her best to resist, but the wheel breaks everyone....eventually. It's just a question of time."

Closing his eyes now, Roan shook his head. "No....no they won't. They no longer need to. The fact that they lured us in like that and ambushed us again so easily, right in our own Goddamned part of the country, means that Gustav Adelebrn was right. We've got a Judas among us what's been tellin' the Stormsongs everythin' they want and need to know. So why would they bother to torture Hester for what they've already got?"

Šarlatová opened her eyes and searched Roan's face for an answer. "What then? Why not just kill her like they've done to so many of the rest of us? Why take her prisoner?"

"Mark my words, *dívka*, they are goin' to execute her publicly. And they'll make quite an ugly display of it."

"Why? As a warning to us? As if we didn't already know that the Stormsongs were a bunch of cruel and heartless...."

"Not as a warning, *dívka*," Roan interrupted. "As a trap. They know full well that we're not just goin' to sit with our thumbs up our assess while they do God knows what to her for God knows how long. That Archduke is a maggoty piece of rot, for sure. But he's no idiot. He knows we'll come for her, and he'll be ready."

Šarlatová scarcely hesitated before she summoned her resolve and, using her bow as a crutch, managed to get to her feet. "Then we'll just have to be ready, too."

She and Roan shared a long and meaningful moment staring at one another. Without any words, much was expressed as they locked glances and eventually embraced. "What happens to one of us...." Šarlatová started.

"Happens to all of us," Roan finished.

For Vanessa, *soon* turned out to be just a few hours later. When most of the screams coming from *das Gott Haus* had quieted down, and all but a few of the Brigittine nuns had retired for the evening, Vanessa padded softly back into the large hall, careful not to alert anyone of her presence.

Looking in every direction to make sure she had not been seen, she stole silently towards Stephen's bed, not sure if she would be able to wake him quietly. But it didn't matter. He was already awake.

"Is it an angel that's coming to see me then?" he asked, much too loudly.

"Shhhhh. Do you want to wake up every nun in Europe?"

"If it would get me out of this bed, for sure."

"That's not why I'm here. You need to stay here until you have recovered. But I need to ask you something first."

Elated to have some company, Stephen was more than willing to answer anything Vanessa might ask of him, and sensing that she might be up to something clandestine, he leaned in closely as she knelt by his bed – a little too closely, in fact. He ended up with his face being scant inches from Vanessa's ample and appealing bosom.

"Stephen!"

"What?"

"My eyes are up here!"

"Yes – of course. I'm sorry. What is it?"

"Who's been to see you? Besides me, of course."

"I don't understand."

"Have any of my father's men been to see you yet?"

"Yes."

"Who?"

"Lord Ernst Gundrham and Lord Lanzo Oddvar were both here not an hour ago. Why?"

Scanning her surroundings yet again to make sure that they were still alone, Vanessa asked, "Did they discuss what's to become of the prisoners we captured."

"Yes, they did. Your father is quite brilliant, actually. He's going to stage a public execution of both of them, along with several other prisoners, in the hopes that the heretics will come swarming out of the woods like a brood of termites. Once they have, we'll be able to send all of them to meet their false god, and we'll be halfway done with this so-called uprising." Stephen paused for a moment when he saw a look of disapproval flash across Vanessa's face. "Why do you ask?"

"I figured as much, but I wanted to be sure."

"Why?"

"I don't know. Maybe it's nothing. But there was a woman with them by the river."

"So?"

"Well, she didn't look like the others. She wasn't pale at all. In fact, her skin was quite dark. Like a Greek, maybe, or an Italian. She could almost have passed for a Turk if not for her red hair. That's the wildest, reddest hair I've ever seen." Vanessa then paused, seeming to try to recapture some earlier thought.

"And what is your interest in this girl then? Please tell me you're not...."

"What? A *Tribade*? Don't be silly, Stephen. And don't you go picturing me doing....*that* with another woman, red-haired or other-wise." Vanessa punctuated her point by jabbing Stephen in the arm.

"Ouch!" he protested playfully. "Then what is your interest in this woman?"

"I don't know. I only got one really good look at her, but...."

"But what?"

"But I would swear that I have seen her somewhere before."

The staging of public executions in the seventeenth century was part art and part science, with the art coming in the form of theat-ricality. The affairs were elaborately staged spectacles, brimming with suspense, tension, and terror. And because they were such popular and festive rituals, they were, like any festival, widely at-tended by people from all socio-economic backgrounds. And for those unable, or unwilling, to attend in person, graphic accounts and descriptions were routinely printed and sold.

Like any other form of "low-end" entertainment (bear bait-ing, bull baiting, cockfights, and the like), executions performed at *Schloß Stormsong* were traditionally performed outside of the walls of the castle. In fact, for centuries, public executions, which had most often come in the form of hangings and beheadings, had been performed at "Torben's Tree."

Torben von Stormsong had been the patriarch of the family in the twelfth century who had popularized the public executions of murderers, rapists, thieves, and other common criminals. The hang-ings themselves were not actually performed on the tree; instead, the executions were carried out on a wooden scaffold nearby. During such festive occasions, seats could be purchased for a nominal fee, but most spectators simply stood around the tree jostling each other for the best possible view. Travelling vendors peddled fruits and pies, and spectators could even buy a pamphlet or ballad that re-counted the various crimes and depraved lives of the criminals being hanged.

The form of execution depended primarily upon the social class of the condemned and, to a lesser extent, the severity of his or her crime. Upper class individuals generally received a hu-mane and, at least by comparison, painless beheading. If the ex-ecutioner's axe was sharp and his aim precise, the beheading could be accomplished quickly and relatively painlessly; however, if the blade was blunt or if the executioner was clumsy or inebriated, the process could require multiple strokes, resulting in a much lon-ger and more gruesome death. The determining factor, bizarrely enough, was the size of the gratuity paid to the executioner by the condemned.

Witches, however, were generally burned at the stake or drowned, while traitors and heretics might be drawn and quar-tered. Regardless of the form of execution, various parts of the body (most often the head) would then be displayed publicly as an attempt to deter others from committing the same crime. Having "confessed" to a litany of crimes and heresies, Hester's sentence could take any one of a variety of forms. But regard-less of the procedure employed, after her sentence was carried out, she was to be disembowelled and burnt, with her ashes blown in every conceivable direction – and there seemed to be precious little that Šarlatová or any of *die Volks Knechte* could do to prevent it.

Chapter Seventeen

It was a great day for an execution.

Because the weather was unusually warm for June, and because her execution was to be the first one at Torben's tree in several months, Hester's hanging was extremely well attended. In fact, Šarlatová had never seen a crowd as large as this one at an execution before – a fact that worked to the distinct advantage of *die Grüne Gauner* and other members of die Volks Knechte. The larger the crowd, the easier it would be for the outlaws who intended to disrupt the proceedings to remain concealed. While she didn't have a precise head count, Šarlatová was fairly certain that at least one of every five people in attendance today was one of hers.

The festive atmosphere appalled Šarlatová, but she did her best to ignore it so that she could focus on the problem at hand – securing Hester's rescue. As she and Roan worked their way through the crowd, she did her best to survey the scaffold to determine precisely where Hester would be brought up. Roan, on the other hand, had to focus on just blending in. At nearly seven-feet-tall and weighing more than three-hundred and fifty pounds, that was no easy task for the mountainous Moravian. However, a pronounced and practised limp, combined with a feigned stoop, seemed to normalise his size, at least a little. To further enhance his chances of not being paid much mind, Roan had smeared his arms and legs with fresh shit that his horse had obligingly produced earlier that morning.

For her part, Šarlatová had to cover her distinctive red hair with a rather plain coif, and both she and Roan had shed their signature green cloaks and hoods. Like Roan, Šarlatová displayed a limp, but hers was not born out of practice. On the contrary, the limp was the residual consequence of the significant wound she had suffered in her right thigh. While it continued to bother her and had not completely healed, everyone one of *die Volks Knechte* who had witnessed the wound marvelled at how quickly and easily it was healing. The general consensus seemed to be that Šarlatová's remarkable healing ability was some welcome byproduct of her....*ability.*

"I haven't seen Hester yet, Roan. But it looks like they're set up for more than one execution today," Šarlatová whispered. But, before Roan could respond, a hawker who was selling meat pies turned her way.

"I hear they're beheading as many as a dozen today," the hawker whispered back, wrinkling his nose when he caught wind of Roan.

"Is that a fact?" Šarlatová asked, hoping to dismiss him easily.

"It is," he offered, his voice now well above a whisper. "Apparently the Stormsongs, God bless them, have captured a whole nest of stinking heretics....nest of vipers, if you ask me....and they're going to give them a right bit of God's justice today. Praise Jesus. And it's about time, too. Executions are good for business, and we haven't had enough of them lately. I've sold more of these today than I have in months." Producing one of his flaky, tender pastries, baked to a rich golden brown, the hawker added in a hushed, conspiratorial tone, "See, I use tough meat to start with. But I cook it at higher temperatures than most bakers, and that makes the meat tender. Use too tender of a cut, and the meat actually gets all stringy when you cook it. And that's my secret. I have some left. Care for one?"

Disgusted by the crass commercial transactions going on at what could soon be her friend's death, Šarlatová said nothing. Roan on the other hand, couldn't resist. "We're not hungry. But I tell you what. If'n you don't stop talkin' about your fuckin' pies, after this business is done, I'm goin' to drag your sorry ass back to your bakery, and into the fuckin' oven you're goin' to go. And when you're all cooked up, I'm goin' to eat you slowly and shit you out fast. How'd that be, you Popish prick?"

The hawker couldn't have been more stunned if Roan had slapped him in the face, which might have occurred next if he tarried any longer. So, exercising rare discretion, he retreated quickly and quietly.

Šarlatová looked disapprovingly at Roan. "The whole point is to try to not bring attention to ourselves," she hissed.

"Sorry, *dívka*. But there's nothing I can do about being big, Protestant, Moravian, and right all at the same time."

Before Šarlatová could respond, a trumpet blast from atop the scaffold signalled that the well- rehearsed proceedings were about to commence. More than a dozen men and women were assembled on the scaffold surrounding Torben's Tree, but it appeared that Hester was going to be the opening act.

A man that neither Šarlatová nor Roan recognised stood front and centre and pronounced Hester's lengthy indictment to the assembled crowd. "This wicked woman is a heretic and a traitor. She hath grievously offended our good Emperor Matthias, his holy eminence Pope Paul V, and the Lord our God." What Roan and Šarlatová saw next prevented them from hearing the remainder of the fallacious indictment against Hester.

As the man spoke, a breaking wheel was rolled up a short ramp and on to the scaffold. Astoundingly, woven throughout the spokes of the wheel was the battered and broken body of Hester Neuss. So shocking and incomprehensible was this image to all of those present, it was generally assumed that this display was some form of cheap theatricality. It simply wasn't physically possible for an actual human body to be stretched and extended this way. Consequently, confident that what they were seeing was all just part of the day's drama, the assembled crowd produced a loud and raucous ovation at Hester's arrival.

Feeling physically ill, Šarlatová turned to Roan. "That can't be Hester, can it?"

"*Ja.* That's her alright, *dívka.* Fuckin' bastards!" Šarlatová could see that Roan was not going to stay silent any longer. When she heard him curse and saw him reach for the pommel of his sword, she stopped him.

"Wait, Roan. If that is her, she can't possibly still be alive. Can she?"

"I pray to God not. But if she is, what more can they do to her than what they've already done?"

"Nothing. They won't touch her again. I'm going to end her suffering right now."

"How? What could you possibly....? No, *dívka,* you can't. You can't use your...." Roan struggled for words. "Not to take a life like that....can you?"

"I don't know. I've never even considered trying."

"Then don't consider tryin' it now, *dívka.* Think of what you're about to do. If you use your....if you use it to take Hester's life, even if it is an act of mercy, you'll be crossin' a line for sure. And there's no tellin' if'n you will ever be able to uncross that line. Please don't do it."

Šarlatová was quite certain that she had never heard Roan use the word please before. But she was not going to let this unusual display of courtesy on his part dissuade her from her decided course of action. "Roan, if I can end her suffering just one minute sooner than the hangman, then *God Himself* would call it an act of mercy."

Roan shook his head in disagreement. "Others would call it murder, plain and simple."

"And are any of those *others* here right now?" she snapped. Seeing that Roan was not going to say anything more, she added, "And if it's murder and not mercy, then I'll just have to take my punishment as I go. If I have to suffer for my sins, then so be it."

The startling flash of anger in Šarlatová's gorgeous green eyes signalled to Roan that the question had now been decided. With the debate over, Šarlatová lowered her head and very softly, imperceptible to all but Roan, began to sing. But unlike before, her power manifested itself quietly, like a song inside of her head – neither loud, nor powerful, but delicately reaching out, like tendrils through the air….searching.

Given the sounds of celebration going on around him, Roan couldn't make out the words Šarlatová was singing. He also couldn't hear the lengthy, rambling list of false charges against Hester, which was only now drawing to a conclusion.

"And while it remains royal policy, consistent with the teachings of Jesus Christ's universal Catholic Church, that we shall not suffer a witch to live, so gracious and merciful is our beloved Archduke that, even now, if this wicked woman were to set aside her treason and her dedication to the Dark One, she might obtain his favour and be granted a pardon. What say you, woman?"

The crowd took several long moments to quiet down. Once they did, the orator repeated his question. "What say you, woman?"

Through the long and awkward silence, during which the expectant audience waited impatiently for an answer from Hester, nothing could be heard except for Roan's whispered voice. "Whatever you're goin' to do, girl, best do it quick."

Šarlatová simply shook her head and stopped singing. "I couldn't reach her. She's already dead."

Finally, the orator bellowed, "In most obstinate refusal to recant, you have deeply offended the Archduke. Your sentence is…." The audience hung expectantly on his next word. Wondering whether they would witness a beheading, a hanging or something far more gruesome, and entertaining, they waited in hushed silence until the orator shouted, "Death by beheading!"

The crowd roared so loudly that Roan had to shout in order for Šarlatová, who was standing right next to him, to hear him. "If'n she's already dead, what's the point in cuttin' off her head?"

Šarlatová paused in thought as she surveyed the crowd. "There is no reason. But the rest of the people here don't know she's already dead. It's all a show, Roan. It's just an act. One designed to bring us out in the open."

"How do you know that, *dívka*?"

"Because when I reached out for Hester, I found someone else instead. I was able to read his thoughts as easily as I can understand my own."

Roan stared in amazement at Šarlatová. He was both awed and frightened by this latest revelation. Having known about Šarlatová's "gift" for some time now, he was not taken completely aback. But within the past few weeks, he had seen her use it to heal Theodore Berger from a fatal wound, attempt to euthanize Hetser, and now read the thoughts of another. He began to wonder if there was any end to Šarlatová's ability, and he both expected and dreaded that he would soon have the answer.

Suddenly realising that, if Šarlatová was correct, all of *die Volks Knechte* in attendance were in grave danger, Roan took her by the arm and began directing her through the crowd; as he did so, the orator was signalling for the assembled men and women to quiet down. "But before we deliver God's true justice to this concubine of Satan, we shall let her suffer a little longer...." It was not until this point that the assembled crowd came to realise that the hideous carcass woven so impossibly through the spokes of the breaking wheel was not some gruesome puppet but was, in fact, a human being – a human being who was, to their thinking, still alive.

This sudden and dramatic realisation caused a great deal of unsettled murmuring and jostling in the crowd and forced the orator to raise his voice. "And while she suffers, we shall take up the case of this next brigand."

Šarlatová and Roan stopped cold, and upon turning back around to face the scaffold, they both saw a bruised and beaten man being carried up to the platform. As the man was lifted up on display so that all present could gaze upon his shattered body, Roan and Šarlatová caught a good look at him. The man had been beaten so badly that his face was the colour and shape of a bruised and deformed plum – rendering him almost unrecognisable. The bruising and the blood had disguised and distorted most of his facial features, but there was just enough left that Šarlatová and Roan had no doubt that they were looking at the face of their dear friend, Herman Jobst.

"You're not going to watch?" Archduke von Stormsong asked of his daughter. Standing at the top of *Schloß Stormsong's* White Tower, the warm wind was whipping enough that Vanessa's father's words were lost in the air.

"I'm sorry, father. What did you say?"

Turning towards her with a thinly veiled expression of contempt, the archduke asked again. "You're not going to watch?" He was referring to the fact that, unlike himself, Vanessa was standing well back from the tower's edge, making it impossible for her to see what was going on several hundred feet below.

Der Weißer Turm (the White Tower) was the tallest of three towers within the Winter Palace of *Schloß Stormsong*. On the far eastern end of the compound, this tall and round cannon tower dated back to the sixteenth century reconstruction of the castle. Since 1581, it had also served as a prison and featured a dungeon with monumental vaults and several circular openings in the floor through which particularly troublesome or offensive prisoners could be lowered, by way of a series of pulleys, into the oubliette.

The walls of the massive tower were eight feet thick which allowed for the housing of some of the largest cannons in Europe. The tower's facade, like much of the Winter Palace, was made of pegmatite, a form of granite composed of interlocking crystals of widely varying textures, patterns, and sizes (some up to several feet in length). But, because the granite crystals varied little in colour (pegmatite crystals are primarily white, cream, or light grey), the entire tower had a bleak, glacial look to it – something that Vanessa found quite appropriate given that her father's current appearance, like her own mood upon entering this tower, was equally bleak and cold.

The top level, where Vanessa and her father stood, had no roof and had been designed as an observation post for military purposes, but today it served as a veranda from which the archduke could view and enjoy the festivities.

"You know I can't bear to watch these....*rituals*, father," Vanessa explained. As she spoke, Vanessa's thoughts were not on this particular execution, but upon a different one her father had made her witness when she was but twelve-years-old. With the promise of a "surprise," he had led her to this very edge of the White Tower to oversee the execution of a dozen or so felons who had been condemned to death. Her father had assured her that they were all criminals and heretics, members of something called *die Grüne Gauner,* and that they deserved to die, but Vanessa had baulked at having to witness their executions firsthand.

Repulsed by his daughter's display of weakness, the archduke had invited her to use the convicts as an opportunity to engage in some target practice with her surprise – a small, white, repeating crossbow. Although intrigued by the device, Vanessa had immediately refused to participate in something so barbaric and had wept when her father had forced the weapon into her hands and had ordered her to fire on the condemned men – and women – down below.

When she had continued to refuse, the archduke had bent down on one knee and, in a rare and surprising display of gentleness, had wiped away her tears and promised her that if she would take just one shot, then he would release all of the prisoners from their sentences.

Having seen this as an opportunity to escape the ordeal, Vanessa had taken up the weapon, aimed carefully at the men below, and had fired a bolt that struck precisely where she had intended it to – nowhere near any one of the condemned men. Vanessa had then relaxed, feeling some comfort from the fact that her acquiescence to her father's twisted demands would result in the commutation of the sentences of the men and women below. However, when her father had taken the weapon from her, he had proceeded to open fire on the band of condemned criminals. With remarkable speed and accuracy, he had placed a bolt in the head of each of the four women below, causing the condemned men to cry out in grief. As Vanessa had fled the top of the terror in sheer disgust and terror, her father had ordered that the men not be executed until the following day; apparently, he had wanted them to look upon the dead women for several hours before being executed themselves.

Despite the warmth of the day, that horrific memory, combined with the whipping wind at the top of the tower, caused Vanessa to feel a tremendous chill. But neither the memory nor the swirling winds affected her as much as the chilling voice of her father when he said, "Yes, daughter, I know that all too well. I suppose I was hoping that your recent.... *activities*....had led to your outgrowing your childish squeamishness."

Vanessa didn't even know where to begin. The *activities* of which her father spoke were all assignments he had ordered himself; additionally, Vanessa had been deprived of being childish since she was four years old. The death of her mother and stillborn brother had seen to that. Finally, there wasn't a squeamish bone in her body. Vanessa had witnessed, experienced, and participated in a range of sadistic, bloody, and violent ventures – all in the service of her father, emperor and God – and she had not baulked at any of them. But she could never say any of that to her father, and he knew that as well as she did.

"It matters little anyway. It shall soon be done, and with it, I think, the better part of this so-called rebellion."

Puzzled, Vanessa asked, "Forgive me, father, how is the execution of a dozen or so heretics going to accomplish an end to the rebellion? If anything, all you will do is start a war with these so-called reformers."

"You disappoint me, daughter. I'm not going to start a war; I'm going to end one. These executions are but a ruse; in fact, the woman....the witch....whatever her name was is already dead. And the others will soon be, too. I care little for the crimes of a solitary witch and a handful of underfed brigands. It's their *confrères* in whom I am interested."

Vanessa never understood her father's fascination with all things French. From doors to art, furniture to vernacular, and wine to women, he seemed to enjoy all things Gallic as much as he did all things Germanic. Could his admiration for Cardinal Richelieu really run that deep? As far as Vanessa was concerned, the French language was fine for traitors and spies, just as Spanish was fine for boy lovers and criminals. And while Latin was the language of salvation, for warriors and patriots there could only ever be one true language – German.

"Their *confrères*, father? Do you really think that the accomplices of these few criminals will come rushing to our gates in surrender just so that they might stop the executions?"

"That's precisely what I think, daughter. Say what you will about these....*Volks Knechte*, or whatever they call themselves these days. They are heretics, traitors, criminals, and pagans. But they are fanatically loyal to one another; I'll give them that much. I imagine that there are quite a few of them down there already, and when the time is right, Lord Oddvar will rain fire down upon the assembled crowd and wipe them from the face of the Earth."

Vanessa's emotions, and corresponding facial expressions, vacillated between alarm, shock, horror, and outrage. "But....how will you separate the outlaws from the....?" But she already knew the answer to her own question. And the vacant, almost disinterested, expression on her father's face confirmed her awful suspicion. There would be no attempt to separate *die Volks Knechte* from everyone else.

Vanessa's education and training (or indoctrination) had taught her that good didn't just need to triumph over evil, it had to make evil pay – dearly. But what her father was suggesting was not good triumphing over evil; it was madness! Every man, woman, and child below, whether Protestant or Catholic, rich or poor, young or old, was going to die today – and, unless she could do something to stop it, the blood of innocents would once again be on her hands.

Chapter Eighteen

———⚜———

Herman Jobst would have never been called handsome – not even before his lengthy session with Monsignor Mučitel, but the bruised and broken rag doll that was now brought up onto the scaffold was no longer just homely. He….it….was hideous.

Because he had not been located after the battle of *der Donau Fluss,* it was widely assumed that Herman had died during the attack. In reality, he had fallen from his *Schutzengel* perch where he, Simon, and Šarlatová had provided a withering coverfire during the assault. But, after having slain only three or four (he wasn't sure which) Stormsong men, the branch of the fir tree on which he had taken up his position gave way, dropping him some thirty feet to the ground. The fall itself hadn't been the problem, but the angle at which his left leg had hit the ground was. With a thunderous and sickening snap, Herman's left leg had shattered, and when he touched a ragged end of bare bone that had broken through both his skin and his pant leg, he had nearly passed out.

As he had lain there writhing in agony for the duration of the battle, desperate to escape the searing pain that shot from his leg all the way up his spine, he had begged and prayed that he would pass out. But, because he had been unable to, once the fighting was over, it had not been difficult for the remaining Stormsong men to find him. His screams had led them to him with better accuracy than a map could ever have.

He had been taken back to *Schloß Stormsong* in the same cart as Hester, and he had been handled just as roughly. In fact, he had passed out even before Hester had and hadn't managed to regain consciousness until he was well within the walls of *der schwarze Beichtvater's* "confessional." It was there that he had quickly become acquainted with "the rack."

The rack, like most things in Europe, dated back at least as far as ancient Greece. It was designed around a rectangular, wooden frame with the victim's hands and feet chained to rollers at either end of the oblong structure. During the questioning, the interrogator would turn the handle at one end, causing the ropes to pull either the victim's arms or legs – or both. With enough time and enough torque applied to the rotation of the handle, the victim's cartilage and ligaments would be stretched and torn. With even more tension applied to the ropes, the victim's bones would snap with a grotesque cracking sound, and eventually his or her limbs could be torn completely from the body.

As terribly effective as the physical agony was at producing confessions and answers to questions, the psychological torture was just as great. Once the subject broke – and everyone broke, eventually – and the physical torture was over, the victim was faced with the prospect of being disabled permanently, living with one or more limbs completely useless.

Herman Jobst had been a gifted potter and a talented archer, but he was not a terribly large or strong man. His thin but sinewy arms had given way very early on, and his legs had not lasted much longer. Within just one hour, Monsignor Mučitel had broken Herman's body, if not his spirit. When he was finally released from the rack, he had essentially been rendered a quadriplegic. But, seemingly impossibly, when two of the priest's acolytes had hoisted his broken body off of the apparatus, Herman had managed to cough out, along with a mouthful of blood, one final statement of defiance.

"You haven't won anything!"

Interpreting that simple comment as an insult and a challenge, the Monsignor had allowed Herman a few hours of recovery time. Then, once shock had set in and had begun to replace his pain with a cold numbness, the priest had ordered Herman to be returned to the confessional.

During his second visit to Monsignor Mučitel, Herman had been introduced to yet another barbaric procedure, this one known as combing. The priest had watched silently as his acolytes had taken iron combs, which were intended to be used to prepare wool for spinning, to scrape and tear at the flesh of Herman's face. After mere minutes, Herman's ears, nose, lips, and eyelids had been flayed to the point that he was virtually unrecognisable. The process would have gone on longer, but Mučitel had been under orders to ensure that the victim was left at least passably recognisable to his friends. The priest had not understood why this was important, but he had known better than to question orders from the archduke.

The consequence of all of this was that Herman was virtually unrecognisable to all but his closest friends. Unfortunately for all in attendance, Herman's closest friend, Günther from Oldenburg, was in the crowd and recognised him immediately, and before the orator could even begin to read a list of fraudulent charges against Herman, Günther leaped into action.

Screaming a torrent of indecipherable obscenities, Günther produced a single-edged falchion and began to slash his way towards the scaffold. Almost instantaneously, Stormsong men and *Volks Knechte* leapt into the fray, and within seconds the previously festive occasion degenerated into a violent maelstrom of blood and metal.

At the first sign of violence that he was not personally directing, the orator fled from the scaffold, but not before shouting to the executioner to proceed. The large, black-hooded, axe-wielding brute stepped toward the breaking wheel where Hester's dead body remained impossibly entangled within the spokes. With one mighty swing he split her head clean in two, spraying blood and bits of bone and tissue across the platform. As he turned then to where Herman had been dropped when the violence began, he raised his massive axe again, but before he could land a second blow, a well-aimed arrow flew from Šarlatová's bow and pierced his throat. Dropping the axe and clutching in vain at his wound, the executioner stumbled backwards, slipped on a pool of blood left by Hester's decapitation, and fell to the floor of the scaffold where he was immediately set upon by the other would-be-victims of his axe.

As obscenities and blows were freely exchanged between the two warring factions, and as the non-partisan spectators attempted to flee, Archduke von Stormsong watched from above with interest but without passion. Having been initially startled when Vanessa had dashed towards the nearest flight of stairs and had scrambled down the steps two or three at a time, the archduke was now observing the proceedings quite calmly. He knew that Lord Gundrham, operating under his own orders, had placed archers and arquebusiers at every embrasure within the White Tower, and that he was simply waiting on a command from the Archduke to unleash hell on the crowd below.

However, he couldn't bring himself to give the order. Watching with a morbid fascination, he simply couldn't look away from the violence at hand, and he didn't want to bring it to a premature end, especially now that his daughter had unexpectedly entered the fray. As bizarre and twisted as his relationship with his only child was, he still felt a perverse and paternal pride every time Vanessa took a life, and she had not yet been given enough time to record a kill or two....or more. Additionally, he didn't want Vanessa to be in the line of fire when Lord Gundrham's marksmen let loose. Far too much time and effort had gone into making her the weapon that she was to simply throw that away with a quick and convenient fusillade. So he decided to wait just a little longer before issuing the ultimate order – an order that never came.

Hundreds of feet below, as she surveyed the tide of battle, Šarlatová quickly realised that, for at least the third time in as many weeks, *die Volks Knechte* were going to be slaughtered by Archduke von Stormsong's men. Already, Hester Neuss, Herman Jobst, and only God knew how many more, had fallen in the early stages of this awful civil war, and Šarlatová, never fully understanding what it was about war that could possibly be considered "civil," decided in that moment that the one-sided massacre of her people would end – today.

And so she began to sing, *"ο Κύριος είναι ο ποιμένας μου."* As she did, the warm dry air turned instantly cold and wet. As the sun instantly vanished between lashings of cold, driving rain, the wind howled like a rabid wolf in search of its prey, almost drowning out Šarlatová's voice. But as the sound of the wind intensified, so did her voice, at first just matching but ultimately superseding its noise. *"δεν θελω στερηθη ουδενος."*

As both the wind and the sound of Šarlatová's voice grew ever louder and battled against each other for supremacy, the violence all around her settled as the combatants on both sides paused to take in what was happening. The whipping wind, the icy cold blasts of rain which were quickly turning to sleet and then to hail, and the rolling thunder all served to both pacify and terrify the adversaries and non-combatants.

Far above, Archduke von Stormsong caught a glimpse of Šarlatová as her coif blew from her head and uncovered her wild, whipping mane of red tresses. In fact, as Šarlatová's singing intensified, it seemed to the archduke that her fiery hair had actually come alive, positively glowing like vermillion snakes as the strands whipped and whirled around her head. From his vantage point, he could not, however, see Šarlatová's eyes, both of which were totally drained of colour. In fact, unbeknownst to the archduke, what had been strikingly gorgeous green eyes mere seconds before were now both an opaque milky white.

While the archduke could not see Šarlatová's eyes, his daughter could. Vanessa came sprinting from inside the White Tower and pulled up within just a few hundred yards of Šarlatová. Impossibly, even though her eyes no longer had either a visible pupil or iris, Šarlatová could see perfectly well, and the instant that she saw Vanessa come careening toward her, she stopped singing.

There was something almost feral about Šarlatová now. Her face contorted into something savage, something inhuman. As she stared Vanessa down, Šarlatová bore the countenance of a wrathful goddess, sent to rain down judgement on the mortal world.

While multiple witnesses would later claim that several minutes had elapsed when the two voluptuous women locked eyes and froze, in reality it was only a second, or two at the most. Then, the brief but intense stalemate was shattered when Šarlatová started to screech. The high, shrill, piercing cry was unlike anything Vanessa had ever heard before, and it was as if Šarlatová's voice had physical depth and weight to it. The sounds she began to make contained as much power and force as the bizarre weather that had been conjured around both her and the crowd, and as that weather continued to intensify and darken, so did Šarlatová's voice. Her voice and the atmospheric pressure seemed to become one, and both reached a point where they had so much substance to them that everything else began to feel heavier and heavier under their combined weight; and finally, when the sound and pressure both became unbearably oppressive, everything....simply....shattered.

Being the individual furthest from where the scaffold had once stood, Vanessa was the first person to be able to regain her feet. What she saw defied all belief and description. The scaffold had been reduced to a smouldering pile of rubble. All of those who had been on or even near the scaffold – Hester Neuss, Herman Jobst, the orator, the executioner, Günther from Oldenburg, the other men scheduled to be executed, and all of the spectators nearest to where the scaffold once stood – were simply no longer there.

The foul weather had been reduced to a light, steady rain, but the flames that licked around the shattered area simply would not die. In fact, the flames burned a constant, eerie blue-white and appeared to neither increase nor diminish.

As a blue-grey haze drifted across the devastated site and settled like a fog around both the combatants and spectators, some of whom were just now beginning to regain their feet, several others continued to lay where they had fallen. Dead. Injured. Or simply too stunned and too frightened to move. As she surveyed this damage and began to look for the stunning redhead who had evidently caused all of this carnage, Vanessa saw the impossible. Torben's Tree, an ancient spruce which, like all spruce trees, did not flower, was not only undamaged, it was blossoming! Pink and purple flowers of all sizes and shapes were, in some inconceivable way, sprouting all over the tree. Blooms that belonged on flowering cherry, pear, crabapple, plum, and magnolia trees – some of which did not exist in any part of Germany – were everywhere.

Struggling to take all of this in, Vanessa produced her sword and continued her survey of the area. The dichotomy between the fresh, brilliant blossoms and the dead and broken bodies was something that she simply could not comprehend. She wondered what sort of force or power could be capable of simultaneously doing such damage *and* such beauty.

As others slowly began to recover their senses and footing, Vanessa gripped her sword tightly with both hands and swung the blade from side to side, pointing it at each and every person in the vicinity. She was uncertain if she would encounter the beautiful redhead again, but she intended to be prepared either way. As she slowly and cautiously worked her way around the devastation, her anticipation of another meeting began to mix with a strong sense of foreboding and trepidation, but in such a way that heightened her senses to levels she had ever experienced before.

Despite her heightened senses, Vanessa could not locate the mysterious redhead, or anyone else who seemed to pose a threat. It was as if she and her cohort of criminals had simply vanished into the blue-grey haze that continued to drift across the ruined site. However, while Vanessa could not see Šarlatová from her vantage point, the archduke could from his.

Stationed high above the battleground, Archduke von Stormsong continued to survey the damage. On a ridge several hundred yards south of the castle, for just a second or two, he caught sight of a slow moving giant. Next to him, appearing to lean on the massive man for support, was the tall, slim red-haired woman. As he briefly glimpsed the woman who had wreaked such damage upon his castle and his plan, the Archduke felt a mix of both anger and admiration, and pondered what the arrival of this remarkable woman meant for the future of the civil war in Bohemia. More importantly, he wondered what might she mean for the future of the entire Holy Roman Empire.

After having waited for a second or two, the archduke turned to depart from the platform, and as he did so, he smiled devilishly, remembering an apropos series of lines from a nearly twenty-year-old English play that had become one of his favourites.

"O serpent heart hid with a flowering face! Did ever dragon keep so fair a cave? Beautiful tyrant! Fiend angelical! Dove-feathered raven, wolvish-ravening lamb! Despised substance of divinest show! Just opposite to what thought justly seem'st, a damned saint, an honourable villain! O nature, what hadst thou to do in hell, when thou didst bower the spirit of a fiend in moral paradise of such sweet flesh? Was ever book containing such vile matter so fairly bound? O that deceit should dwell in such a gorgeous place!"

While the archduke considered those lines and departed the platform atop *der Weißer Turm*, his smile broadened....and he began to laugh.

Chapter Nineteen

Her head felt like it was made up of a thousand pieces of shattered glass, and her throat was so raw that she wasn't certain she'd ever be able to speak again – which was just as well. After the havoc she had unleashed outside of *Schloß Stormsong*, Šarlatová wasn't sure that she even wanted to speak again, much less sing.

During their escape, she and Roan had been separated from the rest of *die Volks Knechte*, most of whom were presumed to be dead or dispersed in every possible direction. That was just as well, too. After what she had wrought, most likely killing Herman along with an untold number of Stormsongs, innocent bystanders, and her own people, the last thing in the world she wanted was to face anyone who had seen her do it. She was most hesitant about facing Günther from Oldenburg. Assuming incorrectly that Günther was still alive, and further supposing that Herman had already died before everything exploded (which was far from a safe assumption), she might find herself in a position of having to explain to Günther how and why she had prevented him from avenging the life of his fallen friend. Knowing that Günther was renowned for his ribaldry and risqué sense of humour, Šarlatová began to wonder if he would ever be whole enough to tell a joke ever again.

"Have something to eat," Roan suggested, passing Šarlatová a hunk of slightly mouldy bread that he had been carrying around with him for several days. "I'll go lookin' for some meat later."

Šarlatová reluctantly accepted the bread, but she could not bring herself to partake of it, nor to say thank you to Roan. "How do you feel?" he asked her, not sure if he wanted to hear the answer. Šarlatová simply shook her head and grunted.

"That bad?" he asked.

Šarlatová didn't look up at Roan who stood over her as she sat back against the sturdy trunk of a fir tree. But she did manage to whisper, "Even my hair hurts."

"Well, least ways you got your voice back," he offered, realising immediately that that was precisely the wrong thing to say. Šarlatová looked up at him with a look that a frightened child might give to a parent after having been caught doing something wicked or cruel. And then she broke. The tears came hard and fast, and Roan knelt to embrace her as her body was wracked with heavy sobs. The weeping she was doing was coming from someplace inhuman. It was as if she was mewling like an animal, mourning for something that could never be undone.

"I killed him. I killed Herman," she sobbed. "I killed them all."

We don't know that yet, is what Roan wanted to say. But all of the evidence supported the conclusion that she had. So he just continued to hold her and stroke her hair, all the while whispering, "Shhhh. It'll be alright, *dívka*. It'll be alright."

"How can anything ever be alright, Roan? You saw what I did....what I'm capable of. You saw....what I am."

Roan had no words of comfort to offer her. He couldn't tell her that a part of him was now terrified of what she had become....or at least what she was capable of. Like a father who finally realises that his child is not what he thought she was, he felt a profound sadness and longing for simpler times.

Desperate to change the subject, Roan asked, "I've never told you about my wife, have I, *dívka*?" When Šarlatová didn't respond, Roan took that as his cue to continue. "She was quite something. Berta was unlike anything I've ever....well, she was as ugly as sin, but that woman could cook like no other."

Šarlatová sniffed a little and wiped her nose as she tried to stifle a laugh. "What's funny about that?" Roan asked. "Men are always so concerned with what a woman looks like. Makes no sense to me. Over the course of your life you'll be eatin' your woman's food a lot more than you'll be...." Šarlatová laughed a little and hugged Roan even more tightly than before.

"Never mind. Anyway, she was mine and I was hers. That's it and that's all of it. But she died of *die Weiße Pest* (the White Plague) before we could have any children. Nasty thing, that. We tried everythin'. Took her to see priests, nuns, even what few doctors we could find. Even tried the royal touch, but you can imagine how that went. Nothin' helped."

Well into the seventeenth century, European monarchs were believed to be religious deities with magical, curative abilities. It was commonly and mistakenly believed that, because they were thought to possess the divine right of sovereigns, the touch of a monarch could cure diseases. So prevalent was this belief that, in some parts of Europe, diseases like scrofula became known as *das Böse des Königs* or *le mal du roi* (the King's Evil).

"Why are you telling me this now, Roan?"

"Well, because it was shortly after she died that I found you.... or you found me. I'm still not sure which it was. And you've been my daughter ever since. Blood is just blood, *dívka*. In every other way....every way what really matters, you are and always have been my daughter."

"And?" prompted Šarlatová, not sure of where Roan was going with this.

"And you always will be my daughter, *dívka*. Nothin' that happened back at that awful place will ever change that. Get me? Nothin.' Just like Berta was my woman and I was her man, you are my daughter and I'm your father. That's it and that's all of it."

Knowing that this was the closest that Roan could come to saying what he really meant, Šarlatová made it easier for him. "I love you, too....*Vater*."

148

"You weren't there, Stephen. You didn't see what she was. What she was capable of."

Vanessa was visiting Stephen in the *das Gott Haus* again. She'd gone there straight after confronting her father about the horrific strategy he had planned to employ during the execution. Stephen was supposed to have been released from the Bridgettine nun's care – or Mother Superior Ludmilla's custody, as he referred to it – but he had recently developed a significant infection in his wound site and had become pale and feverish.

"I certainly heard what she was capable of. That sound – what was it? First the shrieking, then the explosion. I thought the entire castle was going to come down."

"So did I, Stephen. That's my point. I've never seen, heard, or felt anything like it. It was like she was possessed."

"She who? Who was it?"

Vanessa looked around conspiratorially to make sure that no one, most especially Mother Superior Ludmilla, was listening. "The redhead! It was her again! I saw it….*her*. Her hair was wild, and her eyes….I am simply at a loss to explain…."

"And you're certain that you're not becoming infatuated with her?"

"That's disgusting, Stephen. If you keep imagining things like that, you're going to need to go to confession."

"*Disgusting*, is she?" he asked with a sly grin.

"*It's* disgusting, Stephen. Not her. She's not disgusting. She's gorgeous, and sort of dark…. and dangerous."

"She certainly sounds dangerous, alright. But what is your fascination with her?"

"You mean besides the fact that I shot her in the leg with a crossbow bolt; that she somehow healed from that wound in no time at all; that she magically resurfaced at the precise time of the scheduled executions of her fellow outlaws; that she conjured a storm with just her voice, and that she then proceeded to decimate….no, annihilate dozens of people? You mean other than that?"

"Well….when you put it like that…."

A tense silence settled over the two, with neither one sure how to restart the conversation. When Stephen sensed that Vanessa was going to leave if he didn't say something more, he reached up and took one of her hands in his. Using the fingers on his other hand, he slowly traced circles in the palm of her hand, and as he did so, Vanessa felt a rush of heat shoot straight up from her hand and into her head and neck. So stunned was she by this unexpected physical response, that she didn't even hear his next question.

"So what is it then? It sounds to me like you feel some sort of personal connection to this…. wild woman….this red witch. Is that it?" When she stared back at him, flushed and dumb- founded, he released her hand and repeated his question.

Vanessa paused and considered her next words very carefully. "Not a personal connection, no. That goes too far."

"What is it then?"

"I don't know. I just feel….no, I *know*….that I have seen her somewhere before. I felt that after the encounter by the Danube, and I feel it even more so now."

"Forget the girl for a second, Vanessa. What did you say to your father?" Stephen asked.

"About what?"

"About what he was planning to do. That's pretty Machiavellean, even for your father."

"Machiavellian? You really are becoming quite the scholar, aren't you, Stephen?"

"Don't side step the question, Vanessa. What did you say?"

Vanessa paused and sat down next to Stephen on his bed. "It was awful."

"What he was planning to do, or what you said to him?"

"Both, actually. I think I may have said something to the effect that he's so focused on being a powerful Catholic that he's inca- pable of being a good Christian anymore. And then I may have said something to the effect of *Praise God you weren't keeping the inn in*

Bethlehem, because Mary and Joseph would still be wandering in the desert. Or something to that effect."

"Wow! You actually said that? To your father? What else?"

"I don't know. I was angry and I think I said something like *You probably think Jesus wasn't saved until He had His first communion....at the last Supper.* It was awful, Stephen. Just awful! Then again, so was what he was planning. I've always known certain things about my father, but I didn't think he was capable of....that."

Stephen was enthralled. "What did he say in return?"

"He said that it is far better to be feared than loved. Apparently he's been reading *der Prinz*, too."

Der Prinz (The Prince) was a political manifesto written sometime around 1513 by Italian diplomat and pioneering political philosopher Niccolò Machiavelli. It was informed by the behaviour of a number of the "new monarchs" of the fifteenth century – power hungry tyrants like Louis XI of France; Isabella I and Ferdinand II of Spain; Henry VII of England; and, most directly of all, Cesare Borgia of Italy. It was designed to serve as a sort of instruction manual for future European rulers. One of the first works of modern political philosophy, its general theme was that the ends of a Prince's behaviour (power, glory, survival, etc.) justified whatever means he needed to pursue in order to achieve those ends. It was a personal favourite of Archduke von Stormsong's and he used it as a sort of "how to manual," not only for wielding and maintaining power, but also for managing his personal relationships.

"I don't know, Vanessa. Your father is a brilliant and powerful man, and there is much to admire about him. But he absolutely terrifies me. I know the red-haired woman you saw is capable of great and terrible things, but when I think of what your father is capable of...." Despite the fact that Stephen trailed off, Vanessa knew precisely what he meant. In fact, she then proceeded to talk at great length, revealing to Stephen a great deal about her own fears and reservations about her father – things she had never shared with another soul, not even Father Joseph. She had been pouring her heart out to Stephen about the complexity of that relationship for several tortuous minutes before she realised that he had fallen back into a deep sleep.

"Sleep well, Stephen," she sighed. She then kissed him on the forehead and proceeded to leave *das Gott Haus*, knowing full well that Stephen's warning about her father would stay with her awhile, and she knew that there would be no sleep for her tonight.

"So what's the story with the girl with the blue cloak and the big tits?" Roan asked Šarlatová just before she nodded off to sleep.

"What?" she groaned sluggishly. "What girl?"

"The one what shot you at the river. She was there again when…. when it all happened."

"And what of it?" Šarlatová asked groggily, doing her best to signal to her friend that she simply wanted to go to sleep.

"You were lookin' right at her, *dívka*, when everything….well, you were lookin' right at her. And that's when your voice changed."

"What of it, Roan?"

"Nothin,' I suppose. It just seemed to me like you knew her from somewhere before, that's all. Forget it, *dívka*. Get some rest."

But as Roan finally settled down to sleep, his observation stayed with Šarlatová, and she was wide awake now. There would be no sleep for her tonight.

Chapter Twenty

"The secret to pacifying the Catholics lies within their churches." said Count von Thurn. "Until we understand that and start to act accordingly we're going to continue to lose this war."

Heinrich Matthias, *Graf von Thurn und Valsassina*, was a Bohemian noble and one of the recognized leaders of the Protestant revolt against the Emperor. As he addressed an assembly of *Volks Knechte* leaders and leaders within his own Bohemian National Army at a secret church within the village of *Velkà Lhota* (an area some one-hundred-seventy miles east of Prague that was populated by fewer than three-hundred people), he began to outline a new strategy in the young war.

"I don't know if I would even call it a war. So far, it's been a one-sided rout." Count von Thurn was not yet aware of what Šarlatová had done at *Schloß Stormsong*, but it would have made no difference. To his thinking, regardless of what had or had not happened recently, the Bohemian Protestant rebels were not yet fighting their war to win it.

Count von Thurn was a wealthy, educated, and well-respected nobleman who held land both inside and outside of Bohemia. Educated in Italy, he fancied himself a diplomat and a man of considerable political acumen and power. However, he lacked patience, diplomacy, and any sense of tact. Despite that, or perhaps because of it, he had tremendous appeal to the poorer classes within the empire, and his experience as a professional soldier – combined with the fact that he was almost completely devoid of scruples when it came to decision making – made him a natural leader of men.

"What are you suggesting?" asked Dobroslav Demantius, one of the count's lieutenants.

"That we fight this war the same way the Dutch did against the Spanish Catholics, and the same way that the Huegenots fought against the House of Guise. We launch a *Beeldenstorm*!"

Beeldenstorm (or Bildensturm, in German) was a Dutch term for outbreaks of destruction of religious icons and images that had occurred in Europe throughout the sixteenth century. This "iconoclastic fury" – which had been launched by repressed Protestants in the Spanish Netherlands and in France, places where Catholic majorities still held sway – had resulted in the destruction of untold amounts of Catholic art, ecclesiastical furniture and fittings, and church decorations. Most of the destruction had been the result of non-sanctioned actions committed by angry mobs and crowds, and – like the St. Bartholomew's Day massacre, which all of this had been designed as a retaliation against – it was all performed inside churches and other places revered by Catholics.

According to the Catholic Church, numerous outbreaks of unprovoked iconoclasm had taken place throughout Switzerland, France, the Low Countries (Belgium, the Netherlands, and Luxembourg), and the Holy Roman Empire. Protestants, however, continued to argue that these attacks had all been motivated by what had been done *by* Catholics *to* Huguenots (French Protestants) at the St. Bartholomew's Day Massacre in France in 1572.

Regardless of which version was correct, Huguenots and Dutch Calvinists had been storming Catholic churches and other religious buildings to desecrate and destroy church art and images for more than fifty years. And while official records were scant and sketchy at best, anecdotal evidence suggests that rebelling Protestants had even gone so far as to defecate in confessional boxes and fornicate on top of altars within Catholic churches like the *Onze-Lieve-Vrouwe- Kathedraal* (Cathedral of Our Lady) in Antwerp.

"It is worth noting, my lord," said Jarmil Jassinius, one of Count von Thurn's most trusted strategists and political advisors, "That the strategy you're recommending resulted in the War of the Three Henrys in France and the establishment of the Blood Court in the Spanish controlled Netherlands. In both cases, these attacks helped to further fuel the unrest, rather than pacifying the Catholics."

"It is also worth notin', *my lords*, that the Dutch ultimately won their independence from the Spanish Catholics and that the French Protestants won substantial rights, includin' religious toleration, with the issuance of the Edict of Nantes." This came from Gustav Adelbern, who had little ability (and even less patience) when it came to diplomacy and political strategy.

"And at what cost?" asked Jarmil Jassinius, turning to face Adelbern. "Two million dead so far? Some say it's as many as three million already, and could be as many as four million before it's all over. And neither war is remotely close to being over. Now that religious civil war has broken out here, too, how many will die? Five million more? Ten million more?"

"Then what do you suggest we do, Lord Jassinius?" asked Count von Thurn. "All present know that your word is unimpeachable. And your counsel is trusted by all present. But surely you are not suggesting that we simply roll over and play dead while this insidious Hapsburg control over our lands and people grows?"

"Not at all, my Lord. I'm simply trying to raise the issue of escalation. What is now a regional, religious conflict could quite quickly and rather easily evolve into a continental power struggle involving Spain, England, France, Sweden, Denmark....and God only knows who else. A war like that, on a scale like that, would be unlike anything any of us have ever seen before."

"That's why wars are fought by men, not by women!" was Gustav Adelbern's massively oversimplified response. "And the day I'm afraid to fight a French whore or a Spanish bastard is the day I eat my own ass and shit out sunshine!"

Jarmil Jassinius leaned in towards Gustav and asked, "If you've already eaten your own ass, how could you shit sunshine, my friend?"

An awkward silence ensued until Gustav broke it by saying, *"Ach,* fuck it all to hell. It made sense when I was thinkin' it over."

The raucous laughter that followed Gustav's embarrassing admission was welcomed by all present – none more so than Count von Thurn, who was tasked with piecing together a unified army out of piecemeal Bohemian military units and bands of disorganised outlaws, and then using them to engage one of the largest armies in all of Europe. If he couldn't find some way to get these vast and disparate groups to coalesce into something resembling an organised fighting force, then the Hapsburgs would have little trouble routing them and hanging them all like a group of common criminals.

"Freunde," he began, his voice gaining a stentorian resonance that communicated authority. "I realise that what I'm asking of you is frightening to some, distasteful to others, and foreign to us all, for it is not in our nature to make war. But let me remind you that we did not seek, nor did we provoke this war. What I….no, what we accomplished at *Hradčany* was not the first blow. On the contrary, first blood was drawn more than two-hundred years ago when Jan Hus was burned at the stake!"

Invoking the name of Jan Hus earned the Count a chorus of nods and sounds of approval, for Hus, a Bohemian theologian and Protestant reformer who was burned at the stake in 1415 for alleged heresies against the doctrines of the Catholic Church, remained a seminal figure in the hearts and minds of many Bohemian and German Protestants. In fact, because Hus could be heard singing psalms as he was burned alive, he had attained a legendary, almost supernatural, status among his followers (the Hussites), and the current civil war in Bohemia was really just an extension of the Hussite Wars fought between Protestants and Catholics in the Holy Roman Empire during the fifteenth century.

Sensing correctly that the use of Jan Hus' legendary status had gained for him additional attention and reverence, von Thurn decided to go one step further and quote the martyr directly. *"And I would not for a chapel of gold retreat from the truth!* And the truth is, lads, that, God willing, someday you will return to your homes, and your farms, and your families. Someday the suffering we've experienced and the destruction we've witnessed will be the things of songs and legends. But that day is not yet. For now, I pray you stand with me as my brothers- and sisters-in-arms, and remember that governments and churches do not make wars – men do. And men like Pope Paul, Emperor Matthias, and Archduke von fucking Stormsong have waged unanswered war on us for far too long!"

The sounds of approval began to grow, and many of the assembled men (and women) began to strike the handles of their axes and pikes against the wood floor of the church. Others stamped their feet.

"What say you then?" barked the count. "Will you stand with me? Will you now take the fight to our oppressors?"

Each subsequent question was answered by a louder positive response than the one before, and as he whipped the assembly into a fevered pitch, the count decided that now was the appropriate time to pitch his strategy. "Then will you do what is necessary?"

"Auf jeden fall!"

"Will you fight this war to win it?"

"Auf jeden fall!"

"Then let us apprise this Pope, this Emperor, and this *Archduke* that, on this day, the battle …. has finally….been joined!"

In passing years, none of the assembled would be able to re-member for sure, but in that precise moment every man and woman present was certain that the deafening response they offered could be heard all the way to *Schloß Stormsong* – and as the men and women at his command whooped, hollered and stamped their feet, the count, who like the archduke was a great admirer of Shakespeare, bellowed a line from *The Tragedy of Julius Caesar*: "Then let us cry havoc, and let slip the dogs of war!"

Part Two:

The Storm Builds

Chapter Twenty One

The woman was unlike anything Šarlatová had ever seen before, and she was fairly certain that it wasn't just the significantly degraded vision in her left eye that caused her to think so. Even without both eyes working together at full capacity, Šarlatová could clearly see that the woman's skin was much darker than even her own. In fact, whereas Šarlatová's skin was copper brown, like an autumn leaf, this woman's skin was burnt umber – and was so rich and warm in colour, that Šarlatová thought for a moment that maybe she had been carved from the earth itself. Her smouldering doe-brown eyes, dark and puffy lips, and broad, refined nose gave her face a majestic quality, and her velvet-black hair spiralled down her shapely back in rope-like strands that Šarlatová had never seen before. All of that, combined with her statuesque figure, led Šarlatová to believe that, despite her shabby clothing, this stately-looking woman must have been a noble of some kind or another – perhaps an exotic, foreign princess who had been forced for some reason to travel in disguise. In fact, she judged her to be every bit as breathtaking as the raven-haired bitch with the blue cloak and the white crossbow – just in a very different, and much more exotic way.

Šarlatová's initial assessment could not have been more wrong. She knew of the existence of slavery, of course, and unlike most Europeans of the time was repulsed by the concept. While she knew that the Bible justified the keeping of slaves and that the practice was sanctioned by the Catholic Church, she could never quite square the teachings of Jesus Christ with the keeping of human beings as property. Nevertheless, regardless of her opinions on the subject, Šarlatová had never, at least to the best of her knowledge, encountered an actual slave – European, African, Hispaniolan, or otherwise. At least not until now.

The men with the remarkable woman could never be described as stately, foreign, or exotic, however. Ignoble, base, and ugly would best describe the vulgar trio that was "escorting" the dark beauty through *der Kunratice Wald*, one of the many forests in and around Prague – the same forest, in fact, in which Roan and Šarlatová had been residing during the early Summer days following the "incident" at *Schloß Stormsong*. Once again clad in their signature green cloaks and cowls, they were virtually impossible to see in the thick Bohemian foliage. However, the dark beauty seemed to have no trouble spotting them. As the three ruffians dragged her along a rugged but passable trail via a thick rope leash around her neck and wrists, she looked into the woods and locked eyes with both Šarlatová and Roan. As they each put a finger to their lips and mouthed *Shhhhhh*, she responded with a blank expression that gave no indication of whether or not she had understood their message.

"Where does he find these apes?" one of the brutes asked the others.

"*He* who?" asked the one holding the woman's leash.

What do you mean *He who?* Who else do you think I'm talking about? That mad priest….what's his name? Father Michael?"

"Monsignor Mučitel," corrected the third man.

"Right, that's what I said, Mučitel. Where does he find these animals?"

"He doesn't," the third man corrected again. "The archduke finds 'em. He has people in Portugal who shop for 'em. They go to Africa, pick 'em out like they're buying a pair of shoes, and bring 'em back here. The Archduke uses them for all kinds of things."

"And he told you all this himself, did he? Was this when the two of you was having tea together?" joked the second man.

"Shut up! Just because I knows a thing or two about the way things work and you don't, don't go being an *Arschloch*."

"Okay, Herr Petrarch! Or is it Dante....or Francis fuckin' Bacon himself we've been talkin' to? Since you know so Goddamn much, what do you suppose the blessed archduke was usin' this one for?"

The third man looked at the dark beauty, who had still not said a word nor revealed either Roan's or Šarlatová's presence to the men, and he examined her as a butcher might inspect a slab of meat. "I suppose it was most likely kitchen duty for this one," he surmised.

"Kitchen duty!" laughed the second man. "All the way from Africa to scrub dishes, is she? *Blödsinn*! If she's not been warmin' the archduke's bed, then I'm Charlemagne himself."

While the three men were crude, misogynistic, and uneducated, their assessment wasn't too far from the truth. Since the mid-fifteenth century, when the slave trade had been blessed by none other than Pope Sixtus IV himself, Lagos, Portugal, had boasted a slave market for the purchase of imported African slaves. The *Mercado de Escravos*, as it was known, had been stocked with Mauritanian and other West African slaves ever since Prince Henry the Navigator, a major sponsor of Portuguese slave voyages, first started launching expeditions into Sub-Saharan Africa. During the fifteenth and early-sixteenth centuries, slave owning was initially extremely rare in Europe. Only the wealthiest families could afford them, so owning any was a significant symbol of social status and prestige. But like all things – palaces, orange trees, slaves – nothing was beyond the reach of Archduke von Stormsong's wealth.

"What do you think?" Roan quietly asked Šarlatová from the cover of the forest. "Doesn't look like money to me, but they're bound to have some food, which we haven't for two days now."

Šarlatová said nothing. She couldn't take her eyes off of the striking black woman, and she hadn't heard a word Roan had said.

Interpreting her silence as tacit approval to proceed, he slipped quietly from the trees (or as quietly as his massive frame would allow, anyway) and began to follow the four travellers. It wasn't long before Šarlatová followed after him, and even less time elapsed before Roan alerted the travellers to the fact that they were being followed.

"Guten morgen!" bellowed Roan, terrifying all three men, the dark woman, as well as most of the wildlife within five-hundred miles. *"Ach du lieber! Entschuldigen Sie, bitte!* I didn't mean to startle you," he lied.

Roan's massive size completely shielded Šarlatová from the view of the three men, but it mattered little. Whether they were being accosted by two people or by just one extremely large one, they were unnerved by being approached at all on the road to their destination.

"What do you want, you fat bastard?" asked the first man in a fabricated display of bravado. As he asked, the other two circled around their prisoner and produced a pair of small daggers.

"Fat? You think me fat? And after I haven't eaten in two or three days? How could I be fat when it's starvin' that I am? In fact, I was thinkin' how nice it might be to break bread with you three fine….*gentlemen*. What say you?"

The man in front responded by saying, "I say piss off and move along, *du fetter Wischer*!"

Repeating his performance from several weeks earlier, Roan said, "Such language, *Jungen*. And in front of such a fine lady, no less."

"She ain't no fine lady," responded the man holding the dark woman's leash. "She's a slave. A fugitive slave no less. She run away from *Schloß Stormsong*, and we're taking her back."

The man in front turned around and snapped at the leash holder. "Shut up, Christoph. You talk too fuckin' much. It ain't none of their business what we're doin' with this black bitch."

Roan decided to finish replaying the scene that he and Šarlatová had acted out with Countess von Sternberg just a few weeks ago. "I wasn't speakin' of *that* lady, boys. I was speakin' of *that* one!" With that, he stepped aside, revealing Šarlatová who already had her bow out, with not one but two arrows nocked and aimed. Without adding a single word to the performance, and keeping her impaired left eye shut tight, Šarlatová fired both arrows at once, placing one in each of the men's left thighs.

As the two men dropped to the ground, howling in pain, the front man stood frozen in fear, his face affixed in a way that belied his earlier false bravado. "Please don't kill me," was all he could muster.

Roan closed the distance between the two of them with but one stride. "Believe me, *du schlanke Wischer*, if I wanted to kill you, you'd already be feedin' the worms." With that, he whipped his massive head forwards, smashing it like a weapon into the shorter man's face. With a sickening crunch and a thick spray of blood, the smaller man's head snapped back and he dropped to the ground, bloodied and unconscious. "Well now. That's done. So let's see what's for breakfast, shall we?" Roan asked.

After Šarlatová, Roan, and the mysterious dark woman had pillaged the bags and belongings of the three wounded men, they made a hasty retreat about six miles further south from where they had encountered the group. Then, upon building a small cooking fire, they proceed to dine on all that they had taken from the slave catchers.

As Roan and Šarlatová devoured the meal that they had "recovered" from the satchels of the three wounded men, Roan kept glancing back and forth between his two female companions.

"So, how are we going to communicate with this one?" Roan asked.

"I don't know," Šarlatová admitted around a mouthful of boiled eggs. "I've already tried French, German, Italian, Spanish, and English. She hasn't seemed to understand any of them."

The beautiful black woman nibbled politely at the bread and cheese that Roan had given her and attempted to follow the conversation by focusing her eye contact on whoever was speaking at the time.

"Where did you learn all of that gibberish anyway?" Roan asked. "You're the only person I know what can speak all them different languages."

"I don't know, I guess I just picked it up somewhere," Šarlatová said dismissively, not really paying much attention to Roan's question.

"Just picked it up?" Roan repeated in amazement. "You've been speaking all of them ever since I first met you, when you was just a girl. From the time you was about twelve or thirteen years old you was spoutin' all kinds of things I could never understand. Quotin' from books I'd never heard of, usin' words that nobody understands and...." At this point, Roan began to suspect that Šarlatová, still transfixed by the beautiful stranger, was not listening to a word he said. So he decided to test her. "And that's right about the same time that I grew a nice pair of big tits....nice bright orange ones.... three of 'em, actually....all right there on me back....and instead of producin' milk, they shot beer right out of the nipples...."

To each one of Roan's increasingly preposterous statements, Šarlatová simply offered a short "Mmmhmm."

After rolling his eyes in exasperation, Roan offered a small piece of salted pork to the black woman who, still saying nothing, looked at it, sniffed it, and politely refused it, smiling at Roan nonetheless.

"How about that, *divka*? Never met neither man nor woman what wouldn't eat a nice piece of salted pork....except for that one time I met that woman what had two heads, wings, and a dragon's tail...."

Still no indication from Šarlatová that she was listening.

"....and would you please at least pretend to pay attention when I'm talking to you?" he shouted.

Šarlatová and the dark woman, both startled by Roan's unexpected outburst, jumped. Then, upon realising they'd both reacted the same way, began smiling and laughing at each other. Roan, however, was not laughing and was growing increasingly perturbed. He simply said, "Women….you'll be the death of me yet!" Then he proceeded to polish off the rest of the pork….and the bread….and the cheese.

"So what do you suggest we do with her?" Roan asked, once his mouth was at least partially free of food. "You're not plannin' on takin' her with us, are you?"

"That's precisely what I'm planning on doing," Šarlatová admitted.

"Christ, *dívka*! We don't know a thing about this woman. We can't talk to her. We don't know where she's goin'….we don't even know her name."

"We know precisely where she's going. She's going to the same place we are. Back to *Schloß Stormsong*."

"Schloß Stormsong? And what in the hell for? Everyone within two-hundred miles of that place is lookin' for us, and they all want us dead!"

"Which is precisely why no one would think to look there. Besides, we have to go there. That's the only place we're going to find any answers about how the archduke is always one step ahead of us. If we do have a Judas amongst us, and I'm now inclined to agree with you that we do, then that's where we'll learn who it is."

Roan swallowed the remainder of what was in his mouth and paused just a moment before asking, "And just how in the Hell do you think you're going to get in. It's a fuckin' stronghold, not a *Kneipe* (tavern). Are you thinkin' you can just walk up to the front gate, say *Wie geht's?* Then flash 'em your tits and ass and they're just goin' to let you in?"

"That's exactly what I intend to do, Roan. And you're going to help me. Both of you are," she finished while smiling at the beautiful slave girl.

"How's she goin' to help?" Roan asked, as the black girl smiled back at Šarlatová.

"She's going to be the key that unlocks the front door."

Chapter Twenty Two

"What do you mean, you don't know where she is? It's quite simple! Is she....*or is she not*....still here?" Stephen demanded of Sister MaryHelen. Among the Bridgettines, Sister MaryHelen was widely considered to be the kindest nun in the convent. Not meek, but very gentle, so it took a lot for Sir Stephen, gentleman that he was, to bark at her this way. But the fact that Vanessa had seemingly disappeared in the course of the night was enough to move him past any semblance of chivalry or good manners.

"I can only tell you what I know, Sir Stephen. She appears to have left the castle, but no one seems to know where she went." To display that she didn't appreciate being barked at, Sister MaryHelen removed the dressing from Stephen's neck with considerable more effort than was necessary, causing him to wince in pain.

"Damn it, sister, leave that alone! And find someone who has some fucking answers!" Just as Stephen was prepared to curse at Sister MaryHelen again, he saw Mother Superior Ludmilla making a beeline in his direction, and from the look on her face, she was none too happy to have one of her nuns scolded quite so vehemently – at least not by anyone other than her.

But before she could reach Stephen, Father Joseph intercepted her, calmly spoke some soothing words about grace and mercy, and sent her back in the direction from which she had just thundered. Exhaling in a way that one might upon being shot at and missed, he shook his head, relaxed his grip on his Latin Vulgate Bible, moved in Stephen's direction, and motioned for Sister MaryHelen to move along.

"What seems to be troubling you, Sir Knight?" he asked upon sitting at Stephen's bedside. "Is your infection bothering you again?"

"Father Joseph, you know that I respect all men of the cloth. And even if you were not a priest, I would still respect you for the love and care you have provided to Vanessa over these many years. *But as God is my judge*, if someone doesn't start giving me some answers, I'll...."

"You'll what, Sir Stephen?" the priest asked. "You have barely recovered enough to be able to sit up; you still lack the strength to stand, and you haven't the first clue as to where our lovely Raven has flown. So what, pray tell, do you intend to do?"

Father Joseph had always had a way of calmly cutting to the heart of the matter. It was one of the things Vanessa had always loved best about him. In this particular case, his candour and soothing voice were enough to settle Stephen back down – which was a good thing considering that his fever had only recently broken, and that he was still far from good health.

Once he saw that Stephen had calmed down, at least a little, Father Joseph handed him the Bible he was carrying. "I brought something for you."

"With all due respect, father, even if I hadn't been reading the Good Book for nearly twenty hours a day the past few weeks, I still would not need your generous gift. I do have a Bible of my own, you know. And, like you, I have committed vast portions of it to memory."

"Good lad," he said, patting Stephen on the knee. Coming from anyone else, Stephen would have felt that this comment and this action were condescending, at best. But coming from Father Joseph, both were taken as they were intended – as a proud and fatherly recognition of a son's accomplishments. "But you don't have one like this," he added while passing the Bible into Stephen's hands. "I think you will find that this one is quite full of....*revelations*." With that, Father Joseph traced the sign of the cross on Stephen's forehead, offered him a quick blessing, and then just walked away.

Waiting a few moments until the priest had gone, and checking to make sure that no one was paying any attention to him, Stephen slowly opened the Bible and turned immediately towards the back of the book. There, tucked in between two pages of the book of Revelation, was a small, hastily written note that read:

Dearest Stephen,

I'm terribly sorry that I didn't have time to say goodbye before I left. Even if I had had the time, I could not have risked being seen speaking with you – not with what I intend to undertake. The truth of the matter is that my father has sent me on another mission. This time, I am meant to find and kill a man by the name of Gustav Adelbern. I know not what his crimes may be, nor do I care. My days of being anyone's executioner are over! However, under the guise of that assignment, I am leaving Schloß Stormsong for a time. I simply must find that strange woman who did such damage here. I don't know if it is the risk that she poses to the Empire that compels me to find her, or the fact that I am virtually certain she and I have met before. In any case, I simply cannot rest until I've rediscovered her. Rest well while I am gone, but please make no effort to follow or find me. If, and when, I do return, I will share with you all that I have learned. But for now, God has very different paths set out for the two of us, and I pray that He guides and protects us both as we go our separate ways.

Your friend forever,

Vanessa

"If, and when, I do return? Very different paths for us? As we go our separate ways? Your friend forever?" Stephen muttered aloud, continuing to repeat to himself the most troubling lines from Vanessa's note. Crestfallen, he shook his head, crumbled the note into a ball and held it against his chest, hoping and waiting for sleep to reclaim him once more.

As a heartbroken and angry knight lay deep within the halls of *Schloß Stormsong,* hoping to find sleep as a way of avoiding his sorrow and frustration, a Moravian giant lay deep within the surrounding forests, giving up entirely on the prospects of finding either rest or sleep. His own anger and frustrations were far too great to allow for any sleep to come.

His anger, of course, stemmed from what had recently happened at *Schloß Stormsong,* and at what had been happening for the weeks and months before that. The pain he and his wife had experienced when they were unable to have children struck him very deeply, and the loss he felt when Berta died made him feel like he had actually lost some physical part of himself, leaving him confident that he would not feel completely full ever again. But the events of the past few weeks and months seemed to have permanently impaired his ability to feel any additional loss. The shock of witnessing so many deaths of so many friends and brothers-in-arms had left him numb, which he viewed as a gift. Whereas most people were disoriented by loss and acted as if they no longer had a place in the world, Roan was now able to simply carry on as if nothing had happened. He no longer felt the pain associated with such loss. Instead, he felt only anger. He was angry at his friends for dying prematurely, angry at those who had caused their deaths, and angry at himself for not having prevented their deaths from happening. But, above all, he was most angry with God.

Because of Šarlatová, he knew well what the Bible taught. Ephesians, chapter four, verses thirty-one and thirty-two said: *"Let all bitterness, and wrath, and anger, and clamour, and evil speaking, be put away from you, with all malice. And be ye kind one to another, tenderhearted, forgiving one another, even as God for Christ's sake hath forgiven you.*" But Roan always thought that those verses were hypocritical. After all, did not God himself exercise wrath and anger when he sent a flood to destroy the entire population of the world? And wouldn't he do so again during the "End Days?" And wasn't the evil in the world God's fault in the first place, for didn't he allow unprecedented and wholesale famine, plague, and war to go on, right under His very nose? Roan knew the counterargument, of course – that it was man's free will that had brought evil and brokenness into the world. *But the shoddy state of the world is an awful heavy albatross to hang on Adam and Eve's necks just for eating one fuckin' apple,* he always thought.

And if man truly does have free will, then so be it, he thought. *I shall exercise my own free will by killing every murderer, rapist, and traitor I can get my hands on.* Each time Roan took a life and sent one more soul to Hell, he felt more and more anger and less and less of anything else. Eventually, he figured, he would feel nothing at all. Nothing but anger. And then there would be no stopping him.

As he continued to recline against a birch tree, which was only slightly thicker than his own massive torso, and as he pondered the relief it would bring him when he was finally dead and reunited somewhere with Berta, he took in the rolling peaks of the mountains around him and noticed the different shades of green embedded within the surrounding forest. As he watched the overhead clouds float by, casting shadows from the moon and making some parts of the forest darker than others, his thoughts, like the clouds above, slowly drifted and wandered, eventually landing on the fate of the two young women sleeping nearby.

While Roan's anger centred around his many fallen comrades, his frustrations lay with only one person – his adopted daughter. Roan had long known that Šarlatová had no amorous interests when it came to men. And, for just as long, he had suspected that she....

preferred the company of women. But until this morning' events, he hadn't had any actual confirmation of that suspicion. Now, having seen the way Šarlatová had stared at the beautiful runaway slave all day, he knew that she was feeling....well, something. The fact that his adopted daughter might be *eine Tribade* didn't bother Roan in the least. Experience had taught him that the quality of one's life depended almost entirely upon the love one shared with others – regardless of what form that love took. And while the Christian church taught that homosexuality was a sickness and a sin, Roan knew all too well that the clergy was full to brimming with all sorts of sexually deviant and promiscuous men and women – the very same men and women who had taken vows of chastity. And experience had taught him that this was fairly typical of clergy members – preaching one thing to the flock and practising another behind closed (or cloistered) doors.

Even if the clergy wasn't crowded with hypocrites, something Roan had a very hard time imagining, he would still be incapable of judging Šarlatová for her so-called "sins." While he was by no means an educated man – in fact, he could hardly read – Roan was as familiar with certain passages of the Bible as any other man. Almost from the time he met her, Šarlatová had been regaling him with stories from the "good book," and one of his favourite passages came from chapter three of the Gospel according to John. As he recalled, verse fifteen of that chapter read "whosoever believeth in Him should not perish, but have eternal life." *Whosoever* – meaning that God's promises were intended for *all people* who believed that Jesus Christ was the Son of God And while he hadn't read it first hand, Roan was fairly certain that nothing in John's gospel qualified the term whosoever. In other words, all people meant *all people.* Period!

Nor was his concern that Zahara – at least that what he assumed her name was, for she had repeatedly pointed at herself while smiling and saying something that sounded like *"Jina langu ni Zahara"* – was, apparently, *eine Muslimin.* Like most Christians, Roan knew

173

next to nothing about Muslims, or their faith, or their culture, but the very few he had encountered in his life had seemingly all been oppressed by Christians, not oppressors *of* Christians. And all he knew so far about this particular Muslim was that she was beautiful beyond description, seemed harmless enough, and always faced East and knelt in obeisance when praying to whatever god it was that Muslims prayed to.

No – his primary concern was that Šarlatová's obvious attraction to this striking woman was clearly already clouding her judgement. He couldn't really blame Šarlatová. The flicker in Zahara's eyes when she smiled could, by itself, render anyone helpless, clouding their judgement quite easily. But Roan was so preoccupied with protecting Šarlatová and keeping her alive long enough to reconnect with the rest of *die Volks Knechte* that he had forced himself to remain immune to the woman's charms. Besides, regardless of how charming and striking she was, the sudden appearance of this beautiful woman was quite troubling to Roan. While he highly doubted that she was another one of Archduke von Stormsong's elaborate traps, he couldn't be entirely certain. Additionally, he was extremely concerned that Šarlatová's ill conceived plan – which was to try to convince Zahara to return to *Schloß Stormsong*, have her pose as a fugitive slave that he and Šarlatová had captured, and, in so doing, gain access to the castle – was desperate, dangerous, and highly unlikely to provide any actual information regarding the Archduke's strategies or tactics.

But what scared him most was the possibility of losing the one person who mattered most to him – mattered to him at all, really. As he ran his dirty hands through his equally dirty hair, he sighed. What would become of him if something were to happen to Šarlatová? Would losing her reopen those old wounds? Would the walls he had so dutifully and painstakingly constructed around his heart come crashing down? Or would losing her light a fire of anger in him even brighter and more intense than anything he had experienced before?

He feared that he might soon find out.

Chapter Twenty Three

"What do you mean, you don't know where she is?" Stephen continued to shout again and again. But it was as if no one could hear him. Sister MaryHelen, Mother Superior Ludmilla, Father Joseph....even the archduke himself were all present, all huddled together in *das Gott Haus*. But they either couldn't hear Stephen, or they were simply ignoring him.

Yelling even louder, he rose from his bed and no longer felt delirious with fever. The wound in his neck now completely healed, he felt stronger than ever. *So why can't anyone hear me?* he wondered in frustration.

Wandering around *das Gott Haus*, which seemed both smaller and darker than usual, Stephen tried to engage several of the nuns in conversation, but to no avail. Growing increasingly frustrated and anxious, he decided to look for Vanessa himself. *What was it she had said in her note?* he asked himself. *I think it was something about leaving....or not coming back....But what was it? And why can't I remember?*

Stephen roamed around the halls of the das Gott Haus, eventually leaving the great hall when he was certain that he had heard Vanessa's sweet voice. *Is she screaming? No - she's calling my name, isn't she?* Growing more and more confused and less and less patient, Stephen began to scream her name – or at least he tried to. Now, he could not even hear his own voice. He continued to try to speak, but nothing happened. *Has the wound inflicted upon me by the giant at the river cost me my voice?* he asked himself. *No – that's not possible. My wound is healed. I can't even feel it anymore. I can't feel anything. But I can hear. I hear Vanessa! She's here – somewhere. But where?*

As he roamed the familiar halls of *Schloß Stormsong*, he became lost time and time again. *How is that even possible?* he asked himself over and over. *I know every inch of this fortress. But it's like I've never been here before. Everything is smaller, darker, and different. Why?*

Yet again he heard Vanessa's voice. But this time he was quite certain that she wasn't calling his name. No – she was definitely screaming, crying out in pain. Without a moment's hesitation, Stephen reached for his blade, but it was as missing as his voice. The only thing strapped to his belt was a book – a Bible. But not just any Bible – it was the one Father Joseph had given him.

Rushing to open it, desperately hoping to find some additional clue that would guide him to Vanessa, Stephen opened once again to the book of Revelation. This time there was no note. There was only verse four of chapter twenty-one: *"And God shall wipe away all tears from their eyes; and there shall be no more death, neither sorrow nor crying, neither shall there be any more pain."*

What does that mean? he asked himself. *If there's no sorrow, no crying, and no death, why is Vanessa weeping the way she is? Or is she? Perhaps she isn't crying. Perhaps she's....* Stephen closed his eyes to listen more intently. *Yes – she's not crying. Nor is she screaming. In fact, she's....she's singing!*

Stephen had never heard Vanessa sing before, but he was certain that it was her voice that he now heard, angelically singing *"Et abstergt Deus omnem lacrimam ab oculis...."*

Her voice was louder now, clearer. He was certain that he was getting closer to her. *Or is she getting closer to me?* he wondered. It didn't matter. Her voice was louder, and crystal clear as she continued to sing *"Eorum et mors ultra non erit neque luctus...."*

She was terribly close now. Perhaps in the next room.

"Neque clamor...."

Is it just my imagination, or is it getting colder, and darker? Stephen wondered. But he quickly dismissed those concerns; nothing else mattered to him now – not when Vanessa was so close. Stephen could actually hear her voice as if she was standing next to him.

"Neque dolor...:"

He then opened a door he had never seen before, and entered a strange room within *Schloß Stormsong* that he had never even seen before. *But how is that possible?* he wondered. And as he entered the foreign chamber, he saw Vanessa. She was completely nude, spreadeagled and tied securely to a wooden table, bathed in the glow of her own perspiration. He'd never seen her like that before – and she was lovely, more lovely than any work of art he'd ever seen. The shape of her breasts, the curve of her thighs, and her long, strong limbs seemed wonderful to Stephen. But what most captivated his attention, what seemed to him most perfect was the valley at the end of her throat. That simple, insignificant hollow was something he could never forget. Something clean and pure, the memory of which he could draw upon in the future. If he could but press his lips against the perfect, white skin of her slim, supple throat just one time, then he would consider his entire life well-spent.

But as he ached to feel the touch of her warm skin on his, something suddenly seemed imperfect. *No! Not just imperfect, he thought. Something is horribly wrong! She has scars! She's been hurt! She has fresh wounds, too! She's still being hurt! Who did it to her before? And who is still hurting her now?*

As Vanessa turned to face Stephen, apparently feeling no sense of shame or modesty about her total exposure, she flashed him a smile – but one that was somehow laced with sadness and regret. And as she finished singing, *"Erit ultra quae prima abierunt,"* the dark priest standing over her turned to Stephen and flashed an altogether different kind of smile.

Then, with Stephen's limbs somehow frozen in a way that rendered him incapable of doing anything about it, Monsignor Mučitel produced a slim blade and abruptly silenced Vanessa's singing….by slicing her slender throat wide open.

At roughly the same time that Stephen awoke, screaming and sweating, from his nightmare, Roan was finally just slipping into a fitful slumber of his own. But the shadows and figures that occupied his dreams were not part of a nightmare like Stephen's. Rather, they were images of the past, as he reminisced, half-awake and half-asleep, about the moment when he had first met Šarlatová.

Despite the fact that sound did not travel very far or very well through the dense foliage of *der Pfälzerwald* (the Palatinate Forest) which overlay the border between France and the Holy Roman Empire, Roan had heard the shrieking and shouting quite well. The shrieking sounds seemed to be coming from a young girl, while the shouting was definitely coming from a group of fully grown adult males.

As Roan had topped a small rise in his quest for a red deer he had earlier shot at and missed, he had noticed a crowd of men gathered around a clump of trees. Squirrelled away, high up in the branches of one of the tallest trees, was a young girl who couldn't have been more than twelve-years-old. The men yelling at her from below had begun to hurl small rocks at her, and one had even begun to climb up into the tree after her.

What had impressed Roan the most about the young girl was her poise. Not only had she looked quite comfortable in her precarious position within the dead and dying branches of her tree of choice, but she hadn't looked at all scared. In fact, she had seemed to be having fun at the expense of the men who couldn't quite reach her with either their stones or their taunts. She had been eating from a bag of apples, occasionally spitting seeds down upon her would-be-assailants and grinning from ear to ear when her seeds struck with greater accuracy than either the men's rocks or insults.

"Come down here, you little bitch, or we're going to show you what's what!" one of the men had yelled – to which the girl had simply stuck out her tongue and spat another seed.

"And what have we here?" Roan had asked. "Have we captured some sort of demon? Or is it the Devil himself what requires four grown men to chase it up a tree?" Roan had then taken another quick glimpse up into the trees where he had seen the red-haired girl continuing to devour the bag of apples. "No – not the Devil. Looks to me like you've managed to tree a small girl. Well done, *Jungen*."

"Move along, stranger. This doesn't concern you," one of the four men had warned. Roan had seen that his sheer size had already unsettled the group, for three of the men had already placed their hands on the pommels of their swords.

"Didn't say it concerned me," Roan had responded. "In fact, I isn't concerned at all. And it looks like she ain't too concerned neither. Kinda makin' *Trottels* out of you boys, I'd say." The girl had responded to Roan's observation with a smile and a nod – and another bite of apple.

"Who are you calling a *Trottel*?" the man who had been trying to climb the tree had asked.

"Christ!" Roan had answered. "You really are a Trottel if you don't know when you're being called one."

The four men hadn't known what to do with Roan. It was clear that they had wanted him to move along and go about his business, but it was equally clear that they hadn't had any idea how to compel a man so large to move.

The girl up above, meanwhile, had watched the interaction with great interest, and had continued to attempt to polish off the entire bag of apples while she followed the dialogue. Finally, she had been unable to hold her tongue any longer. "*Vati*, can we go home now?" she had asked Roan who had wrinkled his brow with a look of curiosity.

"*Vati*? You this little cunt's father?" one of the men had asked in astonishment.

179

Playing along, Roan had answered, "*Ja!* I am. Can't you see the resemblance?" He had stroked his red beard and had ruffled his red hair as the girl up in the tree had run her own hand through her long, lustrous red locks. Roan and the girl had made eye contact then and had shared a conspiratorial grin – and that had been the moment when he knew….

But at this point, Roan fell into an even deeper slumber. No longer loitering in the pleasant twilight between wakefulness and sleep, he succumbed completely to his exhaustion and was no longer in control of his thoughts nor in command of the dream.

The little girl was still in the tree, but she seemed even younger than before – perhaps only eight or nine now. And the four men were no longer simply common ruffians chasing an apple-stealing girl up a tree. Rather, they were fully armed and armoured Stormsong men. No longer were they hurling small rocks at the girl – now they were firing arrows. And one after another hit the intended target. The little redhead had shafts sticking out of both arms and both legs, and while the wounds bled considerably, she still just kept smiling and laughing, as if she didn't have a care in the world. In fact, while he couldn't be certain, Roan thought she might actually be singing to the men below.

Just as he drew his sword and prepared to have at the men, Roan noticed that his feet were completely mired in a thick, almost clay-like mud, and try as he might, he couldn't get free. In fact, the more he struggled, the more he sank, until he was almost up to his knees in the muck. As he glanced up at the girl, he noticed that she was shaking her head in disapproval, and just as she gave a defeated shrug of her shoulders, one final arrow pierced her left eye, knocking her over and causing her to crash to the ground with a sickening thud.

While the girl still refused to cry, Roan could see that both of her legs had been shattered by the fall and now protruded hideously from her body at gruesome, impossible angles. But neither the arrows that had penetrated nearly every part of her, nor her grossly twisted legs prevented the four men from attempting to take turns with her.

As Roan continued to struggle to free himself from the mud that seemed to thicken by the second, he hurled a variety of curses and warnings at the four Stormsong men, but they simply ignored him and proceeded to partially disrobe in preparation for what was to come next. But what came next was far more shocking than the prospect of seeing four grown men rape a wounded and crippled eight-year-old girl. The girl just....smiled, and then she began to sing.

She started by singing *"καὶ ἐν τῷ συμπληροῦσθαι τὴν ἡμέραν τῆς πεντηκοστῆς ἦσαν πάντες ὁμοῦ ἐπὶ τὸ αὐτό,"* and while Roan had no idea what she meant nor even what language she was using, the Stormsong men seemed to know, for they each took one or two steps back away from the mangled little girl.

Then, the girl's voice built in both volume and intensity, and she sang *"καὶ ἐγένετο ἄφνω ἐκ τοῦ οὐρανοῦ ἦχος ὥσπερ φερομένης πνοῆς βιαίας καὶ ἐπλήρωσεν ὅλον τὸν οἶκον οὗ ἦσαν καθήμενοι,"* causing a loud and violent wind to suddenly burst from the heavens and blow through the forest, nearly lifting the men off their feet.

Finally, as the girl sang *"καὶ ἐγένετο ἄφνω ἐκ τοῦ οὐρανοῦ ἦχος ὥσπερ φερομένης πνοῆς βιαίας καὶ ἐπλήρωσεν ὅλον τὸν οἶκον οὗ ἦσαν καθήμενοι,"* it appeared to Roan that eerie tongues of fire had come to rest on each of the men's heads. But far from being enlightened or gifted in some way by the strange flames, the men began to writhe and contort beneath them. Slowly and torturously they were consumed by the fire, and as their bodies withered away, the little girl just kept singing, each of the men's sickening screams seeming to give new breath and new life to her song.

Ultimately, the light and heat of the flames, fed by the violent wind that had not yet abated, were too much for Roan, and he was forced to raise his arm to shield his face. Then, just as quickly as it had begun, the wind was gone.

The song was over.

The flames were extinguished.

And all that remained of the men were charred husks where they had once stood, and circling between them, as if inspecting her work, stood a fully grown, completely unharmed Šarlatová. She stood for a moment over each man, and when she turned Roan's way, she flashed him a ghoulish smile. But more disturbing to him than her sinister expression was the fact that she....she simply had no eyes. Where her eyes had been only moments ago were now just pools of milky white. And as she approached him, Roan could feel himself being drawn into those pools – deeper and deeper until not even his screams....

....his screams should have woken both Šarlatová and Zahara, as well as anyone else within five miles of their encampment. But when Roan caught his breath and brushed away the strands of his hair that had become pasted to his massive forehead by his own sweat, he glanced around. It took him only seconds to determine that both Šarlatová and Zahara were gone.

Chapter Twenty Four

"What was I thinking?" Vanessa asked herself as she rode her favourite stallion, Starke, through a series of trails in the northern-most region of *der Kunratice Wald*. She'd been riding, seemingly in circles, for several days now and had been asking herself that same question almost the entire time.

When she had first set out from *Schloß Stormsong* almost a week ago, her plan had seemed so easy. Instead of hunting down her father's latest victim in the escalating Bohemian civil war, she would deliberately disobey him; ride out, instead, to find the strange red-haired woman who had done....whatever it is she had done at the execution of the captured heretics; confront the woman; and, assuming she survived that encounter, find out the truth about her.

Days ago, that plan seemed so obvious and simple. It was only after she had been riding aimlessly throughout *der Kunratice Wald*, for what already seemed like a month, that she came to the realisation that her plan was ludicrous. First, how was she going to find the woman? Saint Thomas More had once used the phrase *"looking for a needle in a meadow,"* but finding one person within the entirety of the Holy Roman Empire was going to be more like looking for one needle....buried within a pile of other needles.... hidden in the world's largest meadow. Vanessa now estimated that her odds of just randomly finding this woman, without knowing her name or anything about her other than her hair colour and her....abilities....were about as good as being struck by lightning. Twice. On the same day.

Vanessa had never been impetuous. In fact, virtually every decision she had ever made in her life had always been carefully calculated, meticulously planned, and faithfully executed. Yet, here she was, wandering hopelessly through the woods like *Hansel und Gretel*, the characters in Martin Montanus' *Gartengesellschaft*. She had left *Schloß Stormsong* with practically no supplies, even less of an idea where she was going, and no clue what she would say or do when, or if, she ever found this remarkable but hauntingly familiar woman.

Seeming to sense Vanessa's frustration with her spontaneous and ill-conceived plan, and seeming to agree with her that the plan had, in fact, been hasty and foolish, *Starke* fluttered his nostrils in both directions and snorted loudly.

"No one asked you," Vanessa said, scolding her trusted mount. "I already know it was a stupid plan. You don't need to tell me that." To this, *Starke* added an even louder snort.

"Fine….it wasn't a stupid plan; it was no plan at all. But that still leaves open the question of where we go from here." Again, as if conversing directly with Vanessa, *Starke* snorted and shook his head in the direction of a brook running through a small glade just ahead.

Taking her trusted friend's cue, she guided him in the direction of the brook. "Okay. But not for long. We still have miles and miles of aimless wandering to do yet today." *Starke* snorted again.

As Vanessa dismounted and prepared to feed and water the equine know-it-all, she stroked his mane and scratched behind his ears, which, as always, produced an exquisite sound of contentment. It had always seemed to Vanessa that, when scratched just right, *Starke* would actually purr, almost like a kitten – and, as he did so now, Vanessa smiled at him, taking delight in both the sight and the sound of the magnificent animal.

The sleek, black Friesian stallion was seventeen hands tall and had a wild, six-foot-long mane. He had been given to her as a gift from her father at the age of four, and she supposed that her father had thought that *Starke* could fill the void left in her life by the absence of her mother, who had died trying to birth her baby brother. And while the trauma that these losses had caused in her life could not be overcome by any gift, not even one as magnificent as *Starke*, Vanessa couldn't imagine having been able to survive all of that loss without the horse. Father Joseph, Stephen, Mother Superior Ludmilla, and *Starke* had formed a sort of barrier. A quaternity intent on trying to shield her from the darker things in life – like her father.

At twenty-five, *Starke* was one year older than Vanessa. And despite the fact that he had received the finest care and nutrition throughout his life, he should have, like most horses, already entered the senior stage of his life. Like most horses his age, he should have begun to slow down years ago, performing with less speed and vigour, and losing much of his grace and agility. But for some inexplicable reason, that was not the case with *Starke*. In fact, as if he remained intent on continuing to live up to his name (which meant strength) he seemed to become stronger, faster, and more nimble with each passing year. And there was no doubting the horse's intelligence. In fact, Vanessa was quite certain that Starke was at least twice as smart as half of the population of Europe. *After all*, she thought to herself, *Horses never went around throwing other horses out of windows, or casting spells on each other, or, worst of all, inflicting terrible punishments on their children.*

It was this intelligence that she was relying upon now. "What are we going to do, *Starke*?" she asked as she fed him an apple from one of her saddle bags. "We're almost out of food; we're just wandering around *der Kunratice Wald* in circles; I don't really know what I'm looking for, and I wouldn't know what to do even if by some miracle I did find what I was looking for."

At first, Vanessa misread *Starke's* expression as he finished off a second apple. "Are you laughing at me?" she asked. But as she did, she saw a nervous flicker in his eyes that could only mean one thing. They were not alone.

Rabbi Avrem ben Mordecai's feet hurt. His back hurt. And his bald head, which lacked cover from a yarmulke or any other protection from the sun, was tinged pink with sunburn. Unlike Vanessa, he had only been travelling for a few hours. But, also unlike Vanessa, he had not been riding a horse, and he had been forced to walk more than twelve miles north through *der Kunratice Wald* before he had finally found a boatman willing to ferry him (a Jew with very little money in his pockets) across the *Vltava*.

Having already crossed the river and having started his journey back south towards his destination, he had decided to take some comfort from the crystal clear waters of a brook that ran off of the *Vltava* and through a glade in *der Kunratice Wald*.

While he had been listening to the entertaining "conversation" between the young woman and her horse, the rabbi had not been watching them. Therefore, he had no way of knowing that Vanessa, alerted to his presence by *Starke*, had spun and produced a shockingly white crossbow, which was aimed directly at his head.

"Don't move!" she ordered slowly, keeping her weapon trained on the rabbi.

"I have no intention of moving, young lady. Especially not now that I have found some water. But I can assure you that I am no threat to either you or your companion."

"Which is precisely what someone who is a threat would say," Vanessa noted. The rabbi, a short, bald man who appeared to be around fifty years old nodded. His round, almost pudgy, face was accompanied by a slightly humorous expression, with the result being that he couldn't possibly look less threatening. But none of that mattered to a trained warrior like Vanessa.

"True enough," conceded the rabbi. "Let us try this, shall we? I'll go back to washing my hands and face. You can go back to talking to your horse. And we'll both do our best not to irritate or kill each other. Fair?"

"I suppose," said Vanessa, not lowering her crossbow one inch.

"After all, young lady, *'That which is hateful to you, do not do to your fellow man'* is the maxim by which we are to live, isn't it?" asked the rabbi.

"Close. But the precise language of Matthew's Gospel is *'Therefore all things whatsoever ye would that men should do to you, do ye even so to them: for this is the law and....'"* but before Vanessa could finish, the rabbi interrupted her.

"Yes, it is, young lady. But I was not quoting from the New Testament. Instead, I was referring to the Torah. Actually, to be even more precise, I was referring to *Hillel der Ältere* (Hillel the Elder), the Babyloninan scholar and teacher of the Torah.

"Then....you're....a Jew!" Vanessa observed matter of factly.

"I had better be. If not, the mohel who performed my circumcision owes me quite an explanation." Rabbi ben Mordecai laughed at his own joke, but it was clear from Vanessa's expression that she either didn't understand the joke or that she just didn't find it funny.

"Please....I mean to do you no harm, and if you'd like to come over here, I'd be happy to share what little food I have with you, and your friend." As evidence of his offer, the rabbi produced a handful of raisins.

Vanessa had lowered her crossbow all the way by now, but she still stood in place. She wasn't sure what to make of this man, or of this encounter. As she stood there, silently taking a measure of the situation, *Starke*, having seen the handful of raisins, snorted loudly and trotted over to the kneeling rabbi.

"*Starke! Nein!* Just leave him...." But it was too late. *Starke* had already gone over to Avrem and nuzzled him, lapping up the entire handful of raisins with one giant swish of his thick, pink tongue

Laughing again, and stroking the stallion's magnificent mane, the rabbi said, "See there. We're friends already."

"Hmmm. We'll see," was as cordial of a response as Vanessa was willing to offer for now. Experience had taught her not to trust strangers, especially when the stranger in question was bearing gifts. And while she did lower her weapon, she wasn't about to lower her guard.

Damn it! Roan thought to himself. *I let my guard down for all of five minutes, and the girl fuckin' disappears on me.* Roan knew better than to shout Šarlatová's name; shouting would only draw attention, and that was the last thing we wanted to do right now. But he also knew that he needed to find her – and quickly, before she and the foreigner headed off to *Schloß Stormsong* without him. If the girl was intent on executing some harebrained plan, he wanted to at least make sure that both he and *Schwert* went with her.

As he drew *Schwert* from its scabbard and began to move quietly in expanding circles in an attempt to find Šarlatová, a thought occurred to him. *What if she and Zahara had not left him to start their journey towards Schloß Stormsong? What if, instead, Zahara had done something to Šarlatová?* Experience had taught Roan to never trust strangers, and the sudden appearance of this particular, and exotically beautiful, stranger had sounded alarm bells within his head even before Šarlatová's disappearance.

Throughout all of his travels and battles, Roan had never killed a woman, but the thought of killing one now didn't give him even a moment's hesitation. If the runaway slave had harmed Šarlatová in any way, he wouldn't have any misgivings about ripping her arms off and beating her to death with them.

Sweating profusely and growing increasingly frustrated, Roan decided to do something entirely out of character. He stopped, and he listened. He'd seen Šarlatová do this a number of times while on hunting trips. She had a savant like ability to close her eyes and close her mind off to everything around her except sound. Then, relying on nothing but her hearing, she would let loose an arrow shot that always found its mark. In his attempt to hunt for her, Roan thought he might as well give it a try.

It took less than a minute before his breathing slowed and his mind stopped racing, and less than a minute after that, he heard it. A woman's voice. She was close by, and she was crying. Not wanting to waste another second in trying to determine if it was Šarlatová or Zahara, Roan opened his eyes and charged full speed in the direction of the sound.

He hadn't travelled more than a few hundred yards when the ground disappeared beneath him. He had come across a significant slope that had been shielded by some foliage, and instead of continuing to run on a horizontal plane, he was sliding, tumbling head over ass down the long, steep, and muddy slope. His trip finally ended when he crashed to the bottom of the hill and somersaulted quite ungracefully into a large….and deep….and unusually cold pool of water.

This, of course, prompted an outburst of hysterical laughter from Šarlatová and Zahara – the same laughter that had earlier sounded to him like crying. The angrier he got, and the more he thrashed around trying to regain his footing, the funnier it became to the two girls, both of whom were quite muddy and soaking wet themselves. It took only a few seconds for Roan to deduce that the girls had both fallen down the same hill and met the same wet result in the same pond, probably less than five minutes ago – and it was their laughter that had both awoken and alarmed him.

Finding absolutely no humour in the situation, Roan finally managed to get to his feet and tromp leadenly toward the edge of the pond. The look on his face was enough to quiet both girls, at least momentarily. But when he reached into his tunic and extracted an oversized and wriggling eel, they started all over again.

Angrily tossing the eel back into the pond, Roan glared at both of them menacingly. But undeterred by Roan's attempt to intimidate them, Šarlatová quickly added, "You look madder than a wet hen, Roan."

"*Ja*....do I now?" he asked sarcastically. But before he could say anything more, Zahara stifled her own laughter long enough to add, "You know, we could have eaten that eel. I think you should go back in and get it for us."

Mouth agape, Roan stared at the soaking wet, and apparently bilingual, slavegirl. By way of response, she flashed him that same disarming smile she had displayed earlier. Šarlatová finally stopped laughing long enough to say, "Zahara speaks perfectly beautiful German, by the way."

"Oh, does she now? And ain't that just the devil's piss?" he snapped at Šarlatová who was pressing water out of her long, red hair. "And how long have you known that?"

"I don't know. A couple of hours. You were snoring so loudly that she came to me, woke me up, and told me that she was certain that a wild boar was loose somewhere in the woods."

Roan turned towards Zahara for confirmation and she simply shrugged her shoulders. "Actually, I didn't say boar. I said bush pig, you might call it a warthog, because in my country, only bush pigs make sounds like....well, what you were making while sleeping." She smiled again.

Inwardly growing to dislike that damned charming smile, Roan asked, "And is it in *your country* that you learned to speak German? Fluently, no less?"

"Of course not," Zahara said demurely. "I have been a slave in *this country* for many years now, so I thought it would be wise to learn the language."

"Then why did you pretend not to when we first met?" the angry, wet Moravian demanded.

Šarlatová interjected on Zahara's behalf. "I already asked her that same question. She said that, since she had no idea who we were, or what our intentions were, or what we might do with....or to her...."

"I decided to use caution instead of courage," Zahara added. And there was that damned smile again. At this point Roan was convinced that she knew precisely what kind of an effect that smile had on people, and the fact that she continued to use it just angered him even more.

"And exactly how many words in the German language do you know?" Roan asked.

"All of them, I think."

"Verdammt noch mal!" Roan shouted.

"Including those three," Zahara added.

"And once 'the bush pig' woke you up, what led the two of you down here?"

"We were looking for water," Šarlatová laughed. "And it looks like we, and you, found it."

Roan just stood at the edge of the pond, still knee-deep in the water, trying to process everything that had just transpired. As he did so, Šarlatová began to take sympathy on him. "It's perfectly okay to laugh, Roan. If you think about it, the whole situation is really quite funny."

"Quite funny? *Ja?* I suppose 'tis. Alright, come here and help me out….the both of you."

Šarlatová and Zahara both got up, stepped down to the edge of the pond, and offered a hand to help Roan out. Seizing both of their wrists in the massive ham hocks he had for hands, he gave one enormous jerk that sent both of the women flying headfirst back into the water. As they came back up, spitting out cold water and cursing his name, Roan stepped out of the pond, beaming with childish pride. "Now I'm laughing. *That* was quite funny! Now help me find me fuckin' sword!"

Chapter Twenty Five

⸺◦⸺

"So, what *are* you doing here?" Vanessa asked the Jewish stranger.

"Now that is an interesting and difficult question, young lady. Do you mean, what am I doing in Prague? Or do you mean, what am I doing by this particular brook? Or do you mean, what am I, a man of the cloth, alone and unarmed, without a mount, doing in such hostile territory?"

Vanessa pondered the rabbi's questions while she chewed on a handful of almonds she had gotten from him. "Let's start with the last one."

Before introducing himself, the rabbi finished eating a crust of bread and brushed the crumbs off of his hands. "My name is Rabbi Avrem Meshulam ben Mordecai…" he started but then stopped when he saw Vanessa laughing to herself.

"I'm sorry; why is that funny?"

"Rabbi Avrem Meshulam ben Mordecai? It's just that it seems like it was very important to your parents that you knew that you were Jewish."

The rabbi smiled. "Yes, in naming me, my parents threw the entire Torah at me," he admitted with a chuckle. After Vanessa responded with a polite smile and a perfunctory nod of her head, he continued. "I am from *Židovské město*. It's a small Jewish quarter of Prague, on the eastern side of the Vltava. If you know of it at all, you perhaps know of it as *Josefov*."

"I know of it."

"Excellent. Well, approximately three centuries ago, the Bohemian King Přemysl Otakar II issued *Statuta Judaeorum....*"

"Statutes of the Jews," Vanessa added before the rabbi could translate for her.

"Yes, quite right! Well done again. Well, those statutes granted Jewish communities, like *Židovské město*, a limited degree of self-administration. But in the late-fourteenth century, a pogrom – do you know what a pogrom is?"

"Yes. Unfortunately, I do."

"Yes. Well, unfortunately, I do, as well. All Jews do. In the late-fourteenth century, during the reign of Emperor Sigismund of Luxembourg, a pogrom led by Christians, executed on Easter Sunday no less, resulted in the massacre of hundreds, if not thousands, of Prague's Jews, with most of the rest of them being concentrated within a walled ghetto in *Židovské město*. But a century or so later, we were granted rights to a relatively open atmosphere of economic and religious activity by the nobility in Prague."

"Until...."

"*Until*....we were expelled by the Hapsburgs in 1542....and again in 1561. But we returned each time, and in spite of everything, the ghetto became prosperous....extremely prosperous, especially towards the end of the last century. In fact, you could say that life under Emperors Maximillian II and Rudolf II was a sort of golden age for Jews in Prague."

"But...."

"*But*, in spite of our prosperity, or perhaps because of it, our current emperor has apparently instituted and sanctioned a new pogrom against us. So, I am going to travel to Vienna to speak with him and to petition him to....well, soften his heart and change his mind."

Shaking her head in disbelief, Vanessa asked, "And you really think that the emperor will see you? And that upon seeing you that he will....I'm sorry....did you really say, 'soften his heart?' Is that what you're expecting will happen?"

"That's precisely what I am *praying* will happen," the rabbi responded. "And, for that matter, what I honestly expect *will* happen."

"Why?" asked Vanessa, dumbfounded.

Producing and biting into an overripe peach, the rabbi continued. "Well – first of all, there is precedent. In the year 1520, when Charles V was our emperor, Rabbi Josel von Rosheim came to him to plead for his people and their inheritance, and he did better than that. In fact, he obtained comprehensive privileges for *all* of Germany's Jews. But, in the same year, charters were issued authorising the expulsion of Jews from *Rosheim* and *die Vogtei of Kaysersberg*, both in the westernmost reaches of the Empire. With the help of God, Rabbi von Rosheim interceded with Charles V again....and succeeded, again – this time having the expulsions from Rosheim and die Vogtei of Kaysersberg rescinded altogether. For one hundred years since, by dint of our supreme efforts, we have succeeded time after time, often with great difficulty, in obtaining concessions from emperor after emperor. So, I am now travelling to Vienna to beseech our current Emperor for similar concessions. But, since it is just across the *Vltava*, I intend to stop first at *Schloß Stormsong* to speak with the Archduke. It is widely known that he has the ear of our Emperor, and I intend to bring our plight to his attention first."

"And what makes you think that my....that *he*....the Archduke will concern himself with....?"

"With the plight of a bunch of Jews? Why not? We do worship the same God, after all. A God who has worked many miracles for us before. Perhaps you're familiar with the parting of the Red Sea? It is, after all, written about in the Bible." Vaneesa laughed out loud, which caused the rabbi to smile and ask, "What's so funny?"

"Nothing. I'm sorry. It's just that....you're a Jew, and here you are counting on the *Catholic* Emperor and the *Catholic* Archduke to....what? Be good Christians by helping out their Jewish brothers and sisters? Really? That's your plan?"

"No, of course not," the rabbi responded guardedly. "One can never count on anyone, least of all self-professed Christians to be good anythings."

"Now wait just a minute. I'm a Christian. A Catholic to be precise, and I take great offence to that. You seem to be making a judgement about all Christians."

"Fair enough, young lady. But let's put it this way. When we met just a few minutes ago, my first instinct was to offer you food and water. Yours was to assume that I had hostile intentions and to threaten me with a deadly weapon. I'm quite certain that you're more fluent with Luke's Gospel than am I, but which of us has, thus far, behaved more like a good Samaritan? You....the Catholic? Or me....the Jew?"

This caused Vanessa to laugh again.

"And why are you laughing now?" he asked.

"Because in the past few weeks, I've been reprimanded by a priest, a nun, a rabbi, and a horse. There just has to be a joke in there somewhere." This caused the rabbi to laugh out loud and to offer the last few bites of the peach to Vanessa. She reluctantly accepted and took a bite.

After a few awkward seconds of silence, she spoke up again. "Wait a minute. Earlier, you said 'first of all – there is precedent.' That implies there is a *second of all*. What is it? What's the second thing you're counting on?"

The rabbi wiped some residual peach juice from his chin before looking directly in Vanessa's eyes and exhaling loudly through his nostrils. "The same thing we Jews have always counted on, young lady. Faith."

Two days after Vanessa had vanished from *Schloß Stormsong*, the event which had triggered Stephen's horrifying dream, Mother Superior Ludmilla had finally released him from *das Gott Haus*.

More precisely, she had thrown him out, barking, "Du mußt be-schäftigt sein, du träge Faulpelz!"

Physically, Stephen was fine. He had fully recovered from both his wound and the lingering post-wound infection. Spiritually, how-ever, he was devastated. He was heartbroken by Vanessa's absence and by her parting note which had relegated him to the status of "friend" – far from the role he wanted to play in her life. Additionally, while he was recovering, he had lost his position as Captain of the Guard. Because the archduke had determined that he was physically unable to discharge his duties and had added that he was, *"As soft as an old banana"* for allowing himself to be bested so easily in the first place, he had been replaced by Ernst Gundrham's bastard son Rowland, whose greatest accomplishment in life thus far had been outliving his half-brothers – Gundrham's three legitimate sons. Unlike his father, Rowland had none of the qualities necessary to be a good leader. Rather than possessing his father's bravery and abil-ity, he was ambitious, cruel, and intoxicated with his own inflated sense of self-worth.

In this sense, Stephen felt very much like Pedro Luis Borgia, the famed fifteenth century Captain General of the Papal Forces who, upon being suddenly stricken with a serious illness which rendered him incapable of fulfilling his duties, was replaced unhesitatingly by Pope Callixtus III with Rodrigo Borgia, the pope's favourite nephew.

He was still a knight, of course, but the other identities he had so carefully carved out for himself had all been stripped away. He had long fancied himself the most gifted swordsman in the whole empire – other than Vanessa, of course – and that had been taken away in an instant by, of all things, a giant bite from a giant of a man. Additionally, for as long as he could remember, he had en-visioned he would become Vanessa's betrothed – maybe not now, and maybe not tomorrow, but eventually….and forever. And with one brief note, that had been stripped away from him as well. And now, the cruellest cut of all. While recovering from wounds he had received in the service of his master, his master had relieved him of his title and his ability to perform that service. In fact, even his cape, a gorgeous cerulean blue that bore a gold cruciform sword outlined in red, which was the *Stormsong Familienwappen* (family coat of arms), and that indicated the current holder of the title of captain, had been taken from him in his sleep.

Consequently, when he was released from the care of the nuns in *das Gott Haus*, he had no idea where to go, nor what to do. Unfortunately, as he wandered the castle aimlessly, like a stray dog searching for food, he ran into his new Captain, the vainglorious Rowland Gundrham. Everything about him screamed petulant, spoiled brat. Even the way he waited at the bottom of a staircase, standing at a jaunty angle, one leg slightly raised, as if posing for a portrait, screamed pretentious-little-son-of-a-bitch.

Just seeing his ferret-like face made Stephen's stomach churn; and the way he approached, sashaying so that the signature blue cape would flap outward while he walked, just served to further Stephen's anger and nausea.

"Ah, Sir Stephen, I was just coming to see you. But I see you have finally broken free from the clutches of the Mother Superior and her legions of nuns." The comment was a veiled insult, and it struck Stephen hard.

Choking back what he really wanted to say, he responded with "Yes, my lord. They provided me with excellent care while I recovered."

"I can see that," responded Rowland, reaching out with his gloved hand to touch the spot on Stephen's neck where he had been wounded. "And it's a good thing, too. Nasty wound you received, wasn't it? What was it again? An arrow strike? A blow from a battle axe?"

"No, my lord. It was a bite."

"Yes....yes, of course. Now I remember hearing something about that. At first, I thought you had been bitten by the archduke's daughter while you two were making love with your faces. But then I recalled that she has no amorous interest in you, so I knew it had to be something else entirely."

Trying not to rise to – or, more appropriately, sink to – the level of the new Captain's taunts, Stephen tersely said, "Yes, my lord. It was quite severe. Not the bite itself, but the ensuing infection afterwards was…."

"Quite. One never knows what these Bohemians might do with their mouths. It's a miracle you weren't infected with rabies, or worse. I couldn't afford to have one of *my*….perfectly *adequate* knights running around with rage like a mad dog."

One of my knights? Stephen thought. *And* perfectly adequate? *Please God, I pray you give me five minutes on the field of battle with this bastard so that I can show him what raging like a mad dog is really like.*

Interpreting Stephen's silence as licence to continue, Rowland added, "I myself have never been laid low by….a bite. But it does me good to see you up and around again after only a few weeks of recovery."

"Perhaps if my lord had ever taken part in a skirmish, or even just seen one up close, rather than from behind a parapet, he'd be more familiar with what can happen on a field of battle." Stephen regretted the verbal slap as soon as he had said it, but he couldn't bring himself to take it back.

"You had best watch yourself, you little mongrel. Just because you naively harbour some illusion of one day occupying the archduke's daughter's bed and filling her cunt with your…."

"You watch yourself, too, *my son!*" The warning, which was heavy with unspoken meaning, had come from Lord Gundrham himself. He had been watching the encounter from a distance and had only decided to intervene when his idiot son had made reference to the archduke's daughter a second time. Fearing that Stephen might lose control and chop his bastard son in half with one swing of his sword, and knowing that Stephen could easily do it, he stepped in to both protect and reprimand Rowland.

"Father," Rowland hissed. "I didn't know you were there."

"I would hope not. Because if you had known and had still behaved like a petulant little cur, then I would have to wonder if you were even dumber than my earlier estimates."

Stephen did his best to stifle a smile, but enough emerged that Rowland's face grew hot with anger. "Go along now, *son*," Lord

Gundrham commanded. "Sir Stephen and I have much to discuss, and we're almost certain to be using words that you don't fully understand."

If God had blessed Rowland Gundrham with even an ounce of common sense, the pompous bastard would have retreated quietly and quickly. Alas, God chose not to, and so the slighted child held his ground, which only deepened and prolonged his humiliation in front of Stephen.

"Go along where, my Lord?" he asked.

"To *das Gott Haus*, of course," replied his father. "Now that Sir Stephen has recovered from his injury, the nuns will have sufficient time to tend to your....medical procedure."

Both Rowland and Stephen looked befuddled by this latest comment, but only Rowland was dense enough to ask the question. "And what medical procedure would that be, *father*?"

"The one where the nuns extract your head from your ass! Now go! The *adults* need to talk." Lord Gundrham's voice became increasingly gravely as his anger grew.

"As you command, father," hissed Rowland. But he just couldn't let things go at that. Before departing, he took one last, irritated look at Stephen and spat out, "We *will* finish this later, *Sir* knight!"

"Go!" repeated his father. "Else I'll have to turn you over my knee and...." But before he could finish, his son executed an extravagant turn, making certain that his distinctive blue cape swirled ostentatiously around him, and had departed in a huff.

Allowing him some time to get out of earshot, Lord Gundrham sighed and turned his attention to Stephen. "Listen, lad. I know that you long for the archduke's daughter, but we both know that that's never going to happen." Stephen hung his head as Rowland's father continued. "Chin up, lad. There are plenty of suitable wives out there who aren't named Vanessa von Stormsong. And when you find one, I pray you'll do me one favour."

"Yes, my Lord," Stephen answered, his expression still sullen.

"Look at me, Stephen. When you find the right one, I pray you do not pick a stupid one. And if you do, don't impregnate her without first marrying her."

"And why is that, my Lord?" Stephen asked.

Swinging his head in the direction of his departed son, Lord Gundrham said "Because look what happens when you do."

With that, both men shared a deep and knowing laugh. Then Lord Gundrham put his arm around Stephen's shoulders in a fatherly gesture and guided him away from where his son had gone. "Come with me now, lad. We have much to discuss."

Chapter Twenty Six

"So where has he gone?" asked Count von Thurn. "I was under the impression that he was leading an army of more than twenty-thousand men our way, and that he was intent on using those men to root us out and destroy us. Now you tell me that he's not with his men at all? So where is he? And more importantly, where are those men?"

Count von Thurn was not a terribly patient man. And the conflicting intelligence he was getting from his commanders about enemy troop movements was trying what little patience he had. Dobroslav Demantius and Jarmil Jassinius glanced back and forth at each other, trying to determine who would be the first to break the bad news. Ultimately, it was Count von Thurn himself who spoke first.

"Oh, for Christ's sake, would one of you go already? I'm not going to flay you just because you've lost track of Lord Gundrham. Although I should on account of your shitty timing." The men were gathered in *Hrad Karlštejn* (Karlstein Castle) the home that Count von Thurn currently shared with Kateřina Cibulka, a widow who, despite being Catholic herself, was sympathetic to the cause of Bohemian Protestants, and one of Count von Thurn's many mistresses. Where the count's wife currently resided was open to anyone's guess.

The large Gothic castle was located about twenty miles southwest of Prague in the Beroun region of Central Bohemia. Founded in 1348 by then Emperor Charles IV, the entire area, including the impressive structure, had, ironically, been awarded to von Thurn by the Catholic Emperor Rudolph II for his many accomplishments in the battles against the Turks in Hungary.

When Lords Jassinius and Demantius had first arrived at *Hrad Karlštejn*, they had been compelled to wait outside of the Count's bed chamber, listening to the sounds coming from within. Kateřina's cries and the count's grunts were all that were necessary to keep them from entering without permission, or even knocking a second time. When the Count had finally finished, he had smacked the widow, whom he commonly referred to as his *kleine Zwiebel* (little onion) on the ass and had sent her to the kitchen with instructions to find the blind cook and ask him for some of his lovely sausage. When she had departed, still doing her best to get properly dressed, Thurn's commanders had let themselves in. The count then began to meet with them while he lay naked in the still warm bed, not bothering to cover any part of his exposed, and wet, anatomy.

Sensing correctly that the count was furious for having had his....*time*....with the widow disrupted (even though he had sent for them himself and had told them to meet him here in his home), the lords quickly deduced that any delay in answering the count's questions would only increase his frustration and their peril. Ultimately, it was Lord Jassinius who spoke first. "My lord, to the best of our knowledge, Lord Gundrham has returned to *Schloß Stormsong*."

"Why?"

"Apparently there was some....*incident*....there, during a routine execution of some.... criminals, and Lord Gundrham was recalled by the archduke to....I suppose....investigate the *incident*."

"The execution was far from routine," added Lord Demantius. "Apparently some woman associated with *die Volks Knechte*...." He paused and looked to Lord Jassinius for help.

"Yes? Some woman what?" demanded the count.

"Well, apparently, she engaged some form of dark magic. She effectively obliterated the gallows and killed or wounded an untold number of Stormsong men and *Volks Knechte* in the process."

Lords Demantius and Jassinius watched as Count von Thurn sat up in bed, seemingly much more interested now than before. "What more do we know about this woman?" he asked as he stroked his beard and moustache.

"That's all we know for now, my Lord," admitted Lord Jassinius, finally stepping in to aid Lord Demantius. "But for the spies we have in *Schloß Stormsong*, we would not know even this much."

Count von Thurn closed his eyes as he considered all that he had just learned. Not only was someone within the ranks of *die Volks Knechte* capable of dark magic, but apparently Lord Jassinius now had spies – *plural* – within the Stormsong camp. Closing his eyes so that he could best think how to use these assets to his advantage, he began to hum softly.

After several moments, he finally broke the silence. "So, it would appear that we have the benefit of having a witch in our ranks. And, having revealed herself, she has drawn Lord Gundrham back to *Schloß Stormsong*."

Knowing better than to interrupt von Thurn when he was thinking out loud, Lords Jassinius and Demantius simply nodded in agreement.

"But that still leaves open the question of where his twenty-thousand men went."

"Yes, my lord," agreed Lord Demantius. "*If* it's twenty-thousand men, and we don't know that for certain, they have most definitely *not* returned to *Schloß Stormsong* along with Lord Gundrham."

"Then where the hell are they?" barked the count.

"Unfortunately, we simply do not know – not at this time, anyway" admitted Lord Jassinius.

"Then might I suggest that the two of you find out? Preferably *before* they come crashing down upon our very heads!"

"Yes, my lord," they echoed in unison before departing the small home.

The count laid back down and considered his options. *Should I seek out this sorceress?* he asked himself. *Or should I simply leave her alone and take the chance that she'll appear again, and on my side? And should I send my troops looking for Gundrham's men? If they're without their commander, there might be an opportunity here. Then again, that might be precisely what he wants me to do. Wouldn't it make more sense to find some lovely high ground and take up a defensive position and wait for the emperor's army to come to me?*

As he lay in bed considering both the strategic and the tactical situation, he heard the door to the bedchamber reopen. Kateřina Cibulka reentered cursing him playfully. "You *Schweinehund*! You said to go down to the kitchen and ask the blind cook there for some of his lovely sausage."

"And?" the count asked with a smile, knowing the answer before he even asked.

"And he took out his *Schwanz, du Arschlecker!*" she shouted, feigning anger.

The count laughed loudly and deeply, his attention momentarily diverted from any more thoughts of war or power politics. He grabbed Kateřina by her wrists, pulled her back into bed and decided to have another go at her. Military strategy was important, of course, but Count von Thurn never let anything, not even war, come between him and a warm, wet, and willing widow.

"Your....*plan*....simply will not work," Zahara told Šarlatová and Roan. "You have already helped me, and so I am happy to help you. And there's actually very little risk to me, because I've escaped *Schloß Stormsong* before, and I am confident I can easily do so again. But your plan is ludicrous!"

"What, precisely, is your objection to my plan?" asked Šarlatová.

"It's the two of you. Šarlatová, you cannot escort me into that place. Your hair alone is far too distinctive...."

"But I could...."

"And even if you could somehow conceal your hair," Zahara interrupted, "You would still stand out far too much. Your figure alone...."

"Which I could hide."

"Makes it virtually impossible for you to pose as a man. Furthermore, your left eye is quite peculiar. It doesn't have the same colour as your right eye at all." This comment caused Šarlatová and Roan to exchange nervous glances with each other – something that the very perceptive slave girl did not miss. "And someone is sure to notice that, and whoever notices it is sure to start asking questions."

Nodding vigorously in agreement, Roan interjected, "And that's why it's got to be me what brings you back."

Zahara grinned at Roan and patted him on the knee in a maternal but almost condescending fashion. "You seem to be a nice man – at least when you're not wet...." This caused Šarlatová to smile and Roan to growl. "But you're quite possibly the largest human being I have ever seen. You cannot simply walk into *Schloß Stormsong* without drawing at least some attention to yourself. And, as is the case with your lovely daughter, attention means questions, and questions mean trouble."

As Roan and Šarlatová looked at each other, both weighing their options, Zahara continued. "And do not forget that I am a slave – a runaway slave at that. Whoever returns me to that place will do so expecting a reward. You can't simply bring me back, refuse the bounty and, instead, simply start looking around for....whatever it is that you're hoping to find."

"Who said anythin' about refusin' the bounty?" Roan asked. "I say we take you back, get the bounty, and then get the hell back out of there before anyone is wise to what we're doin'."

"That gets us nowhere, Roan. And we're not risking Zahara's life for some money."

"Alright....but we oughtn't be riskin' it for the slim chance that we'd learn anythin' either. What do you think will happen anyway? We collect the bounty and then just have a sit down with the

205

archduke himself? He tells us all of his diabolical plots and plans, then we gather our things, find Zahara, and all walk out the front gate? It's fuckin' madness I tell you." Roan had raised his voice more than he intended and had adopted a tone he didn't often take with Šarlatová. He could tell by her silence that she was hurt by his appraisal of her plan, but he didn't care. *Better that she gets her feelings hurt than that she gets killed,* he thought to himself.

A few moments of awkward silence passed among the three before Zahara gave voice to her own plan. "It's quite simple. I owe you a debt for freeing me from the archduke's men. I will repay that debt by reentering his castle....on my own. I will then attempt to find out whatever I can about the Archduke's plans for this war, and I will escape, again. Once I have, I will share with you whatever I discover."

Šarlatová stared meaningfully at the slave girl. "Why would you do that for us? You just got out of that dreadful place. And you'd voluntarily go back....*alone*....for two people you've only recently met?"

"I told you. To repay a debt. We have a saying in my country: *Nini kinatokea kwa mmoja wetu hutokea kwa kila mmoja wetu.* I don't think it translates well into your language, but while caring for others....even strangers.... may not be important in your culture, it is in mine." The way she said that, and the way she looked at Šarlatová when she did, made it clear that there was more to it than that. Zahara was holding something back.

"Even if we allow you to do this...." Roan started.

"*Allow* me? Are you my slave master now, too?"

"I'm sorry. I didn't mean it that way. I simply mean that if we permitted...." Zahara's face darkened into more of a scowl than before. Flustered, Roan attempted to rephrase. "If we *asked* you to do this for us....how do you plan to get back into the castle without an escort?"

Zahara flashed a knowing smile Roan's way. "That's the easy part. I'll simply go back in the same way I got out. Right through the front door."

Stephen's meeting with Lord Gundrham did not go as expected. He hadn't expected the battle-hardened commander to attempt to soothe his ego, nor to heap praise upon him. But he had expected that their conversation would have something to do with the Archduke's decision to relieve Stephen of his command. He couldn't have been more wrong.

All Lord Gundrham wanted to speak about was the red-haired witch who had wrought so much havoc at the most recent execution. He advised Stephen that this woman was of much greater concern to both him and the archduke than all of the troops the Bohemians could throw into the field, and he confided in Stephen the fact that he was virtually certain that the archduke knew more about this woman than he was willing to admit.

"I've known the archduke for years," he told Stephen. "And I know when he's being less than truthful. You'll recall that Lord Lanzo Oddvar was personally present for the executions and was instrumental in the Archduke's plans for that day."

"Yes, my Lord. But what of it?" Stephen asked.

Lord Gundrham looked about to make sure that no one was listening before he had revealed to Stephen that, "Lord Oddvar has gone missing. No one has seen him nor spoken to him since the botched execution. When the archduke recalled me from my men, I assumed it was because he was assigning the command of those men to Lanzo."

"And now?" Stephen asked.

"And now I think that Lord Oddvar is on some secret mission for the archduke. Or that he and the Archduke had some advanced knowledge of what was to transpire that day. I'm not certain either way. I intended to speak to Bishop Riphaen about my concerns, but...."

"But what?" Stephen inquired.

"But he, too, cannot be located at present."

Upon hearing this, Stephen sat back, trying to make sense of all that he had just learned. "What do you suppose is at work here?" he asked Gundrham.

"I really don't know. That's why I'm enlisting your aid. I don't care for all of this....*palace intrigue*, and I haven't the brain for it. I'm a simple soldier, and if there is a threat to the empire, then I am duty bound to find it and destroy it. But I'm no longer certain who....or what....the real threat is."

Stephen was flattered that Lord Gundrham, of all people, had come to him for help. Trying not to show how honoured he was, he simply asked, "What is it you wish me to do, my lord?"

"Just this. Find out what you can and report back to me. You can start by asking questions of Lady Stormsong. I know that the two of you are close, and she knows her father better than anyone."

Stephen blushed hotly and shook his head. "I'm sorry, my lord. Van....I'm sorry, Lady Stormsong is gone, too. She departed *Schloß Stormsong* some days ago."

"Where? And for what purpose?" Lord Gundrham asked.

While he would not later be able to say why, Stephen chose to lie at that moment. "I know neither where nor for what purpose, my lord," he said.

"Then perhaps that's where you should start. If you discover where she's going or what she intends to do....then perhaps we'll be able to unravel the rest of this mess." Lord Gundrham paused before continuing. "Sir Stephen, I trust you more than I trust my own son – idiot that he is – and I have never felt the need to ask you to exercise the most extreme caution and discretion. And I don't feel the need to ask you that again now."

"Understood, my lord. This shall remain between the two of us, and I will not fail you."

"I pray that you don't, Sir Stephen" Lord Gundrham responded. "Because if you do fail, I fear we're all going to end up floating adrift. Adrift in a sea of blood and dark magic."

Chapter Twenty Seven

There was something familiar and reassuring in Rabbi Avrem ben Mordecai's round, open face – perhaps he reminded her of Father Joseph – but regardless of what it was, the more that he spoke with her, the more comfortable Vanessa felt with him. And *Starke* had been an even easier convert. So long as the rabbi kept feeding him from a rapidly dwindling supply of raisins, Avrem could do no wrong in the stallion's eyes.

In fact, Vanessa had chosen to accompany the rabbi on the remainder of his short journey southwest towards *Schloß Stormsong*. Unfortunately, that meant that she was travelling back in the direction from which she had just come. But, given that she had no idea where she was going anyway, one direction was as good as another. She was just as likely – or unlikely – to casually run into the stunning and mysterious redhead while travelling with the rabbi as she was going to while travelling anywhere else. And she found Avrem's company quite stimulating.

"You speak of faith," she said as both walked alongside *Starke*, giving him a break from carrying both of them. "But of all people, Jews have the least reason to maintain faith in our Lord."

"Really?" asked the rabbi. "Why do you say that?'

Vanessa drew up short and cast a look of disbelief at her travelling companion. "Are you serious?" *Starke* added a wet snort, as if he meant to echo Vanessa's incredulity.

"I'm perfectly serious. Why would a Jew have reason to doubt God's grace and mercy?"

"I don't know. Perhaps we could start with the fact that your people were enslaved in Egypt for more than two-hundred years."

"Yes, and God sent us Moses to lead the Exodus out of Egypt."

"But only after more than two centuries of slavery!"

"You're a Christian, young lady. You should know that God works in his own time. What is two-hundred years to the creator of the universe?"

"Fair enough. But two-hundred years means a great deal to human beings. And what of the Diaspora?"

"What of it?" the rabbi asked, clearly enjoying having such a bright and inquisitive student with whom to converse.

"You know as well as I do that the First Jewish-Roman War culminated in the destruction of Jerusalem, which resulted in the displacement of the Jews from their....*your*....symbolic homeland."

"Jerusalem was not....*is not*.... just a *symbolic* homeland, Vanessa. Nevertheless, you are an excellent pupil of history." It surprised Vanessa just how much the rabbi's compliment meant to her. Equally surprising to her was the pleasant feeling she received from his use of her name. "But you've forgotten the story of Bar Kokhba," he added.

"I have not. You're speaking, of course, of Simon ben Kosevah, who led the Bar Kokhba rebellion against Roman Emperor Hadrian."

"Outstanding!" praised the rabbi. "Top marks!"

"I hadn't forgotten the story, rabbi. I had left it out because, after four years of devastating warfare, in which far more Jews were killed than Romans, the uprising was suppressed – and the Jews.... *your people*....were taken as slaves to Rome and were forbidden access to Jerusalem! Surely that's not the basis for your faith in God?"

"And what happened to *my people* next?" he asked, suspecting that Vanessa already knew the answer. "We immigrated to Iberia and North Africa and France and the Rhineland. And we have prospered everywhere we have gone."

Vanessa was positively exasperated by that point. "And everywhere that you've prospered, you have also been subjected to abuse, pogroms, massacres, ghettoization, discrimination, and per-secution....the very sort of cruelty that sent you on your journey in the first place!"

Vanessa was practically shouting now, which caused the rabbi to turn to face her. "Why are you so angry, Vanessa? What has gener-ated so much anger towards God? Certainly, it's not the suffering of the Jewish people – a race and a religion of which you take no part."

"I'm not angry at God," Vanessa lied. "But I don't understand how you can feel so much loyalty to a father....any father who al-lows so much pain....an absent father who, instead of.... Look, a father is the one who's supposed to....I mean, he's supposed to rep-resent.... He's supposed to help you make sense of the world, to tell you what's right and what's wrong....to be your moral compass."

Correctly sensing that Vanessa was on the verge of tears, and that her angry rant had nothing to do with God, Avrem took her by the shoulders, and while Vanessa was several inches taller than him, he attempted to look her directly in the eyes. "I hear you, Vanessa. Do you understand? I hear you."

She paused for several long moments before attempting to speak again. "Do you mean that....I mean....that you also....?"

"Yes," he answered, knowing precisely what she meant. "I *also*.... But the sins my father committed with me and with my family....none of those are the fault of God in Heaven. He is my real Father, my Heavenly Father. You want to know, despite all of the pain and suffering I have endured, how can I still have faith in Him? I'll tell you. The Jewish relationship with God is a covenant dating all the way back to Abraham. We keep God's laws, and he brings blessings into every aspect of our lives – *every* aspect, even the pain and the suffering. He is always with us. Do you understand? He works in the world every day and is a part of everything we do. That's not just true of Jews, Vanessa. That's true of Christians, too – at least it's supposed to be. Of course, we interpret the Bible differ-ently, and we don't agree on who or what Jesus was. But Christians and Jews agree that we have a Father in Heaven who loves us. A

Father who is there with us – not just when things are good, but always and forever. Does a child stop believing in the innate goodness of his parents the first time he falls and hurts his knee? No! And it's no different with our almighty Father. Don't lose faith in Him, Vanessa. I assure you that He has never lost faith in you."

The impact of the rabbi's words struck Vanessa like a blow across the face. She remained silent, doing her best to stifle her tears, for several long seconds before she could compose a response. "You certainly have a talent for trivialising the momentous, rabbi. Comparing five millennia of suffering to the skinning of a child's knee…."

The rabbi matched Vanessa's wry smile with one of his own and interrupted. "And you are equally talented at complicating the obvious, my child. Believing that the sins of your biological father in any way reduce the presence of your Heavenly Father in your life…."

After another long pause, Vanessa finally sniffled, "So where does that leave us?"

"Well, unless I miss my guess, that still leaves us a few miles north of *Schloß Stormsong*."

As Vanessa broke into a mixture of tears and laughter, Avrem placed his soft hands on her strong and sinewy arms and gave them a comforting little squeeze. "You help me find my way to *Schloß Stormsong*, Vanessa, and I'll help you find your way back to your Father."

The rabbi had no way of knowing just how much irony and double meaning existed in what he had just promised. And Vanessa prayed that he never would.

At around the same time that Vanessa was getting a lesson in theology from Rabbi ben Mordecai, four royal soldiers were sitting around a table just outside the entrance to *Kostnice v Sedlci* (the

Sedlec Ossuary), a Catholic chapel located beneath the *Hřbitovní kostel Všech Svatých* (the Cemetery Church of All Saints) in the central Bohemian town of *Sedlci* (Sedlec), some fifty miles east of Prague.

The ossuary was believed to contain the skeletons of between forty- and seventy-thousand people whose bones had been carefully arranged to form decorations and furnishings for the chapel, including a chandelier of bones which hung from the centre of the nave. Because it also contained a coat of arms of the House of Schwarzenberg (an aristocratic German family that had once been one of the most prominent noble families in all of Europe), and because it was rumoured to be the final resting place for a number of prominent Catholic clergymen, it was considered to be a priceless relic of German Catholic history. For that reason, it was routinely guarded by royal soldiers.

These particular royal soldiers were in a very jovial mood. The promise of cold drinks and warm female companionship when their shift ended led to a cheerful disposition that was further heightened by the telling of stories, mostly false, of various sexual conquests. As the four soldiers regaled each other with their exaggerated tales, they did not notice the half dozen black cloaked men who entered the ossuary as a group, each with swords drawn.

The initial strike came very quickly, as the first two men in the sextet simultaneously plunged their swords into the nape of the neck of the soldier who was seated, with his back to the group of invaders, closest to the entry of the ossuary. In the fraction of a second that it took the other three guards to respond, two other members of the invading force stepped forward, each one producing a wheellock pistol – a firearm with a smoothbore barrel and a shorter wooden handle than most other seventeenth century pistols. Both men fired a half-inch lead ball into the unarmored chest of the first guard to stand, knocking him to the ground and killing him almost instantly.

As the two remaining guards attempted to overcome their shock at what had just happened and struggled to unsheathe their swords,

Count von Thurn stepped from behind the fifth and sixth members of his team of soldiers. He calmly surveyed the bloody carnage that his men had wrought and turned to face the terrified survivors.

"Do you know who I am?" he asked the two. At first, neither one said nor did anything, but when the count raised his own weapon – a puffer wheellock pistol (a popular German design which was larger than most other wheellock guns) – at them, one of the two dropped his sword and blurted out, "*Ja!* I know who you are."

"Really?" asked the count. "Then tell me, who am I?"

Shaking, the unarmed soldier stammered, "You're the man what's going to kill the both of us if we don't do exactly as you say." It came out sounding more like a question than a statement, but it must have sufficed because von Thurn and his men all laughed.

"Quite right!" answered the count as he turned towards the other, still armed soldier and fired a .62 calibre smooth-bore round from the eleven-inch steel barrel of his pistol. The round caught the unsuspecting soldier in the mouth and ripped off half of his jaw. As the wounded soldier fell to the ground, desperately clutching what was left of his shattered face, Count von Thurn stepped over him and stood face to face with the lone survivor of the team of guards.

"My name is *Jindřich Matyáš Hrabě z Thurn-Valsassina*, but your hapless emperor most likely knows me as Heinrich Matthias Graf von Thurn. I want you to watch everything we do here. Miss nothing and remember it all. When we have left, you are to tell everyone you come across what happened here. If you do, I'll let you live. Do you understand?"

The relieved but still terrified guard nodded silently which caused the count to pat him on the cheek. *"Guter Junge,"* he said to the soldier. Then he turned to his six men, nodded, and said, "Well, let's get on with it, then."

"Get on with what, my lord?" asked one of the men who had earlier fired his pistol.

"Get on with lighting a fire that they'll see all the way to Vienna."

Chapter Twenty Eight

"Thank you for meeting with me, Father Joseph," Stephen said.

"Of course, my son. How can I help you?"

The two were meeting, at Stephen's request, in *der Tiroler Saal* (the Tyrolean Hall), one of the newest additions to *Schloß Stormsong*. It was Stephen's thinking that, if they spoke while casually strolling through this ceremonial hall, they would arouse less suspicion than if they met in secret in some dark corner of the fortress.

Der Tiroler Saal had been designed by Elias Holl, one of the most important German architects of the late Renaissance, and had been built between 1602 and 1606. It was a massive ceremonial hall that was intended for both the reception of official guests of the Archduke and the display of his impressive collection of statuary; in fact, several life size terracotta and stucco sculptures by Dutch Mannerist Adriaen de Vries were exhibited there. The walls of *der Tiroler Saal* were decorated with ornamental pilasters and Renaissance stucco reliefs, and a row of wooden columns in the centre of the hall supported a panelled coffer ceiling and underpinned the double-span-roofs.

Hoping to give the impression of someone who was simply seeking the advice of a priest, hiding in plain sight as it were, Stephen walked alongside Father Joseph and asked, "Father, what do you know about everything that happened during the most recent execution?"

Father Joseph sighed and shook his head in disbelief. "Well....I know that the phrase *most recent execution* is....I don't know....

absurd? Absurd and an abomination. Yes, I understand that the church's Catechism teaches that civil authority may commit lawful slaying. But *lawful slaying*? As if such a thing were possible. Even the most passing understanding of the ministry of Jesus Christ must inevitably lead to the conclusion that that executions are a sin, because they are an attack on the very...."

Father Joseph suddenly realized from the look on Stephen's face that he had not come for a scholarly sermon about capital punishment. "I'm sorry," he apologised. "I got carried away. What was it you wanted to talk about?"

"Thank you, Father. I wanted to know what you had heard regarding the woman who did....whatever it was that she did that has stirred up so much activity."

"Ah – *die rote Hexe* (the red witch). Yes. Well, I witnessed the entire affair, because I was going to say the funeral mass for all of the....deceased....when the madness was over."

Stephen was stunned. "Funeral mass? But none of them were Catholic, father. They were all Protestants....heretics! Is that even allowed?"

Father Joseph stopped walking, which forced Stephen to do the same. "Yes, my son. It is permitted. In the instance when a person of another Christian faith dies and has no way to receive the rites of his own church, then he – or she – may be given a Catholic funeral mass.... with the approval of the local bishop, of course."

"And Bishop Riphaen consented to that? I'm more than a little surprised."

"Don't be. At first, he steadfastly refused to grant me permission. But then I reminded our good bishop that Jesus Christ Himself was not Catholic, and that He, too, was tortured and executed – just as savagely as those heretics were. So, I asked the bishop if he would have denied Christ the benefit of a Catholic funeral mass once His body had been taken down from the cross."

"And?"

"And....that's when he came to view the matter the same way I did. Just because we are Catholics, doesn't mean that we have to surrender our ability to think independently, Stephen. I simply did what was right, and so did the bishop, albeit after a little prodding. But that's not what you came to see me about either. What do you want to know about that woman?"

"Let's start with what you saw."

Father Joseph exhaled very deeply and took Stephen by the arm so that they could resume walking through *der Tiroler Saal*. "I saw *eine rote Hexe* at work, Stephen. I don't know any other way to describe it. She was a witch….and a powerful one at that."

"How much do you know about witchcraft, father?"

"Sadly, far too much, Stephen. There are several references to it in the Bible, of course. Deuteronomy condemns anyone who casts spells or consults with the dead. It says *'There shall not be found among you anyone that maketh his son or his daughter to pass through the fire, or that useth divination, or an observer of times, or an enchanter or a witch, or a charmer, or a consulter with familiar spirits, or a wizard, or a necromancer. For all that do these things are an abomination unto the Lord: And because of these abominations, the Lord thy God doth drive them out before thee.'* And Exodus states that *'Thou shalt not suffer a witch to live.'* Even Martin Luther, a heretic in his own right, taught that witchcraft was a sin against the second commandment and that the penalty for it must be death. But that's not really what you're asking, is it?"

"No….it's not, Father. Vanessa was an eyewitness to what happened, too. And she was almost certain that the woman….the witch….that….well, that she knew her somehow."

Father Joseph sighed ominously before asking, "So what is your question, Stephen?"

"My question is, could Vanessa be right? Could it be possible that she….I don't know…. knew that woman somehow?"

Stephen couldn't quite read the expression on Father Joseph's face while he pondered the question. "I suppose you would have to ask that of Vanessa."

"I would," Stephen whispered tersely. "But as you know, she has vanished. And, apparently, she's in pursuit of that woman....the witch. There are lots of questions I'd like to ask her, but she's not here to answer any of them. So, I want to ask you, and I want you to tell me the truth, what is going on? What do you know that I don't?"

Father Joseph stopped walking again and looked directly at Stephen. He rubbed his halo of white hair as he pondered how best to answer Stephen's inquiry. When it appeared that he wasn't going to say anything at all, Stephen decided to prompt him.

"Father Joseph, you know that I love Vanessa. I have since.... well, forever I suppose. My heart and my soul belong to her – totally and completely. There's no more question about that than there is about whether or not the sun will rise in the east tomorrow morning. Yet if there's anyone on God's green earth who cares for her more than I do, it's you. I'm not asking you these questions because of some morbid obsession with the occult, nor because I have some macabre fascination with what *'die rote Hexe'* can do. I am asking them because I'm afraid for Vanessa. For reasons I can't begin to understand, she's gone off in search of this woman, and I fear that she's in mortal danger. Vanessa is in trouble, Father, I know it in my heart. And I'm asking you for help."

Father Joseph studied Stephen's face for a long time before he sighed again and relented. "Meet me in the archduke's library within the hour," was all he said before he turned and walked away.

"What did you just say?" Roan asked Zahara. The three had been travelling closer to *Schloß Stormsong* for several days, and now that they were within just a few miles of the fortress, Zahara had chosen to share with Šarlatová and Roan her plan for reentering the castle.

"You heard me. In my country, I am from a small tribe called *Jalad Wukar.* In Arabic, one of the languages spoken by my tribe, that means "skinwalker." But in your language, you would probably call us *Gestaltwandlerin* (shape shifters). There are a very few of us, and the women of the tribe – no one knows why, but it's only the women who can….*walk in the skin of others.*"

Roan and Šarlatová continued to stare at Zahara as they attempted to process what she had just told them. "So you're going to….I'm sorry….*enter someone else's skin* so that you can gain entry into *Schloß Stormsong?*" Roan asked sardonically.

"No. I'm afraid it's not quite that simple. In my case, I have never been able to walk in the skin of another human being. So I will enter the same way I left….by walking in the skin of an animal. But that does not mean that I physically enter the other being's skin," she added.

"Then what is it that you do?" asked Šarlatová, who was hanging on Zahara's every word.

"When a *Jalad Wukar* walks in the skin of another, it means that our physical body takes the shape….or at least the form of something else."

"What does that mean?" Roan asked, fearing that he already knew the answer.

"It means that, for a short time, I will….*tahawal*? No….*kubadil-isha*? What is your word? *Transform*? Yes, transform into something else. But I can only do it for a short time. If a *Jalad Wukar*….I'm sorry….a *Gestaltwandler*….walks in the skin of another for too long….well, then she runs the risk of not being able to come back into her own skin. The longer the wait, the greater the chance of not being able to *tahawal*….I'm sorry….*transform* back."

After Šarlatová and Roan continued to stare at the former slave girl, she finally asked, "Why is that so hard to believe? After all," she was looking at Šarlatová now, "You of all people should understand that Allah has gifted some of us with powers and abilities beyond what is common to most."

Šarlatová was stunned. "What? How did you….?"

"I sensed it in you. The very first time our eyes met. Even before you freed me from those men, I knew. I felt a connection, and I was drawn to you. I am certain that you felt something too."

Šarlatová blushed and looked at Roan who just continued to stare at Zahara. "So you're going to do what now?" he asked her. "You're going to....*walk in the skin*....of some animal. You're goin' to slip into the most heavily guarded citadel in the Empire....and do it as what....a fuckin' polar bear?! Then you'll just wander around until you learn somethin' about the archduke's strategy for winnin' this war? Then come back here, and tell us all about it? Have I gotten all of that right?"

"Well, I do not know what a *'fuckin' polar bear'* is, but essentially you have the rest of it right, yes."

"Roan, she's simply trying to help," Šarlatová said to Roan, much in the same way that a parent would scold a child.

"I'm sorry, *dívka*. I really am. What you can do with your voice....that's one thing, and I've barely been able to wrap me head around all of that. But what this girl is talkin' about....well, it's just bat shit crazy, is all!"

"Now it is I who am sorry, friend Roan. What is *'bat shit crazy'*?" The simple and direct honesty of Zahara's question broke the tension that had hung heavy among the three travellers and caused both Roan and Šarlatová to burst into laughter. Once Zahara was certain that they were not laughing at her, she began to laugh, too. Then, by way of a follow-up question, she innocently asked, "Does the *'fuckin' polar bear'* eat the *'bat shit'*?" which simply added to the hysterical laughter.

When the laughter had finally subsided, Roan and Šarlatová discussed a strategy with Zahara, even though neither of them could yet believe that she would actually be capable of executing it. Incredibly, she was to take the shape of a cat, enter *Schloß Stormsong,* eavesdrop as best she could on the archduke's soldiers, commanders, or anyone else she might encounter, and then simply leave, spending no more than a maximum of two hours inside the castle – even though Zahara assured both of them that she could safely hold the form for longer than that.

With the plan agreed upon, the three had waited until the sun was just going down to move within a few hundred yards of the outskirts of the fortress. Then, under a canopy of heavy foliage and the added cover of the lengthening shadows provided by the coming darkness, they had chosen a spot from which to launch their incursion. Once they had, Zahara had moved away from Šarlatová and Roan and had removed all of her clothing before sitting in the seiza position on the forest floor.

When it finally came time to begin, neither Šarlatová nor Roan knew what to expect, but neither could overcome their natural curiosity. Both reneged on their shared promise of granting Zahara some privacy and peeked through the foliage to watch whatever was about to happen. Zahara's concern had not been one of modesty or shame; she simply wanted to be able to concentrate without having to perform in front of an audience. And she had no reason to be modest, as both Šarlatová and Roan quickly noted. Zahara's body was flawless. Every muscle and every curve seemed to be in precise and symmetrical proportion; her skin was absolutely unblemished (which Šarlatová found very unusual, considering that Zahara was, in fact, a slave), and it seemed to both of her admiring voyeurs that she was a living, breathing piece of art. In fact, Šarlatová was quite certain that nothing ever sculpted by Bernini, Donatello, or even Michelangelo himself could compare to the beauty of the statuesque figure before them.

Šarlatová had never felt carnal cravings before. Certainly, she'd had plenty of sexual encounters in her past, but that was not the same thing as desire. She'd been used by more men than she could count, forced to do things beyond description, and she had first been violated at the age of twelve or thirteen. But she'd never felt desire before. At least until now. Now, the feeling that Zahara's dark skin caused in her stomach could only be described as hunger.

Every move the dark woman made was relaxed and unhurried, and it was easy to imagine those slow and sensual motions taking place while Zahara's body was writhing and contorting underneath her own, sharing the same space and the same long breaths. Zahara's sweat covered limbs were all grace and muscle, and Šarlatová desperately wanted to sink herself into that supple brown flesh, to reserve nothing, to envelop her and then dissolve, panting and dripping wet, into her limber body.

Had the circumstances not been so dire – and bizarre – the sight of this flawlessly tantalising exemplar of feminine perfection would have aroused the most basic and carnal of desires within Roan as well. But those considerations were subordinate, at least for the moment, to his curious preoccupation with what Zahara was attempting to do.

She sat with legs bent, buttocks resting on her heels. As she folded her hands in her lap and straightened her back, she took a series of deep, cleansing breaths. Then, suddenly, she acted as if she was being stung by a thousand bees. She scratched and tore at her previously perfect skin as it began to rapidly grow hair – then fur. Her bones appeared to break and reorganise as her muscles tore and shrank. Her face became a distorted mask of pain as her fingernails and toenails mutated into claws. When Zahara reached a grotesque midpoint where she was no longer fully human but not quite fully animal, Roan's stomach began to churn. But even as he turned his head to vomit, Šarlatová could not take her eyes off….whatever it was that Zahara had done to herself.

Finally, when the transformation was complete, a shot of adrenaline rushed through Zahara's veins and she darted with uncanny speed from the spot where she had disrobed only moments ago and took up a spot directly in front of Šarlatová.

Šarlatová reached down and picked up what appeared to be a perfectly healthy domesticated cat. The soft, clean fur, as well as the large, round eyes, and the small, delicate paws combined to create an animal that was just as implausibly perfect as Zahara herself. Had she not witnessed the transformation firsthand, Šarlatová would have no way of knowing that this cat that she held in her hands had only moments earlier been a fully grown woman – at least not until she looked the animal directly in the eyes. Šarlatová saw in the cat's eyes the same smouldering intensity that she had earlier seen in Zahara's.

Then, just as Roan began to regain his composure, the cat.... Zahara....seemed to become infused with a second rush of power, strength, and speed, and it....she....shot from Šarlatová's hands and darted through the trees. Then, without bothering to break stride or look back, it.... she....darted gracefully and powerfully in the direction of *Schloß Stormsong*, leaving Roan and Šarlatová to stare at each other, each mystified by what they had just seen and both wondering what the other one was thinking.

Chapter Twenty Nine

Archduke von Stormsong received word about the assault on the *Kostnice v Sedlci* while he was visiting *Stephansdom* (St. Stephen's Cathedral) in Vienna. Originally built as a Romanesque Basilica in the twelfth century, and then rebuilt in the fourteenth century as a cathedral in the classic Gothic style, *Stephansdom* was the mother church of the Roman Catholic Archdiocese of Vienna. Constructed over a period of sixty-five years and standing on the ruins of two earlier churches, the structure – with its white limestone exterior, signature multi-colored roof tile, and massive south tower which offered a commanding view of the rest of the city – was one of Vienna's most iconic buildings.

During the 1529 Siege of Vienna – the first attempt by Suleiman the Magnificent to capture the city – it had served as the main observation and command post for the defence of Vienna against the more than one-hundred-thousand Ottoman invaders. While the massively out-numbered Viennese defenders were ultimately able to protect both the cathedral and the city itself, the two-week-long siege by the Ottomans had left the limestone structure scarred in many places, turning the exterior from white to black. The archduke had recently commissioned a project to restore the earlier, pristine edifice, and it was that project that had brought him to Vienna in the first place.

As von Stormsong strode through the *Stephansplatz*, the square at the centre of Vienna that housed the *Stephansdom*, Lord Lanzo Oddvar, who had accompanied the archduke on his visit to Vienna, approached in a state of agitation. Despite his military acumen and leadership skills, Lord Oddvar was not a physically impressive specimen. He was heavyset and had a kind face that belied his ability to order his men to their deaths, and his skin, which was the colour of sour oatmeal, accentuated his already unhealthy appearance. However, it was his facility for getting straight to the point, not his outward appearance, that concerned the Archduke most days.

"Yes, Lord Oddvar," the archduke said tersely, clearly upset with having his examination of the cathedral's restoration interrupted. "What is it that has you so worked up this morning?"

"Just this, Your Highness," Oddvar said as he attempted to pass a written report to von Stormsong. The archduke, who had a peculiar aversion to being handed things, didn't even look at the document. Instead, he simply shot Oddvar a look that said *Just tell me already.*

"This is a report from *Kostnice v Sedlci.* It would appear that a group of armed men, under the command of Count von Thurn, entered the ossuary, brutally murdered three of the four guards on duty...."

"Brutally murdered?" interrupted the archduke. "Why do men say such things? As if there is any way to murder someone other than brutally."

It was clear to Lord Oddvar that the archduke wasn't paying close enough attention yet, but he decided to press on anyway. "Yes.... well....leaving one survivor as a witness, they....they desecrated the ossuary in the most vile ways imaginable."

"I can imagine a lot," admitted the archduke. "Be specific, Lord Oddvar."

"I'm sorry, Your Highness. I was hesitant to say. It appears that they destroyed the chandelier and the Schwarzenberg coat of arms. They also....urinated and defecated upon several of the tombs and....smeared the walls with the blood of the three slain guards."

Now Lord Oddvar had the archduke's undivided attention. "Continue," he ordered.

"It would appear that, in a gesture of mockery, they dispatched a donkey, around whose neck they placed a sign proclaiming it to be the emperor. And the brigands had apparently written a rather insulting note on a scroll that was then placed….inside….inside the donkey's anus."

Looking to be slightly amused by this, the archduke asked, "What did the note say?"

Oddvar swallowed hard before answering. "Suffice it to say, Your Highness, that they have suggested that both you….and our beloved emperor have….had….inappropriate relationships…. with your own mothers."

The archduke actually smiled. "Is that all, Oddvar?"

"No, Your Highness. It is not. It would appear from the report of the lone survivor that von Thurn and his men….cut off the ears and fingers of the deceased and….kept them as trophies."

"There is nothing new there, Oddvar," the archduke answered. "I would remind you that these Bohemian barbarians have been taking trophies like that since before either one of us was born."

"Yes….but….Your Highness, clearly this affront must be answered. Count von Thurn…."

"Count von Thurn is rather cleverly trying to bait me into a fight on his terms, Lord Oddvar. And I will not blindly stumble into his trap. I will, of course, deal with these heretic brigands, but I will do so at a time and place of my own choosing. In the meantime, I have more pressing matters that require my attention. And our *'beloved emperor'* is beloved by none, least of all me, save perhaps his own family, and I would wager that even they have their reservations."

Oddvar hung his head as he summoned the courage to respond. "Begging your pardon, Your Highness, but is the colour of a cathedral more important than winning the war in Bohemia?"

Stormsong surprised Oddvar by displaying neither frustration nor anger. "You disappoint me, Oddvar. I always thought you were smarter than that. I care not about the colour of this cathedral, or any other cathedral, for that matter. This restoration is simply a gift from me to our soon-to-be new emperor, who may very well be crowned here. The pressing matter is the location of that little red witch who revealed herself to us at the execution. She is a direct threat to the entire empire, and eliminating that hazard is my primary consideration."

"Yes, of course. But if you'll allow me to speak freely...."

"Because you've been holding back so far?" snapped the archduke. "Go ahead, Oddvar. But do be quick about it. I've not yet had breakfast this morning."

"Of course, Your Highness. You have a rare facility to....to not get caught up in the emotion of a thing at the time that it happens. It is something that I both admire and envy, but I wonder if that facility is failing you just now. Isn't it possible that you are dramatically underreacting to the actions of von Thurn? He has, in fact, raised an army against you. What could be more of a *'direct threat'* than that?"

"Well said, Oddvar. And you're right, to an extent. Don't let my measured response to the abominable actions of these Bohemian traitors fool you, though. They will all be rooted out and exterminated with the power and fury of our Lord's own thunder....exterminated like the rodents they are – but all in due course. Have you not considered that if we can locate and capture the red witch that we could harness her power against our enemies and use it to destroy them all? If we capture her, then we could, like Daedalus from the Greek legends, kill two birds with one stone."

"I had not considered that, Your Highness. But how are we to locate her? And, if we do.... how can we be certain that we can capture her?"

"Leave that to me, Oddvar," answered the archduke. "That's being taken care of even as we speak."

Vanessa Stormsong and Rabbi ben Mordecai were within less than an hour's ride from *Schloß Stormsong* when they decided to stop for a short while. *Starke* needed rest and Vanessa and the rabbi both desperately needed to bathe before requesting an audience with the Archduke.

Avrem went first and was already reclothed in garments that were still wet from having been washed in the stream that was leading them all the way to their destination when Vanessa emerged, naked and wet, from the water. As she was wringing water out from her long and thick black hair, the rabbi spoke up.

"Please don't think this inappropriate, but I couldn't help but notice the scars on your back when you went into the water."

"You watched me?" Vanessa asked. She wasn't at all upset with the rabbi for having done what most other men would have in his position, nor was she embarrassed with false modesty. More precisely, she was trying to divert the rabbi's attention from the most recent wounds that Monsignor Mučitel had left on her body. She knew those scars were like silent narrators of her suffering at the hands of the dark priest, but she had not expected the rabbi to notice them.

"I did. And did you know why?"

"Because you're a man and I'm a twenty-four-year-old girl who is nice to look at, so you decided to take a peek?"

"No. First of all, I am more than twice your age – certainly old enough to be your father, if not your grandfather. Second, I am a Rabbinic Jew, and you are a Christian, and the Talmud prohibits marriage....or even....*relations*....with anyone who isn't a Jew."

"*Relations*?" Vanessa asked, offering a coquettish grin to the rabbi, who was now averting his eyes while she dressed.

Unfazed by Vanessa's coy response, the rabbi continued. "Third, I am a happily married man who is not easily led astray by carnal instincts."

"Okay, rabbi. You've made your point. So why *did* you look?"

"Because you didn't take off your boots. In all my life I've never seen anyone bathe while keeping his – or in your case, her – boots on."

Vanessa chuckled. "I'm sorry, rabbi. Are you certain it was my *boots* that attracted your attention?"

Avrem sighed and shook his head. "Vanessa, while I am quite certain that you are very accustomed to having an inordinate amount of attention focused on your chest, and while I'm also sure that you are equally accustomed to using your....*assets*....as a way of flustering your male admirers, I assure you that it was not your breasts that drew my attention."

"Fair enough, rabbi. I always keep my boots on – even when I bathe – because one never knows when trouble might develop, and I much prefer to fight, or flee, with my boots on. That's it, and that's all of it."

"Very well, and I must admit that I find it hard to imagine you fleeing from....well, anything or anyone. But is it from fighting that you received the wounds on your back? I see that they are healed, but the number and colour of the marks indicate that you've had more scars inflicted upon you than most people your age."

Very eager now to change the subject, Vanessa simply dismissed her wounds and scars by saying, "They're nothing, rabbi."

"They're not nothing," Avrem continued, undaunted by Vanessa's evasiveness. "They speak volumes about the pain you must have suffered when they were inflicted upon you."

"As we sin, so must we suffer," said Vanessa automatically, not intending for her comment to be loud enough for the rabbi to hear.

"Meaning what, exactly?" the rabbi asked.

"Meaning that every drop of blood drawn by the sword must be paid for by another drawn by the lash," Vanessa responded.

"According to whom, Vanessa?"

Vanessa paused while she finished redressing and hoped that the rabbi would let it go at that. But as soon as she was fully clothed, she saw him staring at her, and it was clear that she was going to have to answer his question. "I have been asked....forced, in fact, to do horrible things in the name of the Lord, rabbi. And it is for those actions that I have been punished."

"If your actions are in the service of God, why must you suffer for them?"

"Because vengeance is mine, sayeth the Lord."

"So, because you're usurping God's power to punish, you have to suffer for it? Is that it? And what about those who have asked.... forced you to undertake these missions? Do they suffer no penalty?"

"Those are complicated questions, rabbi," Vanessa admitted as she started to resaddle Starke. "And these are complicated times."

Despite the fact that he sensed correctly that Vanessa's patience for this line of inquiry was nearing an end, Avrem couldn't resist the temptation to have the last word. "Very well, Vanessa. But please allow me to share with you one or two things that are not complicated. First, violence does not live alone. It is incapable of living alone. For violence to exist it must, necessarily, be intertwined with falsehood. And it appears to these tired old eyes that you are a victim of many falsehoods. God does not require violence; in fact, he abhors it. God doesn't require anything. Not even worship. Wanting or needing praise is a human failing, and I suspect that the creator of the universe is above all of that – literally and figuratively."

"I sense a *'finally'* coming on," mused Vanessa, eager to end the conversation.

"*Finally* – violence, war, and punishment? These things don't come from God; they come from men – men like your father, the Archduke." Vanessa spun in the rabbi's direction, shocked by his revelation that he knew who she was.

"Just because I walk slowly, and eat slowly, and bathe slowly, doesn't mean I think slowly, Vanessa. I've known precisely who you were almost from the moment we first met. The Stormsong *Familienwappen* on your breastplate and on the cross you wear around your neck sort of give it away. And when you told me your first name....well, everyone in the empire knows that the archduke has but one heir, and that her name is Vanessa."

"Very well. So, you know who my father is. What of it?"

"Well....I suspect that the lies you've been told, the ones that have led you to such violence and pain and suffering, all begin with him."

"With all due respect, rabbi, you don't know the first thing about me or my relationship with my father!" Vanessa snapped.

"Yes, I do, Vanessa. Remember that I have a father, too. Not an archduke, of course, but a Father in Heaven - the very same one you have. And I have been His faithful servant for more than twice as long as you have been alive, and I can assure you that He wants nothing from you but yourself. It is relationship with you that He craves, Vanessa – not scars, nor punishments, nor the horrible things you've been led to do in His name. And anyone who would tell you otherwise – including your father, the archduke himself – is either a liar or a fool. And there endeth the lesson."

The two mounted Starke and rode for several miles in utter silence, each one pondering the assertions made by the other. Ultimately, it was Vanessa, her head still reeling from the earlier conversation, who broke the silence with a laugh. "I suppose now I have heard it all."

"What do you mean?"

"'Here endeth the lesson?' A rabbi quoting from the Anglican Book of Common Prayer? You are a strange one indeed Avrem ben Mordecai."

Without missing a beat, the rabbi responded with, "Perhaps, but I'm not the one who bathes with boots on, *Vanessa von Stormsong*." With that, they continued on at a slow pace, and they heard *Starke* snort in a way that sounded to both of them remarkably like laughter.

Chapter Thirty

Within thirty minutes of his conversation with Father Joseph, Stephen had made his way to *Schloß Stormsong's* library. He knew that the archduke was currently in Vienna, so he expected to have the room all to himself, but he could tell in no time at all that Father Joseph had already been there. The strong odours of goat-cheese and Benedictine *Weihenstephan* hung heavy in the air, and they mixed with the natural musty smell of the library to produce an identity marker as strong as a fingerprint.

"Father?" Stephen called out, less to see if the priest was still there than to make sure no one else was in die *Bibliotheca Stormsong* with him. Once he was certain that he was alone, Stephen began to wander through the compulsively organised stacks. Dividing the collection into five different sections was one thing. But the rigid order in which the archduke kept his books was beyond organised – it was obsessive. Stephen knew quite well that an entire team of servants was dedicated to keeping this collection fanatically clean and neurotically organised. Legendary were the stories of how Stormsong servants were punished by being assigned to shelf duty in the library.

As he meandered through the collections, Stephen had to resist the overwhelming temptation to misplace a title….or two….or twenty. But when he made his way into the Science and Mathematics shelves, the temptation became overpowering.

While he never claimed to have special knowledge of or expertise in the area, Stephen had long been fascinated by science and its never-ending ability to challenge – and prove wrong – old beliefs and incorrect assumptions. So, when he came across an early edition of Copernicus' *De Revolutionibus Orbium Coelestium* (On the Revolutions of the Celestial Spheres), he simply had to take a look. First printed in Nuremberg in 1543, the work was Polish astronomer *Mikołaj Kopernik's* (Nicolaus Copernicus') magnum opus. Offering an alternative to the Ptolemaic view that the universe was geocentric, *De Revolutionibus Orbium Coelestium* correctly formulated a heliocentric model of the universe that placed the sun, not the Earth, at the centre.

While Kopernik likely was heavily influenced by Greek astronomer *Aristarkhos ho Samios* (Aristarchus of Samos), who had formulated his own "central fire" theory eighteen centuries earlier, it was *Kopernik's* work, published just before his death, that had helped to jumpstart what was already being called the Scientific Revolution, a revolution which the Catholic Church had immediately and vehemently opposed. In fact, because the Church's chief censor – Bartolomeo Spina, Magister of the Holy Palace – had already expressed a desire to stamp out the "Copernican doctrine," Stephen was surprised to find the work among the archduke's collection. The Stormsongs had never been known to embrace anything that ran counter to Catholic doctrine or theology. Perhaps the archduke's interest in the work stemmed from the fact that *Kopernik* had been born and had died in a region of the *Königreich Polen* (Kingdom of Poland) that had been part of the Holy Roman Empire for the past century. Likely it was some misplaced sort of nationalistic pride that led Archduke von Stormsong to include such a controversial work in his collection. Whatever the reason, it was a thrill for Stephen to simply hold it in his hands, but fearing that he might leave some incriminating evidence if he went any further, he returned the book to its shelf, careful to align it perfectly with the volumes on either side of it.

Stephen continued to wander through the library, looking for Father Joseph or anything that the priest might have left for him.

But he could find no note nor any other clue as to why he had been summoned here by a priest who had, evidently, either already come and gone or not yet arrived.

In frustration, Stephen turned to leave when he saw something extraordinary. In the library's literature section, one book was askew. A red leather volume with fully gilt pages stood ever so slightly on edge, jutting out unevenly at an angle that would be imperceptible to anyone who wasn't familiar with the archduke's fastidious arrangement of his books.

Stephen approached as one might draw near to a hissing cobra. Treading cautiously and quietly, he slowly withdrew the volume from its position on the shelf and opened it. The title page declared that this was a first edition of a fairly new work by Spanish author Miguel de Cervantes Saaverda. Stephen wasn't familiar with *Don Quixote,* but it wasn't the story that intrigued him. Instead, he was fascinated by the fact that three of the perfectly gilt pages had been bent, ever so slightly, so that they stood out from the rest. Stephen knew that the Archduke would never allow such "desecration" to be done to one of his books, so he quickly ascertained that the pages had to have been bent by someone else.

Sitting down at a nearby table, Stephen briefly glanced around to ensure that he was still in the room by himself. Confident that he was, he opened the book to one of the bent pages. What he saw there shocked him even more than the bent pages. Someone had actually, ever so faintly, underlined one of the passages. It read: *Finally, from so little sleeping and so much reading, his brain dried up and he went completely out of his mind.*

What could that possibly mean? Stephen wondered to himself. But before he could formulate an answer, he had already turned to a second of three marked pages. There again he found a faintly underlined passage which read: *The truth may be stretched thin, but it never breaks, and it always surfaces above lies, as oil floats on water.*

Mystified a second time, Stephen sat back in his chair and wondered what sort of game Father Joseph was playing with him.

Fiddling with his left earlobe, a nervous habit he had developed whenever he was lost in thought, he noticed a cat with rich, warm, burnt-umber fur that was perched on a windowsill across from him, seeming to study him as carefully as he was studying *Don Quixote*. Choosing to ignore the cat for the moment, and exhaling in frustration, Stephen turned to the final bent page. This time, no underlined passage greeted him; instead, written ever so lightly in tiny, printed handwriting was a cryptic line that read: *The piece you seek is right in front of you.*

What the hell does that mean? Stephen asked himself. *The 'piece' I seek? Did he mean 'peace'? No, he wouldn't have spelled it that way. What piece? A piece of a puzzle? A piece of….*

Just as Stephen felt like he was making some headway, the cat – as if shot from a cannon – leapt down from its perch and landed on the table directly in front of Stephen, startling him so much that he tipped over backwards in his chair and fell to the ground.

"Damn feral cats," he cursed as he got back to his feet. But the cat that had startled him and that continued to loiter on the table in front of him didn't look like any stray animal he had ever seen before. The fur was much too clean and the paws too well manicured. *This cat must be someone's pet,* he thought to himself, but Archduke von Stormsong didn't strike him as the type of person to either keep pets, or to allow them in his home. Out of curiosity, he reached for it, but just as he did, it shot past him and through the stacks of shelves with a speed that Stephen didn't think possible.

Resisting the urge to give chase in order to ascertain to whom the cat belonged, Stephen bent down to retrieve the book he had been examining. To his dismay, the engraved frontispiece – the decorative illustration opposite the book's title page – appeared to have been scratched when it fell. Now there would be no concealing the fact that he had been rifling through the Archduke's prized collections of books. Desperately hoping that he might be able to repair the damage, he carefully examined the image on the frontispiece, which was of a knight, on horseback riding towards….riding towards….

Wait a minute, Stephen thought to himself. *The frontispiece? The front-is-piece?* The front....*is*....piece? *The* piece....*is....right in* front *of*....

Momentarily forgetting all of the polite decorum and courtesy with which the archduke's books were expected to be handled, and operating in the same manner in which a small child would tear open a wrapped present, Stephen ripped the attached frontispiece away from the book. Once it was free from the book, he flipped the illustration over to examine the back of it. What he saw there took his breath away and immediately sent him running, as fast as he could, in the direction of *Schloß Stormsong's* mews.

While Stephen panted and puffed his way through the web of corridors that was *Schloß Stormsong*, the cat who had accidentally set him running towards the mews in the first place made her own tour of the castle.

Her size and agility rendered every conceivable part of the compound accessible to her, and the innocuous nature of a feral cat protected her from even the slightest suspicion. After all, who in his right mind would suspect that a cat was eavesdropping on conversations – privileged or otherwise?

And so it was that Zahara made her way from one part of the castle to another, stopping only when some conference or exchange of dialogue grabbed her attention. But after a little more than four hours (more than double the amount of time she had agreed upon with Šarlatová and Roan) of prowling and spying, she had come up with next to nothing – aside from the joy of startling a boyishly handsome man half to death in what appeared to be a library.

Ultimately, as she was pondering aborting her mission, she made her way to *die Schwarze Straße* (the Black Street), a lane within the compound that had been added as part of the sixteenth century reconstruction and renovation of the castle. Taking its name from the blacksmiths who lived and worked there, *die Schwarze Straße* was lined on one side by a series of small work- shops and on the other by a row of even smaller houses, each one painted the same drab grey-green colour.

What Zahara noticed first, and would have even without her en-hanced feline sense of smell, was the redolence of the street. The combination of human sweat, fire forged metals, and cooking aro-mas produced a lively and distinctive scent that was powerful, but surprisingly agreeable – at least to a cat, anyway. Specifically, it was the odour of fried onions that led her towards a particular home, but as she padded in its direction, her attention was quickly diverted by the sound of metal on metal.

In seventeenth century Europe, blacksmithing was thought to be an integral part of the seven mechanical arts, every bit as impor-tant as masonry, weaving, cooking and hunting, and virtually every town in Europe had a *smithy* who produced objects from wrought iron or steel. The work, which involved forging metal and then us-ing tools to hammer, bend, and cut that metal into shape, was both difficult and dangerous, but it was also essential to the creation of tools, hardware, cooking utensils, and weapons.

As with most things, the Stormsongs had more than their fair share of blacksmiths, and more than two dozen had found full-time employment on *die Schwarze Straße*. Ever since the unpleasantries that had occurred in May, during the third Defenestration of Prague, *die Schwarze Straße* had been alive with activity. However, precious few tools, hardware, or cooking utensils were being produced. For the past five months, the vast majority of the work being done by *Schloß Stormsong's* smiths was devoted to producing castle forged swords, lances, shields, and axes.

The fuel to heat the smiths' fires was charcoal – which was largely free of sulphur and, therefore, vastly superior to coal as a fuel. The distinct, earthy smell of charcoal smoke, combined with the repetitive peal of cross peen hammers on iron, lured Zahara away from her pursuit of food. As she padded along the outskirts of one smith's shop, she overheard a conversation that was nearly as hot as the coals themselves.

"Would you pay attention to what you're doing?" barked one man who was short, but thick through the arms and chest. "You've been doing a shit job on those swords all day!"

"I don't care!" retorted a second man who was surprisingly thin and pale. His haggard and unshaven appearance was testimony to just how tired he was. "I've made more fucking swords in the past five months than I did in the past five years before that. I'm exhausted, and I don't give a shit who knows it!"

"You're an idiot," the first man observed. "You know what's going on, don't you? Word is that the archduke has planned some big offensive for this autumn, or maybe the winter. He's going to help the emperor out by attacking all of the Bohemians and Protestants from here all the way to *die Weißenberge* (the White Mountains)."

"All the way to *die Weißenberge*, huh? I don't understand what the emperor cares about all that rubbish for. I hear that he's as sick as a dog and will be dead before the year's out," answered the pale smith.

"There's a lot of things you don't understand. And how do you know the emperor is sick? Did he tell you that himself? And even if it's true, I'm sure that five seconds after he's dropped dead, they'll find some other pisser in the family who will want to do the exact same thing. So, we keep working until someone tells us not to." The short, barrel-chested man punctuated his point with a few particularly sharp blows from his cross-peen hammer. "Anyway, what do you care about how many swords we have to make? You're getting paid isn't you?"

"*Ja*….I suppose. But while I'm getting *paid*, I ain't been getting *laid*." Both men laughed hard at the crude retort. After the laughter died down, the pale smith waited a few seconds before adding, "You know how long it's been since I seen my wife's *white mountains*?"

This produced a second round of laughter even greater than the first one. Taking that opportunity to sneak away, Zahara just heard the first man respond by saying, "I'm betting it hasn't been any longer than it's been since *I* seen your wife's white mountains." But she did not stay to witness the fight that ensued afterwards.

Knowing that she had not really learned anything, but feeling an urgent and primal pull to vacate the form of the cat and to return to her own skin, Zahara began to make her way back out of *Schloß Stormsong* the exact same way she had when she had escaped several days earlier – right through the front gate.

Chapter Thirty One

———✥———✥———

Kostel svatého Ducha (the Church of the Holy Spirit) dated back to the first half of the fourteenth century and was originally built as a convent for Benedictine nuns. It was located in Prague, on the boundary between the Old Town and *Josefov* – next to the *die alte Synagoge* (the Old Synagogue). In fact, during the reign of Emperor Ferdinand I, those living in the nearby Jewish Quarter had been prohibited from attending services at *die alte Synagoge* and were forced, instead, to attend Catholic masses at *Kostel svatého Ducha*. The exterior of the church consisted of several Gothic buttresses and high windows, while the interior featured a single nave, an elongated presbytery, and an impressive fourteenth century Pieta, believed to be the work of famed German architect and sculptor *Peter von Gemünd*.

While the parallelepiped tower at the north side of the church had been heavily damaged during the Hussite wars of the first half of the fifteenth century, the historic church had never faced the prospect of total annihilation – at least not until the arrival of Prince Christian II.

Born in 1599, Christian II was the second (but eldest surviving) son of Protestant Prince Christian I of Anhalt-Bernburg, a German prince of the House of Ascania who was the governor of *die Oberpfalz* (the Upper Palatinate) and chief advisor to Frederick V, Elector Palatine. As heir to the throne of the principality of Anhalt-Bernburg, the nineteen-year-old Protestant Prince Christian II was overflowing with youthful bravado and (having studied in

Switzerland, France, Italy, and England) education. Able to speak four languages fluently and extremely eager to win his father's approval for something other than scholastic achievement, he had volunteered to command a regiment of arquebusiers in the civil war against the hated Catholic Hapsburgs. His first assignment, as ordered by his Father, was to march that regiment some two-hundred miles southeast towards Prague to "strike a blow" against the control of the Imperial forces that had exercised military control over Anhalt-Bernburg since the thirteenth century.

Christian's appearance and manner were deceptive, and both belied his true nature. He had the sweet cherubic face of a baby, a mop of startlingly red hair, and conducted himself with such polite and refined etiquette that he teetered on the edge of ostentation. His clothing, in which he took great pride, went well beyond the bounds of flamboyance. Besides his signature suede tunic, he also regularly wore a black velvet cape adorned with rubies the size of strawberries and *Juften* leather boots that were sewn with gold brocade and pearls. His horse was similarly caparisoned in the colours of the house of Ascania – red, green, gold, and black. However, beneath his respectable (albeit pretentious) demeanour lay a cold heart that was full of pride and that was completely desensitised to violence.

Those who knew the prince well knew that he genuinely believed that he was better than those around him and that he was the master of all situations. However, the only art in which Christian's actual ability was equal to his perceived skill was in using weapons to inflict pain. Perhaps because of this skill, or due to his complete inability to show empathy or even kindness towards others, the prince did not react to violence the same way that other people might. Instead of feeling moved emotionally by terrible violence, he seemed to be unfazed by it at all. He simply didn't care about the suffering of others; in fact, he seemed to take great delight in them.

So it was little surprise to Christian II's men that, upon having selected one-hundred and twenty of them from his eight-hundred man regiment of arquebusiers, he marched them into the heart of

Židovské město (Josefov), divided them into four platoons of thirty, and arranged them in a semi-circle around the entrance to *Kostel svatého Ducha*. As a Saturday evening wedding mass was approaching its conclusion, each of the four platoons erected a series of fork-rests (long, thin stakes with a U-shaped rest at the top to serve as a mount for the arquebusier's firearm) in positions less than one-hundred yards from the entrance to the historic church. Then, just as the Catholic congregation was dismissed from mass, Prince Christian, in an extremely theatrical and pompous display, placed a bamboo flute to his lips and blew. Each time he did, a different one of the four platoons opened fire. Spread out in a strategic-battle-array, and engaging in well-timed volley fire, the arquebusiers unleashed round after round until they had nearly exhausted their ammunition. In all, Christian blew the flute twenty times, meaning that the four platoons fired a total of six-hundred rounds.

When the smoke cleared, both literally and figuratively, the edifice of the church was pockmarked with black scars, and nearly half of the congregation of two-hundred, including a young, slim, and prematurely grey priest, lay dead or wounded, while the other half cowered in fear inside the church. Turning his survey of the carnage into a theatrical performance, the young prince knelt down next to one of the least severely wounded parishioners and whispered in his ear. "Before your soul descends into Hell, I want you to know that it was the Prince of Anhalt-Bernburg who sent you there" Then, in a mock display of sympathy, the Prince gently placed one hand on the wounded man's chest and patted it lightly. At the same time, he withdrew a short, slim blade from his belt and slowly slipped it into the man's side, working his way past the man's ribs and slowly puncturing his lung.

Before standing, Christian examined his blade and chose to leave the dying man's blood on it. He then straightened up to his full height and, before addressing his troops, struck a heroic pose by placing one boot on his victim's chest. Waiting just long enough for a well-timed gust of wind to cause his velvet cape to billow out boldly behind him, the black-clad and black hearted prince addressed his troops.

"Warriors of Anhalt and Bernburg, and loyal servants of our rightful king, Friedrich V the Elector Palatine, today you have struck a blow for freedom from our Catholic oppressors and for independence from our most Unholy Roman Empire."

This comment was met by a round of sniggering from the prince's troops.

"Years from now, your children and your childrens' children will sing your praises for what you have done here today. Now, I pray you accompany me inside so that we may finish our most noble mission."

Zahara had entered the castle more than eight hours ago. As Šarlatová and Roan huddled together in the spot where she had made her remarkable transformation, they began to worry. Shivering in the cold of an unusually damp September morning, they had no way of knowing exactly what time it was, but they knew it was nearly dawn.

"At what point do we stop waiting?" Šarlatová asked.

"And do what else? Go in there after her? Two people that the entire Catholic universe is looking for are just going to waltz into the largest castle in Europe....to try to find a cat?"

"When you put it that way...."

"Well what other way is there to put it?" Roan asked. "I'm as worried as you are, dívka, but there's not a damn thing we can do until...." The sound of snapping twigs stopped the Moravian giant mid-sentence. As Roan silently drew *Schwert* from its scabbard, Šarlatová deftly nocked an arrow and locked her aim on the source of the sound. Although the sight in her left eye had still not completely rebounded from the last use of her....*gift*, she could see perfectly well out of her right eye and remained as skilled of a marksman as Roan had ever known.

As the two waited quietly behind a stand of trees, the sound of leaves rustling drew their attention slightly left of the earlier sound. There, panting heavily, and lying on its side was the same cat that had departed from their company several hours earlier. The cat appeared to be exhausted and in some distress, but not having any clue what to do about it, neither Šarlatová nor Roan dared approach.

They watched for several minutes that felt to both like several hours, but they witnessed no improvement in the cat's….that is, Zahara's….condition. Eventually, they exchanged a knowing glance. Without saying a word, Roan expressed to Šarlatová that, perhaps, it was time for her to employ her ability again, but she forcefully shook her head. "You used it to heal Theo…." he started.

"And look what happened when I used it the time after that," Šarlatová protested.

"That was an accident. I'm sure that this time…."

"No!" Šarlatová's objection was both louder and sharper than she had intended. But while she was scared of revealing their position to any guards patrolling the perimeter of the castle grounds, she was much more terrified by the prospect of having to use her power again – even if it was to save a life.

Before Roan could continue the argument, the cat made a sound – one that Roan was certain was completely unlike anything any animal had ever produced. As it mewled, the animal writhed and contorted as if going through some sort of seizure. When it finally settled down, it was no longer breathing heavily. In fact, it appeared as if it wasn't breathing at all.

Friedrich V, the Elector of the Palatinate and the unofficial King of Bohemia, was a simple man, and he did not have the qualities expected of a good sovereign. Only fourteen-years-old when he was orphaned by the death of his father, Friedrich was the logical choice to become the new head of the Protestant Union – a military alliance founded by his father (Friedrich IV). When a series of Protestant princes (most notably, Christian I) aligned with him and rebelled against Emperor Matthias, those same princes offered him the Bohemian crown. However, it was not his namesake nor the accomplishments of his father that had motivated the Bohemian nobility. Rather, the nobles hoped to gain the support of Friedrich's father-in-law, James VI of Scotland who was also James I of England. However, James vehemently opposed the takeover of Bohemia from the Hapsburgs, and the lack of the expected support from the English caused many of Friedrich's allies in the Protestant Union to reconsider their support of the twenty-three- year-old king. Nevertheless, after some initial hesitation, Friedrich ignored the warning of his British father-in-law and accepted the Bohemian crown.

Surprising to no one, Friedrich displayed many of the weaknesses common to someone so young. Specifically, he suffered from a lack of decisiveness, and from an overestimation of his own strength and abilities. For the most part, his counsellors and ministers were able to control him, because in most things he did not have a clear opinion one way or another – except when it came to the trappings of royalty.

The young, well-built king dressed himself expensively and fashionably, and he preferred   celebrations and entertainment to the daily grind of decision making. However, having been declared an outlaw by Emperor Matthias, he had been forced to flee Prague within months of being crowned. The brevity of his reign as the King of Bohemia earned him the derisive sobriquet *der Winterkönig* (the Winter King).

Just as the young Christian II was desperate to win his father's approval, so was Friedrich V eager to win the respect and admiration of the Protestant princes who had persuaded him to assume the Bohemian crown in the first place. And so it was that he found himself personally leading three regiments of men into the Rhineland town of *Kirchberg* (Church Hill).

The denizens of *Kirchberg*, like most in *das Heiliges Römisches Reich*, had first learned Christianity from Byzantine missionaries, but during the fifteenth and sixteenth centuries, they saw the forced introduction of Protestantism – first at the hands of the *Utrakvisté* (Utraquists) and later in the forms of both Lutheranism and Calvinism. However, despite the repeated imposition of Protestantism upon them by various lords or military authorities (including, most recently, Friedrich IV), the people of *Kirchberg* remained steadfastly, albeit unobtrusively, faithful to the Catholic Church and adopted for their patron their own King Wenceslas – a Catholic. The fact that the "Reformed Faith" – which was the officially prescribed belief in Kirchberg – was not being practised had not gone unnoticed, and it was something that Friedrich V intended to remedy once and for all.

Sometime between 1460 and 1485, *Michaelskirche* (Saint Michael's Catholic Church) was erected in *Kirchberg*. Built on the foundations of three stone predecessors, the church was outfitted with a large and new main portal, a new porch on the south side of the building, and a fifteenth century sandstone pulpit, thus making the church one of oldest and most historically significant buildings within the *Hunsrück* district of the Rhineland-Palatinate; consequently, even though it was impossibly far away from both Prague and Vienna, at the furthermost western end of the empire, *Kirchberg* remained an irresistible target for Friedrich's attempt to gain credibility in the eyes of his Protestant supporters.

On an unusually cold morning in early September, Friedrich V, supported by more than two-thousand troops, descended upon the town of *Kirchberg* and made his way straight to *Michaelskirche*. Although it was not raining, the air had a heaviness to it – the sort of grey-green colour that portends a coming storm. It was as if the weather knew what was to come.

Chapter Thirty Two

Ever so slowly, blissful unconsciousness progressed into a dreamlike, foggy awareness which itself then transitioned slowly and painfully into reality. Zahara had never known pain like this before. Certainly, every *Jalad Wukar* knew the pain associated with skin walking. But this was unlike anything she had ever felt before. Having held the cat's form for so long, she feared she wouldn't be able to leave it. And that fear was matched by the sensation she felt as she slowly, painfully transmuted her way back out of the cat's skin.

Despite the fact that the sun had just risen, the light was blinding to Zahara's eyes. She felt as if she had no eyelids at all, and worse – despite the damp chill in the air – the heat from the morning sun burned her skin. *So this must be what it feels like to be born,* she thought to herself. Like a newborn child, she was incapable of communicating, or controlling her limbs, and she felt herself slip into and out of consciousness on multiple occasions. But, as her bones began to recast and brace, and as her muscles rebuilt and strengthened themselves, the pain began to intensify to the point where she no longer had the ability to slip back into an insensate fog. And while she had not eaten in hours, her stomach tightened and spasmed, causing her to retch uncontrollably. Finally, when the sour taste in her mouth came up in the form of a thick, sulfury stream of….something that appeared to be a cross between blood, bile, and hair….the retching ceased and she rolled over into a foetal position. Naked, bathed in sweat, and her breath coming in short, hard gasps, she stared silently at Roan and Šarlatová who remained crouched nervously around her.

The looks on their faces communicated to Zahara that they shared the same questions. *What happened? What do you need? What can we do?* Doing her best to fake a smile, Zahara summoned what little strength she had left before whispering, "I guess I just got lost."

Then, mercifully, everything went black.

The report was absolutely unbelievable. The crimes committed by Count von Thurn had shocked the emperor. But what Christian II had done....well....*There must be a special place in Hell reserved for a man like that, the emperor thought to himself. Man? No – not a man. Only an animal could do what he had done. And his name? Christian II. Why was it that the worst sins always seemed to be committed by people named Christian?* he wondered. And now, to add to the list of atrocities committed by Count von Thurn and Prince *Christian* II, came the report as to the atrocities committed by Friedrich V at *Michaelskirche*. "It simply shocks the conscience," the Emperor said upon beginning to read the report.

Emperor Matthias was an ailing man, suffering from a malignant heart condition which he attempted to conceal but which gave his already angular face an uncompromising quality that was further intensified by extremely narrow eyes – eyes that were now locked onto the contents of the document in front of him.

"Yes, Your Imperial Majesty,....there simply are no words," Cardinal Melchior Khlesl, the emperor's chief adviser, agreed.

For the past six years, Khlesl had served as the head of the emperor's privy council. Like the emperor himself, Cardinal Khlesl aimed, first and foremost, to preserve the dominance of the Roman Catholic Church and the Hapsburg dynasty (in that order). However, unlike most men of power in the empire, Khlesl was a pacifist who sought to make peace between the Catholics and Protestants. Consequently, he had considered not bringing this latest bit of news to the attention of the emperor. However, fearing that his influence over Matthias might ebb if someone else supplied him with these updates, the Bishop had brought the report to the emperor almost as soon as he had received it.

As the emperor read further about the *Bildersturm* going on in Bohemia, he became suddenly irritated by the presence of others, and desired to be left alone. With a dismissive flick of his hand, he dispersed his army of advisors and attendants – which was just as well. His closest advisors knew what else was in the report, and they wanted no part of being anywhere near the emperor when he read what Friedrich V had done.

According to multiple eyewitnesses, the Protestant prince had, upon entering the town of *Kirchberg*, made his way straight to *Michaelskirche*. He and his men had then reportedly entered the church, brazenly washed their hands in the baptismal font, and over-turned the church's irreplaceable pulpit, destroying it in the process. Apparently, as the prince had swaggered his way to the high altar, some of his troops had taken to urinating on the two side altars, while others had used the confessional boxes to violate some of the women of the congregation. And any man who had attempted to intercede, or had even just protested too loudly, had been executed on site.

From there the pompous prince had apparently lectured the congregation on the importance of fidelity to the "Reformed Religion," promising them that their temporal sacrifices at the hands of rebellious princes would be rewarded in Heaven, and that those fanatics who clung to the "cult of Catholicism" would never know what it means to look God in the face.

And as outrageous as these affronts were, they were easily equaled, if not exceeded, by what Christian II and his men had done in *Židovské město*. After having slaughtered almost every attendee at a wedding mass in the *Kostel svatého Ducha*, he and his men had used the blood of their victims to inscribe two messages on the interior walls of the church. One read *Erinnern St. Bartholomew*, and the other read *Für Gaspard de Coligny*.

Admiral Gaspard de Coligny was a French noble and a leader of the Huguenot cause during the sixteenth century French Wars of Religion. Just four days after the infamous Saint Bartholomew's Day Massacre in August of 1572, an attempt was made on his life in Paris. As he made his way home one evening, an unknown assailant fired from an upstairs window down onto the street below. While de Coligny was not killed, the bullets tore one finger from his right hand and shattered his left elbow. The would-be-assassin managed to escape. Two days later, while he was recovering from the earlier attack, Coligny was set upon again – this time in his own home.

A team of men killed his servants, stabbed him in the chest with a sword, and threw his body out of his own front window, onto the street below. Ultimately, his attackers beheaded him in the street. Because both attempts on Coligny's life, as well as the wedding day massacre itself, were linked inextricably to the militant French Catholic Duke of Guise, Protestants in France and throughout Europe had raised Coligny to the level of martyr, and the fact that the Duke of Guise and many of his men were themselves later assassinated by the French Catholic King Henry III had not dampened the fire of outrage felt by many Protestants. The despicable actions of Christian II and his men were ample proof that the anger towards Guise, dead now for thirty years, still raged among European Protestants.

"Damn them! Damn them both! Damn them both to hell!" the emperor shouted out loud, even though there was no one else left in the room. *Can't they understand what I'm trying to do here?* he asked himself.

Long before he had become Holy Roman Emperor in 1612, Matthias' personal motto had been *Concordia lumine mair.* A firm believer that *strength derived from unity*, he had long hoped to bring about a compromise between the warring Catholic and Protestant states within his empire, which was precisely why he had elevated Cardinal Khlesl to the position of de facto head of the government.

In fact, as early as 1578 (years before he even knew who Khlesl was), as Governor-General of the Spanish Netherlands, Matthias had set down rules for religious peace within most of the United Provinces of the Netherlands. Fifteen years later, at the age of thirty-six, he was appointed governor of Austria by his brother, Emperor Rudolph II. There, guided by Cardinal Khlesl, he forged the Peace of Vienna, which guaranteed religious freedom in Hungary and granted additional political power to the people of Transylvania.

Additionally, during his first six years as emperor, he had granted religious concessions to Protestants in Austria, Moravia, and Hungary. But this record of conciliatory policies had long been opposed by the more intransigent and ardently Catholic members of the Hapsburg dynasty, including at least two of his brothers. Now – old, ailing, and without an heir – Matthias feared he could no longer prevent a take-over by the more militant factions within his own family.

Already his younger brother, Archduke of Austria Maximillian III, was collaborating with their cousin, Ferdinand of Styria, and Archduke von Stormsong to supplant him. He often wondered how much longer he could stand against the Protestants, the Bohemian rebels, and the radical Catholics within his own family. It appeared that he had to either abandon the conciliatory policies upon which he had staked his reputation, or allow himself to be unseated by those who wanted to wage wholesale war throughout the empire. And the actions of these rebellious Protestants were not making things any easier.

Why can't Protestant nobles like von Thurn, Christian, and Friedrich see that things will be far worse off for them if either my brother or my cousin supersedes me? he thought to himself. Must I crush them all, simply so that I might remain in power? And if that is the case, why do I hesitate? Am I not God's anointed servant? Why should I stay my hand, delaying the inevitable, if He has already sanctioned ahead of time all that I might do?

As doubt began to invade his thoughts, Emperor Matthias began to wonder if the failure of his religious and administrative policies was itself a sign from God. *Could He be so displeased with me? Might that be why He has left me without an heir?*

Seven years ago, when he was fifty-four years old, Matthias had married his first cousin, Archduchess Anna of Austria, who was twenty eight years his junior. The closest they had come so far to conceiving a child was four years ago when rumours about Anna's significant weight gain led Matthias to believe that she might be with child. In reality, her increased girth was due to an overactive appetite.

Considering for the first time the possibility that God wanted him to put an end to his attempted diplomacy, and realising that inaction was a much greater threat to his remaining political power than any course of action that he might pursue, the emperor made his decision. He promptly called for the return of Cardinal Khlesl.

"Yes, your Imperial Majesty," the cardinal said upon reentering the throne room and bowing.

"Send for Archduke von Stormsong, Melchior. I would speak with him."

"Yes, your Majesty. When would you like to see him?"

"Now, Melchior. Right now!"

Chapter Thirty Three

As impressive as the entirety of Vienna was, the archduke was far more enthralled by one tree within *Stephansplatz*.

Der Stock-in-Eisen (staff in iron) was a midsection of tree trunk into which hundreds of nails had been pounded over the years. The practice of keeping *Nagelbäume* (nail trees) had been a well-known and time-honoured tradition in southeastern Europe since at least the twelfth century, when travelling smiths and apprentices would hammer a nail into a tree trunk for good luck – the thinking being that hammering nails into trees, much like tossing coins into fountains or wishing wells, could bring one health, fortune, and happiness.

While *Nagelbäume* could be found in most cities throughout the empire, this particular tree, a forked spruce which likely started to grow around 1400, was held in place by five iron bands dating back to 1575 and was surrounded by many legends. According to one, a thief had hammered the first nail into the tree as he was fleeing the forest. Another told of a locksmith's apprentice who had been denied permission to marry his master's daughter and stole a valuable nail and pounded it into the tree as an act of defiance. But the one that most intrigued the archduke was the legend that the Devil had placed the tree trunk in iron and driven the first nails in himself. And while no one could articulate just why the Devil would do such a thing, the legend had persisted, even going so far as to claim that the Devil had (again, for reasons passing understanding) kept careful watch over the tree for the past two-hundred years.

Something about this fabled tree and the bizarre myths surrounding it had always appealed to the archduke; and as he was already in Vienna's *Stephansplatz*, overseeing the restoration of *Stephansdom*, he had the opportunity to regard it once again. However, also because he was already in Vienna, it did not take long for word of the emperor's summons to reach him, and he was just as unhappy with having his time with *der Stock-in-Eisen* cut short as he was with being sent for by a man (even his Emperor) whom he felt was his inferior in every way imaginable.

"I beg your pardon, Your Highness," Lord Oddvar said upon approaching the archduke. He never understood what von Stormsong's fascination with this stupid old tree was, but he hated to interrupt the Archduke nonetheless. "But a rider just arrived from Vienna. He's been travelling straight through the night, and he bears an urgent message from His Imperial Majesty, Emperor Matthias."

"And just what is in this message that is so urgent that it warranted interrupting my solitude this morning, Lord Oddvar?"

"It would appear that His Imperial Majesty has summoned us.... that is, summoned you. To an audience. In Vienna, Your Highness."

Sighing heavily, the Archduke responded, "Very well. Let's go see what that impotent old cripple wants now."

Lanzo Oddvar knew that there was no love lost between the Stormsongs and this particular Hapsburg monarch, but it still shocked him to hear the archduke refer to the emperor in such insulting terms.

"Begging your pardon, Your Highness, but do you really think it is wise to refer to our emperor that way? After all, he is elected by the Grace of God, our Emperor, King in Germany, Hungary...."

"Yes, yes. I know all of his titles, Oddvar. I know them by rote. But simply because a man holds three dozen titles does not mean that he is worthy of my respect. In fact, I would wager that the more titles a man holds, the more incompetent he is. And this emperor's incompetence is more than equal to his number of titles. It simply knows no bounds."

"Your Highness?"

"Think about it, Oddvar. When he was made Governor of the Netherlands, it was without the backing of and against the will of his uncle, Philip II of Spain. When he finally returned to Austria, after having bent over backwards to appease the rebellious Dutch Protestants, he attempted to become elected bishop three times, and failed each time. He then attempted to become the Polish King and failed yet again. Within two years of having finally wormed his way into the governance of Austria, the farmers there revolted and he had to resort to hiring mercenaries to quell that pitchfork mob. He waged traitorous civil war against his brother Rudolph, accidentally triggered *der Huldigung Streit* (the Tribute Quarrel), and inadvertently helped to create *der Horner Bund* (the Horner Confederation)."

It was clear now to Oddvar that the archduke was not going to let him get a word in, so he mutely nodded, prompting the recitation of the emperor's failures to continue.

"He married his first cousin, whom he has been unable to im-pregnate, managed to father a bastard of some unknown whore, and has authored one conciliatory policy after another to the Protestants who are forever bemoaning their lack of religious freedom. And he has, thus far, done absolutely nothing to avenge what was done to Counts von Chlum and von Martinitz this past May. He spends his entire day cowering behind the purple cassock of that damned pacifist bishop, whose advice, if we can call it that, has allowed the empire to dissolve into a ghastly farce of what it once was. He is old, weak, and stupid, and he fails completely to comprehend any of the basic obligations of the monarchy, and all of this a time when the empire must, by needs, be governed by a vigorous and powerful man."

"Yes, Your Highness. Of course. But he is, in fact, still...."

"Yes, Lord Oddvar. You're quite right, of course. After all, while he is totally incompetent to govern, controlled and governed by oth-ers who have given him evil counsel, and completely unwilling to listen to good counsel, he is still our emperor....*at least for the moment*. Let us go see what doth trouble him today."

Lord Oddvar had no idea what the archduke had meant by "at least for the moment," but he was afraid that he soon would.

The term mews referred to royal (or otherwise magnificent) stables, so called because they were originally built where monarchs' royal hawks were once mewed, or confined at mew (moulting) time. Stephen had saddled and mounted the first horse he could find upon entering the mews at *Schloß Stormsong*. He would have been better served by waiting for one of the grooms or stable boys to select a proper one for him for, in his haste, he ended up with a disagreeable mare named Kimber. While the mare certainly looked to be a great and powerful animal, and while she was capable of tremendous bursts of speed – albeit only for short periods of time, she had a demeanour that suggested that she would rather sleep or eat than run. She was no nag; on the contrary, she was one of the finest looking and physically strongest animals Stephen had ever seen in *Schloß Stormsong's* mews. The simple fact of the matter was that Kimber was incorrigible; she just wasn't going to do *anything* she did not want to, and apparently getting Stephen to his intended destination in a timely manner was just not one of her priorities.

As he alternated between berating the lazy animal out loud and silently cursing her in his head, Stephen continued to study the map he had found inside of *Don Quixote*. The map pointed the way to the island town of *Lindau im Bodensee*, and for several days now, that had been his destination.

A former fishing settlement set along an important trade route between Bavaria and Italy, the beautiful town of *Lindau*, with its sturdy Linden trees and its complex maze of narrow streets, existed on an island on the eastern side of *die Bodensee* (Lake Constance), placing it extremely close to the borders of both Switzerland and

Austria. While the town had exchanged hands many times over the years, it had been made a Free Imperial City in 1275 by King Rudolph I (the first German king from the Hapsburg line), and apparently – unbeknownst to most, including Stephen – the Franciscan monastery that had been founded in *Lindau* in 1224 (and subsequently closed in 1528) now belonged to the Stormsong family.

Despite being an extremely well educated man, Stephen was not familiar with *Don Quixote*. After all, the second part of Cervantes' masterpiece had only been written three years earlier. However, had he been acquainted with the comic foibles of the man from la Mancha, he would have laughed. Here he was, a chivalrous knight so desperately in love with a beautiful woman who didn't love him that he had undertaken a knight's quest to discover the truth about said woman's enemy – an equally stunning and mysterious, red-haired witch.

He wasn't quite tilting at windmills, but he was pretty close to it. At minimum, he felt that he was living out a farce that belonged in some Shakespearean comedy. Like the King of Navarre in *Love's Labour's Lost*, his infatuation and childish romantic notions had set him on a path that most would find either comic – or tragic. Comic because he had no more sense of what he was doing than Vanessa did when she hastily departed *Schloß Stormsong* several days earlier. Tragic because his nobility and chivalry seemed to be rendered useless and outdated by the senseless violence and the jarring deprivation of the times, and because his quest was almost certain to end where it began – with his love for Vanessa still painfully unrequited.

That gut-wrenching realisation hurt Stephen far more than the painful injury from which he had only recently recovered. While he knew that there was no such physical ailment as a broken heart, he still felt a deep physical pain in his chest when he thought of Vanessa.

To most, trite phrases like *heart-broken* or *love-sick* were simply poetic metaphors. But the physical pain Stephen felt was no trite metaphor; on the contrary, it was as real as any other serious bodily injury he had ever incurred. However, as he was not the type to gently nurse his wounds, he simply refused to lay in bed, pining away for a woman who didn't love him. Instead, as he had always done whenever he had suffered a setback of one kind or another, he intended to put one front in front of the other and press forward.

So, almost completely undaunted by either the absurdity of the situation or the increasing lethargy of his mount, Stephen pressed on, determined to reach the defunct Franciscan monastery at *Lindau am Bodensee*, where he hoped to discover why Father Joseph had so cleverly and covertly arranged for him to go there in the first place.

Chapter Thirty Four

Vanessa, Starke, and Rabbi ben Mordecai arrived at Schloß Stormsong just a few hours after both Stephen and Zahara had left it. While she was hesitant to meet with her father again so soon, Vanessa felt compelled to do what she could to aid the rabbi in his efforts to win some concessions for the Jews of *Josefov*.

Upon entering the main gates of her home, Vanessa felt a mixture of both disappointment and relief when she learned that her father had left for Vienna during the time since she had left on her quest to find the red witch. She was even more disappointed (but, again, somewhat relieved) when she learned that Stephen had also left *Schloß Stormsong*, without so much as a by your leave from anyone. When she learned that Bishop Theodor Riphaen and Lord Lanzo Oddvar were also unaccounted for, she began to grow curious and concerned. It was then that she sought out Father Joseph and found him in the unlikeliest of all places – *das Hirschgraben* (the Deer Moat).

The Deer Moat (or *Jeleni příkop*, the name by which the locals knew it) was a natural ravine that extended for nearly a mile along the north side of the castle. The moat was so named because the land on the other side of it had served as a breeding ground for deer since the thirteenth century. Although the fire of 1541 that had destroyed much of the castle and the surrounding lands had also driven nearly all wildlife away from *Schloß Stormsong* for several decades, the deer had once again repopulated and now roamed freely on the grounds adjacent to the moat.

Vanessa was surprised to find Father Joseph standing on one of the many muddy bridges that crossed the moat; after all, he was no Saint Francis of Assisi. Unlike the venerated Italian Catholic preacher, Father Joseph was not known to be a great patron of nature or wildlife. On the contrary, he was much more comfortable indoors than outside. More than once, he had remarked to Vanessa that nature was to be avoided at all costs because it was dirty, dangerous, and full of things that could poison, bite, and maim. While Vanessa found that nature was one of God's greatest panaceas, capable of easing anxiety and improving one's overall outlook on life, Father Joseph avoided it at all costs. In fact, he often referred to nature as "God's smiling killer," capable of swallowing ships or reigning fire from above, which was why it was so surprising to her that she found him on a bridge overlooking *das Hirschgraben*, especially on a particularly cold late-September morning.

In a reversal of one of their previous encounters, this time it was Father Joseph who sensed Vanessa's presence before seeing her. "Bless you and welcome home, my little Raven," he said without turning to face her. But Vanessa immediately noticed a heaviness to his voice that had not been there when they had last met.

"Father Joseph? How did you know it was me?"

The short and round priest turned to face Vanessa and her companion. But the usually robust and affable clergyman, with his double-chin and signature halo of white hair, seemed to have aged several years since Vanessa had last seen him. His shoulders appeared more stooped than usual, and his gentle brown eyes lacked the sparkle that she was used to seeing in them whenever he saw her.

"I have my ways, Raven. Just as you do. *And*....I was expecting you," he said cryptically.

"What *ways*, Father Joseph? And how could you have been expecting me? I only recently made the decision to return. And why are you outside in the cold? You hate the outdoors. In fact, have you ever even seen *das Hirschgraben* before today?"

260

"Nature appeals to me these days," he responded wistfully. "I feel closest to God when...." The priest trailed off, seeming to be lost in thought.

Just as Vanessa removed her blue cloak and approached him, fully prepared to wrap it around him in an attempt to comfort him, he seemed to come back to himself for a moment. "Ah, but you have a guest with you, don't you? And who might this be?"

"I am Rabbi Avrem ben Mordecai," said the rabbi as he approached to shake Father Joseph's hand.

"Wunderbar! How nice to meet a fellow man of the cloth! Well, may God bless you, too, Rabbi ben Mordecai, and welcome to *Schloß Stormsong.* But what is it that brings you here .... alongside our little Raven?" he asked with more than a hint of suspicion in his voice.

Hoping to ease the father's mind, Vanessa answered for the rabbi. "We ran into each other in *der Kunratice Wald.* He came here with me to seek father's help with....something. We didn't know that he had left for Vienna."

"To seek your father's help with what?" inquired the priest.

"Is there somewhere we can speak, Father Joseph?" asked the rabbi.

"What's wrong with right here?"

Turning to look at Vanessa and receiving a nod of approval from her, he began. "Father, I am from a small part of Prague called *Židovské město.* Perhaps you've heard of it? It is well known for its old synagogue and the *Kostel svatého Ducha.* Despite a rather troubled past, Jews and Christians in *Židovské město* have learned to peacefully coexist and even prosper over the past three hundred years. At least until recently. You see, of late...."

Father Joseph interrupted as if he had heard nothing but the name of the town. *"Židovské město,* you say? You mean *Josefov?"*

Vanessa and the rabbi turned and looked at each other. "Yes, father. Have you heard of it?" Vanessa asked.

"Oh yes, my child. I'm quite afraid that I have heard of it. Quite recently, in fact. Have you not heard? Christian II, the young prince of Anhalt-Bernburg just….well, I'm afraid he did unspeakable things there."

"Did what *things*? And to whom?" the rabbi asked. But before Father Joseph could answer, he added, "This *Christian*, is he another marauding Catholic, doing the bidding of the Archduke? Trying, once again, to cleanse the empire of Jews? Trying to serve God by eradicating people instead of sin?"

While Vanessa placed a hand on the agitated rabbi's arm, Father Joseph responded. "He most certainly is not a Catholic! He is a Protestant – a brigand and a heretic of the House of Ascania, and I assure you, *rabbi*, that any harm he did to your people was measurably outweighed by the atrocities he committed against the Catholics at *Kostel svatého Ducha*."

"You'll understand and excuse me, father, when I say that I neither trust nor believe you! And even if I did, do you think for one minute that it matters which *type* of Christian committed these latest sins? Catholic? Protestant? What's the difference? To us, you're all one in the same – ravenous vultures who will not be sated until you have devoured your pound of Jewish flesh." With that, the rabbi spun on his heel and began to quickly make his way off the bridge. As Vanessa redonned her cloak and moved to follow him, Father Joseph reached out and grabbed her by the arm, exerting more pressure on her than she had thought the old priest was capable of.

"Vanessa! Please don't go! Much has happened since you left, and we need….that is, *I* need to speak privately with you."

"About what?" Vanessa snapped, with more edge to her tone than she had intended. About my absent father? About my missing friend? About the violence that my family keeps perpetrating on innocents? Tell me, Father, what is it that you have been keeping from me?"

Father Joseph released her arm and stood staring at her as if he had been struck dumb. He gave Vanessa the impression that he had so much to say that he didn't know where to begin.

Frustrated and angry, Vanessa said, "I have to go, father. I promised the rabbi I would help him, and I intend to see that promise through."

Vanessa waited for a few more seconds, hoping that Father Joseph would stop her by offering some clue as to what secrets he was keeping from her. But when all he could offer was, "Bless you, little Raven. May God go with you," she spun around and took off after the rabbi who was now running back in the direction from which they had just come. And in her haste, she noticed neither Father Joseph's trembling lower lip nor the solitary tear that streaked down his right cheek. She also never heard him say, "Bless me, Father, for I have sinned."

Chapter Thirty Five

Zahara had been asleep for several hours since her foray into *Schloß Stormsong*, and during that time, Šarlatová and Roan had stood watch over her, trying to conceal themselves as best they could in the foliage surrounding the castle.

Hiding in the shadow of the place they most wanted to avoid had been a tenuous enough proposition, but doing so while trying to care for Zahara had been an even riskier enterprise – especially when their food had run out. Impatient and hungry, Roan had decided to try to work his way around to the north side of the massive fortress where there were rumoured to be hundreds of deer freely roaming about.

He had gotten close enough to deliver a shot from Šarlatová's bow when an argument on one of the many bridges leading back towards the castle had caused him to reconsider. From the distance he was from them, Roan had not been able to see well enough to determine who the three people were, nor were the voices loud enough for him to have heard what they were discussing. But none of that mattered. He simply couldn't afford to be seen; so he had cursed his bad luck, had crept back away from *das Hirschgraben*, and had retreated back to the spot where he had left Šarlatová and Zahara.

"Keine Glück?" Šarlatová asked as Roan dropped her bow into her lap in frustration.

"Ja....keine Glück. I had a bead on a nice big stag what would have kept all of us fed for a week, but some fools got too close, so I made me way off."

"It's okay. I'll give it a try later," Šarlatová offered by way of consolation. But Roan knew that she would not leave Zahara's side until the remarkable black woman recovered and awoke.

"*Nein.* There's lots of little towns and villages scattered around here. I'll go into one of them and find something there. You stay here with her."

"We have no money. How are you going to pay for food?"

"Who said anythin' about payin' for it?"

Šarlatová smiled. *Good old Roan*, she thought. *It's comforting to know that some things never change.*

"How much longer do you think she'll sleep?" he asked Šarlatová.

"I don't know," she admitted. "I've never seen anything like that before."

"*Ja....*there's been a lot of that lately, *dívka.*" This comment earned Roan a sharp glance from Šarlatová, but he chose to ignore it and continued. "Anyway, we can't hide out here forever. Sooner or later, someone's going to discover our little refuge here, and we'll end up in stocks inside of that damn castle. Or worse, and I'd hate to see the Stormsongs do to you....or her, especially after what they did to Hester and Herman."

The responding cold tone of Šarlatová's voice and the vacant, trancelike expression on her face both seemed extremely menacing to Roan, and he felt a cold chill go down his spine when Šarlatová said, "They won't hurt us, Roan. In fact, they'll never lay a finger on me or on anyone close to me ever again. As God is my judge, they won't."

Not knowing what else to say, and discomforted by just how scared he was of this girl he had known for fourteen years, Roan said nothing at all. As he stared down at her, he contemplated just how little he really knew about this girl. He knew nothing of her family and didn't even know her real name – then again, Šarlatová didn't know either of those either. And, how much did it really matter? After all, as he had told her many times, a man has two families

– the one he's born with and the one he makes for himself. And he had made Šarlatová a part of his family long ago. Still, much like the girl herself, he had, until recently, had no idea just how powerful she truly was. While not educated in any formal sense, Roan was by no means stupid. However, he could make no sense of what he'd seen Šarlatová do at the execution of their friends. And he understood even less the....*abilities*....of this African girl with whom his adopted daughter was so obviously taken.

Frustrated by the ever increasing complexity of the world around him, Roan fell back to two of his oldest friends – profanity and food. "Fuck it all. Whether we're stayin' or goin,' I'm hungry enough to eat the shit right out of a dead horse's ass. I've got to find us some food."

The fact that Šarlatová didn't acknowledge him at all further confirmed for Roan that she was simply....elsewhere. She was apparently buried so deeply within her own thoughts that she was barely even aware of his presence. Grunting and walking away in a huff, Roan repeated to himself what he seemed to be thinking all too often lately – *Dívka, you'll be the death of me yet.*

Built sometime during the thirteenth century, *der Alte Stier* (the Old Bull) was the most popular Kneipe (tavern) within walking distance of *Schloß Stormsong*. It was one of the traditional centres of social and political life in Bohemia, a meeting place for both the local population and travellers passing to or from *Schloß Stormsong*. It offered various roast meats, as well as simple foods like bread, cheese, salted pork, and bacon, but unlike most of its competitor establishments, *der Alte Stier* served very little wine. It did, however, serve beer – lots and lots of beer.

Consequently, this particular *Kneipe* had become a refuge for rogues, scoundrels and outlaws. In fact, the crowds it attracted made it so disreputable that educated men and proper women avoided it completely, and it came to symbolise opposition to the rigid class structure endorsed by both the empire and the church. As a result, proper authorities like the church, and "society types" like the Stormsongs regularly condemned the drunkenness that was so prevalent within.

Drinking itself was tolerated amongst the men, as long as they lived up to both the rules of the tavern and the societal norms and demands of their roles as husbands and fathers. However, the whoring, swearing, gambling and knife fighting that went hand-in-hand with the drinking were viewed by "proper German society" as morally degenerate and, therefore, subject to constant regulation – thought by local authorities to be best achieved through a myriad of taxes.

Control however, wasn't the only reason for the complex web of confusing, and often contradictory, taxes. Ever since the Hapsburgs had gained control of Bohemia in 1526, they had kept the taxes there particularly high because Bohemia, which was unusually wealthy in both agriculture and commerce, was able to yield more taxes than any other part of the empire – so much so that the taxes collected from the Bohemian people provided for more than half of the cost of the administration of the entire Empire.

Roan entered the raucous establishment intent on "finding" some food that he could bring back to the refuge he was sharing with Šarlatová and Zahara. At first, he was quite encouraged to see that Emma Wagner was tending bar. She was a former member of *die Roten Teufeln* (the Red Devils) who had chosen to leave the group and had decided to pursue more legitimate employment after her husband, Max, had died as a result of injuries suffered during one the Red Devils' raids. While she bore no ill will to the group, after Max's death she had decided that she didn't want her two children, Sonja and Johann, to grow up to face the same prospect that their father had. However, that had in no way changed her sympathies or allegiances, and as the new owner of *der Alte Stier*, she did all that she could in that capacity to support any of the various bands of outlaws within *die Volks Knechte* – and that made her a trusted friend.

267

Unfortunately, it appeared to Roan that his trusted friend was, at the moment, in need of some support of her own.

"I told you already that we haven't sold that much beer here this month," Emma was saying to the two Imperial tax collectors who were standing uncomfortably close to her while she tried to tend to the crowd of men seated at or near the bar. "How are you going to tax me on twelve kegs of beer when I ain't sold but six or seven this month?"

Exasperated, and wanting to vacate the increasingly tense scene as soon as possible, one of the tax collectors replied, "It's quite simple, Frau Wagner. When we were last here, you had eighteen kegs on hand. You now have only six. That means that you've gone through twelve of them, or...."

"Or they've been stolen from me."

"Again?" asked the second tax collector.

"Again," responded Emma, defiantly crossing her arms over her broad chest. Like most of the women who worked at *der Alte Stier,* Emma was hard-faced and brawny, and she had eyes that were much too small for her large and round face. Those small eyes were currently locked in a defiant stare on her two antagonists.

"Frau Wagner," continued the second man, "Everytime we come here, you claim that you have been the victim of some robbery or another. What are we to make of that?"

"You can make of it whatever you want, *Herr* tax collector. Maybe it just means that the Archduke and the Emperor need to do a better job of takin' care of their people so that they're not always so hungry that they need to resort to stealin' from me just to keep their bullies full. Maybe while your wealthy bosses are buildin' castles and sendin' their children to expensive schools and armin' their troops, they could set aside a little somethin' for schools or roads or buildin' some hostels for the poor. But until they does, people is going' to keep stealin' to feed themselves, and I can't pay taxes on what's been stolen from me."

That comment was met by a chorus of cheers from most of the men assembled in the tavern, making the two tax-collectors even more nervous and uncomfortable. The two knew full well that men in their profession had been reviled for more than two thousand years. Mentioned many times in the Bible, tax collectors had been routinely criticised and condemned for their perceived greed and collaboration with the Roman Empire; and, because modern tax collectors routinely amassed great personal wealth by demanding and collecting payments well in excess of what was levied by the Emperor, they were hated as much by seventeenth century Europeans as they had been by Jews during the time of Jesus. Feeling a sense of impending danger emanating from the hostile crowd within *der Alte Stier,* these two particular tax collectors wisely decided to vacate the premises so that they could return at a later date, and in larger numbers. However, as they turned to make their escape, they were blocked by Roan, whose massive form filled the entire doorway.

"Guten Tag," he offered as he put his massive hands on the shoulders of the two men. "Now you two look like good God-fearin' Christians, so I bet you know all about Jesus' parables about the tax collectors, don't you?"

"Of course," offered the first man, swallowing hard and finding the size of Roan's hand in comparison to his own shoulder very disconcerting.

"Sehr gut! Then you know that Luke's gospel tells a story of a pharisee and a tax collector who went to the temple to pray, *Ja?"*

Misinterpreting Roan's question as support for their position and occupation, the second man said, *"Ja!* The pharisee prayed about how good he was, but the tax collector asked for God's mercy because he knew he was a sinner. And Jesus said that it was that tax collector who went home justified before God."

"Das ist richtig, mein Freund!" Roan complimented, slapping the man hard on the back. "In fact, Jesus said *'Everyone who exalts himself will be humbled and he who humbles himself will be exalted,'* didn't He?"

Practically beaming now with the sense of security that came from having this massive man on their side, the two tax collectors smiled, laughed, and nodded in agreement. But just as they did so, Roan's face darkened and he pulled the two men close to him – so close that they could smell his body odour and feel his hot, foul breath on their faces.

"But herein lies the problem, boys. There ain't no Jesus Christ in this here tavern. Ain't no saints or pharisees either. In fact, it's nothin' but sinners in here. And if the two of you doesn't get the fuck out of here right now, I'm going to be *exalted* by everyone here when I *humble* you....right up the ass....with either my fist or my sword!"

The ripple of laughter that spread throughout the tavern was a reaction both to Roan's statement and to the wide eyed look of sheer terror on the faces of both of the tax collectors. However, before the two men could make their retreat, a rugged soldier – one nearly as big as Roan himself – rose from a table he was sharing with three other soldiers.

"Halt!" he ordered. Moving Roan's way, he added, "You will release those two men. And you will show them the proper respect that their title requires, for they serve the empire and they serve you."

As the other three soldiers stood in support of their brother-in-arms, Roan took note of the Stormsong coat of arms displayed on the breastplate of all three soldiers and licked his lips in preparation for the fight that he knew was about to take place.

Releasing his grip on the two tax collectors and shifting it to the pommel of *Schwert*, Roan smiled at the three soldiers. "Okay? How about you all *serve* the empire and *serve* me right now....by coming over here and polishing my balls for me?"

As the four soldiers drew their swords, Emma barked, *"Nein!* Take it outside, Roan!" But the massive Moravian defiantly held his ground, standing quietly and calmly in front of the approaching soldiers.

"Now you boys have two options, as I see it. You can either put those swords back in their scabbards, or *we* can put them away for you. But I don't think you'll like where *we* put them."

270

"And just who is this we you're talking about, brigand?" asked the first soldier. "I don't see anyone here but a fat, foul-smelling, red-headed bastard. Shouldn't take me more than a few seconds to teach you a lesson."

In response to the soldier's challenge, more than a dozen other men stood, producing axes, swords, pikes, and a variety of clubs. One at a time, each one announced "I am *we*."

Hopelessly outnumbered, the four soldiers sheathed their blades, slowly approached the tax collectors, and very calmly and quietly escorted the two terrified men out of the establishment.

Once the six had left, but before the two dozen Bohemians who had risen in Roan's defence had retaken their seats, Roan looked to the barkeeper and asked, "Now, Emma, tell the truth. How many kegs of beer did you sell last month?"

Without missing a beat she announced "Twenty-two!"

The resulting chorus of laughter from within the walls of *der Alte Stier* could be heard half-way to *Schloß Stormsong*.

Chapter Thirty Six

Since they had left *Schloß Stormsong* so suddenly, and because their trip to *Židovské město* was expected be a relatively short one (made even shorter by the fact that Vanessa had the money to hire a boatman to cross the *Vltava*), Vanessa and Rabbi ben Mordecai hadn't bothered to resupply for the short trip that they had ahead of them. However, within just a few minutes of having left *Schloß Stormsong,* both travellers had realised just how famished and tired they both were. Therefore, Vanessa had planned for them to stop at *der Alte Stier* to purchase some food and drink. However, upon arriving, the sounds of raucous laughter from within *die Kneipe*, as well as the sight of four of her father's soldiers angrily pacing back and forth in the area outside of the establishment, led her to advise the rabbi that they should simply press on and try to find some food somewhere else.

"I'm not afraid, Vanessa," the rabbi assured her.

"I realise that, rabbi," Vanessa responded. "I know that many within the clergy have taken to carrying arms as they travel through this country, so the fact that you do not speaks volumes about your bravery. But it's not a question of courage, it's a question of discretion. We want to get back to *Josefov* as quickly and as *quietly* as possible. Going into that rowdy *kneipe* right now doesn't improve our chances of doing either one."

"Fair enough," responded the rabbi. "But we are in desperate need of food….and water."

"And whose fault is that, rabbi? If you hadn't left *Schloß Stormsong* in such a hurry, we would have had time to eat, rest, and resupply."

"When one's house is on fire, Vanessa, one doesn't dither about. Rather, one seeks to extinguish the flames as quickly as possible. And it would seem that, once again, my house is on fire."

After several minutes of silence passed between them, Vanessa finally noted that, "Rabbi, it seems to me that *your house* is always on fire."

Avrem laughed uncomfortably. "That is, unfortunately, true, Vanessa." Then he paused for a moment, seemingly lost in thought. "Do you know how my people came to be in *Židovské město....* *Josefov....* in the first place?"

Vanessa simply shook her head, prompting the rabbi to further her education into Jewish history. "During the fifteenth century, when the Moors were gradually being driven from Spain, many Jews fell under suspicion for their alleged cooperation with the Moors. Many Jews had been forced to convert to Christianity and became known as *conversos*. Anyone of these *conversos* suspected of deviating from the strictest Christian orthodoxy or of secretly maintaining Judaic customs and rituals while posing as Christians were tortured mercilessly. So, in order to avoid this oppression, countless Jews fled Spain....or were expelled....and came to every other part of Europe."

"And is that how your family came to be here?"

"No....no. My family had already been here for several centuries prior to that. But that's how my wife's family came to be here. And, as an only child whose mother died when I was very young and whose father was....well, suffice it to say that her family is now my family." The rather unusual expression that crossed Vanessa's face caused the rabbi to ask, "What? What's wrong?"

"Nothing....I mean....it's just," Vanessa stammered. "It's just that.... we seem to have rather a lot in common, Avrem. We're both only children. We both lost our mothers at an early age, and apparently we both have....shall we say....*complicated* relationships with our fathers."

"You know something? I think that's the first time you called me by my name, Vanessa. And, yes, we do have much in common.... even more than you realise."

"Meaning what?"

"Meaning that you and my second eldest child share the same name."

The look of utter surprise that crossed Vanessa's face caused the rabbi to laugh out loud. "I know. I can't believe it myself. Granted, she's not *Lady* Vanessa *von Stormsong*, but she is *Vanessa* ben Mordecai, and she is as lovely and articulate as you are. I see much of her in you."

Blushing, Vanessa sought to deflect the focus of the conversation away from herself. "Tell me about your family, Avrem. What are they like?"

Avrem smiled at the mere mention of his family. "Maria and I have been married for more than twenty years. Her family was originally from Oyeregui, in the Spanish kingdom of Navarra, but I met her in *Židovské město*, which is where her family, the Barberos, eventually settled after fleeing from Spain. Her parents, believe it or not, are still alive and live not too far from us and our three children – Talya, the oldest, is sixteen; Vanessa is twelve; and Caleb is a very mischievous little six-year-old. They are the light of my life, Vanessa. And there is literally nothing I wouldn't do for them. They, more than anything else, are what set me on my journey to see the emperor....or your father.... in the first place."

For reasons she couldn't quite identify, Vanessa felt compelled to wait a few moments before saying anything else. After what felt like an appropriately long period of silence, she finally said, "Well, Avrem, they sound absolutely wonderful, and I can't wait to meet them. Now let's get moving so that we can reach them before...."

When Vanessa cut herself off, an ominous silence hung heavily between the two for just a moment. It was Avrem who finally broke that silence when he completed Vanessa's thought for her. "You mean....before....it's too late?"

Vanessa couldn't bring herself to respond to the rabbi, so she remained silent, a silence that was far more meaningful than anything either of them could have said. They simply stared at each other for a moment, nodded, and continued on their way.

The time had come. It was time to meet with the emperor. Actually, it was time to replace the Emperor, thought Archduke von Stormsong. But that would have to wait. For now it was simply time to play the part of a loyal and dutiful subject.

Ostensibly, *das Heiliges Römisches Reich* was a monarchy; however, the title of emperor was not legally hereditary, and the heir could not simply crown himself "Emperor" without having been personally elected. The seven electors were all rulers from various German principalities. The electors from Cologne, Mainz, and Treves were all Catholic Bishops, while the electors from Saxony, Brandenburg, and the Palatinate were all Protestant princes. These six, together with a seventh elector (the King of Bohemia), formally selected a "King of the Romans in Germany," and their selection only became Holy Roman Emperor when crowned by the pope. The last emperor to have been crowned without election was Charles V in 1530; since then, all of his successors were made Emperor by election. But even that was only true in theory. While *das Heiliges Römisches Reich* symbolised the late mediaeval ideal of a single, universal Christendom, and while its ruler was the only Christian monarch with an Imperial title (thus, elevating him above all other crowned heads), that ideal was very distant from reality. The truth was that the empire was a disparate collection of more than two-thousand towns, more than one-hundred-fifty-thousand villages, and more than twenty-four million people, and the notion that one man, any one man (even an emperor), could maintain hegemony over such a vast and varied array of localities, was sheer folly.

However, since at least the middle of the thirteenth century, the Stormsong family had tried. In fact, they now exerted such tremendous influence over the King of Bohemia, and the rulers of the Palatinate, Saxony, and Brandenburg, that the family held a de facto majority within the College of Electors. Thus, Archduke von Stormsong could essentially elect or select whomever he wanted to serve as the next emperor. However, that process was only initiated when there was a vacancy on the throne. And so long as the current emperor, Matthias, lived, the throne would remain inconveniently occupied.

To the archduke's thinking, the *Concordia lumine mair* policies that Matthias had adopted were far too conciliatory towards the Protestants within the empire. After all, were not the Protestants both heretics and criminals? Should not these infidels be dealt with in the most severe way possible? Certainly with the recent actions undertaken by wretched monsters like Count von Thurn, Christian II, and Friedrich V, the Protestants had finally taken off their masks and revealed themselves to be what the Stormsongs had long known them to be – traitors. Not only to the empire, but to the one true God.

And how had this emperor chosen to deal with such apostate rebels? By trying to make peace with them! And when that, as von Stormsong had easily foreseen, had failed, what had he done next? He had summoned the archduke to an audience within *die Wiener Hofburg* (the Hofburg Palace in Vienna) so as to pick his brain for a new strategy. And now, to add insult to injury, the emperor had apparently decided that Cardinal Khlesl should be present for the archduke's strategy session with the emperor, and it was the cardinal himself who summoned von Stormsong into the Imperial apartments with a simple wave of his chubby hand. *As if this feckless little scrap of humanity has the authority to so much as summon me to wipe my ass!* Archduke von Stormsong thought, upon being called into the emperor's residence.

From approximately 1279, *die Wiener Hofburg* had been the primary residence of the Hapsburgs in Vienna. At first, the original building was everything but a residence. Instead it was an important component of Vienna's military fortifications and was constantly being expanded to better suit that purpose. It wasn't until the middle of the sixteenth century that Emperor Ferdinand I had moved the royal residence to Vienna and had begun the expansion of the existing wings by adding some new buildings, including the Imperial apartments.

Despite having been here on more than one occasion in the past, Archduke von Stormsong was still impressed by the dozens of rooms which constituted the Imperial apartments. The exceptionally ornamental and theatrical style of furniture, art, and decoration included rich stuccoes, ceramic tiled stoves, and magnificent chandeliers made of Bohemian crystal. The deep gold in the lush tapestries was accented by gold brocade chairs and gold tones in the muted patterned carpet. But the sheer opulence of these rooms stood in stark contrast to the very simple wooden chair that had been offered to the archduke by Cardinal Khlesl.

Choosing to abandon any sense of pretence or protocol, the archduke began with a simple statement. "You summoned me, Your Imperial Majesty."

"Indeed," answered Cardinal Khlesl for the emperor. "You are aware, are you not, of the recent events at the *Kostnice v Sedlci*, and at *Michaelskirche* in *Kirchberg*, and at the *Kostel svatého Ducha* in *Židovské město?"*

Cardinal Khlesl was a small, hatchet-faced, colourless man, with a tight-shut, thin-lipped mouth. He was precisely the type of man who, according to the archduke, should measure his words with a teaspoon, but who, instead, doled them out by the bucketload.

Refusing to respond to the impudent little cardinal, the archduke looked to the emperor and said, "Yes, Your Imperial Majesty. I am aware."

"And....?" asked the cardinal.

"And I am, of course, appalled, Your Imperial Majesty. But, I am also somewhat relieved to hear that you are aware of them, too, Your Imperial Majesty. I was under the impression that Cardinal Khlesl's pacifism had so clouded his judgement that he was simply no longer bringing you the latest news of *der Bildersturm* which has been set loose within the empire."

Cardinal Khlesl's face flushed red with anger. "You would agree, wouldn't you, *Johann*, that sending offers of amnesty *to* and trying to promote some sort of peaceful dialogue *with* these rebels is infinitely more desirable than open civil war."

"Johann, is it?" thought the archduke. "Yes, *Melchior*, I would agree that peace is much preferable to war, but I would also remind you that the lion does not negotiate with the lamb. And these rebels, as you have called them, are heretics and traitors. They have steadfastly refused to consider your peaceful overtures, thus confirming the fact that they are not gentlemen with whom one tries to reach an agreement or compromise by discussion and negotiation. They are common criminals and should be dealt with accordingly."

"You disagree with my attempts to arrive at some compromise, Archduke von Stormsong?" asked the emperor.

"I do, Your Imperial Majesty."

"It is easy for you to do so, Archduke von Stormsong. It is not your empire that hangs in the balance," barked Cardinal Khlesl. Choosing to temporarily ignore his de facto chief-of-staff, the emperor waited a moment before asking a follow-up question.

"What then would you have me do, Johann?"

The archduke paused dramatically. He knew he had an opportunity here, and one that he could not afford to squander, but he also knew the risks of attempting to overplay his hand. "I would not presume to tell you how to run your empire, Your Imperial Majesty." This prompted a derisive snort from the cardinal. "But nor should anyone else – least of all a pacifist who has never even seen a field of battle."

Silence hung heavy in the apartment for several moments. Then, just when the cardinal was certain that Matthias was going to dismiss the brazen archduke, the emperor stood and said, "Have you ever seen *der Schweizertor* in *die Alte Burg*, Johann?" When both the archduke and the cardinal stared at the emperor, failing to catch his meaning, Emperor Matthias followed up with, "Come then. Let me show it to you"

As both the emperor and the archduke stood and made to leave the room, Cardinal Khlesl immediately moved to follow close behind them. However, Emperor Matthias placed a hand on the Cardinal's shoulder stating, "That will be all for now, Melchior. I shall meet with you again later."

Cardinal Khlesl stood in shock and disbelief as his peace-loving emperor and the war-mongering archduke proceeded to leave the room – together and without him.

Chapter Thirty Seven

Das Reinheitsgebot (purity order) was a set of regulations dating back to 1516 which limited the ingredients in beer brewed within the Holy Roman Empire to water, barley, and hops. Roan knew that Emma Wagner's beer, like most in the region, also contained yeast, but he was certain that there was a secret, fifth ingredient that Emma refused to identify. There must have been, he thought; for water, barley, hops, and yeast alone could not take hold of a man the way that Emma Wagner's *Doppelbock* had taken hold of Roan – on more than one occasion. In an attempt to divine what that secret, addictive fifth ingredient was in the strong, malt beverage before him, and in acceptance of Emma's gratitude for having helped her, once again, avoid her taxes, Roan had worked his way through six large steins of the house brew before he finally remembered that he had come to *der Alte Stier* to acquire food for Zahara and Šarlatová – not to get drunk. But that error made him no different from most of the denizens of the Holy Roman Empire. In fact, seventeenth century Germans were celebrated throughout Europe for their seemingly insatiable appetite for drink, and the Germans did not deny the claim. In fact, they seemed to celebrate both the accusation and their inherent vice, arguing through a national proverb that *Germans pour their money away through their stomachs*.

But before Roan could even say a word about Zahara and Šarlatová , Emma placed a towel in front of him. Wrapped up inside were two warm loaves of bread, a slab of salted pork, and a few small pieces of cheese. Thankful for Emma's kindness but embarrassed by his need for her charity, Roan meekly uttered, "Bless you, Emma. But you know I can't pay for any of this. I haven't got...."

"Hush, now, Roan," Emma interrupted. "You pay me when you can, and that's all there is to it. Lord knows you saved me a fortune chasin' off them damn, dirty tax collectors, and you and my Max were practically brothers. That makes you kin. And even if you wasn't, what happens to one of us...."

"Happens to all of us," Roan finished. *"Danke vielmals*, Emma. Speaking of *all of us*, have you seen anyone from *die Volksknechte* in here recently?"

"Not for some time, Roan. The last one I saw was *der Oberst*. Ever since Max's death, he stops by from time to time to look in on Sonja and Johann and to help me out. But even he hasn't been by in weeks." Emma was referring to Sebastian Mauer, who had started leading the band of *Roten Teufeln* (the Red Devils) just before Emma had left the group. "Why do you ask?"

"Only because we've all gotten scattered to the winds ever since..."

"Ever since what, Roan? And where is Šarlatová, by the way? The entire time I've known the two of you, I've never seen the one without the other."

Roan paused, hesitant to reveal too much. It wasn't a question of whether or not he could trust Emma; on the contrary, he knew her to be the soul of discretion. But not wanting to burden her with more than she already had to bear, Roan held back. "It's nothing, Emma. Thank you again, and I'll be sure to let Šarlatová know you asked about her."

"You're going to do better than that, Roan. You're going to repay me by bringin' that lovely *divka* with you the next time you come by....and by not waitin' so damn long before you do. Now off with you before you scare off my respectable and *payin'* customers."

With a knowing laugh and a nod, Roan took his food, swallowed the last off his sixth beer, and headed out the front door of *der Alte Stier*. But as soon as he did, he heard someone shout "That's him there! That's the one." And just like that, Roan found himself surrounded by at least two dozen armed, armoured, and angry Stormsong soldiers.

Die Alte Burg (the old fortress) was the oldest part of *die Wiener Hofburg*. It dated all the way back to the late-thirteenth century and had been constructed by Ottakar of Bohemia, the last of the Babenbergers (the ruling royal family that had preceded the Hapsburgs). It had originally been designed as a simple fort within Vienna's city walls, with four turrets surrounding a square courtyard which was itself then surrounded by a moat with a drawbridge at the entrance. But over the centuries – as possession and control of the fortress passed from the Babenbergers to the Hapsburgs – the old fortress of *die Wiener Hofburg* underwent constant change and expansion.

In the fifteenth century, *der Burgkapelle* (the castle chapel) was added, and during the mid-sixteenth century the façade was renewed in Renaissance style. It was also around this time that *der Schweizertor* (the Swiss Gate), a distinctive red and black piece designed by Italian architect Pietro Ferrabosco, was added, causing *die Alte Burg* to become more commonly known as das *Schweizerhof* (the Swiss Courtyard).

Something about the Swiss Wing of his primary residence appealed greatly to Matthias. Whenever he needed a quiet place to which he could escape so as to avoid the many competing demands for his attention, it was here that he went.

Matthias was much shorter than the archduke, and his long angular face and severely retreating hairline – not to mention his bizarre and fastidiously groomed moustache – gave the impression that he was both cold and severe. In reality, however, he was cheerful; his humour was earthy, and his heart was both big and unpredictable. As evidence of his cheerful disposition, the emperor had offered the archduke a glass of wine from his own personal collection.

"What do you think of the wine, Johann?" he asked as they made their way towards *der Burgkapelle*. But before the archduke could respond, the emperor continued. "This particular red is from the town of Chinon in Touraine and has been cellared for more than ten years. I prefer dry and light bodied wines these days, and this one has particularly strong notes of blackcurrant and anise which I adore."

"Yes, Your Imperial Majesty. I, too, find it quite delightful. However, with all due respect, I should tell you that my taste in wine is reputedly deplorable."

Having gotten the emperor to smile at his self-deprecating joke, the archduke decided to strike. "But you did not bring me here to discuss wine, Your Majesty. Nor did you bring me here to give me a tour of *das Schweizerhof.* Rather, I suspect that you brought me here so that you could get both of us away from Cardinal Khlesl for a moment or two. Am I right?"

The emperor said nothing, but the look he gave the archduke confirmed everything he had just said. It also gave the archduke the sense that he had an opening here – an opening that, if exploited just right, might enable him to use the emperor's good nature (along with his innate weakness and lack of decisiveness) to his own distinct advantage. The archduke also knew that, in situations such as this, whomever spoke first was destined to lose. So he waited, for what seemed like an eternity, until the emperor finally broke the silence.

"I am at a loss, Johann. I desire peace….but my empire is on the brink of war. I long for a son to continue my legacy after I am gone….and yet my wife is as barren as a desert." The archduke wondered precisely what legacy the emperor was referring to, but he chose to remain silent, waiting ever so patiently for the question that he knew must come next. "What am I to do?"

Archduke von Stormsong resisted the overwhelming temptation to smile, took a sip from his wine, and sighed thoughtfully. "Have you prayed on these matters, Your Imperial Majesty?"

"I have, Johann. Repeatedly. Time and time again I have prayed for wisdom. But none has ever come. That is why I seek your counsel."

Even though he knew precisely what he intended to say next, the archduke hesitated as if he was thinking. "I think, Your Majesty, that you have to think less about yourself and more about your adversaries."

"Meaning what?"

"Meaning, Your Majesty, that Cardinal Khlesl hasn't advised you very well….if at all….as to what it is that your enemies really want."

The look of confusion on the emperor's face was all that the archduke needed by way of a cue to continue. "I suppose that he has told you that peace is possible because your adversaries are motivated solely by religion. They are not. Religion is merely a pretext for much deeper and more complex ethnic and political motivations. The immediate crisis of the defenestration has already passed, and any united front the rebels may have once held has already begun to devolve into its component parts."

"Go on."

"The rebellion has multiple leaders, and each one wants something different. For men like Count von Thurn, the rebellion is about religious liberty, but it's also about national freedom, and power. For those like Christian II and Friedrich V, it is much more personal than that. Christian is just a boy who wants his father's approval, and Friedrich seeks the respect and admiration of the Protestant princes who persuaded him to assume the Bohemian crown in the first place. Meanwhile, still others, like Gustav Adelbern and the other so-called *leaders* of *die Volks Knechte*, see the war as an economic campaign for the rights of the poor against their sovereign."

"Cardinal Khlesl never put the rebellion in those terms," the emperor admitted.

"I'm sure he didn't, Your Imperial Majesty. He lacks the strategic vision necessary to see all of the pieces on the board. But

I assure you that each party within this seemingly united front is prepared to sacrifice the interests of the other; so let them do that. In fact, encourage it! Set them against each other. That's how you will put an end to this so-called rebellion and achieve peace within your empire."

"But how do I do that?"

There it was. The emperor had finally asked the penultimate question. The archduke was now mere moments away from putting into place a strategy that would eliminate any and all opposition to the crown; and, once the crown was on the head of someone he had installed rather than on Matthias', von Stormsong would be the de facto ruler of the empire.

"Your Majesty, do you know what the difference between gods and kings is?" Not waiting for a response, the archduke answered his own question. "The difference is that gods don't aspire to become kings. But kings do aspire to become gods. And each of the *leaders* of this unlawful rebellion fancies himself a king in his own right. We need only devise a strategy by which those disparate kings come to fight against each other for control of this revolt – to see which of them is to be the *god* over the others. Once they start fighting amongst themselves, who will remain to fight against you?"

The wait felt like it would last forever. The archduke feared that he had erred in explaining this to the emperor in terms of man's desire to be God-like. After all, who suffered from delusions of divinity more than *der Kaiser des Heiligen Römischen Reiches*? He decided to try a different tactic.

"Think of it this way, Your Majesty. The events of the past few months have brought to the surface many animosities that have been simmering within the ranks of our enemies for years. You... .I mean *we*....need only find a way to get those conflicting forces to engage in internecine warfare, and what better way to do that than by creating the perception of a leadership vacuum within their ranks?"

This time, the wait seemed even longer, and the archduke could actually feel the beat of his own heart pulsing in his forehead and ears. Then it happened.

"And do you have such a strategy in mind to accomplish this, Johann?"

The archduke smiled ever so slightly. "I do indeed, Your Majesty. I do, indeed."

Chapter Thirty Eight

At the head of the group of soldiers in front of Roan was the most ridiculous looking man he had ever seen.

He was mounted on a high charger which was covered with red and blue satin. In addition to an absurdly long blue cape with a gold cruciform sword outlined in red, the man wore a ridiculously large cap that was festooned with a great many jewels, including two double rows of five rubies, each as large as a *Linsenbohne* (lentil bean). He was also accompanied by four richly dressed musicians with silver trumpets who announced his presence by playing their instruments loudly and unceasingly, and by two royal lancers (mounted knights who were usually attended by a group of one or more armed retainers).

Roan did not know who Rowland Gundrham was; but even if he had, he would not have guessed that, beneath all of the bastard's pomp and swagger, lay a deep vulnerability. Quite simply, despite his displays to the contrary, the young captain felt out of his depth. Within the safety of *Schloß Stormsong's* walls, he had grown accustomed to behaving however he pleased, his status guaranteed without question. But outside of the security of those gates, things were quite different. Rowland could not avoid sensing that the Bohemian locals regarded him as nothing more than a young upstart, a bastard devoid of noble blood. And as a manifestation of this sense of inadequacy, he seldom forgave even the most minor slight and was liable to wreak drastic revenge for any perceived insult. In fact, on one occasion when a local satirist had alluded to the bastard's childish behaviour, Gundrham had had the man's tongue cut out and nailed to his forehead.

In this instance, having been informed hours earlier that a local ruffian had insulted a group of Stormsong men at *der Alte Stier*, Gundrham had felt personally slighted. And he decided to rectify the situation in person, but making certain that he did so with the appropriate amount of both flair and security.

"That's him there! That's the one," repeated one of the tax-collectors, shouting to be heard above the blaring trumpets. The two tax-collectors and the four Stormsong soldiers whom Roan had earlier driven away had evidently returned with twenty other men, not counting the pompous little shit who led them and who finally silenced his trumpet players with a wave of his hand.

The men accompanying the overdressed little *Pferdearsch* (horse's ass) wore uniforms that identified them as Stormsong men. But even if they hadn't been wearing uniforms, Roan would have easily identified them as soldiers based on the grimly set jaws, solemn eyes, and stiff postures they all shared.

"Do you know who I am?" asked Gundrham.

Roan paused for a moment to survey the troops in front of him before he spit on the ground and answered. "Nope. But if I had me either a *Taler* or a *Florin* for every little shit what ever asked me that stupid question, then I guess I'd be the one wearin' the fancy hat."

With a facial expression that would have been more apt if Roan had spat directly in his face, Gundrham responded, "Hear me well, you filthy...." But Gundrham lost the thread of insults he was attempting to weave and had to start over. "You are a filthy....damn it! It matters not. I am Rowland Gundrham, the Captain of the Guard for *Schloß Stormsong*, and both you and the owner of this.... *establishment*....are thieves and outlaws."

"And?" Roan asked, spitting on the ground again.

"And....and I intend to arrest both of you and bring you both before the Archduke himself so that he may administer the emperor's justice for your felonious and nefarious behaviour." Emboldened by the troop of soldiers behind him, Gundrham straightened up a bit in the saddle as he made his pompous pronouncement.

"Felonious and nefarious?" mocked Roan, with a little laugh. "Those are some fancy words coming out of your pretty, little mouth there, *Herr Captain*! In fact, the next time I feel like havin' me a fuck, I might just use your mouth. I'd wager it's at least as sweet as me own wife's *Fotze*, God rest her soul." As Gundrham struggled to process Roan's verbal assault, the giant Moravian dropped his towel full of food and made an elaborate show of withdrawning *Schwert* from its scabbard, adding, "Or maybe I'll just fuck you in the ass with this!"

Roan was prepared for the sound of two dozen swords being unsheathed, but he was not expecting the sounds that came from behind him.

"What have we got here?" asked one of the dozen or so men, and women, who had been alerted to Gundrham's presence by the blaring of trumpets and who now stood behind Roan, wielding a wide assortment of weapons.

"Looks like we've got a little Fotze what thinks he's a knight," answered one of the others in the group that had spilled out of *der Alte Stier.* The motley assembly, sufficiently inebriated and more than a little amused by Roan's crude comments, chuckled loudly, while Gundrham, angry and humiliated, shouted just as loudly to his troops.

"Arrest them! Arrest them all! Damn you, arrest them now, else I….."

But before Gundrham could finish, an arrow zinged from the trees surrounding *der Alte Stier* and tore his oversized, jewel-encrusted hat from his head, pinning it to a nearby tree. As Gundrham placed his hand on his forehead to make sure that it was still intact, his men turned their individual and collective attention to the trees from which the almost-deadly missile had flown. But before they could take any further action, four more perfectly aimed arrows found their targets – the instruments belonging to the four musicians who had been on either side of the captain of the guard. Despite the fact that none of the four suffered anything more significant than a scratch, all four fled to positions behind the rest of the troop. One even squealed and another wet his pants. Not one bothered to retrieve the silver trumpet that had been knocked from his hands and to the ground.

As the troop of soldiers was trying to process what had just happened, Emma (who had just stepped outside and who was still polishing a beer stein with her spit and a dirty dish rag) decided to use the confusion to her advantage. "Oh, Roan, I forgot to tell you….I hired me some extra security. You see, someone keeps stealin' me beer, before I can even pay taxes on it. So's I hired me a few lookouts. Best damned archers you've ever seen, and they don't mind hangin' 'round the trees all day, so long as I feed them three times a day."

Having no idea what had just transpired, Roan turned around to look at Emma. Only when she flashed him a conspiratorial wink did he decide to play along with her little charade. "Is that so now, Emma? Just how many of these *damned fine archers* did you hire then?"

Spitting again into the glass she was "cleaning," Emma responded, "I can't keep track. Eight or nine, maybe. Or maybe it's a dozen now. I never could count so good."

The looks on the faces of the remaining Stormsong men said it all. Not only had they lost any element of surprise or intimidation, but they now faced, in addition to the dozen armed brutes in front of them, possibly as many as a dozen skilled archers, apparently hiding in the trees around *der Alte Stier.*

Before the men could overcome their collective hesitation and indecision, Roan decided to press his newfound advantage. He stepped forward to where Gundrham's ridiculous cap was pinned to a tree, removed the arrow, and placed the cap upon his own, massive head. "There now. It don't look so ridiculous on me, does it?"

"*Ja,* 'tis a fine cap indeed, Roan," answered Emma. "Fits you like it was made for you. But what are we to do with the rest of these fancy little fucks who came here to stir up trouble?"

Still unclear as to what was transpiring, but confident either that Šarlatová was covering him from a *Schutzengel* position in the trees, or that Emma had at least some idea as to who had fired the remarkably accurate shots, Roan looked to the rest of the troop of soldiers. "Well, Emma, I figure if they leave their horses and their weapons...."

"And their boots!" added one of the men behind Roan.

"And any food or money they might have on them!" said another.

"And the fancy trumpets," added one more.

"Well....then, I suppose we can let bygones be bygones," Roan finished. Then, as he looked up into the surrounding trees from which the five arrows had flown, he readjusted his new cap and asked ominously, "So....what say you now, boys?"

Lindau am Bodensee was approximately three-hundred-fifty miles southwest of *Schloß Stormsong.* Hoping that Kimber would be able to average around forty miles a day, Stephen had hoped to reach his destination in eight or nine days. However, the lazy nag, whom Stephen had tried to replace more than once, didn't get him there until the twelfth day of his journey.

He had begun by travelling southwest to a ferry crossing at *Regensburg.* On both sides of the Danube, he had tried to sell or trade the incorrigible horse, but had found no takers. Upon arriving in *Ingolstadt* he had tried again, and had tried one final time upon reaching *Augsburg.* Then, having resigned his fate to being stuck with Kimber, he had begun to make the final stretch southwest towards *Lindau.*

When he finally arrived, Stephen's first glimpse of the historic town took his breath away. *Lindau* was situated on an island of the same name in *der Bodensee* (Lake Constance), and its picturesque buildings (including St. Stephan's church), lively squares, and open alleyways gave it a rich and festive atmosphere that was positively palpable.

The lake itself, which was the largest inland body of water in the German states, was placid, and the water a deep, vibrant aquamarine that connected two parts of the empire (Swabia and Austria) with Switzerland. *Der Untersee* (the smaller part of the lake) lay directly on the border between Switzerland and Swabia, while *der Obersee* (the larger part of the lake) which was Stephen's destination, was where Lindau and the entire Austrian shore could be found.

Surveying the town from a ridge on the eastern (Austrian) side of the lake, Stephen bent forward and asked Kimber for her thoughts. "Okay, you lazy bitch. Do you think you can summon enough strength to take us down there, or do I have to walk the rest of the way?"

Kimber responded by dropping a clump of shit from between her flanks and then craned her head around proudly to view her creation.

Stephen sighed and shook his head in disgust, but "I feel the same way about you, Kimber," was all that he could muster by way of a response.

Chapter Thirty Nine

He had done it.

Archduke von Stormsong had successfully convinced Emperor Matthias to resist the temptation to get drawn into a series of minor skirmishes against the heretic rebels and, instead, to engage the various elements of this motley insurgency in one major battle – a battle which the Emperor's forces would conveniently and purposefully lose. Stormsong's thinking (and now the emperor's, too) was that, after a major "victory," the various "leaders" of the rebels would each claim credit for the win and would each try to assert himself as the rightful head of the movement. Once that process started, the so-called rebellion would begin to fall apart from within.

This strategy would serve two purposes. First, the apparent "defeat" of the emperor's forces would further weaken any political support that Matthias still had amongst the German princes, thus making it even easier for the archduke to supplant him. Secondly, as the archduke elevated Matthias' cousin, Ferdinand, to the status of the new emperor, the rebellion would begin to disintegrate from within, thus giving the appearance that the new Emperor was responsible for ending the civil war.

The only obstacle that stood in the way of the successful completion of the archduke's plan was Cardinal Khlesl.

Born into a Lutheran family of bakers, Melchior Khlesl had studied philosophy at *die Universität Wien* (the University of Vienna), where he had been converted to Catholicism by Jesuits. After having been ordained to the priesthood in 1579, Khlesl had soon been appointed councilor to the Bishop of Passau for Lower Austria. Twenty years later he had been named Bishop of Vienna, and thirteen years after that had been placed by then Bohemian King Matthias as the head of the King's privy council. In that capacity, the extremely shrewd and capable "son of a baker" had become indispensable to Matthias and had assisted in securing the position of Emperor for him in 1612. Ever since, the two had sought, quite unsuccessfully, to make peace between warring Catholics and Protestants.

After having been secretly named a Cardinal by Pope Paul V in 1615 (and then having publicly "received the purple" the following year), Khlesl had been allowed by Matthias to conduct most of the secular political affairs of the empire, wherein he had attempted again and again to reconcile the various religious factions by means of reciprocal concessions. However, his conciliatory attitude had come to be resented by the German Catholic princes and, as indispensable as he was to Emperor Matthias, he remained despised and distrusted by powerful archdukes like Maximillian of Tyrol and Ferdinand of Styria. Despite being surrounded by powerful enemies (or, perhaps, because of that), he had continued to grow even closer to the Emperor, and now held so much sway in Matthias' government that many considered him the de facto head of the Empire.

Archduke von Stormsong knew that separating the cardinal from the emperor would need to be done with a very delicate touch – and with an equivalent dose of subterfuge. Having been dismissed by the emperor, von Stormsong made his way back to the imperial apartments and found the Cardinal precisely where he and the emperor had left him.

Wanting to take command of the conversation right away, the archduke chose to speak first. "Cardinal Khlesl, I owe you an apology."

Immediately suspicious, the cardinal said nothing.

"I owe you an apology for not respecting either you or your title. You are an extremely well-credentialed man who is not used to being spoken to as I did. I humbly and sincerely beg your pardon and forgiveness."

Still deeply suspicious, but also enjoying the humble supplication of the usually vainglorious archduke, the cardinal decided to indulge him. "Is this you speaking, Your Highness, or is it the Emperor?"

Cardinal Khlesl couldn't divine the meaning of the archduke's smirk when he answered, "Both, Your Eminence. Both."

"Very well, Your Highness. The lord and saviour to whom I have given my life taught that it is holy to forgive, and so I now forgive you for your impertinence." There was that smirk again, noted the cardinal.

"Your grace and your mercy are unsurpassing, Your Eminence. And it is upon your supreme generosity that I now depend."

Cardinal Khlesl was absolutely loving this. It was clear now that the emperor had delivered a private but serious dressing down of the archduke and had sent him back to the cardinal to receive some further instruction.

"I am your humble servant, Your Highness. How may I serve you?"

This time, with practised ease, the archduke managed to suppress the smirk. "His Imperial Majesty has decided that one final round of diplomacy is necessary and appropriate before engaging the Protestant Bohemians in open civil war. As you have long led that effort at reconciliation, and as I have long opposed it, the Emperor has decided that it is time for us to combine our efforts."

The confused look on the cardinal's face invited the archduke to continue. "His Imperial Highness has ordered me to return to *Schloß Stormsong* and to bring you with me as my guest," he lied. "There, comfortable in the warmth of my hospitality, you and I are to work collectively to arrive at some kind of peaceful conclusion to the unpleasantries of late."

Sensing a trap, the cardinal asked, "Why can we not simply set ourselves to that task here, in Vienna, Your Highness?"

"My thought exactly, Your Eminence. However, His Imperial Majesty wants us to include in our meetings a certain Bishop Riphaen, one of the best strategic thinkers in the empire, who is currently in residence at *Schloß Stormsong* and too feeble at the moment to make the journey all the way to Vienna." Realising that he had not quite sealed the deal just yet, the archduke added, "And it was, after all, a direct order from the emperor himself."

"Very well," conceded the cardinal. Then, his voice oozing with exaggerated sweetness, he added, "I am the emperor's humble servant. When are we to depart, Your Highness? Within the fortnight?"

"Tomorrow, Your Eminence."

"Tomorrow?"

"Yes, Your Eminence. The emperor is most eager for us to begin. Additionally, I am most eager to rectify an error and to do that which I should have done long ago."

"And what error is that, Your Highness?"

"Long ago I should have introduced you to someone who shares Your Eminence's….passion for peace, and I desire greatly to do that as soon as practicable."

"And who would that be, Your Highness?"

"My own personal confessor, Your Eminence. A priest by the name of Monsignor Mučitel. I am most eager to introduce you to him." This time, there was simply no hiding the smirk.

Vanessa was not sure what to expect upon arriving in *Židovské město*, but based upon what little she knew about the Jewish part of Prague, and upon what Father Joseph had told her about the recent atrocities committed there, she was prepared to witness a nightmarish landscape. Instead, she saw movement, colour, modern architecture, and crowds.

From its early existence, *Židovské město* consisted of settlements surrounding a spacious marketplace on the bank of

Vltava. As far back as the twelfth century, thanks in part to the large market that was held every Saturday, the merchants of *Židovské město* became rich, and to protect those riches, they surrounded the town with a wall (protected by more than a dozen gates) and a huge, semi-circular moat connected at both of its ends to the *Vltava* river. Thanks to this security and prosperity, as well as the development of various trades and crafts, this part of Prague became one of the most important metropoles in central Europe.

Despite the fact that several of the more beautiful buildings bore obvious signs of recent damage, and despite the presence of an acrid odour which attested to the fact that the town was still populated by at least a few unburied bodies, the town was far more active, lively, and beautiful than Vanessa had anticipated.

"It's....it's just lovely," Vanessa admitted to Avrem.

"Why, you sound positively surprised, Vanessa."

"I am, I suppose."

"What did you expect?" the rabbi wondered.

"I don't know. Certainly not anything quite this....quite this perfect."

"Well, it's far from perfect, as you can see. But it is home. At least it will be until the next time we're evicted from it." With that, the rabbi dismounted *Starke* and Vanessa did the same. Together they made their way through the streets and headed towards the *Staronová synagoga* (the main synagogue within the Jewish section of Prague). But as they did so, both began to notice the faces of those going about their daily routines.

The expressions of most of the residents were not so much frightened or angry as they were just dull and expressionless. Nearly everyone's face was pinched and pale, with their eyes downcast and cold. Their blank expressions seemed to indicate that the life behind their eyes had somehow been extinguished and that, with nothing to look forward to, they had simply given up.

The silence between Vanessa and the rabbi became palpable, filling the space between them, until it became so uncomfortable that Vanessa felt compelled to break it.

"What exactly happened here?" she whispered.

"I don't know," ben Mordecai admitted. "But I'm afraid we're about to find out."

Within seconds of Rowland Gundrham's ignominious retreat, the woods around *der Alte Stier* produced a varied assortment of *Grüne Gauner, Dreketen Huren,* and *Schwarzen Schurken.* Among them were Franz Hohenleiter, the leader of *die Schwarzen Schurken*, both of the Berger brothers (Simon and Theodore), and a small group of women, including *Einäugige Agata* (One-eyed Agatha), the leader of *die Dreketen Huren* (the dirty whores). The band numbered approximately two dozen, and It was clear that they were hungry, tired, and desperately in need of clean clothes and a wash.

"Jesus Christ," Roan bellowed. "Just look at this motley crew what came to me rescue."

"And just in time, from the look of things" laughed Franz Hohenleiter as he approached and hugged Roan.

"Christ almighty, Franz! It's a wonder the bastards didn't smell you comin'," teased the giant Moravian.

"Or hear us," added *Einäugige Agata.* "Theo's been farting so loud today I thought there was a storm a comin'."

As the members of the two groups began to exchange pleasantries in the only way they knew how (through a series of bear hugs and punches to each other's chests that were punctuated by rounds of spitting, cursing, burping, and farting), Roan approached the Berger brothers and noted, "That's some fancy shooting what you did there, takin' that boy's hat off without leavin' a scratch."

"Fancy nothin'," responded One-eyed Agatha. "That was my shot, not theirs. And I was aimin' for his throat. I'm only sorry that I missed. I guess I should use my good eye next time."

With that, the entire assembly laughed and began to retrieve the cache of weapons, food, and clothing that had been left by Gundrham's men.

"Let's take everything inside and portion it all out," Roan suggested, looking back into the trees from which he and the others had just come. "Unless I miss my mark, those bastards will be back in even greater numbers soon. And we'd be wise to be gone before they are."

"*Ja*," agreed Franz. "*Einäugige Agata's* aim may not be what it once was, but her judgement ain't diminished none."

Roan looked to Franz with an expression indicating that he hadn't understood his old friend's meaning.

"She's right that there is a storm on the way, Roan," he explained. "It'll be here soon, and it has nothin' at all to do with Theo, or his farts."

Chapter Forty

The official language within *der Alte Stier* was a hybrid of German, Bohemian, Dutch, and Polish; the most common profession of those who drank and ate there was anything that began with the phrase out-of-work, and the average length of stay was anywhere between two hours and two days, depending upon how much of Emma Wagner's *Doppelbock* one imbibed. *Die Kneipe's* ambiance, such as it was, consisted of the stink of unwashed bodies and unemptied chamber pots, tables tacky with spilled beer, and a bluish haze that was a combination of cooking fumes and tobacco smoke.

Against this multi-ethnic backdrop of loud and unemployed drunkards, Roan sat in one corner drinking with Franz Hohenleiter and Simon Berger, while Simon's brother, Theo, and One-eyed Agatha sat nearby trying to outdo each other with dirty jokes and horrific tales of bloody executions.

Theo seemed to have the upper hand with a story about an execution he'd witnessed during which the offender had been disembowelled and had had his entrails thrown upon a fire while he was still conscious enough to watch and smell them cooking. As his brother's telling of this tale grew both louder and more animated, Simon pushed away the plate of pickled herring that was sitting in front of him. Despite the fact that he was surrounded by friends, not to mention the raucous din of the now filled-to-capacity *Kneipe*, Simon felt compelled to speak in hushed, conspiratorial tones.

"This is the best I've been able to gather before Theo and I got reunited with Franz and the others," he whispered. "For the past several weeks, imperial troops have been marching out of Vienna, headed northwest towards Prague, where I imagine they'll join up with Stormsong's men. But all along the way, different bands of *die Volks Knechte* have been harassing them with attacks and small skirmishes, and it seems that they've had to fall back towards Budweis where they're regrouping and rearming."

As Simon laid out the latest news regarding imperial strategy for them, Franz and Roan took turns having at the pickled herring that Simon had passed up. Around a particularly wet bite, Roan asked, "But what's happened to von Thurn, Simon? I saw everyone scatter after that mess at *Schloß Stormsong*, and unless my guess is wrong, I bet that some of us have linked up with his troops. But where are they?"

After looking over both shoulders to ensure that no one was listening, Simon leaned in closer to both men. "Best as I can tell, Von Thurn has put Count von Mansfeld in charge of twenty- thousand men, and he's marching those men towards *Pilsen*."

"*Pilsen?*" said Franz too loudly for either Roan's or Simon's liking. "Why in God's name would any of us want to be in *Pilsen?* Why not just hand himself over to the fuckin' Stormsongs while he's at it?"

Located on the confluence of four rivers in western Bohemia, the city of *Pilsen* had been founded by Bohemian King Wenceslas II in 1295. Now one of the larger cities within the Empire, Pilsen – because it was situated on the crossroads of two important trade routes – had grown into an important commercial, cultural, and administrative centre within the Hapsburg dynasty. It had also become one of the richest and most important strongholds for the Catholic loyalists within the Empire.

"Shhhhhh!" hissed Simon. "Any louder and they'll hear you in *Pilsen.*"

"Fuck off!" responded Franz, before slurping down the last of the pickled fish. Sufficiently scolded, he then added, "No one's listening to us anyhow."

"Both of you shut up and let me think for a second," admonished Roan. After a brief pause, he observed that, "It makes perfect sense. If the imperial army is massin' in *Budweis*, then they're halfway between both Prague and Vienna. And that leaves them several days' march from *Pilsen*. So if von Mansfeld lays siege to *Pilsen*....."

"Then the imperial army will have to march on *Pilsen*," Simon continued. "Whether they're ready or not, to relieve the beleaguered *Pilsners*."

"And von Thurn will already be prepared for that, and could catch them out in the open between *Budweis* and *Pilsen*," finished Franz.

"Precisely!" whispered Simon.

"He is a crafty son-of-a-whore, I'll give him that," commented Roan. "But there's one God awful flaw in all that. Even if the imperial army marches on *Pilsen* from *Budweis*, and even if that's precisely what von Thurn wants them to do, what will happen when the Stormsongs decide to join the battle comin' south out of Prague?"

"Then it will be von Thurn who's caught in the trap, not the other way around," concluded Simon.

"And just as the weather is startin' to turn," added Roan. "It's practically October already, and the first snow will be here just in time to make things miserable for him and his men."

"Then we'll have to gather as many of *die Volks Knechte* as we can and get to *Pilsen* first," announced Franz.

"*Ja*, but they're scattered all over the place. You know that as well as I do," observed Roan, at which the table fell into an awkward silence.

"Where do you come by all of this information, Simon?" asked Franz.

In response, Simon simply shrugged his shoulders, smiled, and proffered, "The best way to keep a secret is by keeping it to yourself."

Somewhat taken aback by Simon's rather cryptic and evasive response, Roan announced, "Well, we can start with what we've got here. We'll send out messengers in every possible direction and put out the word to join up as close to *Pilsen* as soon as possible. Šarlatová and I can start by…."

"Šarlatová?" snapped Simon in surprise. "She's with you? Where? I thought…."

Decidedly put off by Simon's sudden display of curiosity regarding Šarlatová's whereabouts, Roan responded rather bruskly. "*Ja*, she's with me. I know where she is, and only I know. And that's the way it's going to stay….for now."

Holding up his hands in mock surrender, Simon leaned back in his chair. "I'm just glad that she's still…..I'm just glad is all."

Trying to make some sense of the awkward interaction he'd just witnessed between his two friends, Franz decided to break the tension by attempting to take command of the situation. "Looks like we've got our work cut out for us then. Roan, why don't you go and retrieve Šarlatová, while Simon and Theo and Agatha and I get everyone here in order?"

"In order for what?' asked Roan.

"For one thing, to get the hell out of here before that pissant whose hat you stole decides to come back with even more men. Before he does, I can get everyone here organised and moving southwest towards *Pilsen*. In a day or two we can meet up in the spot where….well, you know the spot. Along the way, we're bound to run into more *Volksknechte*, and by the time we reach *Pilsen*, we should have enough to help out von Mansfeld and von Thurn."

Simon said nothing, but he was more than a little bothered by the fact that Franz wouldn't bring him into the confidence he shared with Roan. *"What spot?"* he wondered. *"And why is it a secret to keep from me?"*

At the same time, a sombre expression passed across Roan's face, like dark and heavy clouds hanging over a mountain. He knew that he had no gift for all of Simon's and Franz's talk of strategy and tactics. He simply wanted to take his food, find Šarlatová, and get her as far from danger as was possible. But could he turn his back on the duty he felt to *die Volksknechte* in the battle that he now knew was coming? As he weighed his decision, he felt Franz and Simon staring at him, until he finally nodded to both of them and said, "What happens to one of us..."

"Happens to all of us," they both responded. Then, in a solemn but somewhat stilted display of accord, the three men rose, embraced one another and promised to meet again as soon as possible, with each one wondering just how much faith and trust to hold in the other two.

Peter Ernst Graf von Mansfeld was more mercenary than soldier. The bastard son of the Governor of the Duchy of Luxembourg in the Spanish Netherlands, he had been raised in the Catholic faith and, much like Count von Thurn, had gained renown fighting for the Hapsburgs' Imperial Army during the "Long War" against the Turks in Hungary, ultimately rising to the rank of *Oberst* (Colonel). However, a mysterious and undisclosed dispute (either real or imagined) with Archduke Leopold V of the Austrian Hapsburgs had forced him to leave the service of the Imperial Army and drove him into the arms the Hapsburgs' enemies, where (despite remaining a devout Catholic) he had, for the past eight years, increasingly allied himself with the rebelling Protestant princes.

He was tall and thin, with a complexion the colour of candle wax. Taken together with his remarkably long legs, his receding hairline, thin lips and nose, and sharp, protruding chin all combined to give him an unusually stork-like appearance. But there was nothing bird-like about his eyes. In fact, with almost no discernible eyelashes to give them cover, his dark, clear (almost translucent) eyes practically leapt from his face and left him with a penetrating expression that made it clear to all that he did not suffer fools easily.

Those clear, unsettling eyes were currently fixed on a note that had just been handed to him by a mousy little courier with a freckled face and a high grating voice.

"From Count von Thurn, *Herr Oberst*," the courier had squeaked.

"It's bad enough that von Thurn seems to feel that it is necessary to issue written instructions to me on an almost daily basis, but for the love of Jesus what does he always send such mouses to deliver his commands?" von Mansfeld wondered out loud.

"Mice, *Herr Oberst*."

"What's that, boy?"

"It's mice, *Herr Colonel*, not mouses," the courier responded.

With that Mansfeld switched his gaze from the note to the courier, and without so much as a word communicated that the boy had better either apologise or retreat far away from the count, possibly until his voice changed.

As the boy pursued the second of those options and practically ran from Mansfeld's sight, the Count read von Thurn's latest instruction. For reasons not articulated in the order, Mansfeld was to delay his siege of *Pilsen* for another few days. As his army was still another forty miles northwest of *Pilsen*, accommodating von Thurn would be little trouble. But it left Mansfeld wondering.

"What's he at now?" he wondered. *"He's bypassed Lords Demantius and Jassinius to give me command of more than half of an army that he's only had control over for a few months. Now he wants me to delay the very siege for which he gave me command of those troops. And why on Earth does he have me using that army to march on Pilsen in the first place, rather than on Vienna? Or better yet, Prague? With the men I have under my command, I could easily lay siege to Archduke von Stormsong's precious castle and have him in chains by the end of the month."*

As he considered von Thurn's newest command, Mansfeld gazed up into a sky that had just enough light left to turn the horizon into a swirling palette of purples, pinks, and blues. Then, as the moon began to increase its milky white presence in that heavenly kaleidoscope above him, he prayed out loud to God, "Heavenly Father, You are the one, true, and everlasting God. I humbly beseech Thee to grant me Thy wisdom. Show me Thy will, that I might see it done. Graciously hearken unto me and to those who seek Thee, and grant us Thy almighty power so that we may crush Thy enemies. Amen."

Then, as he completed the sign of the cross and crumpled the written order from von Thurn, he thought to himself, *"And please guide me as to just how much I should trust this pompous Lutheran from Bohemia."*

As he slowly made his way from *der Alte Stier* to the spot where he had previously left Šarlatová and Zahara, Roan, like von Mansfeld, gazed up at the strikingly beautiful sky, and he, too, spoke to God.

However, while von Mansfeld offered a prayer that was a solemn and pious request for guidance and wisdom, all Roan had to offer was a frustrated, angry, and irreverent rant.

"Lord, that sweet *divka* you brought into my life after Berta died sure has saved me. In every way possible. And in Your infinite wisdom, You know she's a hell of a lot smarter than an old ox like me. But some of the shit she spouts about you from the Bible just don't seem to hold up.

"She tells me that the word *Holy* means 'set apart for God's special purpose.' She says it's a condition of purity and freedom from sin. She also says that when the good book speaks of Your holiness, it means Your utter separateness from everything else that exists – all of the unholy shit that plagues this world of yours. But if'n You created everything that exists, then shouldn't all of that be holy, too? How can the creator of this stinkin'-shit-pot-of-a-world be Holy and separate from all of it? Or don't You claim responsibility for the evil in this world? Do You just take all the credit for the good and wash your hands of anything evil and claim that it's 'separate' from you?"

Roan then proceeded to walk in absolute silence for several minutes, waiting impatiently for some kind of answer or sign from God. But, as was always the case, he heard none, so he simply laughed at himself. "Christ, now she's got me talkin' to You out loud. Or am I just talkin' to myself? Either way, if'n You can hear me, please bring some of that Holy down here where we common folk can use it. I don't know whether You know it or not, but the whole fuckin' world You created down here is on fire, and there sure is a hell of a lot of pissants with narrow hearts and small minds in some pretty damn high places who are makin' it…."

Roan suddenly cut himself off in mid-sentence. Having arrived at the precise spot where he had left Šarlatová and Zahara just a few hours earlier, he now saw nothing. No weapons, no clothes, no food. No indication at all that they had been there, other than a sizable pool of blood where Šarlatová had earlier stretched out for some much-needed rest. But as for the two women, they were nowhere to be found.

Part Three:

The Storm Breaks

Chapter Forty One

———◦———

The main synagogue of the Jewish community in Prague was also the oldest synagogue in Europe. Dating back to the last quarter of the thirteenth century, the beautiful, Gothic structure consisted of a two-nave hall that was divided by two pillars and was vaulted in five parts. The middle of the synagogue contained an elevated pulpit with seats for prominent members of Prague's Jewish community placed around it, and the east-facing tabernacle contained the Torah, which was not meant to be touched by human hands. The entrance hall on the western side of the building, built at the beginning of the fourteenth century, consisted of two treasuries for tax collectors and two brick gables, while the main nave contained a tympanum (a vertical recessed triangular space forming the centre of a pediment) which was decorated with a relief of vine leaves and grapes meant to represent the twelve tribes of Israel as branches extending from a single bush.

Like most synagogues in most Jewish towns throughout the empire, this one had historically not only served religious purposes, but had also allowed *Josefov's* rabbis to meet with and educate their pupils; and until it had its own town hall, all of *Josefov's* public affairs were dealt with there. Additionally, the main synagogue was a place for documenting the long and sad history of Prague's Jews. Towards that end, the north and south walls of the synagogue's main hall contained Hebrew inscriptions that were meant to serve as reminders of the massacres of Prague's Jews in 1096, and again in 1389, and again in 1469, and again in 1609. During just one of those infamous pogroms (the one in 1389), possibly as many as three thousand of Prague's Jews were massacred in the ghetto on Easter Sunday, and the walls of the tabernacle had been permanently stained with the blood of the victims who were seeking refuge within the synagogue.

As Vanessa and Rabbi ben Mordecai surveyed the new damage done to the synagogue, she was the first to notice the presence of blood stains that were not old. Apparently, during Christian II's massacre at *Kostel svatého Ducha*, a dozen or more of the Jews in the ghetto had intervened by lending aid to the Catholic victims of the assault. For having had the audacity to interfere with the Protestants prince's diabolical acts, those Jews had been brutally executed on the grounds of the synagogue. And, as a twisted warning to not interfere with the business of his so-called "reformed religion" again, the prince of Anhalt-Bernburg had ordered that the blood of his Jewish victims be splattered above the entrance to the synagogue and on the walls of the tabernacle. The young prince had apparently even gone so far as to make a joke about having brought to *Josefov* a new, reformed version of Passover.

All of this information had been relayed to Vanessa and the rabbi by a team of men who were currently in the process of repairing the damage done to the synagogue by Christian II's invaders. In response to Vanessa's questions about what, precisely, had occurred there, one of the men barked at her, "The same thing that always happens when Jews prosper. We get punished for it by Christians."

Before she could offer any response, Avrem defended her by saying, "Nothing that happened here is the fault of all Christians, Yaakov. Christians aren't to blame, least of all this young girl. This wasn't the work of Christians, Yaakov. It was the work of mad men."

"Ken at beemet tzodeket, Ravi," said a second man. "But you do understand Yaakov's meaning, don't you? Persecution....suffering....these continue to be the primary occupations of all Jews."

With a mixture of both anger and sadness in his eyes, Avrem responded by saying, "But, Efrayim, without suffering and persecution, what would we have? Persecution and suffering are the only things that we Jews can truly call our own. Without them, what else is there that's truly ours?"

With that, the rabbi turned and began to walk slowly away from the blood-stained entrance to the old synagogue, causing Vanessa to ask, "Where are we going now, Avrem?"

"Why home, Vanessa," he responded softly. "To see what's left of it."

Upon entering the town of *Lindau*, Stephen knew not where to begin his search; for that matter, he didn't know what he was searching for. Having finally reached his destination, despite Kimber's continued attempts to slow him down, he wandered into *Lindau's* market square feeling very much like a lost child.

As he examined the map he had discovered in the archduke's copy of *Don Quixote*, Stephen continued to recite the passages from the book that had, ostensibly, been underlined by Father Joseph.

"Finally, from so little sleeping and so much reading, his brain dried up and he went completely out of his mind."

But whose brain? Stephen wondered. The archduke's? The emperor's? Or was it, perhaps, Father Joseph's? Who do I know who has gone completely out of his mind?

"The truth may be stretched thin, but it never breaks, and it always surfaces above lies, as oil floats on water."

What truth, though? he wondered. And what lies is the truth supposed to surface above? Are the lies from the person who has gone completely out of his mind? Or did someone else's lies cause that person to lose his mind in the first place?

"The piece you seek is right in front of you."

"The hell it is!" Stephen said out loud. "What piece, Father Joseph? Is it the map? Or is it something else? Damn it, father! Why couldn't you just have said *'Go here! Find this! Do that!'* Why did you have to be so damned cryptic?"

As several townsfolk passing through the marketplace began to stare in Stephen's direction, he suddenly realised that he had just been speaking aloud. Realising that he must have looked like a crazy man to the passersby, he immediately apologised. *"Entschuldigung, Sie, bitte.* I....I have a lot....I'm not feeling well."

In apparent acceptance of his explanation, the *Lindauers* simply nodded courteously and continued on their way, while Kimber snorted as if to say *"You're not feeling well? I'm the one who had to carry you all this way, and for what?"*

Ignoring Kimber's latest derisive snort, Stephen began to refold his map, and as he did so, his attention was drawn to the path taken by the passersby who were now walking away from him and chatting in hushed tones to each other.

They were headed through the market square and in the direction of *die Kirche St. Stephan* (Saint Stephen's Church). Originally founded in 1180, *die Kirche St. Stephan* was no longer in regular use, but with its beautiful stucco ornaments and unusual green-domed steeple, it remained one of the most iconic structures in *Lindau*, and all of Bavaria, for that matter.

"Die Kirche St. Stephan?" he whispered quietly to himself. "Well....I suppose that's as good of a place as any to start. Come on, Kimber. Let's see what Saint Stephen has to offer." With that, he dismounted his horse and walked her in the direction of the church.

Upon returning to *Schloß Stormsong*, the archduke had immediately "introduced" Cardinal Melchior Khlesl to Monsignor Mučitel, who had apparently developed a new form of granting penance. In the cardinals' case, the "Black Eminence" had used an especially agonising process of *internes Brennen* (internal burning), which involved inserting a red-hot poker into a funnel-like device that was placed inside the victim's rectum, and the resulting sounds that continued to emanate from *der schwarzer*

Beichtvater's confessional were a constant source of amusement to the Archduke.

Less amusing to him, however, was the constant pleading by Bishop Theodore Riphaen, von Stormsong's own Apostolic Nuncio, to either release Cardinal Khlesl or to end his suffering with a swift and merciful execution.

"Your Highness, I implore you, if not for the sake of mercy, then for political expediency, please release Cardinal Khlesl from his suffering."

"My dear Bishop, Cardinal Khlesl is barely human. He's a fraction of a creature....no....a cancer is a more apt description. He is a cancer on the German body politic and it is well and good that I have it removed."

"But must it be removed so painfully, Your Highness? Would not it be better to simply.... *remove the cancer*....as it were, than to let it linger in such agony? After all, he is a Catholic, and a fellow man of the clergy. Whatever his sins, should it not be for the Lord our God to decide his fate?"

"Perhaps," replied the Archduke absentmindedly. But when it was clear that von Stormsong had nothing more to say than that, Bishop Riphaen interpreted that as his sign to leave. As he moved to do so, the archduke stopped him.

"Theodore, you said something a moment ago. What was it? Something about 'political expediency.' What was that?"

"Yes, Your Highness," responded a cautiously optimistic Bishop Riphaen. Sensing that he might have found an opening into the Archduke's thinking, he decided to press his advantage. "I simply meant that the emperor is certain to hear of what has befallen Cardinal Khlesl. I mean, it's only a matter of time....and now that you seem to have the ear of the emperor, wouldn't it be wiser not to anger him? You know how close he is to the cardinal."

The Archduke paused for a moment. "Perhaps you're right, Theodore. Maybe it is time to reconsider my....position regarding the cardinal. Yes, perhaps it is finally time."

"Yes, Your Highness. So what will you do, exactly? Surely you don't intend to return him to the emperor. Not in the....condition.... he's currently in."

"Of course not. Do you take me for a fool?" But before Bishop Riphaen could respond, the Archduke raised his hand and waved him off. "I mean simply to put an end to Cardinal Khlesl's ....*confession*. Thank you, my dear bishop. As always, you've been most helpful. That will be all for now."

Chapter Forty Two

Roan knew better than to call out to Šarlatová.

Doing so would only invite unnecessary and unwanted attention. But he simply couldn't help himself. Unable to find either of the two girls, he began by whispering Šarlatová's name for several minutes. But when no answer followed, he began to call out for her loudly. And when still no answer came, he began to curse....even louder.

"Son of whore! I should have known better than to leave her with that fuckin' Muslim.... shapeshiftin'....whatever she is. If she's touched so much as a hair on that girl's head, I'll rip her heart out from her chest and serve it back up to her for breakfast, and I don't give a damn what kind of fuckin' animal she turns herself into. Damn it!"

As he continued his search, he wove an exceptionally creative and descriptive tapestry of profanity that, more than once, included promises like: *"An eye for an eye? A tooth for a tooth?* Well, fuck that all to Hell and back. If that girl's been harmed at all, it will be *a heart for an eye and a soul for a tooth,* so help me...."

But he just couldn't bring himself to utter God's name. Then, after several more minutes of searching and calling out for Šarlatová failed to yield any results, Roan dropped his bag of food and sat down right next to the pool of blood, which was the only indication that anyone had been there at all. Uncharacteristically, he began to calm down, closed his eyes and then proceeded to do something even more uncharacteristic for him. He asked for help.

While Roan had generally shown scant evidence of piety, leading more than a few to suspect that he had little more than a purely ceremonial belief in God, as a result of what Šarlatová had taught him these past fourteen years, he had actually acquired at least a surface faith in the existence of the heavenly Father that she so often spoke about. And while he didn't have even a fraction of the relationship that she had with Him (after all, she really seemed to know Him….personally….as if she could actually speak to Him and hear from Him), he had come to believe that God was real. However, it was not until this precise moment, when he had no answers and no hope and could find no solace in anything else that he finally turned to God for help.

He began the way that Šarlatová so often did. "God of Abraham, and Isaac, and….that other fellow….I forget his name, I am unworthy of Your grace, and I don't expect that you give two shits about a worthless old sack of….well….shit like me." Roan paused and muttered under his breath, "Christ, I am really fuckin' bad at this." Then he paused again before attempting an apology. "Sorry about sayin' shit….*twice*. And for sayin' fuck….*twice*. And for usin' Your son's name in vain. But, according to *dívka*, You are a very forgivin' type. So I hope that's all okay."

Roan paused again before conceding, "Look, I'm not goin' to pretend that I'm a religious person, God. And I wouldn't blame you if'n you told me to go….well, you know. But Šarlatová tells me that You have already revealed Yourself to her in so many amazin' ways, and I pray now that what she says is true. Let it be true that You sent Your only son to save sinners like me. Let it be true that the creator of the universe loves me and loves her. Please reveal Yourself to me and show me the path to findin' that girl. She's all that I have, and….."

In that moment, Roan realised just how fragile he was. He realised that he had nothing at all in this world besides Šarlatová, and that he had no way of finding her by himself. And he even acknowledged the fragility of his own faith, cursing himself as a hypocrite for only now turning to God for help, when he could have done so much earlier.

Then, as he sat in stunned silence and placed his hand in the pool of blood next to him, something deep within him gave way, and he uttered words that he never thought he would say. "God, I need You. Please help me. On the blood of Your son Jesus Christ, I ask You for help. I beg of You that You forget my sins and that You show me the way to...."

But before he could finish, Roan heard a piercing scream coming from the direction of *der Alte Stier.* The scream was almost immediately followed by a deep and strong male voice yelling, "Come this way! Over here!"

At first unable to process this unexpected turn of events, Roan quickly recovered and leapt to his feet. Then, completely forgetting the bag of food he had carried with him before, he abruptly ended his prayer by saying, "Well....shit! Thanks, be to Thee....or You.... or....whatever. Just ....thanks, Jesus! Šarlatová never told me that you worked so damned fast."

And just like that, Roan was off, headed in a full sprint back in the direction of *der Alte Stier.*

The archduke wanted to see for himself what Monsignor Mučitel had done with Cardinal Khlesl. And while he was far from squeamish and almost immune to the sights and sounds of violence and torture, even he was unprepared for what awaited him in Mučitel's "confessional."

Cardinal Khlesl's skin, usually pale to the point of being colourless, had turned dark red. His face twitched continuously and, while he appeared to not be consciously controlling it, his whole body periodically convulsed, as if possessed by a demon. A wet, gurgling sound spilled from his throat and blood from ruptured vessels had burst out across his face, arms, and chest. A terrible smell of burning flesh and hair hung heavily around the cardinal, and what little hair remained on his body was singed and glowing orange. Most remarkably, it appeared to the archduke that the cardinal's body had actually shrunk or crumbled so much that, like a rotting piece of fruit, it had shrivelled into a putrid mass of meat and juice.

"You've really outdone yourself this time, Monsignor," complimented the archduke. "Is it still alive?"

"It's hard to tell, Your Highness," hissed the sadistic priest. "But even if he....*it*....even if *it* is, it stopped responding to pain long ago."

"Is that a fact?" With that, the archduke produced a slim blade from his belt and used it to slice the cardinal's ring finger clean from his hand, producing nothing by way of a response from the cardinal himself.

As the archduke toyed with the severed digit, he admired the cardinal's episcopal ring. Traditionally, when the pope elevated a bishop to the cardinalate, he gave him a ring (the style of which was determined by the pope himself) as a symbol of his consecration. This unusually large ring, given to him by Paul V just two years earlier, was solid gold and set with a sapphire, bearing an oblong crucifix on either side of the bezel.

"Have you prepared the note for our dear emperor as I requested?"

"Yes, of course, Your Highness. It requires only your signature and seal."

"Very well. But let's include this with it," he ordered as he handed the severed digit to the priest. With that, the archduke signed his name and affixed his seal to the note that Monsignor Mučitel had written days earlier.

Once the note had been signed and sealed, Monsignor Mučitel donned a thick pair of gloves and very carefully placed the parchment and the cardinal's ring and finger inside of a cane tube. A tube that also contained pieces of a shroud that had recently been used to wrap the cadaver of a prisoner who had died of the plague.

Monsignor Mučitel had absolutely no idea what *yersinia pestis* bacteria was; nor did anyone else in Europe, for that matter. But he did know that whatever was on the shroud was still quite potent, as evidenced by the fact that the young slave whom Mučitel had ordered to place it in the tube had contracted flu-like symptoms just two days after having handled it. That same slave, who had subsuquently been locked away in one of *Schloß Stormsong's* most isolated dungeons, was now experiencing fever, a hacking cough, headaches, incessant vomiting and painfully swollen lymph nodes throughout his hands, arms, and chest. He, like the man whose shroud he had been ordered to place inside the tube, had also developed several dark blotches on his skin and had started to give off a disgusting stench which seemed to leak from every part of his body.

As Monsignor Mučitel sealed the tube and cast the gloves aside, the archduke realised that, if all went well with the delivery of his message, Emperor Matthias would be similarly poisoned by the contents of the tube, and would be dead within just a few days of having received it.

After the archduke had donned his own pair of very thick gloves, the priest delicately handed the carefully sealed tube to him. Then, as he toyed with the deadly device, he couldn't stop himself from smiling. And lifting the tube up as if to toast the sinister priest who had handed it to him, he said, *"Auf die Gesundheit von der Römisch-Deutscher Kaiser."*

The rabbi's homecoming had been a blessed affair – lots of hugs, lots of kisses, and plenty of tears; and after all of the reunions and introductions had concluded, Vanessa had been invited to sit and share dinner with the rabbi's family. Maria had prepared *Cholent*, a savoury stew-like dish that included beef, barley, potatoes, and beans. It was a simple dish, but Vanessa had never tasted anything like it before. Even better was the *Kubaneh*, a slow-cooked bread that Maria had baked for the next day's Shabbat, but which was prematurely pulled apart by hungry hands and used to sop up the last remains of the *Cholent*. The bread had a rich, buttery taste with just a hint of tomato to it, and Vanessa was quite certain she could have eaten the entire pan by herself.

During the dinner, Vanessa marvelled at the dynamic of the family's conversation and dinner rituals. Talya, the oldest, was an extremely inquisitive sixteen-year-old. She looked remarkably like her father, and spoke like him, too. She participated in the family's conversation as if she was an equal to the adults, and she was treated like one by her parents.

Vanessa, the twelve-year-old, looked much more like her mother. She was already beautiful, and with her jet black hair, thin nose, and olive skin, she could have passed for Persian, and she had far more Barberos in her than ben Mordecai. She said little, but she missed nothing. She tracked the conversation like a predator stalking its prey, but her visual scrutiny always came back to Vanessa.

Caleb, the very mischievous six-year-old, was a perfect blend of both mother and father in terms of appearance, but he was quite unlike any of the others in his behaviour. He was extremely loud and fidgety and could not sit still at the table for more than a few seconds at a time. He had to be constantly reminded to eat his food, and whenever he did take a bite, he was back up again almost immediately, constantly asking his mother if he could go "over there." Given how small the house was, there was very little "over there" available, but the lack of space didn't prevent him from trying. Vanessa was amused by the fact that his mother, Maria, constantly played the role of enforcer, trying to impose some structure upon and instil some manners within the boy, while Avrem simply said "Go ahead, Caleb," to nearly everything the boy asked.

When Vanessa inquired about which parent "ruled the roost" so to speak, both Avrem and Maria laughed and indicated that the other was the authority figure in the family. Talya had followed that up with "Well, you know what Alfonso the Magnanimous said about marriage, don't you?"

Maria and Avrem had clearly heard this before, but Vanessa played the role of charitable guest and asked, "No, what did he say?"

Talya immediately brightened and sat up straighter in her chair. Beaming with pride in her ability to educate their beautiful guest, she stated, "Alfonso the Magnanimous was the King of Aragon and Sicily and Naples during the fifteenth century. In fact, he was one of the most prominent political figures of the early Renaissance, and he said that having a happy marriage requires that the wife be blind and the husband deaf."

Vanessa laughed loudly and sincerely and asked Maria, "Is that true? Is your happiness predicated upon your pretending that you don't see what he does and upon his pretending that he can't hear you?"

Maria blushed and smiled. "I don't know. Is it?" she asked her husband.

When Avrem pretended that he couldn't hear Maria's question, everyone laughed and his wife jabbed him hard in the ribs.

"Not so hard, Maria. I haven't finished digesting the *Cholent* yet."

"Ha! With as much as you ate, you won't be finished digesting it until sometime next week," Maria teased, causing Caleb to laugh so uproariously that he fell to the ground. It was clear that he hadn't quite gotten the humour from Talya's story about King Alfonso's keys to a successful marriage, so he attempted to more than make up for it by significantly overreacting to his mother's joke, which he did understand.

After dinner, the conversation turned to the success (or lack thereof) of the rabbi's trip and the recent hostilities that had occurred at *Kostel svatého Ducha*, at which point Vanessa had excused herself to sit outside of the simple two room home. She had made some excuse about needing to stand and stretch her legs after such a sumptuous meal, but the truth was that she felt fine – at least physically. The hospitality of the rabbi's family had warmed her heart (and filled her stomach), but she was still left wanting. The rabbi's near perfect family had left her feeling forlorn and somewhat sullen. She suddenly realised that she would never know what it was like to have a brother or a sister; she would never get to help her mother bake bread, and she would never feel the warmth of her father's loving embrace. The intimacy of the family's conversation, the knowing looks they exchanged, the welcome hugs and embraces they shared all combined to leave Vanessa feeling rather hollow and empty – which was ironic considering how full she was after sharing the family's meal.

She was prepared to reenter the house and offer to help with the dinner dishes when Vanessa, the twelve-year-old, came out and sat down next to her.

"Is your name really Vanessa?" he asked right away.

"Yes, it is."

"Mine, too. But I'm not a princess like you."

Vanessa smiled. "I'm not a princess either. I am a Lady."

"What's the difference?" the child asked.

Vanessa paused. "You know, I'm not really sure."

"I'll ask Talya. She'll know. She knows *everything*," Vanessa responded, rolling her eyes in the process. "But if you are a Lady, shouldn't you know what that is?"

"Yes, I suppose I should," Vanessa admitted, but before she could add more, the child interrupted her.

"Are you Jewish? We're Jewish. Are you? I think you should be, but only if you love God. You do love God, don't you?"

"No, I'm not Jewish, but I do love God….most of the time. I'm Catholic."

"What's that mean?"

"It means that I'm a Christian."

"What's that?" Vanessa asked, twisting her head as a dog might when trying to make sense of some new sound. But before Lady von Stormsong could respond, the child added, "Let me guess. You don't know what that is either."

As Avrem came out to collect his precocious daughter so that he could set her to work at helping in the kitchen, the child stood up and announced to her father, "Daddy, I like your new friend. She's very pretty, but she doesn't seem to know who or what she is."

Avrem picked up his daughter, laughed, and quoting verse two of psalm eight said, *"Out of the mouths of babes*, Vanessa. *Out of the mouths of babes."*

But to which of the two Vanessas the rabbi was speaking wasn't entirely clear.

Chapter Forty Three

Sometime in the early-sixteenth century, after several unsuccessful attempts on his life, Pope Julius II created the *Pontificia Cohors Helvetica* (the Pontifical Swiss Guard), an elite armed force and honour guard unit designed to protect both the Holy See and the Apostolic Palace within the Vatican. As one of the primary duties assigned to them by Julius II, the members of the Swiss Guard were to be present during any masses he celebrated, both to protect him and, if necessary, enforce discipline among unruly worshippers. While the commissioned officers of this official papal escort (captains, majors, vice-commanders and commanders) wore a completely red uniform with golden embroidery on the breeches and the sleeves, the rank and file members were outfitted in a distinctive Renaissance-style uniform, allegedly designed by Michelangelo, which consisted of brightly striped garments, black berets, ceremonial swords, and very intimidating halberds (a two-handed pole weapon approximately five to six feet in length).

Approximately four years later, unbeknownst to anyone but a select few within the Swiss Guard, Julius added to this elite corps the post of Prior General. The purpose of this secret office was to serve as the Holy See's *Canis Iustitia* (Hound of Justice), meaning that his regular duties included travelling throughout Europe to collect monetary levies, censor sermons, snuff out any signs of heresy, and (if necessary) "refer" heretics to the Inquisition. He was even empowered to interrupt priests mid-sermon and forcibly remove them from the pulpit if they strayed into any controversial or unsanctioned territory.

Over the course of the sixteenth century, a series of popes from Leo X to Clement VIII had made frequent and effective use of the *Canis Iustitia* as they each did their best to confront the challenges imposed by what the heretics of the day so blithely called "the Reformation."

The latest holder of the secret title of Prior General was a sinister-looking Jesuit by the name of Father Abaddon Sohar. With his black soutane, heavily scarred bald head that was often covered by a matching black zucchetto, wild and unkempt black beard, flashing eyes, and ghostly-pale skin, this seven-foot-tall giant was one of the most feared and intimidating men in all of Europe. In fact, to the few stunned onlookers who had seen him at work and survived to bear witness to what they had seen, he seemed to possess an almost superhuman power to bend the world to his purpose. Even the Holy See himself, Pope Paul V, had described Father Sohar – only in private, of course – as a "giant in both body and soul who was as difficult to manage as he was violent."

His facial expression, even when called into service by the pope, was perpetually flat and muted, as if someone had chiselled a dull and lifeless affect on his face for all eternity. But everything else about the man seemed to exist on a magnified scale – everything, that is, except for his voice. Having, for reasons unknown to anyone but Pope Paul V and himself, not spoken a single word in the thirteen years of his service to the pope, there were virtually no people alive anywhere in Europe who had ever heard his voice.

Utterly incapable of either reading or writing, and unwilling to intrude on papal secrecy even if he could, Father Sohar knew nothing of the content of the letter he carried with him. He knew only that it was to be hand delivered to Archduke von Stormsong as soon as possible. Had he possessed either the ability or the inclination to read the note, he still would likely not have understood the meaning of the passage which read: *"We are credibly informed that Cardinal Khlesl has been taken from Us, against both his will and that of the emperor's, and that he is, at present, your prisoner. However, should he be returned to Us uninjured and unhurt, you might retain Our Apostolic favour in the same manner in which you formerly enjoyed it. On the other hand, should he be harmed in any way, We would be vexed most grievously."*

The pope had increasingly found himself dithering between two sources of contrary advice regarding what to do with the Stormsongs. There were those within the *Curia Romana* (the official administrative body of the Roman Catholic Church) that advised the Holy See to remain faithfully aligned with the Houses of Hapsburg and Stormsong, while others counselled him to move steadily away from the "treacherous Austrians" and to seek closer ties with the Bourbons in France. Because he hopped back and forth between these two contradictory strategies, and because his sixty-six years on Earth had, unfortunately and comically, left him with only two front teeth on top and two on the bottom, he had earned for himself the nickname *Papa Lepus* (the Rabbit Pope). But on this issue, the capture and imprisonment of a Catholic cardinal, there could be no dithering. A note of warning had to be issued, and Father Sohar was uniquely suited to deliver it.

However, when he wrote the stern warning, Pope Paul V did not know that Cardinal Khlesl had already been killed, nor that his episcopal ring, along with the finger on which he wore it, was already en route to the emperor. But even if the pope had known, he still would have sent Father Sohar, for this was not a diplomatic mission he was sending the priest on. No one in his right mind, least of all Pope Paul V, would ever send a man like Abaddon Sohar on an errand requiring tact or diplomacy. He simply wasn't equipped for that. This was a mission of force, and Sohar knew it. His sole objective was to put the note in the hands of the archduke himself, and to dispatch with extreme prejudice anyone who would stand in the way of that goal.

As he prepared to ride out from the Vatican, on an enormous stallion worthy of his massive frame, so as to begin his long journey to *Schloß Stormsong*, Father Sohar stared blankly at the young groom who had been tasked with saddling his horse for him. Unable to meet the giant's piercing gaze, the groom looked down at his own feet and prayed to himself, *May God bless whoever this man is looking for, and may He grant that person a good head start; because whoever you are, something not human is coming for you. Every monster from every children's story you've ever read is real, and they're all set loose tonight.*

Then, as if he could, through some supernatural ability, actually hear the boy's silent prayer, Abaddon looked down at the groom and did something most uncharacteristic.

He flashed the boy just a hint of a terrifying smile.

Roan, on the other hand, was not smiling. He was running – faster, perhaps, than he had ever run in his life. As he did, everything suddenly became extraordinarily sharp to his senses. Every rock that he jumped over, every pine branch that either his head or his arms snapped, even the minute rustling of his scabbard against his filthy and mud-caked clothes all provided additional stimulus to him and spurred him to run faster and faster.

Try as he might to *not* contemplate what may have befallen Šarlatová, an icy cold sense of doom blossomed inside of him and took such complete hold over his imagination that every other conscious thought began to blur. Roan was so completely focused on reaching Šarlatová that he completely missed the large and shadowy form that lurked just a few hundred yards ahead of him, directly between him and his destination – *der Alte Stier.*

As the sounds of violence – men shouting, women crying, metal striking metal – echoed up into the dense forest around *die Kneipe,* Roan slowed just enough to draw Schwert from its scabbard, and to take stock of his surroundings.

A ghostly wreath of smoke coming from *der Alte Stier* added to the heavy, brooding clouds that already hung low over the entire area, and an acrid smell of gunpowder drifted up into the trees. Convinced now that something wicked was afoot, Roan turned to begin his descent down towards the sounds of violence, but just as he did so, the dark clad figure, nearly as large as Roan himself, burst from the trees in front of him, and tackled him around the legs.

Taken completely by surprise, Roan dropped his sword and went sprawling forward, landing face down on the cold, hard forest floor. As he struggled to make sense of what was happening, he felt the black clad figure climb on top of him, pressing his face down into the earth so hard that he felt the bone and cartilage of his nose crumble like a stale biscuit. As Roan felt blood ooze from his badly broken nose, he continued to hear a cacophony of distressed cries, shouted orders, and sounds of violence. But above the echoes of that harsh, discordant mixture of sounds, he heard the black clad man on top of him whisper, "As you hope to live, do not move a muscle, and do not make a sound."

The second Count of Bucquoy was a consummate study in contradictions. Born in Northern France and bearing an overly French name and title (Charles Bonaventure de Longueval, *Comte de Bucquoy*), he made his name while serving in the Spanish army. Having excelled as a military commander (by his mid-twenties he had attained the status of colonel and was made a general of the artillery by his early thirties), he ultimately pursued a life of diplomacy – serving first as Spain's ambassador extraordinary to France and later travelling to Bohemia to represent Austrian Archduke Albert at the *Diät von Budweis* (the Assembly at Budweis).

Known to be friendly and temperate, he preferred to live a life of splendour, surrounded by his staff of officers from leading European families, yet he did not avoid life in the field, and he often slept in a simple tent among his soldiers. Tending to be somewhat loose with the discipline he maintained within the army (which made him very popular with his troops), Buquoy was always a model of discipline in his personal affairs. Despite always displaying personal courage in battle, he was known to lead his troops in a very cautious, defensive way, so as not to squander their lives by hurrying unnecessarily into a fight (making him even more popular with his men).

Shortly after being elected in 1614, Holy Roman Emperor Matthias made Bucquoy the new commander-in-chief of the entire imperial army. As *Marshal* Bucquoy, he was also an imperial counsellor and a member of the imperial court's war council, but as fate would have it, he was away on leave in the Hapsburg controlled Spanish Netherlands during the defenestration of Prague, and had missed out on the first few months of the "unfortunate situation" as the emperor had taken to calling the civil war.

However, as the late Summer had slipped into early Autumn with no end of the "unfortunate situation" in sight, the emperor had recalled Bucquoy to Vienna, ostensibly to task him with re- taking command of the imperial army and using it to put down the Bohemian Revolt.

His journey having taken somewhat longer than he had anticipated, Bucquoy did not reach his destination in the centre of Vienna until the first week of October. Upon arriving at *die Wiener Hofburg*, his entire travelling party (including a large number of servants, his wife Maria, and their eleven-year-old son, Charles Albert) were immediately attended to. But Buquoy himself was rather oddly and brusquely told to make his way, alone, to *die Stallburg* – the palace's imperial mews.

Having begrudgingly complied with the unusual request, Comte de Bucquoy dismounted, expecting to have been met at *die Stallburg* by at least some dignitary – perhaps not Cardinal Khlesl himself, but certainly someone should have been there to greet him. Protocol demanded it. However, the sixteenth century Renaissance-inspired building, which was not physically connected to the rest of the palace, was completely empty. In fact, both *Josefsplatz* and

Michaelerplatz, the two squares between which *die Stallburg* lay, were also uncharacteristically quiet and vacant.

While he was trying to make sense of this unusual scene, Marshal Buquoy heard someone moving around in the shadows of the stalls behind him.

"Qui s'y rend?" he asked in his native French. Hearing no answer, he stepped closer to the source of the sound and switched to Spanish. *"¿Quién va allí?"* A cold and foreboding tingle creeping down his neck, Buquouy withdrew a rondel (a stiff-bladed dagger usually worn at the waist by knights) from his belt and took one step closer to the stall from which the sound had come. *"Wer geht dorthin?"* he asked in German.

Just then a sickly spectre stepped from the shadows. Covered in blankets, the shrivelled little man appeared to be bleeding from both his nose and his mouth. Racked by violent coughs, his blackened skin was particularly dark, almost oily, around his nose and fingers. As he emerged enough from the shadows of the mews for Buquouy to see his face, the deathly looking and foul smelling figure just managed to wheeze out an answer. "It's only me, Charles. Only your Matthias. Are you prepared to do your emperor one final service?"

Chapter Forty Four

Seeing no alternative to what the man had commanded, Roan lay still and silent. After what seemed like hours, during which the attacker had ascertained that neither of them had been seen or heard, the dark clad man slipped off of Roan and offered him his hand.

"Sorry, Roan," he said, helping the giant Moravian to his feet. "I couldn't call out to you without bringing attention to myself."

Roan rose slowly to his feet and realised that the man who had tackled him was none other than Franz Hohenleiter – his friend and the leader of *die Schwarzen Schurken* with whom he had been meeting just hours earlier.

"Christ, Franz! You broke me nose, *du Schuft!*"

"Quiet!" Franz commanded. "Do you want to bring the whole lot of them up here?"

"The whole lot of who? What the fuck is goin' on, Franz?"

Franz pried apart several branches of the nearest tree so that Roan could see for himself. It appeared that the clown Roan had earlier humiliated had returned, and with the same group of men as before, minus the two tax collectors and the four trumpeters. They had already shot several of the men who had been in *der Alte Stier* earlier and set fire to their still-warm corpses. They were now in the process of arresting the remaining men and requisitioning from the tavern all of the "taxes" that Emma owed – this being accomplished by relieving her of the entire day's profits. Clearly this activity accounted for the sounds Roan had heard earlier, but there was still no sign of Šarlatová.

"They came back just a few minutes ago," Franz informed him. "I got away, and maybe one or two others, but you can see for yourself what's become of the rest."

"They're not arresting Emma....or the children. And they haven't set fire to the tavern. I thought they would have killed everyone and burnt everything to the ground by now," Roan noted, confused.

"It's simple, Roan. Dead men....or, in this case, dead women.... pay no taxes. They want Emma's money more than they want revenge."

"Even so....they came back without any additional men," Roan observed. "It looks like they're back with the exact same men from earlier."

"So?"

"So? When they was here before, we left them with reason to believe that these woods were crawlin' with archers. Why would they come back so quickly? And why without more men?"

Roan stared hard at his friend, desperate for answers. But all Franz did was hang his head, clearly not wanting to tell Roan something.

"Franz? What is it?"

Franz spit to the side in disgust. "We've found our Judas, Roan. It's Simon Berger."

"Fuck that! That's his brother, Theodore, down there gettin' arrested with the rest of them. There's no way that...."

Franz put a reassuring hand on Roan's shoulder and offered him a cloth from his belt. "Here. Wipe the blood off, and hear me out."

Roan hesitated, clearly trying to decide whether or not to join the fray taking place down below them. Reading his friend's expression rather easily, Franz said, "There's nothin' more we can do down there, Roan. Even if the both of was to rush down, we'd be arrested or killed without changin' a damn thing. For once in your life, do the smart thing. Listen to reason, and let me explain what's happened."

Comte de Bucquoy could scarcely believe his own eyes. Here before him was a man who bore a striking resemblance to his emperor and his friend, Matthias. But the deep creases in his face and the lines at the corner of his eyes and mouth were new additions to the face that he should have recognised easily. And this man seemed smaller than the emperor. One of his eyes was swollen shut, while the other was bloodshot and somewhat weepy. Despite it all, this man who claimed to be the emperor smiled, revealing several missing teeth, and reached out for Bucquoy.

"Your Majesty?" he whispered, as the shrunken man reached out his hand. Forgetting all protocol, Bucquoy put one arm around his emperor and took the monarch's hand in his own. Shockingly, the grip of the man's hand was as limp as his hair now appeared to be. Easing him gently to the ground he asked, "What's happened, Your Majesty? And why are you out here alone? Shouldn't you be in bed, tended to by your doctors?"

Shaking his head and waving his hand weakly, the emperor coughed several times before sputtering, "I'm not well, Charles, and I don't want anyone to see me like this. I'm sure I'll be well soon enough, but until then I must maintain the illusion of strength." The emperor followed that up with another round of coughing and gagging that produced more than a little blood around his nose and mouth.

Charles Bonaventure de Longueval, *Comte de Bucquoy* had always been a consummate diplomat. He was courteous and polite; he spoke four languages fluently, and he was equally comfortable conversing with heads of state as he was with common soldiers. But nothing in his repertoire of diplomatic skills was availing him now. This shrunken and battered-looking man before him bore enough resemblance to the emperor he knew and loved to confound him.

But clearly, he thought, *this must be some trick. Some imposter must have....*

Before the *Comte de Bucquoy* could finish his thought, the man he was holding seemed to read his thoughts. "It's really me, Charles. Who else would know that, when you became a knight of the Order of the Golden Fleece, that you had to renounce your position in the Order of Calatrava?"

Bucquoy was about to interrupt to inform this person that this was common knowledge, but before he could, the man coughed again and added, "Or that your commandery was transferred to your son, Charles Albert? Not quite common knowledge that, eh?" he asked, seeming to read the count's mind again. "Or that you've quietly served as Grand Bailiff of *Grafschaft Hennegau* for me these past five years?"

Der Grafschaft Hennegau (the County of Hainaut) was a territory within the Holy Roman Empire that straddled the border of France and the Spanish Netherlands. The fact that Bucquoy was the bailiff (meaning governor) of that territory was due, in large part, to the emperor and had been a reward for his years of faithful and effective service to the Hapsburgs.

Convinced now that the man before him was, in fact, his emperor, Bucqouy begged for forgiveness. "I'm sorry, Your Imperial Majesty. I've just never seen you...."

"It's quite alright, Charles," the emperor responded and tenderly patted one of Bucqouy's gloved hands. "I know I must look.... well....not like myself. But don't let that diminish the weight of what I have to say to you."

"Yes, of course, Your Imperial Majesty. As always, I am your humble servant. What can I do for you? Simply name it and it shall be done."

After another round of wet coughing, the emperor looked up into the eyes of the count and wheezed, "I need you to lose a war for me."

After having found a place to secure Kimber, Stephen entered *die Kirche St. Stephan* with absolutely no idea what he was looking for, nor what he was to do with it, when, or even if, he found it – whatever it was. The phrase "sleeveless errand," meaning something that provided no useful information and was often used to get someone out of the way, was dominating Stephen's thoughts. *Did Father Joseph send me all this way just to get me out of Prague*, he asked himself. *If so, why?*

But Stephen's thoughts were soon consumed by the beauty of the church. Inside the heavy wooden doors, the sounds and the troubles of the outside world fell immediately silent, and he was transported into a world of beautiful simplicity and tranquillity. Built in the late twelfth century, this three-aisled Romanesque church was the largest in *Lindau*. Because it sat on the eastern shore of Lake Constance, the exterior of the church was often enveloped in a grey, woollen blanket of fog. But the bright interior was neither grey nor heavy; on the contrary, it was warm and inviting. The altar, baptismal font, and pulpit were all done in an understated stucco marble, and the white pews reflected the soft light from the muted green stucco ornaments and the brightly colored windows found high on the walls of both sides of the church.

The sense of peace and piety that this simple but beautiful church evoked soothed Stephen and left him in awe. In fact, so dumbstruck was he by its grace and purity that he did not hear the priest who had approached him from behind and who was now standing directly behind him.

"May I help you, my son?" he asked in a resounding baritone voice.

Startled, Stephen spun around to find a short man with a huge round stomach and a bright red face that was dominated by a very large and very flat nose. His heavy and overgrown eyebrows were like dark awnings above coal-black eyes. When he spoke, it was clear that he had lost several of his front teeth, leaving him with a very gummy and comical smile. But there was nothing comical about the priest's demeanour.

He was clad in a long-sleeved cassock made of wool, and the heavy black garment, with purple piping that indicated the father's position as a canon, was matched by a black biretta, surmounted by a purple tuft. The only thing heavier and darker than his vestments was his scowl. It was clear that he was not accustomed to receiving guests unannounced in his church, and he was made even more cautious by Stephen's size and weaponry.

"Yes, father. I'm sorry....you startled me. Yes, you can help me, with...."

As Stephen continued to stammer away in an attempt to formulate a response, the cautious priest examined Stephen carefully. Upon seeing the signature Stormsong coat of arms on Stephen's tunic and the pommel of his sword, the priest's expression brightened considerably.

"Ah! You come to us from *Schloß Stormsong. Entschuldigung, Sie, bitte!* How are things in Prague?" But before Stephen could respond, the suddenly affable priest shook his hand and added, "So, Archbishop von Rodt must have sent you."

Correctly sensing that he was being tested, Stephen responded by saying, "No, father. I was sent here by Bishop Riphaen. We don't have an Archbishop von Rodt in residence at *Schloß Stormsong* at the moment."

"Ach, yes, of course!" the priest responded, flashing his gummy smile. "My memory sometimes is not what it used to be."

Stephen laughed politely, but he was not using his real laugh. Instead, it was a counterfeit sound that he had learned to use when attempting to stall a conversation until he could think of what he wanted to say next. He had learned this art at an early age through his many awkward conversations with Vanessa. But the artifice of his laugh seemed to have had no effect on the priest whose mercurial temperament had shifted from one of suspicion to one of welcoming and now to one of hesitation.

"And....I'm assuming that Bishop Riphaen sent you here to....?"

Stephen's attempts at stalling had run their course. But just before he was going to be forced to admit that he had no earthly clue why he was in *Lindau*, a nun approached from behind the priest and said, rather loudly, "Father Phillip, is this the young man we were expecting today?"

The thick jowled nun had a bulbous nose and an oversized head. She stood more than a foot taller than the priest, who Stephen now knew was named Father Phillip, and her droopy face was punctuated by a deeply furrowed brow and wild nose hairs that had grown out of control. But she projected a blunt and honest affect that set Stephen at ease and reminded him more of a country farmer's wife than a nun.

Father Phillip's reaction on the other hand was much less positive. Clearly perturbed by the untimely intrusion, the priest turned and growled at the nun. "Sister Elsebeth, always so pleasant to see you," he snarled. "Yes, I suppose this young man...." he turned towards Stephen and held out one hand.

"Stephen, father. Sir Stephen to be precise. Bishop Riphaen wouldn't have sent me on such an important mission had I not already been knighted," he lied.

"Yes, of course." Turning back to Sister Elsebeth, he added, "It appears that *Sir* Stephen is the replacement that Bishop Riphaen had promised us."

"Ausgezeichnet!" Sister Elsebeth exclaimed. "Then you'll be wanting to see the monastery right away."

"Yes, of course!" Stephen said, allowing his unexpected rescuer to take him by the hand and begin to lead him away from the suspicious priest.

As the unlikely pair exited the church and made their way together out onto *Lindau's* market square, Stephen was virtually certain he heard Father Phillip behind them exhort something to the effect that *Even ugly women are made prettier when they learn to keep their mouths shut.*

Turning to see if Sister Elsebeth had heard him, Stephen blushed with embarrassment on the priest's behalf.

As if sensing his mortification, the nun patted him on the hand reassuringly and said, "Pay no mind to him, Sir Stephen. He's just a bitter old man and has been for....well....about forty years now."

As Stephen laughed and smiled, Sister Elsebeth took him by the arm. "Now, let's show you what you came to see."

Chapter Forty Five

Vanessa had decided to stay with Avrem's family for several more days. She claimed that it was simply because she wanted to remain there in case anymore trouble arose in *Josefov* from the *verdammte Protestanten*. But the truth was that she felt far more comfortable and at home within the confines of the Mordecai family's small house than she ever had in the luxurious confines of *Schloß Stormsong*. In fact, it was during her extended stay that Vanessa vowed to never again live in a place so big that she might get lost just looking for a place to pee.

Added to that comfort level was the fact that she didn't really know where next to turn in her search for the so-called *red witch*, and those two factors had combined to make her quite comfortable with her decision to prolong her stay with the Mordecais. And she had also come to cherish her time with the rabbi and his family, each member of which had tried, in his or her own way, to make her feel at home.

With Maria, it was always food. She had done her best to stuff Vanessa full of *Boyoz* (a Turkish pastry), *Chraime* (a spicy fish stew with tomatoes), *Pescado frito* (a traditional fried fish dish from the Southern coast of Spain), and her personal favourite) peppers stuffed with rice. Vanessa had never eaten so much rich food in her life, and she was certain that it was Maria's goal to feed her until she was as delightfully plump as Maria herself.

Talya, of course, could always be counted on to impart some knowledge about a variety of topics ranging from ancient civilizations to recent advances in science. Vanessa was as well educated as any woman (or man, for that matter) in the empire, but Talya's conversations always kept her on her toes and often left her with something to ponder for the next several days, or at least until Talya's next "lesson."

Talya's younger sister Vanessa was also very inquisitive, but her questions were not of an academic nature like Talya's. Hers were of a very curious (bordering on nosy), personal nature. Vanessa Mordecai wanted to know everything there was to know about Vanessa Stormsong, and she wanted Vanessa to know everything about her life here in *Josefov*, as well. Lady Stormsong was quite certain that Vanessa Mordecai did not stop talking from the moment she woke up until the moment she went to bed. In fact, she was known to talk in her sleep, and since the sleeping quarters were all very close together, the entire family would often be regaled with young Vanessa's nightly ramblings.

Caleb was both the easiest and most difficult to appease. All Vanessa had to do to please him was agree to play whatever new game he had created that day. But, whether the game was continuously sorting and resorting the kitchen utensils or using household items as loud, percussion-based musical instruments, the game had to be played strictly according to Caleb's rules, which tended to change minute by minute. If Vanessa deviated even slightly from those arbitrary and very fluid rules, Caleb would explode into a torrent of tears, accusations, and abuse.

Vanessa's interactions with Maria and the children came so naturally, that she quickly felt like one of the family. But what she treasured most were her conversations with the rabbi himself. He had no pretence whatsoever. He was kind and direct, and had a peculiarly simple yet honest way of looking at things.

Recently, their regular evening conversations had, as a result of something Talya had brought up earlier, turned to science and medicine, and when Vanessa had expressed a question as to why the "new disease" (which is how polite culture was referring to syphilis) seemed to be unusually fond of priests, especially rich ones, the rabbi had answered her query which his typical directness.

"There are currently something like five-thousand priests in Rome," he had said. "And since, for far too many of them, celibacy simply means not taking a wife….at least not publicly, anyway…. there is an almost equivalent number of prostitutes in Rome. The more priests you have, the more prostitutes you can expect. The more prostitutes, the more priests with the 'new disease.' It's really just a simple question of mathematics."

Vanessa had laughed at the rabbi's peculiar ability to trivialise the monumental, but had then demurely scolded him for his constant abuse of Christians in general and Catholics in particular. And this was a constant source of conversation between the two.

"I don't think poorly of Christians or Catholics or clergy, Vanessa," he had said. "I simply think of them the same way I think of all men, and women, for that matter. They are all God's children, but they are all flawed – saved only by His grace."

Tonight, as the Bohemian sun had begun to set, and as the first purple-blue fingers of evening had begun to thread themselves through *Josefov*, Vanessa and Avrem had returned once again to the question of God's relationship with man.

"My point is this, Vanessa," the rabbi said. "You speak something like seven languages, am I correct?"

"Eight, actually," Vanessa responded, proudly.

"Eight? Fine. So you speak eight languages, and that is wonderful. It's remarkable, actually. But it doesn't matter how many you can speak or how many anyone else speaks, for that matter. Unless and until you speak His language, you're never going to be able to understand Him."

Vanessa just smiled and shook her head. "You don't sound like any other Jew I've ever met, rabbi."

"And just how many Jews have you met, Vanessa?"

"That's a fair point. Still, to hear you speak of God, you almost sound like…."

"What? A Christian?"

"Well, yes, I suppose."

"It's not a question of Christianity or Judaism, Vanessa. They are both just two different sets of rules and traditions. But, at the end of the day, neither of their lists of "do's and don'ts" can change one simple truth. God loves you. In fact, He loves you so much that he didn't just send a messenger to tell you so. He came to do it Himself. And He paid a terrible price to do so."

"Wait just a minute, rabbi. 'He paid a terrible price?' It sounds like you're talking about the crucifixion."

"And what if I am?" the rabbi responded.

Vanessa stared at him dumbfounded for several seconds. "But you're Jewish!"

"So?"

"So, you can't believe in Jesus!"

"Why not?"

"Why not? Because....because it's against the rules....against your rules. It's against your own rules," she stammered incredulously.

The rabbi just grinned and moved even closer to his star pupil.

"Think of it this way, Vanessa. Micah, a *Hebrew* prophet of the eighth century before Christ, said that a saviour would be born in Bethlehem. Isaiah, arguably the greatest *Hebrew* prophet of the Old Testament – who, by the way, is quoted at least fifty times in the New Testament – wrote that this saviour would be born of a virgin, and live in Galilee. Daniel, a *Hebrew* statesman and priest of the second century before Christ, wrote about a band of evil men who would curse this saviour, and mock Him, and gamble for His clothing. And, not for nothing, but Isaiah went on to say that He would be pierced for our transgressions, and crushed for our iniquities, and that His punishment would bring us peace. Now, which of those has failed to happen?"

Vanessa stared at the rabbi, mouth agape. As educated as she was and as fluent with scripture as she claimed to be, no one ever had exposed her ignorance quite like this man just had.

"Yes, I'm Jewish. And I love being Jewish. Ours is a proud people – God's chosen people, in fact. But we have had a very sad and tortured history, and it is our faith and our traditions that have seen us through nearly five thousand years of suffering. So those traditions mean a great deal to me....to all Jews, really. But thousands of years before the birth of Christ, some of the wisest Jewish thinkers in the world said that a Messiah would be born of a virgin in Bethlehem, that He would live in Galilee, that He would be a light to the nations, that He would suffer and die for the sins of mankind, that His days would be prolonged and that the good pleasure of the Lord would prosper. So, either Jesus Christ was precisely who and what He said He was, or all of the greatest Jewish prophets of the Old Testament were wrong. You're an educated woman. Which of those do you think is more plausible."

"Yes, of course, rabbi. I believe in Jesus. I'm a Christian, but you, as a Jew...."

"As a Jew, I am just one of God's children," the rabbi interjected. "But when you ask me whether or not I believe in God the Father *and* in His son? Well, I suppose I must. If I didn't, I would have to reject the prophecies of Micah, Isaiah, and Daniel, wouldn't I? And what kind of a Jew would I be then? So, yes....I believe in the Son of God. But the real question, Vanessa, is ....what do you believe?"

Just as the purples and blues of the night gave way to the brilliant pinks and golds of a shimmering sunrise, Franz finally settled Roan down long enough to describe to him what he had witnessed. At first, the giant Moravian swore a series of oaths that threatened to return the sky to a deep shade of blue. But he finally calmed down, and once he did, nearly an hour passed during which neither man said a word.

It was Roan who finally broke the long and awkward silence. "You're certain then?"

"Of course, I'm not certain! But what else could it mean? After you left, Simon conveniently had to *tend to somethin'*. Not long after that Gundrham shows back up like he never left. And while we was all scatterin' into the trees for cover, I saw him. And there was no doubt in either the look on his face or the size of the purse on his belt." Franz then paused a moment before adding, "I don't like it any better than you, Roan. But the fact is, we've found our traitor."

Roan shook his head in disbelief. "But to betray you and Emma and all the others like that. I just can't…."

"Roan, you're forgetting that he betrayed his own brother. And a man what will abandon his home and family is a man what will abandon anythin'. I suppose we know now why he was always so full of secrets. And didn't it seem odd to you that he was always dressed so much finer than the rest of us?"

"Damn it all to hell! How could I have been so blind? And he was always askin' too many questions, too, weren't he?" Franz just nodded along silently while Roan worked the whole sordid affair out in his mind. "But for what? For some pieces of gold or silver? Is that all we was worth to him?"

Scratching at the ground in front of himself, Franz spit in disgust. "Greed transcends everythin' else, my old friend. It's stronger than love, stronger than religion….stronger even than blood." As Roan looked at him questioningly, Franz stood, scuffed one boot against what he had drawn in the dirt and continued. "It's as old as the Bible, Roan. Why did Judas betray our Lord? For thirty pieces of silver. What did the Roman soldiers do at Golgotha while Christ was being nailed to that tree?"

"They gambled for his garments," Roan answered, citing from memory one of the many parts of Mark's gospel that Šarlatová had taught him over the years.

After another prolonged period of silence, Franz asked, "So what are we to do now?"

"Well I'm for damned sure not going to condemn our friends to death and torture," Roan snapped.

"Meanin' what, exactly? That we're goin' to invade *Schloß Stormsong* all by ourselves? Just the three of us? You and me and Šarlatová can kill more than our fair share of Stormsong men, Roan. But even on our best day, the three of us…."

"Šarlatová is gone," Roan interrupted.

"What do you mean, gone?"

"What do you think I mean? She's missin' too. She's not where I left her when I met up with you and Simon at *der Alte Stier.*"

"You don't think that Simon….?

Despite the fact that there was dried blood all over his face and that both of his eyes were already turning black and blue from the broken nose he'd just suffered, a tranquil expression spread across Roan's face before he sighed and said, "What do I think about Simon? Well….I'll tell you, my old friend. Here's what I think. I'm goin' think of that lyin' traitor as a dead man, at least until I can make him one with my own bare hands." Pausing just long enough to spit out a broken piece of tooth, Roan stood and added, "And then I won't think of him at all."

It should have been a great morning for Peter Ernst, *Graf von Mansfeld*. The German sunrise had already exploded with a nearly indescribable palette of oranges and reds and yellows. Those rays, coming in from the east at a low angle bathed the dewy fields in front of him in a golden light, and provided a limited degree of warmth that was far preferable to the past few wet and miserable days he and his men had spent marching towards *Pilsen*.

But this glorious Autumn morning was lost on von Mansfeld who, having just risen, stretched his long, stork-like legs and groaned. He was growing increasingly impatient as he waited for more news from Count von Thurn. He had thousands of men under his command and was fully prepared to lay siege to *Pilsen*, as originally ordered by the count. But now, having been ordered not to proceed (also by the count), he had heard nothing more from von Thurn for days.

He had, however, received a rather sternly written letter from Charles Emmanuel, the Duke of Savoy. "Charles the Great," as he had taken to calling himself, had been the Duke of Savoy for nearly forty years, and while he was extremely well-educated and quite intelligent, he was also prone to impulsiveness and reckless action when it came to military matters, which is why von Mansfeld wasn't the least surprised that the duke's letter was imploring – demanding, in fact – him to engage the Emperor's troops in *Pilsen* with *"the utmost haste."* After the Count reread the Duke of Savoy's letter, he thought to himself, *"I wish these* Blödian *(idiots) could decide, once and for all, which one of them is in charge of this rebellion."*

Tossing the Duke's letter to the ground, von Mansfeld took a deep breath of the fresh, crisp German air that was, for the first time in several days, free from both rain and fog. *"It's getting colder already,"* he thought to himself. *"It must be early October by now. The first snow can't be too far away."*

Looking out across the impressive array of soldiers under his command, who were scattered like thousands of tiny islands across a vast green sea, von Mansfeld did some quick calculations. Determining that his army (consisting of approximately four-thousand Swiss mercenaries and six-thousand Silesian and Moravian soldiers), which was growing increasingly restless by loitering idly at the edges of *Pilsen*, probably only had enough food and supplies left to stretch into the last week of November, he made his decision. He would consult neither the strategy of von Thurn nor the hotheaded, impetuous temper of "Charles the Great." He would defer, instead, to God.

Dropping to his knees, he looked up and, in a loud and clear voice, prayed, "Heavenly Father, my Lord and Saviour, I humbly come to Thee again. Grant me Thy wisdom. Show me Thy will, that I might see it done."

Before the count could even finish his prayer, a strong wind whipped out from the east and blew the discarded letter from the Duke of Savoy due north – precisely in the direction of Pilsen.

Smiling gratefully at having received such a clear and unambiguous answer from God, the count thought to himself, *"Then it is to war we are to go. Thy will be done."* With that, he stood, made the sign of the cross and signalled for one of his couriers.

Chapter Forty Six

As was so often the case after meals, Vanessa found herself sitting on the front step of the Moredcai family's dwelling, having been excused, once again, from having to assist with the post-meal clean up. And as was also often the case, Rabbi Mordecai soon came out to join her.

They sat together in silence for a few minutes before they both noticed awkward movement in the shadows up ahead. It appeared that a woman and her two sons were struggling mightily to keep a bundle, wrapped tightly in white cloth, affixed atop a donkey who was reluctant to carry the load.

Maintaining their mutual silence, Vanessa and Avrem watched as the three approached the gate to a Jewish cemetery that was only a few hundred yards from the Mordecai's front door. This particular cemetery, as Avrem had already told Vanessa, had been founded less than two hundred years ago, but it was already populated by more than two-thousand tombstones. The oldest grave, according to the rabbi, dated back to 1439 and belonged to the scholar and poet Avigdor Kara.

Upon passing through the cemetery's gates, the woman and her children struggled to get the white bundle down from the unenthusiastic donkey's back. As they did so, Vanessa noticed that one limp arm came swinging out of the bundle. Suddenly realising what was happening, Vanessa immediately stood and made to go assist the three, but Avrem placed a gentle hand on hers as a way of silently communicating his desire that she sit back down.

Eventually, and reluctantly, Vanessa did. But she stared at the rabbi for an explanation.

"I know that family," he said. "That's Ani Asha and her boys Daniel and David. They are saying goodbye to Uri Asha. He has been ill for many weeks and finally succumbed two days ago. But they have no money to afford a burial plot or a headstone. So they will leave him there until someone decides to donate one."

Vanessa had already seen so much death in her twenty-two years on Earth that it had come to seem like a normal thing to her. She had experienced, witnessed and even caused so much death herself, that it no longer seemed like something that needed to be mourned. In fact, death had completely lost all darkness and mysteriousness to her. But this was something else entirely. It was not the death of the stranger that weighed heavily upon her, nor was it the sadness of the family having to part with a beloved father and husband. Rather, it was the simple fact that this was being done with no sense of veneration or ritual. No prayers were offered; no mourners were in attendance to support the family. They were simply left to dispose of Uri Asha's body as if it was an old piece of furniture that was no longer of use – all because the family could not afford to provide the appropriate level of reverence or regard that the occasion demanded.

After having deposited the body within the gates of the cemetery, the family simply led the donkey away in silence. As they retreated out of the circle of light provided by the torches on the cemetery gate, they became increasingly difficult to see. When they had disappeared completely, Vanessa turned again to face the rabbi, but she couldn't produce the proper words to indicate her level of outrage.

His own grief somewhat assuaged by the fact that someone as wealthy as Vanessa could still feel pity for someone as poor as Ani Asha and her children, Avrem said to her, "That's the way it is with poor people, Vanessa. That is why it's of no great concern to them who wins or loses this war. Whichever side wins, they will lose. The poor always do. That's simply the way things are." When he saw a combination of shock and outrage darken Vanessa's otherwise beautiful face, the rabbi sood up and said, "Come with me. There's something I want to show you."

Avrem took Vanessa by the hand, something she was still more than a little uncomfortable with, and led her to one of the newer burial plots in the cemetery. According to the headstone, it belonged to a teacher and religious scholar named Rabbi Yehuda Liwa ben Bezalel.

"We called him Rabbi Löw," Avrem told her. "He died just nine years ago. He was a great and important man, and he was my teacher." The rabbi remained silent for a moment and Vanessa couldn't tell if it was out of respect or sadness. When he spoke again, Avrem said, "He has become associated with the local legend of the Golem."

The rabbi could tell by Vanessa's expression that she did not understand. "A Golem is an artificial being – sort of a giant clay figure that's created and brought to life by some spirit or magic. And a legend has grown around Rabbi Löw that a powerful Golem will one day rise from his grave to protect the Jewish ghetto here from future pogroms."

Vanessa couldn't tell if the rabbi was being serious or if he was teasing her. "And do you believe this legend? It sounds like silly folklore to me," she said, but immediately regretted doing so. It was apparent from the expression of his face, that the legend had some significance to the rabbi.

"Legends are an important part of history, Vanessa. They help keep the memory of great and terrible events alive. And they all have two possible interpretations. The first is the plausible one…. the logical one….which is that they are simply fairytales. Just nonsensical stories made up by parents to keep their children in line, with no truth to them whatsoever."

"And the second?" Vanessa asked.

The rabbi turned to her and smiled the way a father does when he is proud of his child's accomplishment. "Well, I think that man is a romantic at heart. And I think that he will always set aside the dull, plausible explanation for things for the mysterious one – the one that gives us hope and keeps us believing in forces beyond us and greater than ourselves." The rabbi paused as if weighing what to say next. "I don't know if I believe in the legend of the Golem or not, Vanessa. But I do have hope. That's all we, the Jewish people, really have. Faith and hope."

Steeling herself for what was to come next, Vanessa said, "You don't need Golems anymore, rabbi. And you have a hell of a lot more than just faith and hope."

The rabbi was virtually certain that he heard a rumble of thunder in the distance and that he saw lightning flash in Vanessa's eyes when she added, "You have me."

"Sister Elsebeth, I have a confession to make," Stephen said as the homely nun led him by the hand towards the entrance to *Lindau's* Franciscan monastery.

"Nuns don't hear confession, my son," she responded curtly.

"Yes, of course, I know that. What I meant was…."

But Stephen stopped as soon as they entered the monastery. Founded in 1224 by the Abbess Offemia von Pflegelberg, the monastery in *Lindau* had joined *der Franziskaner Orden* (the Franciscan Order) during the fourteenth century and carried on its work despite the fact that Lindau had become an Imperial Free City under King Rudolf I as early as 1275. But during the 1520s, when Emperor Charles V – in an attempt to restore religious and political unity in his empire so as to rally against the impending Ottoman invasion – called upon the Princes and Free Territories in Germany to explain their religious convictions, *Lindau* had accepted the Protestant Reformation according to the terms of *das Augsburg Bekenntnis* (the Augsburg Confession), and the Catholic monastery closed in 1528.

At that time, the sisters who had been charged with running the monastery became, like the rest of the residents in *Lindau*, de facto Protestants. But one of the worst kept secrets in Germany was the fact that the now defunct monastery remained a small community of die hard Catholics. What those nuns actually did in the halls of that former Franciscan stronghold, however, remained a mystery to all but a select few. But as Sister Elsebeth and Sir Stephen entered the halls of the ostensibly defunct building, it became very clear that it remained a hive of activity.

"What's your confession, Sir Stephen?" the nun asked as she pulled him along by the hand like a mother would a child.

"My confession? Oh....yes....my confession. Well, I don't really have the first clue as to what I'm doing here, and I certainly wasn't sent here in any official capacity by Bishop Riphaen."

Sister Elsebeth pulled up suddenly and turned Stephen around so that they were now face-to-face, and uncomfortably close – so close, in fact, that Stephen could smell the hard boiled eggs that the nun had clearly eaten earlier that day. "I know that, Sir Stephen," she said. "And I'll do you one better." She leaned in so close now that Stephen feared she might attempt to kiss him. "I'm not really a nun!"

Italy in the seventeenth century, much like Germany, was less a country than a collection of fiefdoms where, one day, a country might exist. Vastly different dominions like the Kingdom of Sicily, the Republic of Venice, the Papal States, and the Duchy of Milan combined with a dozen or so other nation-states to form a patchwork quilt of geo-political and socio-economic diversity. But there was little to no unity, and what unity there was came as a result of foreign domination.

Ever since the 1559 Peace of Cateau-Cambrésis ended the Hapsburg-Valois War (also known as the Last Italian War), the history of Italy had been one of foreign domination and economic decline. The northern Italian states fell under the indirect rule of the Austrian Hapsburgs while the states in the south came under the control of the Spanish branch of the Hapsburg dynasty. But foreign domination is not the same thing as internal unity, and this lack of any kind of Italian solidarity, combined with a post-Renaissance economic decline, meant that the seventeenth century was an extremely tumultuous time for Italians.

Despite important artistic and scientific achievements, such as Galileo's work in the fields of astronomy and physics or the flourishing of Baroque art and architecture, the bulk of the seventeenth century witnessed an Italy (to the extent that one even existed) that was in overall political and economic decline. And that lack of cohesion combined with the political and economic deterioration of the Italian states to create an atmosphere of violence and discord.

Virtual anarchy reigned in the streets of many Italian states, with the more distinguished aristocrats and clergy forced to fortify their castles with standing, private armies for their personal protection. As early as 1559, the same year as the signing of the Cateau-Cambrésis treaty, Romans rioted in celebration of the death of Pope Paul IV and broke open the prisons of the Inquisition. The Italian carnivals of the sixteenth and seventeenth centuries were even more violent and unruly than usual. Convicted criminals were executed for entertainment; prostitutes and Jews were forced to compete in races during which the riotous crowds hurled insults and sharp objects at the runners, and "sport" often consisted of feats of strength between hunchbacks and cripples.

In short, Italy was a brutal place where men (and women) learned to be brutal and cunning, thinking only of his or her own survival. The use of ruthless force and violence was as common as church attendance.

Father Abaddon Sohar knew full well the dangers that lay ahead of him as he continued his journey towards Prague, but he was on an errand for Pope Paul V, to whom he was blindly loyal. And, to

Sohar, that meant the exact same thing as being on an errand for God. But even if his zeal had not steeled his resolve in seeing this mission completed, his sheer size and his own penchant for ruthless use of force comforted him greatly. He feared not the potential hazards of the trip; in fact, having encountered no trouble at all during the first few days of his journey north towards *Valtellina*, Father Sohar was almost disappointed.

That disappointment was sure to come to an end, however, as he rode into *Morbegno*, a little town on the western banks of the Adda River in the province of *Sondrio*. *Morbegno*, like most of the other *comuni* in the valley, was known for its cheeses, its wines, and its *Bresaola della Valtellina* (an air-dried, salted beef that is aged for two to three months until turning hard and dark red). It was also, like so many other *comuni* in Italy, known for its crime and corruption, and as he made his way closer to *Morbegno's* gates, Father Sohar saw an agitated group of four men – *banditi*, he thought to himself – harassing an elderly merchant and what appeared to be his granddaughter; and whereas most Italians would have seen this as an opportunity to look the other way, Father Abaddon Sohar saw it as a chance to dispense the Lord's justice.

As he approached calmly and silently, Sohar made eye contact with the old man who then called out to him for help. The girl who Sohar took to be the man's granddaughter was silent as two of the four *banditi* held her by the arms.

The girl's torn bodice, the blood on the old man's face, and the overturned cart of fruits, cheese and *Bresaola* spoke volumes about what had already happened – and, more importantly, about what was to come next.

Father Sohar groaned inwardly, rolling his eyes as he did so. He had hoped to stay on the less-travelled roads of *Valtellina*, where he hoped he would encounter very few people. Roads where a dark and determined rider like himself wouldn't have to skulk in the shadows. But it appeared now to the priest that God clearly had other plans in mind.

Assuming that most passersby would do precisely that – pass on by – the banditi initially paid little to no attention to Father Sohar. But as he grew closer, and as both his size and apparent interest in what they were doing became clearer, the four began to take greater notice of the giant priest.

The smallest of the four (*Why were the smallest ones always the loudest ones?* Sohar asked himself) stepped clear of the frantic old man and cautioned the priest to move along. "No souls to be saved here, padre. Best keep about your business."

"Yeah! Or you'll be next," added one of the two men clinging to the traumatised young girl.

No souls to be saved? Sohar thought to himself. *Perhaps not. But there are certainly plenty of souls to be taken.* And, for the second time in a week, Father Abaddon Sohar smiled.

Chapter Forty Seven

The battle for *Pilsen* began long before von Mansfeld's army fired its first shots.

In fact, within weeks of the third "Defenestration of Prague," many Catholic monasteries and unfortified manors loyal to the Hapsburgs, correctly ascertaining that civil war was now inevitable, had been evacuated. Believing that Pilsen represented the best place from which to mount a successful defense against the rising "Bohemian hordes" that were sure to be terrorizing the countryside, these Catholic refugees had slowly made their way to the western Bohemian city.

Living in a centre of commerce and culture that was conveniently situated on the confluence of four rivers, *Pilseners* had many advantages when, four months ago, they began their preparations for a lengthy siege. However, what Pilsen enjoyed in terms of advanced planning and strategic location, it lacked in terms of trained soldiers and gunpowder for its artillery.

Heavily outnumbered and having seen enemy troops begin to collect on the outskirts of the city as early as late September, the beleaguered defenders of *Pilsen* decided early on to completely seal two of the city's gates. They then reinforced the remaining gate with as many guards as possible.

With only one viable avenue into the fortified city left to him, and initially fearing that he lacked sufficient troops for a full frontal assault, von Mansfeld had decided to engage *Pilsen* in a protracted war of attrition, starving the city out and allowing hunger to do what he feared his troops could not. However, spurred on now by the Duke of Savoy's terse letter, as well as the arrival in early-October of some much-needed pieces of artillery, von Mansfeld changed his strategy and began his bombardment of the city.

Realising very quickly that neither the number nor the calibre of his cannons were sufficient enough to weaken the city enough to make a full frontal assault practicable, von Mansfeld changed tactics again, reverting to a strategy of patience. As October grew colder, the *Pilseners* would begin to be weakened by their lack of munitions and potable water. Conversely, Mansfeld was certain that he would be receiving new recruits and new supplies from Count von Thurn on an almost daily basis. Only when his troops reached twenty-thousand in number, which he believed would happen sometime in early November, would Mansfeld engage the city's four-thousand defenders in close quarters combat.

Unbeknownst to Mansfeld or any of his commanders was the fact that Charles Bonaventure de Longueval, the *Comte de Bucquoy* had made a hard ride northwest from Vienna, circled around the Protestant troops to the northeast corner of the besieged city, and slipped inside its walls under the cover of darkness.

Despite the fact that he travelled alone and wore the clothes of a simple farmer, Marshal Bucquouy was recognized almost instantly by the sentries on *Pilsen's* walls. With small, dark eyes set far back in their sockets, cheeks and a rather severe nose both pitted with scars, and a moustache as thin as the rest of him, he was hardly an imposing figure. But when he demanded to know who was in charge, his delicate voice resonated like thunder and he was quickly shown to the quarters of Felix Dornheim, the beleaguered commander of Pilsen's defences.

"Marshal Bucquoy, welcome. We were not expecting you," was all that Dornheim could manage by way of a greeting. With the shadows under his eyes nearly as dark as what remained of his hair, and with his cheeks so sunken that they appeared to have collapsed, Dornheim looked the part of a defeated man.

"Quite! That was obviously my intent, *Monsieur* Dornheim," responded Bucquoy as he took mental note and visual inventory of his surroundings. "I come at the request of the emperor himself. Is there some place where we can speak privately?"

"Yes....of course." With a somewhat effeminate wave of his hand, Dornheim dismissed the men who had brought the marshal to him. "How are things in Vienna?"

"Never mind that, Monsieur Dornheim. We have time neither for pleasantries nor palace intrigue. How go things here? How stands the defence of *Pilsen*?"

As he lowered his head in shame, Dornheim quietly admitted, "Not well, Marshal Bucquoy. Not well at all. We are short of money and supplies. Our food stores grow scarce, and we simply haven't enough trained soldiers. Meanwhile, the heretics further reinforce their position daily, and I fear that they will soon bring enough artillery to bear to pound us into dust."

"You make it sound as if the case is utterly hopeless, Monsieur Dornheim. Is that what you are saying? Is all hope lost?"

Sighing dramatically, Dornheim whispered. "*Oui*, Marshal Bucquoy. *Tout espoir est perdu.* All hope is lost."

"Excellent, Monsieur Dornheim. Your emperor will be most pleased."

Valtellina was an essential part of the die *Spanische Straße* (the Spanish Road), a commercial and military route linking northern Italy to the Holy Roman Empire, France, and the Spanish Netherlands. This critical alpine pass was both the best and fastest way for the Hapsburgs to ship convoys of men, money and material from their holdings in northern Italy to the upper waters of the Rhine, where they could then be dispersed throughout the Holy Roman Empire (controlled by the Austrian branch of the family) or the Netherlands (controlled by the Spanish branch of the family).

Historically a theatre of intense military and diplomatic struggle between Germans, Italians, Swiss, and French, the valley was currently held by *die Drei Bünde* (the Three Leagues), an alliance of anti-Hapsburg forces dating back to 1471, and was commanded by the Protestant Duke of Savoy.

None of that mattered to Father Abaddon Sohar, however. As he made his way like some wraith, skulking in the shadows from Rome to Vienna, he was entirely unconcerned with history, politics, or geography. Completing his mission for Pope Paul V was his one and only concern, and the four men currently blocking his path into the small northern-Italian comune of *Morbegno* were literally and figuratively standing in the way of that mission.

Having been interrupted during the process of committing a robbery, and likely a rape, by Father Sohar, the four irate bandits began to circle around spectre-like priest. Moving like a pack of wolves at the hunt, in wordless communication and coordination, they surrounded the priest and his mount, ready to pounce at the slightest provocation.

"Best keep about your business, padre," the shortest one repeated, displaying a crude but wicked looking knife, while his accomplices readied similarly coarse but deadly blades.

Moving ever so slowly, Father Sohar produced a skin of wine from his saddlebags, took an extra long pull, and grunted with satisfaction as the red liquid burned down his throat. Then, in a gesture indicating a willingness to share, he held the skin out to the short and loud-mouthed leader of the band, smacking his lips loudly as he did so, as if to demonstrate just how exquisite the wine truly was.

Smiling as if to indicate his pride at having cowed such a massive and bizarre looking man, the short bandit reached out to accept the offering. Just as he did, however, Father Sohar distracted him by dropping the wineskin. Then, with a small blade that the short bandit had not seen concealed in the large man's massive right hand, Father Sohar sliced his throat from ear to ear.

As the first bandit fell, desperately clawing at his open wound, and as the other three bandits each displayed a dull, almost bovine-like expression of misunderstanding, Father Sohar used his left hand to produce from within the folds of his cossak an oddly configured weapon that was as strange as it was massive.

The primary barrel of the flintlock pistol was nearly twenty inches in length and held one 12 bore lead round. But what made the weapon so unique was the second cylinder below the main barrel. It was crude, short, and fat – almost as thick as a normal man's forearm. Sporting its own separate trigger, and intended only as a desperate final blow in close quarters, it was terribly inaccurate and was limited by an extremely short range; but because it fired a single lead ball about the size of an egg, it was even deadlier than it was inaccurate.

With speed that belied his massive frame, Father Sohar fired a 12 bore shot towards the man furthest away from him, taking him right through the forehead. The second shot, from the second barrel, was aimed at the bandit closest to him. When it hit, the man's domed forehead, previously crowned with reddish-brown hair, exploded in a shower of blood, brain matter, and shattered bone.

His adrenaline pumping so strong that he was acting almost purely by instinct, the fourth man foolishly lunged at Father Sohar, only to be kicked so savagely in the face by the priest's massive boot, that he was quite certain that his nose and lips had been pushed through to the back of his head.

Sliding down off of his mount for the first time in the fray, Abaddon stood over the fallen fourth man and, picking up the blade the man had dropped when he fell, used one hand to effortlessly pierce the thief through the stomach, effectively pinning him to the ground. There was nothing left to see of the blade except for the crude hilt that protruded from the dying man's chest, and as he tried to rise, only his head and feet came up a little.

So terrified were the two victims of the aborted crime, that they both ran away from the giant priest, screaming *"Diavolo!"* and leaving their wares behind.

Grunting again and wiping away some of the blood and brain matter that had splashed onto his face, Abaddon decided to help himself to some of the abandoned merchant's food. After he finished packing away as much fruit and cheese as he could, he reloaded both barrels of his bizarre firearm and surveyed the carnage he had wrought.

As he prepared to renew his journey, he said a quick and silent prayer for the souls of the four men he had just killed, his lips moving silently as if to gain additional potency by at least attempting to speak the prayer aloud. As he did so, as happened so often when he prayed, a lesson that had been taught to him by none other than Paul V himself came to mind.

It was an obscure French phrase. *How was it worded?* he thought to himself. *Was it "pour encourager les autres?" An action carried out to warn or discourage others? Yes, that was it. How then to best use this unfortunate carnage as a deterrent to any others who might be foolish enough to interfere with my mission,* he wondered. Then helping himself to a particularly appealing piece of *Bresaola*, so dark red that it was almost purple, he decided to take some trophies that he hoped would ward off any other impediments to his journey.

And so, as the snow covered peaks of the Bernina Alps loomed in the distance, wrapped in thin, cotton-like wisps of white clouds, Father Sohar remounted his horse and resumed his journey – this time with four severed human heads dangling, and dripping, in ominous warning from his saddlebags.

Chapter Forty Eight

"What do you mean by that?" Stephen demanded of Sister Elsebeth. "Of course, you're a nun. Why else would you be here?"

"Yes….of course, you're right. Obviously, I am a nun. What I mean to say is that's not all that I am, and that's certainly not why I'm here."

Sister Elsebeth then directed Stephen into a small, unadorned apse just inside the entry to the monastery, saying, "Come in here. These walls have ears, and not all of them are friendly."

"I have no idea what you're talking about," admitted.

Sighing heavily, Sister Elsebeth asked, "Do you know what a *Domkapitular* is?"

The vacant look on Stephen's face was all the answer Sister Elsebeth needed. "It's a canon – a member of a certain, specific body that is subject to a certain, specific ecclesiastical rule."

"A priest then," Stephen offered.

"Yes and no. Father Phillip is the canon here….and he is a priest, but he's a secular priest, just as I am a secular nun."

"I'm lost," Stephen confessed. "How can a nun….or a priest, for that matter, be secular?"

"Since at least the eighth century, maybe even before that, the Church has had secular priests called canons who are, essentially, clerics living with other ordained clergy in a house close to a cathedral or college. And while these secular priests are not ordained by the Church, they are encouraged, but not required, to conduct their lives along with the customary rules and discipline of the Catholic Church."

"Such as?"

"Well....they are expected to demonstrate celibacy, to renounce their wealth and material possessions....things like that."

"Meaning no offence, sister, but what is the value of having priests....or nuns....who are not actually ordained in the Catholic Church?"

"No offence taken, Sir Stephen. And this is where it gets really interesting...."

Stephen could tell that Sister Elsebeth had been desperately spoiling to share this secret knowledge with someone....anyone.... for quite some time. Clearly vows of silence – or secrecy, for that matter – were not strongly "encouraged" for secular nuns, and Sister Elsebeth prattled on like a young girl in school eager to tell what secrets she had divined about the other girls.

"Actually, it's already fairly interesting," said Stephen.

Sister Elsebeth nodded and smiled as if to say, *I know!* She then took a deep breath before continuing her soliloquy. "Let's say you're the Bourbons in France....or even the Hapsburgs here, and the Church needs some special service from you, or you require something special from the Church...."

"Something that neither the Church nor the monarchy would want to ask of a priest...." Stephen added, catching on now.

"Precisely!" Sister Elsebeth exclaimed, punching Stephen in the arm to accentuate the point. "Nothing immoral or illegal, of course...."

"Of course...." Stephen conceded.

"But, perhaps, something that requires a certain skill set or a degree of discretion that could best be served by someone other than an ordained priest...."

"Or an ordained nun," Stephen added, earning himself a huge smile and another punch in the arm from Sister Elsebeth.

"Father Joseph was right, you're as smart as you are tough and handsome."

"Father Joseph? What's he to do with any of this? He's an ordained priest. And how do you even know him?"

"Well of course, he is. But he's the one….along with Father Phillip….who's on our side, by the way….he's just….well, *launisch wie eine nasse Henne*…. But I suppose he has to be. He needs to remain ever vigilant and very suspicious of any newcomers to the monastery here. But he's definitely a friend….and an ally."

Sister Elsebeth's use of the phrase *moody as a wet hen* to describe Father Phillip gave Stephen only a momentary pause before he asked, "A friend of whom? An ally of what?"

This time Sister Elsebeth drew very close to Stephen and whispered in a conspiratorial tone, "Of what Father Joseph is trying to do here."

"Which is what, exactly?" Stephen whispered back in a mocking tone.

Sister Elsebeth's eyes grew very large, and she said, "I'll have to show you in order for you to believe it. Come with me."

A dull ache settled into the left side of her head, just behind her left eye. Earlier it had been like a hailstorm of white-hot nails, but the pain had now settled into a distant noise, like living near a babbling brook, a sound that you heard constantly but never really consciously processed.

And she was cold. It was too early to tell if it was merely a side effect of her gift, or the first hint of something else – something worse. *Or was it just the weather? The nights were cool already, weren't they? The leaves have already changed colour, I think.*

She was suddenly aware of a foul smell. *What is that? Is that my own stench?* Her clothes were torn and stained with mud, blood, and sweat and her hair and skin gave off a powerful, almost tangible reek. *How long has it been since I've bathed? And when did I last eat?*

Why is it so hard to remember? What had I been doing? I was singing, I think. What was it? "Introíbo ad altáre Dei. Ad Deum qui laetificat juventutem meam." *That was from the twenty-third Psalm, wasn't it?* "I will go to the altar of God; to God who gives joy to my youth." *No, that wasn't part of the twenty-third Psalm. What was it from? Who said that?*

Darkness then slipped back over her. She wasn't sure for how long, but when consciousness finally forced its way back into her, painfully and violently, she couldn't remember what she had been thinking. *It was words. What were the words?*

"I will beat the love of Jesus Christ into you. I will beat both of you until you pray that God takes you both to His bosom right now, rather than on the day of judgement."

Were those the words? Who had said them? Was it just now, or was it said before? Who are the 'both of you?' Am I one of the two?

"Can you hear me, Šarlatová?" the voice asked.

Who was that?

"Šarlatová, can you hear me?" the voice asked again. "I think someone is coming. Can you hear me?"

Šarlatová? Who is that? Is that me? Yes....I think that's me. But I can't be sure. 'Someone is coming?' Who? And who said that? I am so tired. I just want to sleep.

Mercifully, but inconveniently, sleep overtook her, blanketing her with a warm and dark cover of senselessness.

"What do you want to do now?" Franz asked Roan. It had been more than a day since Franz had revealed Simon's treachery to Roan, and for the better part of thirty hours, Roan had been in an almost catatonic state. So shocked had he been by Simon's betrayal and Šarlatová's dis- appearance that, in his despair, he had withdrawn from the world and retreated deeply into the recesses of his own brain. When he had begun to fear that his old friend was suffering from some sort of nervous breakdown, Franz had finally decided to press him.

"Roan, what do you want to do now?" Franz repeated. Roan finally showed some indication that he had heard Franz and he turned in his direction, but his expression was as hopelessly blank as the face of a dead man.

"What do you want to do now?" Franz asked for a third time.

Finally, some recognition returned to Roan's face. "What do I want to do now? I'll tell you, old friend. I want to go into *Schloß Stormsong* and rescue our friends. Then I want to find Šarlatová, wherever she is, and see her to safety. And then I want to find Simon Berger, and I want to pull his eyes right out of his head and fuck his eye sockets until death seems preferable to livin'.'"

Sighing remorsefully at just how far his friend had fallen, Franz had softly said, "That's terrifyin'....and oddly specific. I suggest we focus on the third one first. And our best bet to find Simon is to follow his own words....to go to *Pilsen.* As far as our imprisoned friends and Šarlatová....well...." But what Franz didn't say echoed much more in Roan's subconscious than any words he could have chosen to use at that moment.

"Then it's on to *Pilsen* we are to go," Roan had said lifelessly.

Up and moving again, the two had not been walking for more than a few minutes, when the sight of a small cave embedded in a mossy hillside attracted their attention. It seemed relatively small and far from appealing, but as they moved closer to the mouth of the cave, enticed by the aroma of a cooking fire, both men drew up short.

"Roan," Franz whispered, looking at the fresh and massive set of pawprints left in front of the entrance to the cave.

"I see them," Roan whispered back to Franz. "But that's now what worries me." Pausing for effect and taking one very slow step backwards towards Franz, Roan added, "That's what worries me."

Franz looked just a few hundred yards past the cave to see, and smell, what Roan had already detected – a very large and very hungry looking brown bear.

"Fuck," was all Franz could get out before the massive beast took notice of them and started moving in their direction.

Chapter Forty Nine

Anna of Tyrol, by birth an Archduchess of Austria and a member of the Tyrolean branch of the House of Hapsburg, was dying.

By marriage, at the age of twenty-six to her fifty-four-year-old first cousin Matthias, she became the Holy Roman Empress, Queen of Germany, and Queen Consort of Bohemia and Hungary. A life-long devout Catholic and ardent proponent of the Catholic Church's Counter Reformation, she was ultimately awarded the Golden Rose (a rarely conferred honour given as a token of reverence or affection by the Pope). But none of that mattered now. At the tender age of thirty-three, Anna had only weeks to live.

Much like both of her older sisters, Eleonore and Maria, Anna had suffered from poor health almost since her birth. But despite her poor health, she had somehow managed to always remain industrious, good-natured, and genuinely warm and loving. In fact, despite having learned about her husband's ongoing affair with a woman named Susana Wachter, Anna had always remained extremely supportive of him; in fact, after having made her peace with the fact that she would have to share her husband with his mistress, Anna continued to work so well with him that contemporaries began to refer to the couple as *das Arbeitspaar* (the working couple).

In many ways the leader of *das Arbeitspaar*, Anna had accomplished a great deal during her seven year marriage to Matthias. She had convinced her husband to relocate the imperial court from Prague to Vienna and, despite the fact that her primary motivation in doing so was to move her husband further and further away from

Archduke von Stormsong, the new court she had helped to establish became the centre of European culture and commerce. Additionally, again at Anna's urging, the couple had generously supported the religious order of Franciscan Friars, had founded the Capuchin Church in Vienna, and had played an important role in bolstering the efforts of the Austrian Counter-Reformation.

But for all of her accomplishments, Anna was still a weak and frail thirty-two-year-old girl when she took permanently to her bed in the winter of 1617. While she languished in bed, covered in sores, it was assumed that the sorrow of having failed to produce an heir for her emperor had depressed Anna so much that she had simply lost the will to live. While her inability to conceive had assuredly heightened her melancholy, that was not what was killing her. Despondent over her barrenness, Anna had taken to eating, overeating, and then eating again. It was complications stemming from her morbid obesity, not her depression, that ultimately drove Anna permanently to her bed, and the sores that her doctors falsely believed were the cause of her illness were simply bedsores that resulted from her unwillingness or inability to leave her bed.

Nevertheless, despite the fact that she slept almost continuously, waking only to gorge herself on sumptuous meals of smoked eels, Beluga caviar, and suckling pig, she attempted to remain useful to her husband and emperor, and that was the reason why she had requested his presence in her bedchamber.

Matthias had not shared a bed with Anna for at least two years, so it was with great surprise and delight that her chambermaids noted the arrival of the emperor on that cold October morning. However, they were shocked and alarmed to see that Matthias appeared to be in even poorer health than his wife. Islands of black and purple splotches criss-crossed his face and hands; his skin had both the colour and the consistency of parchment, and the shadows cast by the dim light in the room collected unfavourably in the hollows of his cheeks and eyes.

Still, despite the emperor's ghastly appearance, Anna's chambermaids were extremely eager to know the purpose of this rare visit, and they were greatly disappointed when they were all dismissed unceremoniously by a wave of Anna's weak and fleshy hand – only after they had left her with a fresh plate of peach and raisin *Topfenstrudel*, of course.

Once the emperor was alone with his empress, he moved slowly to a chair by the side of her bed and, to delay the inevitable, smoothed his robes so excessively that he turned the simple act of sitting down into a performance. "You look....well....Anna," he lied.

"Ach, du lieber! Then your eyesight is as poor as your judgement, husband. I'll be dead before the year is out. And from the looks of it, so will you."

Matthias coughed a bloody spew into a cloth he kept always at hand and admitted, "Yes, my love. I've not been well of late."

"Well, it's just as well then."

"What is that, dear wife?"

"It's just as well that you follow me into the grave. After all, Archduke von Stormsong has already taken so much of your manhood, that there is scarcely enough left to hold the throne anyway."

Matthias stared at his wife with a combination of shock and curiosity. "Have you not ferreted it out on your own yet, husband?" she asked. When her question was answered by a rather vacant expression on the face of her husband, Anna went on. "What news from Prague? How is Cardinal Khlesl?"

Matthias hung his head. "I fear that Khlesl is no longer with us. May God grant him peace."

"And who is the cause of that, dear husband? Think on it. Stormsong advises you to try to win the war by *losing* its first major confrontation? Then, no sooner has he engineered your defeat than he takes Cardinal Khlesl, your most trusted advisor, from you and has him killed! Do you not see what is at play here?"

Matthias stalled for time by coughing wetly again into his cloth, but Anna returned quickly to her point. "You are a good man, husband of mine, but you are simple, aren't you? Let me explain something to you. Power, my dear, is quite beguiling, and once a man has achieved it, he does not give it up lightly – especially a man like Archduke von Stormsong. He has lied, murdered, manipulated, and engaged in every kind of treachery and deceit imaginable, all to acquire a tenuous hold on power....*your* power – and those are but a few of his failings as a Christian and as a man. Now, with Khlesl gone, with me soon to follow, and with you weak, heirless, and pursuing a policy of fighting a war so as to lose it, his power grows daily." Anna paused both to catch her breath and to make her final point more dramatic. "And no matter how tenuous his hold on power may be today, what will he do *tomorrow* to maintain or increase it?"

As a hint of realisation dawned slowly across his withered face, the emperor took his dying wife's hand in his own. "You're right, Anna. Of course, you are right. How could I have been so blind?"

As a look of steely resolve began to replace his earlier expression of confusion, Matthias tightened his grip on his wife's plump hand. "I hope it is not too late for me to undo what I have done."

"Courage, my husband. When the Lord gives a man a burden, He also gives him the strength to carry it out."

Nodding in agreement, Matthias added, "Yes, I suppose He does. But that's not all. He has given me more than just strength. He has also gifted me with great weapons of His justice. I have, thus far, been loath to use them, but perhaps it is high time that I reveal my claws."

Flashing her husband a knowing smile, Anna felt a tremendous sense of accomplishment and rewarded herself by grabbing another delectable piece of *Topfenstrudel*.

A very resolved Vanessa had decided against returning to *Schloß Stormsong*. *What would be the point anyway?* she had wondered. Likely as not, her father wasn't even there; and even if he was, he was about as likely to help her help the Jewish people of *Josefov* as he was to sprout wings and fly to France. Instead, she had decided she would ride south to Vienna and demand an audience with Emperor Matthias himself. She was cautiously optimistic that she could convince the emperor – who, despite all of his failings, was still a Christian and a fundamentally decent man – to travel back with her to *Josefov* to see for himself just what inequity and injustice were taking place on his watch.

"I have great faith in your heart, Vanessa," Avrem had said. "But I think that there is a far greater chance that the Golem will rise to protect us than that Emperor Matthias will ever set foot here."

Determined to prove him wrong, Vanessa had set out from the Jewish quarter of Prague in the hopes of reaching Vienna in just five days – even less, perhaps, if she really pushed *Starke*, who had grown a little restless with all of the rest he had received since arriving in *Josefov* and was eager to run.

But just two days into her journey, she had been plagued by a severe and mysterious ache in the left side of her brain. It had begun with a moderate sensitivity to light, which she quickly dismissed. Momentary bouts of light sensitivity were something that Vanessa had experienced, and had learned to deal with, from a very early age. But as the second day of her journey drew on, she began to notice that her vision itself was being affected. No longer just bothered by the soft light of the October sun, Vanessa began to experience a cloudiness in her peripheral vision, a cloudiness that was soon accompanied by an increasingly harsh pain on the left side of her head.

Attributing her symptoms to simple dehydration and the presence of too much heavy cream in most of the food she had been served by the Mordecai family, Vanessa stopped to refill her water skins at a bend in the *Vltava river*, just outside of the town of *Český Krumlov*. As she led Starke to the water and bent down herself, a wave of nausea overcame her and she vomited into the cool, clear water.

As if sensing something was wrong, *Starke* initially moved closer to Vanessa, but he backed away again when she began to experience several rounds of short, but violent, retching. When she finally caught her breath, Vanessa sat back on her haunches, wondering what in the world had just come over her.

I'm definitely not pregnant, she thought. *At least not unless God has chosen to bless the world with another virgin birth*. Vanessa had once been told (she couldn't remember by whom) that losing her virginity would be like her first kill. While she could only guess what sex was like, her first kill had been quick, clumsy, and messy. But for all the anxiety it had induced, she had gotten the job done – which was all that mattered. She wondered now if that's what sex would be like – quick, clumsy, and messy. Then, laughing at herself, Vanessa made to stand back up when she was certain that she heard a male voice.

Reacting purely on instinct and with adrenaline now coursing through her body and clearing her head, Vanessa had her crossbow out of her saddle bags in the blink of an eye. But as she swung the weapon back and forth in sweeping, defensive arcs, she soon realised that no one was there.

Great, she thought. *Now I'm hearing voices.* But before she could dismiss the voice as a simple figment of her imagination, she heard it again – this time louder and angrier. And this time it was followed up by….something. Something she couldn't quite identify at first. *A woman's voice, perhaps? But not speaking….singing? No….not singing. Screaming.*

Vanessa had heard many screams over the years. In fact, she had been the cause of far more of them than she cared to admit. But this was unlike anything she had ever heard before. It wasn't plaintive in nature. It was deeper than that….more elemental. It was corporeal….a mixture of both love and rage. Though she couldn't quite make out the words, it sounded to her like someone was having her soul shredded into pieces.

As the original sound of the male voice responded to the tortured screams, she could actually feel the words inside of her. Though she still could not comprehend their meaning, they whirled wildly through her head and body as if they had actually become part of her – or she had become part of them – and a kind of cold electric shock ran through her. Then, just as a sharp rush of breath suddenly escaped her lungs, she opened her eyes – and it was over.

The sounds, the words she could not make out, the intense feeling, the nausea, all of it was simply gone.

As Vanessa tried to make some sense of what had just happened to her, *Starke* continued to back slowly away from her with an inquisitive look on his face that Vanessa would later describe as being one of *"Just what the hell was that?"*

Chapter Fifty

Just the hell was that? was precisely what Stephen was wondering when Sister Elsebeth left him alone, inside the cool, damp corridors of the former monastery. *I have no idea what that verrückte nun is up to. She hasn't made a bit of sense since dragging me in here, and now she's gone God-knows-where to do God-knows-what. And, meanwhile, I am no closer to knowing why Father Joseph sent me on this sleeveless errand in the first place.*

Left completely to his own devices by the bizarre and chatty nun whose parting "wisdom," if he could all it that, had been *'Just remember, these walls listen, and they remember,'* Stephen began to do precisely what she had instructed him to do – that is, roam the virtually vacant halls rather aimlessly. He began in the refectory which was so barren that Stephen guessed it hadn't been used for a communal meal – or for any other purpose, for that matter – in quite some time. Equally neglected was what appeared to be a small, private library that the Franciscan monks and nuns must have once frequented.

A narrow flight of stairs took Stephen to a lower level that appeared to have been modelled after the catacombs in and around Rome. As with the upper level, he found no one here. The entire lower level was populated only by the occasional statue of a saint or martyr, and it seemed to be composed of a maze of dark corridors, each of which was punctuated by dozens of closed and locked doors. His frustration growing by the minute, Stephen came to a final door, this one open and unlocked, at the end of what appeared to be the last hallway in the lower level.

Stepping through the door and ascending a short flight of stairs up, Stephen was instantly transported into an entirely different world. He emerged from the dark and damp covered walkway into what could best be described as a cloister – a massive, open gallery that seemed to stretch on forever.

The cloister was triangular in shape and, in what appeared to be a deliberate representation of the trinity, featured a small, stone chapel at each of the three corners. The high, stone inner-walls of the triangle were adorned by what appeared to be early Renaissance frescoes and the massive, open space between the three walls was dominated by flower and vegetable gardens. The garden nearest to Stephen was populated by red roses, yellow tulips, and white lilies of the valley – all of which appeared to be in full bloom, which should have been impossible given the crisp, cold October air.

Equally bizarre was the fact that several small animals – mostly pigs, chickens, goats, and sheep – all roamed freely throughout the cloister, seemingly completely disinterested in either the flowers or the row upon row of vegetables – asparagus, tomatoes, pickles, potatoes, cabbage, and red onions – most of which were also out of season.

What is this place? Stephen mused. *How is this possible?* As he gazed in wonder at the miracles before him, Stephen suddenly sensed the presence of another person nearby. Making his way towards the centre of the cloister, he saw a man dressed in a capuce and loose black tunic that was girded with a white cord from which hung the Franciscan Crown rosary. The man, whom Stephen assumed was a Franciscan monk, was sitting on a marble bench, surrounded by rabbits and birds, and because he had a Latin Vulgate Bible open before him, it looked almost as if the monk was delivering a sermon to the animals gathered around him.

I swear, if I didn't already know that he has been dead for nearly four-hundred years, I would swear that person was Saint Francis of Assisi himself, Stephen thought to himself.

Looking around to make certain that there was no one else in the cloister but the monk and himself, Stephen slowly approached

377

Saint Francis' doppelgänger and cleared his throat to get the man's attention.

At first it appeared that the monk had not heard him, so Stephen drew closer and cleared his throat even more loudly than the first time. Then, ever so slowly, the man looked up, closed his bible, smiled, and said, "Welcome, Stephen. I've been expecting you."

Eurasian brown bears typically sport dark brown or black fur, and this particular one was no different. The dense fur that covered its massive, five-hundred pound frame was a rich burnt- umber that was accentuated by occasional tufts of velvety-black hair. Its pleasantly small, rounded ears accentuated its equally small, round head, but its paws – which sported three-inch- long, menacing claws – were neither small nor pleasant.

It might have just been his imagination – an unwelcome and unnerving byproduct of sleep-deprivation, hunger, and thirst – but the shape of the bear's dark and puffy lips, its wide but somehow refined nose, and the way its muscles rippled gracefully beneath its skin, reminded Roan of....something. Or someone. He thought for just a moment that he recognized....

Realising that something was suddenly and dangerously amiss with Roan, Franz carefully drew his sword and stepped in front of his old friend, whispering, "Easy, Roan. Don't make any sudden movements. Let me handle this."

As Franz steadied his grip on the large, basket-like hand guard of his *Wallonisches Schwert* (Walloon sword), the bear, sensing the threat, reared back on its hind legs, straightened up to its full height of eight feet, and roared an ominous warning, displaying all forty-two of its deadly teeth. That's when Roan was certain. It wasn't the teeth, but something flashed in the bear's smouldering doe-brown eyes when it roared....something he had seen before. He knew the power of those eyes. They were the same eyes that had weakened him the first time he saw them.

The same eyes that had clearly captivated Šarlatová before.

They were Zahara's.

"I'm sorry....I don't believe I know you," Stephen admitted as he approached the kindly Franciscan monk.

"I suppose not, but I know you Stephen Stallknecht. Although I have not seen you for some eighteen years now, I can plainly see the boy I once knew in the eyes of the man before me now."

The monk motioned for Stephen to come sit on the stone bench next to him. Hesitantly, Stephen did, and the animals that had been gathered around the monk now scattered and kept their distance.

"I do so enjoy nature now," the man mused. "I didn't used to. I suppose that's because I've never been much of a poet. Poets always see nature the way a musician sees notes on the page. Something modest....beautiful....even mysterious. That's why it is always such a source of inspiration to them."

Stephen had absolutely no idea where this conversation was going, nor did he know who this person who claimed to know him was, so he decided to continue to listen politely.

"I have always considered myself more of a man of science.... and nature had, until recently, always seemed a wrathful temptress, daring me, and men like me, to attempt to conquer her and control her. But those efforts have always been in vain."

The man seemed so lost in his own rambling thoughts that he no longer even seemed aware of Stephen's presence. It was as if the strange monk was off somewhere in the very nature about which he was babbling and, not knowing how to bring him back down to Earth, Stephen chose to continue his silent vigil.

"We can delight in nature, but we should never seek to control it," the monk continued. "I know that now. When we seek to control nature, we do so at our own risk. Nature, when offended, tends to exact a severe price, and her retribution can be....outrageous."

Stephen was even more lost listening to the musings of this Saint-Francis-of-Assisi-want-to- be than he was trying to follow the raving lunacy of Sister Elsebeth. *Is there something in the water of this place that drives everyone to madness?* he thought to himself. Then, uncertain of how (or even if) he should restart the conversation, he simply said the first thing that came to his mind.

"I know someone who would both agree and disagree with you," he noted. "Someone who sees nature not as majestic or mysterious, but who does fear its power. Someone who goes to great lengths to avoid encountering nature. In fact, he loathes it in a way that's comparable to how Herod the great loathed first-born children in Judea."

The monk now turned to look directly at Stephen, almost as if he personally knew the person about whom Stephen was speaking.

"But for all of his idiosyncratic animosity towards nature, he knew it to be a gift from God. A gift over which all men, from the lowest cobbler or tavern keeper all the way to the Holy See himself, were granted dominion...." Stephen trailed off, not sure of where he was going with his observations.

"Ah....Father Joseph. I do miss him terribly," the monk admitted.

Shocked to have heard the name of the person about whom he was just musing spoken aloud, Stephen turned in stunned curiosity and made uncomfortable eye contact with the monk.

"Who are you?" Stephen finally managed to whisper.

"Why, my dear Stephen, do you not recognize me after all this time? I'm Vanessa's father. I am Archduke Johann Albrecht von Stormsong."

The siege of *Pilsen* was the greatest non-event of the first seven months of the Thirty Years' War. Commander Dornheim and Marshal Bucquoy daily did their best to bolster the city's meagre defences, but they both knew that defeat was inevitable and, as it so happened, precisely what Emperor Matthias (operating under the strategy advised by Archduke von Stormsong) had ordered. Despite knowing how this campaign was destined to play out, it was their duty to maintain the illusion of steadfast resistance and, in so doing, keep the morale of *Pilsen's* defenders high.

Late October had presented these commanders, and their men, with a welcome surprise when they were unexpectedly reinforced by one-hundred-fifty Dragoons under the command of Henri Duval, Count of Dampierre.

Known to most simply as Dampierre, this popular, thirty-eight-year-old commander was a rising star in the imperial army. Having already established his legacy fighting for the Austrian Hapsburgs during the "Long War" with the Ottoman Turks, he had also been instrumental in assisting then Emperor Rudolph II bring an honourable end to the *Bocskai* uprising (the last time that Protestant rebels in Hungary had fought against the Emperor). Called back into service to, once again, defend yet another Hapsburg emperor against yet another rabble of Hungarian Protestants rebels, Dampierre had ridden hard and fast from the town of *Krems an der Donau* with five companies of arquebusiers from his newly formed regiment of mounted infantry.

But the arrival of these troops, while a boon to the spirits of *Pilsen's* beleaguered defenders, was more than offset by the steady influx of troops into von Mansfeld's already impressive siege army. So confident was von Mansfeld in his ability to take the city any-time he wanted to, he had demanded one-hundred-twenty-thousand *Gulden* and forty-seven-thousand *Florin* to spare the city from his wrath. Having been denied the price he called for, he continued to lob artillery shells into the besieged city. But neither the walls nor the city's stalwart defenders had yet cracked, and a typical day of "battle" consisted of von Mansfeld lobbing a few dozens shells into the city and Bucquoy firing about half as many back – the effect be-ing that the only "casualties" so far had been a few dairy cows who had mistakenly wandered too close to the city's walls.

But as the cool air of October grew both heavier and greyer, both sides knew that November was fast approaching, and they knew what that meant. November would bring the first snowfall. And once the first snow fell, then the city's hungry but dedicated defenders would, too.

Chapter Fifty One

"It's going to take a lot more than a few hours of sleep and a few bites of food to make her whole again," Zahara informed Roan from inside the confines of the cave where she had been protecting Šarlatová for the past day and a half. Franz Hohenleiter could hear her, too, but he was outside the cave, too occupied with retching up his guts from having witnessed Zahara's remarkable transformation from bear back to beautiful woman to fully participate in the bizarre conversation.

"Explain it to me again," Roan requested.

Zahara looked askance at Roan. "Why? Did you not hear me the first two times? Did you not understand me either time? Or do you simply not trust the account that I gave you….twice?"

"Listen, girl," Roan bristled. "Trust is not somethin' I have a lot of right now. So humour me and explain it again."

Zahara sighed heavily and looked over to the other side of the cave where Šarlatová was sleeping fitfully. "You know that women bleed once a month, yes?" As uncomfortable as he was talking about women's menstrual cycles, Roan was eager to get to the story of what had happened with Šarlatová since he had left her, so he just nodded awkwardly. Meanwhile Franz continued to gag outside of the cave.

"Well, when I have been….in the skin of another….for too long, my monthly bleeding comes much earlier and much heavier than it would otherwise."

"That would account for all the blood I saw," Roan said, more to himself than to Zahara.

"Yes. The blood that you thought was Šarlatová's. Blood that you immediately assumed had been spilled by me."

Roan said nothing and just stared down at his boots.

"As best I can figure, Šarlatová saw the blood and, because I still had not woken, became concerned. She must have used her...." Zahara paused and nodded in the direction of Franz, who was just now recovering. "Does he know about....?" Roan glanced back at Franz and shook his head no. Lowering her voice and leaning closer to Roan, Zahara said, "She used her gift to heal me. I woke to hear her singing, and I was....I was restored....instantly"

"But...." prompted Roan.

"But it must have taken a great deal out of her, because she collapsed almost immediately. Ever since, instead of her caring for me, I have been caring for her. Where have you been all this time, and who is that other man? I do not like him."

"I was lookin' for some food for the three of us, and I was.... delayed. As for who he is, he's one of the very few people on the planet I trust right now."

"And why is that?"

"Because his older brother Ulrich was captured, tortured, and executed by the very same people what are after me and Šarlatová. The same ones what enslaved you, too, by the way."

"And you trust anyone who fights against your enemy?"

Roan nodded. "I have to."

"And despite the fact that I was kidnapped from my people, sold into slavery, brought to a foreign land and and forced to do things I am too ashamed to even utter....all by the people you call your enemy....I am not one of those people you trust? Is that correct, friend Roan?"

Before Roan could respond, Franz approached and offered a gruff apology. "I have no idea what I just saw, but I take it the two of you already know each other?" he asked.

Roan and Zahara just stared at each other, neither one acknowledging they had even heard Franz's question. Franz watched both of them carefully and, while neither one of them said a word, he felt that an entire conversation was passing between them nonetheless. After having impatiently indulged them with a few seconds of awkward silence in which to formulate a response, Franz finally grunted and looked to his friend. "Can I have a word with you, Roan?"

Zahara stared intently at Roan, watching him as he weighed his decision. "Roan?" Franz repeated.

"Anythin' you care to say to me can be said in front of her, too, Franz."

Zahara smiled ever so slightly, but Franz reacted as if he'd just been slapped across the face. *"Ja?* Is that a fuckin' fact? Well, here's what I'd like to say….*to the both of you*….then! It's clear that you two know each other. It's also clear that you're both keepin' secrets from me, which I don't like. And the only thing I likes less than that is keepin' company with…. witches….dark skinned or otherwise!"

As Roan stood to defend Zahara from Franz's accusation, a weak voice came from inside the cave. "She's not a witch, Franz. No more so than I am, or you are, or anyone else, for that matter. And wherever Roan and I go, she goes too. What happens to one of us happens to all of us, and that includes her, too."

Zahara, Roan, and Franz all looked into the cave where a newly awakened Šarlatová was just starting to sit up – or at least attempting to. Despite the fact that her three friends were clearly in various stages of surprise, disbelief, and relief, each one smiled at her when she asked, "Now…. who has something to eat?"

Stephen shook his head no when the man who claimed to be Vanessa's father offered him an apple from inside the folds of his loose, black tunic.

"It's okay, Stephen. It's not forbidden fruit from the garden of Eden. Although I must admit that this cloister looks precisely like what I imagine it must have looked like….before the fall, anyway."

Stephen shook his head no again, prompting the monk to wonder aloud, "Why is it that no one ever wants to eat when they have something important to discuss?" Taking a large and loud bite from the apple, he added, "I always want to eat at those times. I find it helps ease the tension."

"I don't think there is any fruit that could ease what I'm feeling right now, whoever you are. And I'm not certain I would describe what I'm feeling as tension. You....you have falsely claimed that you are the father of the woman I...."

"That you what?" the man interrupted. "Go ahead, Stephen. You can complete that thought. It would do you immeasurable good to come out and say it. I already know that you love her anyway. I think the whole empire knows by now, but I've known for some time. And, for what it's worth, I have no objection to it."

Stephen stared at the crazed monk with a look that was equal parts confusion and part shock. "You....wait....what?" was all he could stammer out.

The crazed monk just smiled and took another bite of his apple. "That's not entirely true, of course. I do have objection to it. Strong objection, in fact. After all, she's a beautiful young woman, and I am her very protective father. What I meant to say was that I have no *particular* objection to *you*. I only object in principle, as all fathers are supposed to do, to any boy who shows any interest in his daughter. But she could do much worse than marrying an honourable young man like yourself. I pray to God every day that she doesn't end up with someone like Rowland Gundrham. That child is....well, he's just not right in the head. If God ever made a mistake, it was that child. Although I suppose he's not a child anymore. He must be a grown man now, like you. Or she could end up with a Protestant. God! Which would be worse? The Gundrham bastard or a Protestant? I tell you, Stephen, there are times...."

"Stop!" Stephen implored, much louder than he intended to. "Just....stop, please," he added much more politely. Stephen's head was about to explode, and this crazed man was prattling on like he had just been released from a vow of silence. "I need a minute to think," he confessed as he stood and circled around the bench, trying to process everything he had just been told.

"Yes, of course. I do apologise. It's just that....well, the worst part of being imprisoned in this paradise here is the solitude. For most of my life, I've been surrounded by people. People wanting this or needing that, but now....now I'm imprisoned here with a small guard of nuns and priests. Don't get me wrong, Father Joseph has chosen each one very well. They are all exceptionally capable and loyal and dedicated to the task Father Joseph has assigned to them. But, with the exception of Sister Elsebeth, they hardly ever communicate with me. In fact, most of them act as if I have something contagious they're afraid to catch. So this is the longest and most significant conversation I've had in...."

Stephen looked back down at the strange man whose face he felt he was actually beginning to recognize. "I'm sorry," he interrupted. "Did you just say that you are imprisoned here?"

But the monk just continued on as if he had not even heard a word Stephen had just said. "And I miss the activity. The comings and goings in and out of *Schloß Stormsong*. And all of the daily details, of course. But most of all, I miss my children."

"I'm sorry, did you say *children*? As in plural? Meaning more than one?"

The crazed man looked up at Stephen, and it appeared as if he had a tear in the corner of his left eye. "You heard me correctly, Stephen. I said my *children*."

"That's what I thought you said. Well, now I am certain that you are an imposter. Until now, you told a fascinating and almost believable tale. *Almost*, that is. But you erred just now. Archduke von Stormsong....the *real* archduke.... has but one child. Vanessa."

Just as Stephen felt victorious for having elicited the truth and having revealed this charlatan for what he was, the mad monk seemed to deflate in defeat right before him. "God bless you, Stephen. You are a fine boy, but there is much you don't know."

Stephen bristled at being called a boy – again – and considered walking away from the crazed lunatic, but the man glanced up at him with a look of despair. "Please, sit down….I have quite a story to tell you."

Against his better judgement, Stephen relented and sat next to the madman who then asked, "Tell me, Stephen. What do you know of witchcraft and sorcery?"

Father Joseph was not well.

He looked even worse than when Vanessa had introduced him to Rabbi ben….something or other. He couldn't remember his name. His memory was fading even faster than his once prodigious appetite, and the former colour in his face had faded to an almost onion-like shade and texture. His shoulders sagged more and more; what little hair he had left was rapidly falling out, and his sense of smell was failing so fast that he was the only person in *Schloß Stormsong* who wasn't aware that he now reeked of a foul odour – a pungent cocktail of old piss, new sweat, and dried vinegar.

There was no light left in his eyes, not even when he prayed. And lately, his prayers sounded more like a lyrical lament than a steadfast profession of faith. He mumbled almost constantly, repeating the same verse over and over. He repeated *"And ye shall know the truth, and the truth shall make you free,"* so often that those around him began to fear that verse thirty-two from chapter eight of the Gospel according to John was the only part of the Holy Bible he was still capable of reciting from memory.

When he was not shuttered away, alone and in his room, he was almost always within the confines of *Chrám Všech Svatých* (All Saints' Church), one of his favourite places within the sprawling complex of *Schloß Stormsong*.

Originally constructed as a free-standing building in the Romanesque style, the church had been consecrated in 1185 but was badly damaged by the mysterious fire which engulfed and claimed much of *Schloß Stormsong* in 1541. Subsequently, through a series of successive rebuildings and enlargements, the church slowly became physically integrated into the rest of the massive, ever-growing compound. Usually only accessible from the rest of *Schloß Stormsong* through the massive and elaborate *Vladislavský Sál* (Vladislav Hall), the church allegedly held the tomb of *Prokop Sázavský* (Saint Procopius of Sázava), a Bohemian hermit who was canonised by the Catholic Church in 1204. As if to substantiate that claim, the life of *Prokop Sázavský* was depicted within the church on a series of paintings, one of which consistently captivated Father Joseph's attention far more than any of the others.

As he stood before the painting – which depicted *Prokop Sázavský* holding a book and a whip, and with the devil at his feet – Father Joseph fumbled nervously with his rosary. But instead of repeating by rote the same four prayers over and over again, he did something quite uncharacteristic for most seventeenth century Catholics. He prayed directly to God, straight from his heart, and not through the intercession of *Prokop Sázavský* or any other saint.

"Heavenly Father, I fear that my time here is at an end. And while I am blithe to be able to look You directly in the face soon, I am griefstriken by my failures to do for my Raven what needed to be done. I pray now that any physical, psychological, or theological damage she might have incurred as result of my failings, or of her mother's untimely death, or as a result of her ....her...."

Father Joseph choked a little, unable to utter the word father. "Or of....*his*....sadistic use of her as both a weapon and a political pawn, has not dented her faith. I pray the armour of God over her, Lord, and pray that You do for her what I was unable to do. I pray that You use Your truth to set her free. Reveal Yourself to her as the Father she so desperately needs, before it...."

But before Father Joseph could finish his heartfelt prayer, he heard an all too familiar voice whisper from behind him.

"Father Joseph," hissed an almost giddy Monsignor Mučitel. "His Highness, Archduke von Stormsong would like to have a word with you. You are to come with me....now."

Chapter Fifty Two

Stephen hated onions.

In fact, he hated everything about them.

And the whole sordid saga Stephen had just uncovered was like an onion in every way imaginable.

It had layer upon layer; it reeked terribly, and it had already brought tears to his eyes.

Having heard the entire, incredible, and tragic tale from the man he now suspected to actually be Archduke von Stormsong, he had cried for several minutes. But he had recovered quickly and, at the urgent pleading of the archduke, had resupplied, relocated Kimber, and beat a hasty retreat from *Lindau*.

If this man really was telling the truth, and if he was, in fact, really Vanessa's father, then everything Vanessa thought she knew about herself and her family was wrong. But more importantly, if everything else the man had told Stephen bore equal veracity, then both she and Father Joseph were in mortal danger.

Somehow, almost as if she understood Stephen's need for haste, Kimber found a speed and a determination that had been previously lacking, and she tore through the countryside as if someone had lit her tail on fire. In fact, it was all Stephen could do just to hang on at times, and he was so exhilarated by this radical transformation in Kimber's demeanour that he completely failed to notice the four riders who remained just one or two miles behind him, desperately trying to keep up.

The chandelier was totally incongruous with the rest of the gloomy space. In fact, one of the many people who had died in this place over the years had once observed, in the moments before his death, that it made about as much sense as having an altar in a brothel.

But Father Joseph didn't know that. On the contrary, standing in the cool and damp lower level of *der Roter Turm* (the Red Tower), the shortest and least used of the three towers within *Schloß Stormsong's* Autumn Palace, a place he had never before entered, Father Joseph was transfixed by the chandelier that was as beautiful as it was out of place. Hanging fifteen feet above him and embellished with semi-precious stones, the ten-foot-wide chandelier was designed like a glass bouquet, with flowers of coloured glass, and a jewel glowing at the centre of each of the flower's petals, and it stood in stark and ominous contrast to the rest of Father Joseph's sombre surroundings.

A loud voice called out to him and echoed through the cavernous lower level, causing Father Joseph to look away from the chandelier. As the archduke stepped out from the shadows, Joseph noticed that he had two men with him that he had never seen before.

On either side of the archduke stood what appeared to be twin black African slaves. They were both bald and darker than any Africans Father Joseph had ever seen before. They shared identically wide noses, thick lips, and prognathous jaws. Broad shouldered but with narrow hips, the pair paced back and forth behind the archduke, like panthers sharing a cage. They both displayed surprising grace despite being so bulky, and both of them looked able, and willing, to dismember a man with his bare hands.

Father Joseph had never actually seen them before, but he was fairly certain that he was looking for the first time at the *Akuji*. According to what he had been told by the archduke when he had first purchased the twin slaves, *Akuji* was a Swahili word meaning *dead but awake*. As he stared into the eyes of these two unholy acolytes, who looked to him more like monsters than men, Father

Joseph understood that meaning for the first time. These two legendary berserkers had, over the years, become surrounded by an almost mythical ethos based on how powerful, brutal, and blindly obedient to the archduke they had become. Even in an empire that was regularly punctuated by violence, these two had managed to gain an unparalleled reputation for savage cruelty.

"Welcome to my trophy room, Father Joseph," the archduke said in feigned hospitality.

"Your Highness, I'm afraid you have me at a loss. I've never been to this place before, and I don't know for what purpose you have summoned me here."

"Well of course you haven't," the archduke chuckled. "Few who have seen this place have lived to tell about it. But go ahead.... look around."

Father Joseph decided to play along for a minute, and as he looked up and down the halls of what could only be described as a cavern, he saw row after row of what appeared to be effigies, like the life-size wax figures displayed in the nearly six-hundred-year-old Westminster Abbey Museum in London. But it didn't take long for Father Joseph to realise that these figures were neither wax nor effigies. They were, in fact, perfectly preserved corpses.

As Father Joseph gasped and covered his mouth in shock and terror, the archduke flashed him a depraved smile. "You see, Joseph, I like to keep my former enemies....my vanquished foes, if you will, near me. Dead, embalmed, and dressed in whatever uniform or other attire they customarily wore while they were still alive, they serve as a welcome and constant reminder of my many past victories." Father Joseph was shocked and appalled as Stormsong daintily fingered the delicate lace on the apple-green bodice of the archduke's late wife and Vanessa's mother – Gabrielle Robinette von Stormsong.

"It's true. In fact, one of my favourite habits is to take guests on a guided tour of my.... collection. But that's not why I invited you down here today, Father Joseph."

"It's not?" the horrified priest somehow managed to ask with trepidation.

"No. I don't just want to show it to you. I want you to become a special part of it." Before the priest could respond, the archduke twitched ever so slightly and, with stunning speed and agility that belied his massive form, one of the Archduke's *Akuji* launched forward and kicked Father Joseph in the chest hard enough to send him crashing into the nearest wall. When the stunned priest bounced off and fell to the floor, he curled immediately into a foetal position, unable to find any air. A second kick, this one to his stomach, lifted him clear off the ground and forced whatever air was left to explode out of him like a fiery ball of lead. The sudden and vicious assault left Father Joseph certain that some unseen force was either squeezing his heart or crushing his lungs, while some other force was directing a river of lava to course its way painfully through his stomach and throat. Only when he vomited some putrid combination of bile, blood, and fire did the priest's throat reopen to the rush of sweet air.

"You see, Father Joseph," the archduke said in the tone of a school master disciplining an unruly child, "Spy networks work both ways. They're a two-way conduit for information. You have yours, and I have mine. And that's how I learned about your betrayal of me....about your little secret project in *Lindau*."

Father Joseph was only able to cough out a brief gasp before the second Akuji jerked him violently to his feet and held him up by the scruff of his neck, as if he weighed no more than a child's toy.

"Actually, I've known about it for years. But it served my purposes, so I allowed it. Until you betrayed me by sending Sir Stephen there. And I. Do not. Brook. Betrayal. Lightly." The archduke spoke each syllable as if it was its own completely formed thought, and each word he uttered was accompanied by a tightening of the grip by the monstrosity holding onto the back of his neck. With just one arm, the massive berserker had Father Joseph suspended in air, his feet no longer able to touch the ground.

Impossibly, as if briefly gifted with some supernatural strength, the priest was able to offer a measured retort. "My only concern…. ever….was that I did not…. betray our Lord….Jesus Christ." The last few words came with a wet hacking sound and another discharge of blood and bile.

"Is that so? You're still believing in those defunct fairy tales, are you? Well let's see what help your Lord Jesus Christ can be to you now." As if on cue, the second *Akuji* let the wounded priest fall unceremoniously to the ground. Landing with an extremely sharp jolt to his tailbone, Joseph was certain that he had just shattered several bones in his hips and spinal column, and he flopped over on his left side like a lifeless rag doll. As he did, Stormsong circled around him in a mocking display of searching for something or someone.

"It would appear that He's not coming," the archduke teased in a whisper. "It's really not all that surprising. He tends to steer clear of Prague during the colder months."

"Abba, forgive him," the priest offered in a barely audible prayer. "He knows not what he does. He is ambitious and ruthless; he has murdered friends and terrorized his family. He has consorted with prostitutes and seduced boys. Worst of all, he has dabbled in the occult and embraced the darkness of Your Enemy. But he is not beyond redemption, Lord. No matter what a waste he has made of his life, it is still possible through Thy unsurpassing grace, to help him find some path to salvation."

The archduke had knelt down next to the priest so that he could hear his final prayer. Now that it appeared to be over, he said, "I must admit, Joseph, I am impressed. You really are remarkable. After everything I have taken from you, and as you lie here, seconds away from death, you are praying, albeit in vain, to save me from the darkness. Extraordinary."

All that Father Joseph could offer by response was, "And may perpetual light shine upon him," to which Stormsong stood, shook his head disapprovingly, and tsk-tsked the dying man.

"I'm sorry to be the one to tell you, father, but the truth is, it is impossible to properly appreciate the light without first knowing the darkness. And I know the darkness better than any man who has ever walked this Earth."

"Fear not. For the eyes of the Lord are on the righteous, and His ears are open to their prayers," the priest moaned. Then, just as Stormsong turned to walk away, prepared to let his twin acolytes tear the priest to pieces, Father Joseph added, "And because He hears *her* prayers, *she* is far stronger than you. In the end, you will see that *her* strength comes from *her* faith. And that faith will be your undoing."

"What did you just say?" Stormsong hissed, turning back around to face Father Joseph who managed a weak smile, and made a very slow, very deliberate, and very painful sign of the cross.

Enraged, Stormsong avowed, "On second thought, *father*, I'm not going to keep you in my collection. The presence of a fat and wrinkled old sack of meat like you would just spoil the entire ensemble. Instead, here is what I will do with you. You know, of course, that I have always been fascinated by large guns. Well, I am going to drop you into a vat of molten bronze and melt you down in one of my foundries. Then I'm going to cast you as part of a massive cannon….a piece of artillery that will spew fire and belch death and destroy everything in its path. And that will be your legacy. But before I am done, if your precious little Raven will not use her power to advance my kingdom, then I will let these two abominations ravage her little virgin body again and again and again, until she begs for death! If I can't have her power, no one will!"

Mustering what little life he had left, Father Joseph craned his head up as far as he could manage and uttered, "You think yourself powerful because of your wealth and your weapons. But you can neither purchase nor conquer the light. And the power of your darkness will never vanquish the power of *their* light. *They* are stronger than you!" Then, mimicking Stormsong's earlier rhythm and cadence, he added, "For. She. Is. Not. Alone!"

Stormsong's eyes instantly flashed with violent, red lightning, and Father Joseph simply vanished into a seething mass of fire, bent bone, twisted muscle, and scorched flesh. And for hours after the archduke and his slaves had left the Red Tower, the flames that had once been Father Joseph continued to whip around in a swirling kaleidoscope of horror.

Chapter Fifty Three

Although Gottfried Heinrich, *Graf* (Count) *von Pappenheim* was only twenty-four years old, he was already one of Emperor Matthias' most capable commanders. As the second son of Veit von Pappenheim, Lord of *Treuchtlingen and Schwindegg,* he had mastered several languages during his lengthy and expensive education at *die Universität Altdorf* and *die Eberhard Karls Universität Tübingen.* Pappenheim had subsequently put those languages to use while he travelled throughout southern and central Europe seeking fame to add to his – or, more precisely, his father's – fortune. His various stays in these countries had led to far fewer knightly adventures than he would have liked, but they did contribute directly to his conversion, at the age of twenty, to the Roman Catholic faith, and it was his zeal for his adopted faith that caused him to abandon a promising legal and diplomatic career and take service in the army of Polish King *Zygmunt III Waza* (Sigismund III Vasa) – a religious zealot who fanatically imposed Catholicism all across Poland.

It was in the service of the Polish army that Pappenheim gained his reputation as a skilled cavalry officer, helping *Zygmunt III Waza* impose Roman Catholic doctrine across his vast realm and neighbouring states like Lithuania. Pappenheim, like the Polish king he served, embodied the spirit of traditional inherited wealth and, thus, traditional inherited conservatism, with both showing great scepticism in man's ability to govern himself. Therefore, not only did neither man feel any qualms about imposing a religious despotism upon the Polish and Lithuanian people, but both felt it was actually in the best interests of those "commoners" to be ruled by the heavy hand of a tyrant.

It was during his service to *Zygmunt III Waza* that Pappenheim finally found the "knightly adventures" he had sought earlier in his life, helping the Polish despot launch religious crusades into Finland, Sweden and Russia, and it was during these crusades that Pappenheim came to the attention of Emperor Matthias. In fact, after having heard about the successes achieved by this bright, young, cavalry officer, Matthias had paid a king's ransom to *Zygmunt III Waza* to enlist Pappenheim into the Holy Roman Imperial Army, at the head of an elite regiment of cuirassiers.

Emperor Matthias was extremely partial to cuirassiers – members of cavalry units equipped with an eponymous cuirass (a piece of armour formed of multiple pieces of metal which cover the torso), a sword, and a pair of long-barrelled wheel-lock pistols. Matthias found them to be the "tip of the spear," and appreciated the almost mediaeval romanticism they inspired. To further contribute to the knightly look his new benefactor favoured, Pappenheim insisted that his cuirassiers also carry lances – and to distinguish himself from his men, Pappenheim notoriously sported a "horseman's pick" (a type of war hammer with a very long spike on the reverse of the hammer head).

Operating under orders from Emperor Matthias, Pappenheim's cavalry regiment of nearly five-hundred cuirassiers was dispatched to Prague with orders to arrest the archduke and return him to Vienna, where he would be expected to atone for his treatment of Cardinal Khlesl. Alternatively, if Stormsong resisted, they were to, in the words of the emperor himself, "place the tip of a lance right between the bastard's eyes."

Pappenheim was simultaneously excited to embark on an adventure for Emperor Matthias, especially one that met with his standards for what constituted a "knight's errand," and hesitant at the prospect of having to confront one of his heroes.

Consequently, ever since having received his orders, he had spent much of his free time praying and contemplating verses ten through twelve of Psalm 143. *Teach me to do Thy will; for Thou art my God; Thy spirit is good; lead me into the land of uprightness. Quicken me, O Lord, for Thy name's sake; for Thy righteousness' sake bring my soul out of trouble. And of Thy mercy, cut off mine enemies, and destroy all them that afflict my soul; for I am Thy servant.*

As they daily drew nearer and nearer to *Schloß Stormsong,* Pappenheim's men also began to privately express concern and trepidation about arresting the legendary archduke. But the first one to actually voice those concerns publicly, was Pappenheim's second in command, Friedrich Georg Nehring – a man who was rumoured to be far more to Pappenheim than just a trusted lieutenant. In fact, those scurrilous rumours and stories were so common, albeit apocryphal, that many in the regiment had begun to refer to Pappenheim as *Herr Weichschwert* (Sir Softsword). And while it was clear to many in the regiment that the two men shared a bond of unusual closeness, it was hoped by those same men that the two were simply engaged in some bond of adoptive brotherhood, like that of David and Jonathan in the Old Testament

"Begging your pardon, *Graf von Pappenheim.* But might I have a word?" Nehring asked, standing just outside of his commander's crude and simple tent – just one part of the regiment's encampment near *Herálec,* a small village approximately eighty miles southeast of Prague.

"Of course. What can I do for you, Friedrich? And, when we're alone, you may refer to me as Gottfried."

"Yes, of course, *Herr*….I mean, Gottfried," Nehring said, blushing. "I just wanted to discuss with you some….misgivings….the men and I are having regarding this assignment."

"And what misgivings are those, Friedrich?"

"Well, if I may speak candidly, some have expressed a practical fear, born out of the legends on how ruthless and powerful the archduke is. For others the hesitation appears to be political in nature, the concern being about following orders from….well….from an obviously failing Emperor. And for still others, the reservation is entirely theological, a scepticism about what might become of us – pawns, if you will, in a game between two different Catholic authorities."

"Ja? Is that a fact, Friedrich? Well, let me share with you something valuable I learned at *die Universität Altdorf."*

Nehring, whose own schooling at *die Universität Helmstedt* was exquisite in its own right, bristled at Pappenheim's constant gloating about the quality of his own expensive education – as if the cost of one's education had any rational bearing on its quality.

But Pappenheim proceeded as if he didn't notice – or, more precisely, just didn't care about – Nehring's consternation. "For centuries, science has always told us what is, while morality has always told us what is right and wrong. Conversely religion hasn't concerned itself with what is or what is right or wrong; religion has always promised that there is an eternal kingdom somewhere that is far better off than the temporal world in which we live. Do you get my meaning?"

"Not precisely, no," Nehring admitted.

Shaking his head in an air of patronising superiority, Pappenheim stood and approached his lieutenant. "What I mean, my friend, is that it matters not what we occupy ourselves with in this world, for we are only here for a short time. Whether our mission is successful or not, whether it is morally just or not, matters not at all. All that matters is our fidelity to our Lord Jesus Christ. So long as we maintain that, then our salvation is secure, and we shall all share in our Saviour's promise of a better life." Pappenheim punctuated his point with a brotherly pat on Nehring's shoulder.

"Yes, of course, *Gottfried.* But there is still something that concerns me."

"What is that?"

"Well, of late, I have been reading from Étienne Dolet. Are you familiar with Dolet?"

"Yes, of course," Pappenheim lied. "What of her?"

"Well, before *he* was strangled and burned by the Inquisition, he wrote some very interesting critiques on the rationality of Christianity."

"Then I'm sure the Inquisition was justified in eliminating her….I mean him."

"Perhaps, but I've also been reading from the *Theophrastus redivivus.*"

"And what is the *Theophrastus redivivus?*" Pappenheim asked tersely, this time choosing to abandon the pretence that he was familiar with the text to which his subordinate was referring.

"Well, it's sort of an anthology of….well, free thought. It contains material from brilliant philosophers like Pietro Pomponazzi, Lucilio Vanini, Michel de Montaigne, and Pierre Charron. Even Machiavelli."

"All of those people you just named are either heretics…. or dead….or both. And if that trash is not already on the *Index Librorum Prohibitorum,* I'm sure it soon will be."

The *Index Librorum Prohibitorum* (commonly known as the Index of Forbidden Texts) was a list of material banned by the Catholic Church. First published in the early sixteenth century, it continued to list numerous books and articles which were forbidden to Catholics, ostensibly to *protect* them from immoral or blasphemous material.

Nehring could tell now that he was trying his commander's patience, but he couldn't help himself now that the words had begun to pour from his lips. "Nevertheless, they, in combination with the writings of Copernicus, with which I have recently been preoccupied, raise a compelling question."

"And what is that," Pappenheim asked tiredly.

"What if we're wrong?"

Pappenheim stared back blankly, clearly not following.

"What if this is it? What if this life is all we get? What if there isn't anything more after we die? I guess my point is this. If the promise of eternal life is just a….a fable….then, shouldn't we conduct the one life we have….differently? Perhaps, better?"

Pappenheim just stared back at his lieutenant with an expression of total confusion, as if he had just been told a riddle that he couldn't quite understand.

After several long seconds of awkward silence, Nehring finally offered a halting apology for having so thoroughly vexed his superior. Then, feeling no more need to trample upon the Count's obvious ignorance in these questions of theology, he quietly excused himself and left a forlorn Pappenheim alone to contemplate the possibility that things were not quite as simple as he had previously thought them to be.

Things seemed to be going according to plan. Based on the latest reports he had received, Marshal Bucquoy was convinced that the strategy he had been ordered to employ by Emperor Matthias was succeeding. In fact, just days ago, on November ninth, approximately ten- thousand imperial troops, ostensibly on their way to reinforce the beleaguered defenders of *Pilsen*, had "accidentally" (meaning, on purpose) encountered a larger force of fourteen-thousand Bohemians under the command of Count von Thurn in the small, southern Bohemian town of *Lomnice nad Lužnici* (*Lomnitz an der Lainsitz* to the Germans).

The bulk of the emperor's Catholic forces conveniently positioned themselves in the floor of a valley, between two large ponds – this, despite the fact that von Thurn's Protestant artillery held the high ground on a ridge overlooking the valley. Consequently, the Catholic troops suffered from a withering torrent of artillery fire, sustaining more than fifteen-hundred casualties in the process. However, despite the fact that the troops under his command suffered fewer than two-hundred deaths or injuries, von Thurn chose not to follow the Emperor's troops when they beat a hasty retreat out of Bohemia. Instead, rather than press his easily won advantage, von Thurn decided to march the bulk of his forces northwest to reinforce Mansfeld's troops at *Pilsen*, which meant that, within the fortnight, both von Mansfeld and von Thurn would be participating in the siege of Pilsen. And if the emperor's plan continued to work, they would almost immediately begin to squabble for authorship of the "victory" and control of the rebel army.

Commander Dornheim, however, remained unconvinced that this strategy of deliberately losing battles to the Protestant hordes was a sound one. "I simply don't see the virtue in sacrificing our men this way," he confessed to Marshal Bucquoy. "We should be fighting the war to win it, not lose it. This new strategy...."

"Dornheim, let me explain something to you about this 'new strategy'," Bucquoy interrupted. "Anytime anything 'new' appears in Europe, the same thing inevitably occurs. The English always want to know if it works; the French want to know if it is safe; the Greeks want to know if it was born in Greece; and the Italians want to know what the rest of Europe thinks about it."

Dornheim looked puzzled. "And the Germans? What do the Germans want to know?"

"They don't!" Bucquoy barked.

"They don't what, my lord?"

"They don't want to know. They don't care. They simply follow orders, and they don't ask questions. They just do what they're told, Herr Dornheim."

"Understood, Herr Marshal. But doesn't prudence dictate that we at least make it look like we're trying to win?"

"That's not our task, Herr Dornheim. It is not up to us to question Imperial strategy. It is up to us to do our best to execute those policies. *Verstehen, Sie?*"

"*Natürlich,* Herr Marshal. But let's just pray that we don't get executed....before the policy does." This caused Bucquoy to smile and think to himself *From your lips to God's ears, clever boy. From your lips to God's ears.*

The four riders overtook Stephen just thirty miles outside of *Lindau,* at the free imperial city of *Leutkirch im Allgäu* (the People's

Church at Allgäu). Despite the fact that *Leutkirch*, like most other free imperial cities within the empire, had gone through considerable strife during the Protestant Reformation (Lutheran one day, Catholic the next, then back to Lutheran), the residents of the town cheerfully claimed it to be one of the sunniest cities in the entire empire.

Hoping that *Leutkirch's* reputation was not just a meteorological one, Stephen decided to rein Kimber in and allow the four riders behind him to catch up as he entered the town. He had first noticed them a few miles back, and each time he checked on them, there they were – maintaining a safe but constant vigil behind him.

As the four riders drew near, Stephen relaxed considerably when he saw a red-brick castle floating on a sea of blue waves all set against a gold shield base on their tunics. That *Meer und Schloß* (Sea and Castle) emblem was the coat of arms for *Meersburg*, a small town on the northern shore of Lake Constance. Despite the fact that many of the territories around Lake Constance had joined the Protestant Reformation as free imperial cities, *Meersburg* remained under the secular and episcopal control of das *Hochstift Konstanz* (the Bishopric of Constance), where the Catholic prince-bishops retained almost total power. That meant that the men approaching Stephen were devout Catholics and, consequently, allies – at least in theory.

But Stephen could not yet account for the loyalties of the fifth person who was riding in his direction. While the four *Meersburg* riders were coming at him from the southwest, this fifth rider, a black-clad giant, was approaching *Leutkirch* from due south, riding out from only-God- knew-where. *Perhaps the gates of Hell, by the look of him*, Stephen thought to himself. And while the *Meersburg* men and the giant were clearly not together, it was equally clear that their paths would soon intersect – right at the spot where Stephen was standing.

Chapter Fifty Four

The light sensitivity, cloudiness in her vision, and nausea that struck Vanessa so suddenly just outside of *Český Krumlov* caused her to do something quite uncharacteristic – she stopped to rest. And when the voices returned, some sort of ancient and elemental presence that was both part of her and separate from her, she decided to spend an entire day in bed, and at rest – hoping that the alien and terrifying, but also familiar and intoxicating, presence in her head might go away.

The town where she stopped, *Český Krumlov*, which she knew as *Krumau*, dated back to the middle of the thirteenth century and had developed spontaneously as a place to house all of the servants who worked tirelessly maintaining the castle overlooking the town.

That castle, built in 1240 by the *Vítkovci* family of Bohemian nobles, stood on a steep and rocky bluff towering (both literally and figuratively) above the town and the *Vltava* river. By the fourteenth century, the *Vítkovci* line had become extinct and both the castle and the surrounding town were acquired by King Wenceslaus II, who promoted trade and crafts within the town, and saw it flourish and grow. When gold was discovered in the late-fifteenth century, the town grew even more, fed by an influx of German and Bohemian miners.

To accommodate this consistent growth, and to further promote trade, the town wisely erected a series of hostels, and Vanessa had chosen one of the smaller and unassuming ones to quietly recover from whatever it was that had plagued her on the outskirts of the town.

Fortunately, she did not hear any more mysterious voices during her brief stay in *Český Krumlov*, and, as she almost always seemed to do, she recovered very quickly – at least physically. Rested and rejuvenated, she then decided to continue her journey towards Vienna, but later that morning, as she followed the *Vltava* river through the foothills of the Bohemian forest and approached the town of *Rožmberk nad Vltavou* (*Rosenberg an der Moldau* in German), Vanessa again began to feel weak but irritating whispers in the back of her head.

Rosenberg an der Moldau, whose name literally meant Rose Hill on the Vltava River, was founded in the middle of the thirteenth century and lay on an important trade route leading from *Český Krumlov* through the border passes to *Linz* in Austria. It was first settled by the *Rožmberkové* (the Rosenbergs), a prominent Bohemian noble family who brought order and tremendous prosperity to the town, controlling it for more than three-hundred years.

Loyal Catholics for centuries, the Rosenbergs had defended the interests of Holy Roman Emperor Sigismund during the Hussite Wars of the fifteenth century and had supported Emperor Charles V in his fight against the Turks in the sixteenth century. However, when Peter Vok, an Utraquist sympathiser and prominent member of the Protestant *Moravská Církev* (Moravian Church), inherited the Rosenberg holdings in 1592 as the last of the family line, the union between the Rosenbergs and the Hapsburgs began to break down. And when Peter died childless in 1611, control of the town passed first to Emperor Rudolph II and, more recently, to the French aristocratic Bucquoy family – all still very loyal to the Hapsburgs.

But after his death, Peter Vok became the subject of many popular local legends, most of which falsely characterised him as a perfect and generous gentleman, a chivalrous romantic, and an exemplary Renaissance courtier. Fed by those legends and lies, those still loyal to the memory of the last of the Rosenbergs – easily identifiable because they still wore the traditional *Rožmberkové* coat of arms (a red five-petaled rose on a silver field) – had come to bitterly oppose the Hapsburgs for political, theological, and personal reasons. And because they opposed the Hapsburgs, these few diehards also opposed the Stormsongs. In fact, they hated them.

But despite the fact that she was riding into openly hostile country, and bearing the infamous Stormsong coat of arms no less, Vanessa felt relatively at ease. Her skills and training had left her feeling almost invincible, even when she was far from home. In fact, as she approached the shadow cast by *Schloß Rosenberg* (known to the locals as *Rožmberk* castle), she noticed the similarities to *Schloß Stormsong* and couldn't help but think of home.

Rožmberk, one of the largest and oldest castles in Bohemia, stood on a headland carved out on three sides by the *Vltava* river, and, like much of the town itself, was owned by Charles Bonaventure, Count of Bucquoy. Dating back to the middle of the thirteenth century, *Schloß Rosenberg*, like *Schloß Stormsong*, had originally been designed as a Gothic fortress and later rebuilt as a series of Renaissance palaces, complete with *sgraffito* decoration adorning the outer facades and beautifully painted Renaissance artwork gracing the interiors.

While *Schloß Rosenberg* was nowhere near as large, as imposing, or as beautiful as *Schloß Stormsong*, it bore enough similarity to the only home she'd ever known to cause a momentary wave of nostalgia to sweep over her. Oddly, as she drew closer and closer to the castle, the voices in her head, earlier just faint whispers, seemed to grow in both volume and intensity.

I hardly think she's qualified for such service, Your Highness, an old but familiar voice said. She's but a child....and a girl at that. Meaning no offence, of course.

None taken, a second, more authoritative voice responded. But she will be very well trained; she's already highly skilled, and she will have neither husband nor children to cause outside distractions. And the only thing that seems to matter to her is....pleasing me.

Am I going crazy? Vanessa asked herself. *What are these voices? And from where are they coming?* She now felt that the voices were not just talking to each other, they were talking to her. *No, not talking to me. Talking about me. They are….no….were….they were studying me…. wondering about my loyalty and ability. I remember this conversation. It was six or seven years ago, when I was fifteen or sixteen-years-old. That was when…..*

Best of all, the second voice said, intruding on her attempt to recall the circumstances of this bizarre conversation, *She's cold and distant. She has been ever since her mother passed. Better still, she's cunning, capable, and who could possibly be better suited for recovering….*

Recovering what? Vanessa asked herself, straining to simultaneously quiet the voices in her head and to place these memories. *Am I hallucinating? Or are these voices just some part of an unfinished dream? No, they're not dreams. This happened, didn't it?*

Closing her eyes and concentrating fiercely, she remembered having been….*what? Was it conflicted?* The prospect of proving herself to her father and the others had been….appealing, she remembered. A chance to no longer sit back, powerless as events moved around her. A chance to actually shape those events. At the same time, she remembered that she had felt tremendous reservation. Something had held her back. Not the enormity of the task, nor the violence inherent in what she was being asked to do, but…. something. Something else. *What was it? What had it been? And, for the love of God, why can't I remember what it was?*

So focused was she on trying to simultaneously place and yet silence these voices, Vanessa didn't see the three riders approaching from *Schloß Rosenberg* – not until *Starke* whinnied to alert her to their presence.

But by then, it was too late.

The first shot had already been fired.

Sister Elsebeth was extremely proud of herself.
And I have every right to be, she thought.

Pursuant to Father Joseph's wishes (or, more precisely, those he had expressed in the covert message that had been furtively placed in her hands just two days before Sir Stephen's arrival in Lindau), she had located Stephen within *die Kirche St. Stephan* (*How ironic?* she thought, not for the first time), had rescued him from that droll little Father Phillip (*Who always seemed to be so sullen*, she mused), had escorted him into the defunct monastery where Father Joseph's brilliantly devised scheme remained at work, and had pointed Stephen in the direction of the monastery's *guest*.

While she hadn't heard everything that the two had discussed (after all, her hiding space beneath an open window overlooking the cloister suffered from terrible acoustics), she had heard enough to both confirm her suspicions as to who their mysterious guest truly was and to realise with great satisfaction that Father Joseph's wise and patient plan had, after all these years, finally been set in motion.

Why even now, she thought, *Sir Stephen must be well on his way back to Prague to find Vanessa, reveal the truth to her, save her father, and God-willing marry her.* It all seemed so beautifully romantic and impossibly storybook, that she could scarcely believe she had been fortunate enough to have been instrumental in setting it in action.

Perhaps that's why he has summoned me, she thought, always eager to receive the kind of praise that Father Phillip only doled out on the rarest of occasions.

So it was with eager and childlike anticipation that Sister Elsebeth eased silently through the heavy wooden doors of *die Kirche St. Stephan*. Upon seeing her enter, Father Phillip displayed an uncharacteristically cheerful smile and waved her forward to the baptismal font.

So light on her feet that she was practically floating down the church's main aisle, Sister Elsebeth returned the unusually warm smile and said, "You wanted to see me, father?"

"Yes, my child. Yes. I simply wanted to confirm something. Are you the one responsible for arranging yesterday's meeting between Sir Stephen and our....*guest?"*

Positively giddy and beaming with pride, Sister Elsebeth eagerly responded, "Yes, father. yes, I am."

Before she could say another word, the short priest produced a very thin blade from within the sleeves of his black cossack and slipped it neatly into the space between Sister Elsebeth's fourth and fifth ribs. As she gasped in shock and amazement, he then moved the blade with practised ease slightly upwards and to the left, scraping her left ventricle in the process.

Already effectively dead, the stunned sister struggled slightly and slipped off of the priest's unexpected blade. Then, as she stood back, glancing in horror first at her open wound and then at her killer's face, the priest simply said "Oh, I really wish you hadn't done that, sister."

As her legs gave way beneath her, Father Phillip caught the nun and dragged her limp form over to the baptimsal font. "May God forgive you of your sins, Sister Elsebeth," was all he said as he placed her head into the font and pushed her face down below the level of the baptismal water, holding it there until she finally stopped struggling.

The first shot, a .55 calibre iron round fired from a sixteen-inch, smoothbore wheellock pistol, ripped through the folds of Vanessa's blue cloak as she dismounted *Starke*. The second, fired a fraction of a second later from a twenty-one-inch-long Dutch flintlock horse pistol with a .55 bore three-stage-steel-barrel, tore through the leather of her right boot, just grazing her calf, as she spun away from her horse.

In one impossibly swift movement, as she completed her spin away from *Starke*, hoping to keep him out of the field of fire,

Vanessa fired two shots from her crossbow. The first one struck the front rider, a light-skinned man with curly dark hair that was thinning up front, right through his fleshy neck, just below the chin, ripping him violently from his mount. But her second shot flew wide – a rare miss from this deadly weapon in the hands of an even deadlier warrior.

When her third attempted shot inexplicably jammed her crossbow, Vanessa dropped the weapon and unsheathed her sword. As the remaining two riders foolishly dismounted and drew their swords, Vanessa cocooned herself in a circle of concentration, centred entirely on herself and her opponents. As if in a painting by *Jan van Eyck*, where only the action in the centre mattered, everything on Vanessa's periphery melted away. In fact, so complete was her concentration that, as her enemies bore down on her, she could see individual hairs on their day-old stubble and smell what they had had last eaten.

The second attacker, a tall but fat man with a large red face and a double-chin who likely needed all of his energy just to get out of bed in the morning, strode confidently and stupidly straight at Vanessa. "You just killed my brother, you bitch," he half-barked and half-burped.

With one deft swing at the fat man who had evidently breakfasted that morning on eggs and a *Kartoffelpuffer* (a potato pancake mixed with parsley and onions), Vanessa sliced through his abdomen, spilling that last meal on the ground in front of him. Then, using the momentum of that strike, she pivoted effortlessly into a turn that left her in perfect position to strike a killing blow at the third and final attacker – a pale-skinned teen with burnt-orange hair, a pug nose, and a wide jaw. But as she swung her blade a second time, the near impossible happened.

She missed.

And that potentially lethal miss simultaneously brought her too close to her opponent and left her wide open to a counter attack that came in the form of a savage backhand from the young man's non-sword arm.

Stumbling backwards with the coppery taste of her own blood in her mouth, Vanessa actually smiled. "That's going to cost you," she cautioned as she repositioned for her next strike, which would certainly spell the end for this pimple-faced boy.

"Not as much as it's going to cost you," he responded, just as a fourth man, one she had never seen before, emerged as if out of thin air and struck her behind her left ear with something heavy and hard.

"I told you so," the boy gloated, like a five-year-old who had just won a childish argument. But Vanessa never heard him. Taken completely by surprise, she never had a chance to brace for the strike, or to deflect its power by rolling forward with the blow. As a result, she was already completely unconscious when she hit the ground directly in front of the orange-haired boy.

Chapter Fifty Five

Šarlatová, Roan, Franz, and Zahara had weighed their options. While all four had agreed that it would be too dangerous for Emma and her children to impose upon the hospitality of *der Alte Stier* a second time, they had disagreed on everything else. While Franz had wanted to travel to Vienna to kill the emperor personally (and had described in rather graphic detail how he intended to do it), Roan had wanted to storm *Schloß Stormsong*, just the four of them, to rescue their imprisoned comrades. Fortunately, the discretion and common sense of the two women outweighed the foolish valour of the two men.

Ultimately, the exhausted quartet arrived at a consensus plan to travel towards *Pilsen*. Doing so would accomplish multiple objectives. First, it would, or so they all thought, afford them the best opportunity to locate and deal with the traitor, Simon Berger. Additionally, it would allow them to participate in the rumoured assault on Pilsen, helping the Bohemian army of Protestants to "cast the bastards out" of that important Catholic stronghold. Finally, the journey there, which would have to be conducted on foot, but at a leisurely pace, was sure to last at least three days, during which time both Šarlatová and Zahara could regain their earlier vitality.

As it would turn out, however, very little of that would come to pass.

Vanessa's head was pounding.

She opened her eyes and tried to focus, but a foggy haze wouldn't allow her to do so.

Her mouth was dry, and she felt a throbbing pain in the back of her head and neck. As that pain continued to pulse, her vision cleared just enough to see a sweaty man sitting in front of a fire, but he was paying little attention to his beautiful captive. Instead, he was concentrating on prying dirt out from underneath his fingernails with a blade that was much too large and menacing for the simple task. Feeling no need to parade her ignorance as to her whereabouts, Vanessa did not ask the questions that burned in her brain. Instead, she simply said nothing as she slowly and painfully regained consciousness.

"And he said unto me, it is done, and I will give of the fountain of the water of life freely to him....or her....who thirsts," the sweaty man said. Because he stood and offered a skin of water to Vanessa, and because the pain in her head continued to assault her senses, she chose not to waste any energy correcting his incomplete and slightly erroneous recitation from chapter twenty-one, verse six of the Book of Revelation. Instead, she simply leaned forward (she could not take the skin in her own hands because they were bound tightly behind her) and allowed the man to press the skin to her lips.

It hurt to swallow; the pain in her head was pulsing to an almost drum like beat as it assaulted her in wave after wave, and she could still taste blood where that orange-haired little shit had struck her, but the water was cool and it felt magnificent as it made its way down her throat. "Thank you," she offered hoarsely, but the sweaty man just sat back in front of the fire without responding.

As she surveyed her surroundings in an attempt to determine where she was, the sweaty man went back to ignoring her and resumed working steadfastly on his dirty fingernails. Only when he finally seemed to be satisfied with his work did he turn to Vanessa and ask, "Do you know why there are so many pigeon feathers scattered all over the Vatican?"

Dumbfounded, Vanessa could not formulate a response.

"Do you?" the sweaty man repeated.

"No, I suppose I don't," Vanessa admitted incredulously.

The sweaty man smiled and laughed. "It's because there are a lot of pigeons in Rome, Lady Stormsong." As he stood and reached around behind her to sever the ropes that bound her hands, he added, "They get in through the air shafts and other holes in Saint Peter's Basilica. They leave feathers and shit and a horrible mess everywhere."

Because she was so thoroughly and equally confused as to how this man knew who she was and why he was talking about pigeon shit in the Vatican, Vanessa chose not to do anything other than rub her wrists once the ropes were released.

Seeing her confusion, the man smiled and laughed again. "Not everything is a riddle, my Lady," he said with mock deference. "It was a simple question, and I was just testing to see how hard you had been struck. Pretty hard, I would say, given that you couldn't answer even so simple a question as that."

Vanessa continued to stare at the sweaty man, wondering if he had been struck even harder in the head than she had been.

Smiling, he said, "I imagine you're wanting to know who I am and where you are, right?"

Vanessa nodded her head gently, but even that slight move sent waves of pain shooting from her temples, through her neck, and down her spine.

"My name is Peter, and you are in *das Haus der fünf-blutige Rose* (the House of the five- petaled Rose), and today you murdered two of my brothers."

This time, the sweaty man neither laughed nor smiled.

The four riders reached Stephen first. "Paise, God, you slowed down, Sir Stephen," said one of them. "That mount of yours seems to be charged with a supernatural bank of speed." As the man Stephen took to be the leader of the foursome dismounted, Stephen exchanged a knowing glance with his *supernaturally speed mount.*

If you only knew the truth of it, Stephen thought to himself.

"How can I be of service to you, my lord," Stephen asked politely.

By now, all four of the riders had dismounted, and a second one, this one possessing an oddly shaped skull and a flat snout of a nose, said, "You misunderstand us, Sir Stephen. We are here to serve you."

"I'm not certain I understand," Stephen admitted.

The first rider stepped closer and whispered conspiratorially to Stephen, "We have been sent to both guide and protect you. This is dangerous country and these are dangerous times, my Lord." Something seemed amiss to Stephen. The man was speaking stiffly, as if reciting words that had been written for him.

"Yes, of course," Stephen offered. "But sent by whom."

"By Father Phillip, of course" a third rider with oversized and very hairy ears said too loudly, earning a glare of admonition from the other three riders.

"Father Phillip?" Stephen asked. "But he ministers over the church in Lindau, whereas you four all bear *das Meer und Schloß,* the mark of *Meersburg.*

"Ja....natürlich!" said the fourth rider, a bat-faced little man who had been silent until now. "But just as the grasp of our enemies is long and wide, so is the reach of our allies, like Father Phillip. Come, let us help find you a place to rest. You must be weary from your journey."

Having only travelled some thirty miles or so, albeit at a blazing speed, Stephen was far from weary. However, he was growing somewhat suspicious. "Then you are to escort me all the way to Vienna, I suppose?" he half-asked and half-stated, knowing full well that his true destination was Prague.

"Yes, of course!" all four riders nodded and agreed – much too quickly and enthusiastically for Stephen's liking. But just as he was attempting to formulate another test of the veracity of the claims made by these four men, a long shadow was cast over him. The sun was virtually blocked out by the silent but ominous arrival of one Father Abaddon Sohar.

Stephen was the first one to see it.

The gruesome trophy from *Morbegno*.

The four severed heads, bouncing like some ghastly belt around the massive priest's belt.

Wisely, Stephen said nothing. But when the *Meersburg* men saw what he was looking at, one gasped, two reached for their weapons, and the leader of the group cried out *"Rette uns, Jesus!"*

For the third time in as many weeks, Father Abaddon Sohar just smiled.

Peter led Vanessa out of the building, a Renaissance-style hunting lodge built sometime between 1555 and 1557 in the shape of a five-petaled rose (hence the name *das Haus der fünf- blutige Rose*). As they walked, he related to her several interesting facts. The first was the fact that, as a child, he had been given a strict Catholic education, including training in several languages. The second was that, despite his pathological hatred of the Hapsburgs and the Stormsongs, he – much like the bulk of the group – still considered himself to be an obedient Catholic. But once he became an independent ruler of one of the most influential free thinking groups in the empire, *der Orden der fünf-blutige Rose* (the Order of the five-petaled Rose), he had become an outlaw.

Talking so quickly that Vanessa couldn't ask any one of the hundreds of questions that sprang to her mind, Peter led her through a densely wooded space that eventually opened up into a green oasis. Peter explained that this space, which might as well have been named Eden for how lush and fertile it was, once was the Rosenberg family's personal hunting grounds. Now it was home to *der Orden der fünf-blutige Rose* and, at the moment, it was also home to one of the wildest, lewdest, and most bizarre rituals Vanessa had ever witnessed.

Chestnuts, berries, and even some small eggs were strewn all over the green space, and the women of the group....or tribe....or whatever it was, were all crawling – actually, crab walking would be the more apt term – around naked, despite the cold weather. And every so often the women would attempt to pick up the edible items.... using only their vaginas. The women then transported the items to the men, all of whom were chanting and screaming riotously, and dropped them at their feet.

To show their gratitude, the men then ate the chestnuts, berries, and eggs and even awarded prizes to the women (who Vanessa assumed were prostitutes) who picked up and deposited the most.... or the largest....of the....*treasures*. Often the prize was a simple smack on the ass, but just as often it was a full, unabashed sexual.... *Encounter*? No. Domination might be the better word. But the women were giving as good as they got, often smacking or even biting the men as they coupled with them.

The look of shock and embarrassment, mixed with equal parts disbelief and disgust, that registered on Vanessa's face caused Peter to say to her, "What's wrong? The brothers of *der Orden der fünf-blutige Rose* work hard, and they deserve to play hard, too."

"I see," was all Vanessa could manage at first. "And the women? Are they 'playing hard'? Or are they....*working* hard?"

Peter laughed loudly and said, "They're not prostitutes, if that's what you're thinking. They are all sisters in the Order."

Just then, one of the largest women Vanessa had ever seen approached and looked her up and down. She had to be nearly seven-feet-tall and seemed to be carved entirely out of granite. She was barrel-chested and bull-necked and looked like she spent the entire day lifting large objects above her head and slamming them back to the ground – objects like castle walls, for example. In fact, the only thing feminine about her at all, besides the long blonde hair that cascaded halfway down her back, were her breasts. Inconsistent with the rest of her monstrous frame, they were surprisingly pink, petite, and feminine.

The reason Vanessa could determine this was because the mountainous woman stood before her totally naked and extremely sweaty, and Vanessa could see several red handprints and purple bite marks spread across her muscular body where the men of the order had apparently.... *rewarded* her.

"Peter, I'd be willing to wager that this little princess couldn't pick up so much as a chickpea with her tiny little twat," she noted in a voice that was deeper than most men's.

As Vanessa immediately and reflexively reached for the sword that was no longer on her belt, Peter covered her hand with his own. "Another time, perhaps, Kateřina," he said. Then, as the monstrous woman huffed and lumbered away, Vanessa turned and looked at Peter.

"I don't think I've ever seen a woman, or even a man, that size before."

"Yes you have. She's the one who knocked you senseless earlier today."

"No, I'm afraid you're mistaken. That's simply not possible. I have never felt anything like that before in my life. That had to have been a man, and a large one at that."

"No, it's you who are mistaken, *Lady Stormsong*," he said in a tone lay somewhere between derisive and playful. "It was definitely Kateřina. She and the three Peters were the first to spot you. All four of them immediately recognized the Stormsong *Familienwappen* that you were so brazenly wearing while encroaching on our lands. So they did what they are trained to do."

"I'm sorry....*the three Peters?*"

"Yes, all of the men here are named Peter, and all of the women are named Kateřina"

Vanessa paused for just a second trying to process everything she had just heard. There were dozens of questions she wanted to ask Peter – this Peter. But the best she could come up with for the moment was, "Who are these people? And what is this place?"

"That's quite a long story," he answered. "I suppose it began when Peter Vok and his wife, Kateřina of Ludanice, the last of the Rosenbergs were betrayed and murdered...."

"I thought they both died of natural causes," Vanessa interrupted. "I've read that he died of old age and that she succumbed to some mental illness."

Peter shook his head sadly. "No. That's what you are supposed to think....what the histories claim. But that's not what really happened. They were definitely murdered, and when they were, all hereditary claims to the former *Rožmberkové* lands were immediately forfeited. And Emperor Rudolph II, that selfish bastard, took all of those lands for himself. That's why they were killed. For land and money. Everything was taken but the lodge we just left, and this small space."

"I'm so sorry." Vanessa paused for just a moment to see if Peter might need to display some expression of sorrow. When he didn't, she added, *"For the love of money is the root of all evil."*

Peter impressed Vanessa by saying, "Paul's First Epistle to Timothy, chapter six, verse ten. That's one of my favourite New Testament verses." Then, after pausing quite awkwardly, as if he had more to say about that particular verse, he simply shrugged his shoulders as if completely indifferent to the matter now.

"It's okay. Actually, it's not so bad with what he has here. Each season brings us a unique taste of nature. The spring is wet and full of awakening flowers and trees. The summer is cool and shady. And autumn, like now, brings the beautiful changing of the leaves."

Somewhat surprised to hear this rather strange man wax so poetic about the changing of the seasons, Vanessa asked, "And the winter?"

"Oh, the winter is shit, of course. All we do in the winter is wait until it's spring again."

They both laughed at this and then the man surprised Vanessa again by taking her by the hand. "Come with me. There's one more thing I want to show you before we get started."

Vanessa had no idea what Peter meant by the phrase "get started," but based on the orgy of sex, violence, and games she had seen earlier, she was perfectly willing to indulge this man with anything that would delay whatever was to become of her.

Chapter Fifty Six

———⚬⚬⚬———

"We call this place *der Hof der reiterlosen Pferde* (the Courtyard of Riderless Horses)," Peter said. But the place to which we had taken Vanessa was hardly a courtyard; in fact, it was really just a clearing with a lone spruce tree in the middle. "This is where we celebrate and pay homage to all of our order who have fallen in battle….including the two you slayed earlier today. But fear not. You gave them both honourable deaths…."

"And they were, in fact, trying to kill me at the time," Vanessa interrupted.

"There's that, too."

Vanessa approached the tree and noticed that dozens of pairs of boots had been nailed to it, some of them quite recently. Others looked like they had been there for years. "I'm afraid I don't understand," she confessed to Peter.

"It's a custom that some say dates back to the time of Genghis Khan, who would sacrifice a horse for every fallen warrior."

"Why?"

"So that the dead warrior's horse could serve his fallen master in the afterlife. Others say it dates all the way back to a thousand years before Genghis Khan. Something about the Afghan people representing Buddha as a riderless horse. I don't know. But we can't afford to be sacrificing any horses, so we nail the boots of the fallen to this tree. We can't really afford to lose the boots either, but we need to do something to honour our fallen."

"Why are you showing me all of this?"

"Because we are an honourable people, Lady Stormsong. I don't know where you rank in the hierarchy of your family…" Vanessa interrupted him with a laugh. "Why is that funny?'

"Because my family doesn't have much of a hierarchy. It's really just my father and me." If Vanessa was expecting a show of sympathy, she didn't get one.

"Regardless, you come from wealth and you occupy a seat of tremendous power. Therefore, you can do something to help us."

"Help you how?" Vanessa asked, not really fully vested in trying to do so.

Peter paused dramatically and adjusted his posture, as if he was about to launch into a speech for which he had been preparing his entire life. "So many of the so-called lords and ladies here in this empire are poor. Maybe not poor in the sense that we are here, but poor in every other sense of the word. Poor in spirit. Poor in grace. And poor in humility and compassion. But while they're poor, they think themselves rich, and they choose to live as if they are entitled to…..well, anything and everything. And that dichotomy had forced them to resort to innumerable cruelties, which are inflicted in all manner of ways….and on all manner of people. The boots you see here are proof positive of that."

Vanessa still wasn't sure what Peter was getting at, but she decided to humour him and continued to listen silently.

"We don't go looking for trouble, Lady Stormsong. In fact, we try to avoid it. That's why we still wear the *Rožmberkové Familienwappen*. We're not ashamed of it, and we're not trying to hide it. We wear it as a warning. Had you not intruded on our land….what little land we've been left with….we would have left you alone. But you did intrude on our land, wearing the coat of arms of one of our sworn enemies."

Vanessa attempted to interrupt, but Peter cut her off by holding up his hand. "It's fine. We know now that your intention was not to steal from us. But history has taught us that we can't afford to take that chance. Nations, religions, races, are all the same. They do not distrust each other because they are armed; they are armed because they distrust each other. And we can't afford to trust anyone – least of all Hapsburgs or Stormsongs."

Vanessa glanced away pensively, as if she had somehow just been transported to another time and place. "My father once told me that nations do not make wars; people do."

"Ha….no doubt he was right. People do make wars. Greedy people. When Peter was betrayed and murdered….for a parcel of land….that was the precise moment when I realised that greed is the primary force the Enemy uses to destroy the good will of men. There are really only two problems with people, Lady Stormsong. And one of them is that they are so greedy that they are capable of just about anything.

"What's the other one?"

"What's the other what?"

"The other problem with people?"

"Oh," Peter smiled in preparation of delivering a joke he'd told countless times. "It's that there's too damned many of them."

Vanessa and Peter both laughed.

"If you earn the right to leave here," Peter said, causing Vanessa to blanch at that statement, still uncertain as to what would become of her in this lawless place, "Please remember that. You have the ear of the two most powerful people in the entire empire. Remember what you've seen and learned today."

"I will," Vanessa promised, not sure that she would and surprised at how easily and sincerely she had promised to.

"Well then, now that that's taken care of, let's see about getting you back on the road to wherever you were headed, shall we?"

While Vanessa was eager to resume her journey south towards Vienna, she was not looking forward to whatever it was that she was going to be asked in order to earn the right to do so.

On Saturday, November seventeenth, *Pilsen's* stores of potable water finally ran out.

Two days later, Count von Thurn arrived, reinforcing von Mansfeld's already overwhelming numerical and strategic advantage with thousands of fresh, new soldiers.

And on the day after that, the walls around *Pilsen* began to crack and fall.

Once they did, every shot fired by the vastly superior Protestant artillery carved a deadly path of destruction through the tightly grouped mass of Catholic defenders, sending helmets and heads, weapons and limbs, and any hope of survival flying indiscriminately through the cold November air.

It was on Wednesday that von Thurn and von Mansfeld finally launched their coordinated assault. It took less than fifteen hours of desperate fighting, much of it being close hand-to-hand combat, before *Pilsen* fell. Short of soldiers, supplies and money, Bucquoy and Dampiere fought valiantly. But in the end, it was all for naught.

It took four more days, during which the two Protestant commanders laid waste to the entire area, before *Pilsen* officially surrendered. But already by the time Šarlatová, Roan, Franz and Zahara arrived – one day before the surrender – the place was unrecognisable.

The ground in and around *Pilsen* was slick with and dyed red by the gallons of blood that had been spilled there. Everywhere they looked, the once great town and its surroundings were covered in discarded weapons, dead horses, and human gore. The acrid grey-green dust of warfare seemed to linger everywhere, muting the once vibrant colours of autumn, and temporarily screening the four from seeing some of the worst of the human suffering still playing out on the ground in front of them. But no amount of smoke or haze could shield them from the piteous moans of the wounded and dying, the shrieks of terror, or the appalling stench of human tragedy.

Unbeknownst to the four weary travellers, Bucquoy and Dampierre, in order to evade capture, had both retreated southeast towards *Budweis*, effectively leaving the survivors of the assault leaderless and hopeless. Worse still, the air, heavy and bearing a hint of dampness, promised the coming of a wet snow, the first of the season, which would be but the herald of a long and deep winter, certain to soon fall on these people and add further to their misery and suffering.

As she and the others silently surveyed this desolate wasteland, Šarlatová desperately wanted to take some pleasure in the suffering of….*these people*. After all, *these people*….the emperor's armies…. the Catholic church….they had both caused her and her people tremendous suffering over the years. As far as she was concerned, they were the root of all evil in the world. But some of these victims were women and children, and their faces were just as grim and as dark as the few surviving men. As she and the others moved closer to what remained of *Pilsen*, she could look directly into the sunken, desperate eyes of these defeated and hungry people, and it seemed as if they were pleading with her to do something.

In what she hoped the others would mistake as an act of deference to the dead and the dying, an exhausted Šarlatová, unable to go any further or endure anything more, knelt down and scooped up a handful of debris, allowing the small pieces to sift through her fingers. As she did so, a red and white cloth floated towards her and hovered ominously in mid-air for several seconds. Then, as if with great portent, it fell gently to the ground, right at her feet.

Since 1253, the official state colours of Bohemia had been red and white, and in the fifteenth century they were established on white and red cords attaching seals to documents issued by the King of Bohemia. So it was no surprise that Šarlatová initially mistook the cloth for one of the bicolor white and red banners that were so often carried into battle by the armies of Bohemian monarchs and nobles. But only when she picked it up did she realise that it was not a banner or flag at all. It was a woman's garment. It was a thin, white, adjustable bodice called *ein Jump Mieder* (a jump bodice). Typically worn by pregnant women on account of the garments' adjustability, jump bodices were popularised in France before becoming available throughout the rest of Europe. This particular *Jump Mieder* was relatively unsullied near the top. But the bottom, the part she had earlier mistaken for the bottom red banner of a Bohemian battle flag, was completely saturated with and dyed red by blood. A chill ran through Šarlatová as she tried to imagine what had been done to this pregnant woman and her unborn child to cause so much blood.

As she remained kneeling, Šarlatová exhaled loudly and hung her head in both shame and disgust. Both Roan and Zahara could instantly divine what she was thinking, but it was Zahara who spoke first.

"Do not even consider it, my friend," she whispered, kneeling at Šarlatová's side and putting a comforting arm around her. "Even at your strongest, you could not heal so many. And in your current state, you would only kill yourself in the process."

Šarlatová could feel the heat of Zahara's embrace through her tunic, and as she turned to say something to her, their eyes met and locked. Šarlatová's heart was pounding so hard that she could no longer think of what she had wanted to say. All the while, Franz had no idea what was transpiring between the two women. But Roan knew. And he sensed in that moment, with tremendous sadness tinged with a bit of relief, that he had finally been replaced as the most important figure in Šarlatová's young life.

At the same time that something undefined, but significant nonetheless, passed between her and Zahara, something else inside of Šarlatová hardened. As a child, she had been discarded by her own family like a piece of unwanted furniture, at least until Roan had found her. But even then, as she found some level of happiness as an adult within *die Grüne Gauner*, she had then been treated as an outlaw, even considered a heretic, by the church and government of her own country. But now, witnessing what her own people were capable of doing, she felt like a refugee from the entire human race. In fact, while none of the devastation in front of her was her fault, she had the sensation, and not for the first time, of being less than human.

427

Exhaling deeply, Šarlatová thought, *Now I know that I have to devote my ability, no matter the cost, to ending the wrongs being done to my country, my people, and my friends. God has clearly chosen me for this task that I, and I alone, can accomplish. It's my responsibility. No one else's.*

As if sensing what was going on inside Šarlatová's head, Roan stated, "It's the terrible price of war, *divka*. When one nation takes up arms against another…."

"Nations don't make war, Roan," Šarlatová interrupted. "People do, and I know now what I must do."

Then, as Šarlatová steeled herself, picked up the bloody bodice and stood, Roan saw something both familiar and terrifying flash in her eyes, and all he could think was, *Well, shit!*

"There are only three ways for you to earn your way out of here," a different Peter explained when she and the first Peter had returned from the Courtyard of Riderless Horses. "One, you become one of us." Vanessa looked askance at both him and the Peter who had taken her on a guided tour of this place. "Right, but then you wouldn't really be leaving here, would you?"

"Or, there is the second option," said a third Peter. "We appease the spirits of the two men you killed by sacrificing you in *der Hof der reiterlosen Pferde.*"

Vanessa cocked one eyebrow. "And how exactly would that be done?"

"By nailing you to the tree in the courtyard," offered a fourth Peter.

Vanessa just smiled. "You're not serious, are you?"

"Or," said the original Peter, "There is the third option. You could earn a pardon by besting Kateřina in single, hand-to-hand combat."

A dubious Vanessa pointed out, "So there's really just one option then, isn't there?"

All of the Peters nodded in agreement. "I guess you're right," the first Peter conceded.

"Fine," Vanessa agreed. "I choose the third option. I'll fight. At this point, I would really appreciate the opportunity to beat someone half to death. Which Kateřina?"

"That one," the first Peter said, grinning deviously and pointing to the monstrous woman she had encountered earlier.

As all of the Peters laughed in unison and grinned in eager anticipation of what was to come, all Vanessa could think was *Well, shit!*

Chapter Fifty Seven

Well shit, is precisely what the four men from *Meersburg* must have been thinking when the preposterously enormous Father Abaddon Sohar dismounted his equally large mount, four severed heads swinging from his belt.

"And who might you be?" the rider with the oddly shaped skull and the flat snout of a nose asked, his tone sounding much more confident than he actually felt.

"He might be someone you want to leave alone," Stephen cautioned.

The third rider, the one with the oversized and hairy ears, who was clearly the dumbest of the four, didn't take Stephen's well heeled advice. "He asked you a question, didn't he?"

Seeing where this confrontation was inevitably headed, Stephen took a few steps back, while the first rider, the one Stephen correctly assumed was the leader, placed his hand on the pommel of his sword.

For reasons passing understanding, the fourth man from Meersburg, the little bat-faced one, had crowded close to Sohar's horse and was prying back the cover of one of the priest's saddle bags, clearly trying to get a better look at the unusual two barrelled flintlock pistol.

Without taking his eyes off of Hairy Ears, Sohar slapped the cover of his saddle bag shut, loudly striking Bat Face's hand – which looked like a child's in comparison to Father Sohar's – in the process.

Bat Face leapt back as if he'd been grievously wounded – Stephen thought he might actually cry – and shouted in surprise, causing Snout Nose to reach for his sword, too.

Trying to defuse the situation, the leader of the group stepped forward. "Right....well, just be on your way then, friend. We have business here with Sir Stephen that doesn't concern you."

"That's right," echoed Hairy Ears. "Best be about your business, *father*."

That was the second time someone had told him to be about his business in as many weeks, and he liked it about as much this time as he had the first time. He liked even less the derisive way Hairy Ears had said the word *father* – as if he was merely impersonating a priest.

Sohar offered an ominous growl, as if in warning, which caused Snout Nose to foolishly note, "He's awfully tight-lipped for a priest, ain't he? You suppose he's dumb?"

The others never got a chance to answer. Striking out with a quickness that belied his gargantuan form, Sohar seized Snout Nose by the throat, lifting him, one-handed, at least three feet off the ground.

As Snout Nose struggled to free himself from the priest's vice-like grip, all of the others, including Stephen, reached for their weapons. But Sohar flashed a quick look at Stephen that was part warning and part absolution, silently indicating that Stephen was excused from the punishment that was coming for the four *Meersburg* men.

Hairy Ears was the first to unsheathe his sword, so – as Stephen held up his hands in mock surrender and took another step backwards – Sohar launched Snout Nose into Hairy Ears, and the two ended up in a confused tangle of limbs more than ten feet away.

By the time the leader had unsheathed his blade, Sohar had removed the trophy belt from around his waist and swung it like a weapon. The sound of the four severed heads crashing into the leader's face, and the spray of blood and bone that resulted, was enough to send Bat Face running away, squealing like a five-year-old girl in the process.

As Stephen stood there, dumbfounded, the priest moved to retrieve his trophy belt. *So much for the concept of 'pour encourager les autres,'* he thought to himself, as he lifted the four severed heads.

Then, realising that what had been intended to ward off any unwanted incidents had, instead, actually helped to provoke one, he let the belt fall back down on the leader of the *Meersburg* men, the result being that the unconscious man appeared to have five heads – four lifeless and decaying, and one simply battered and bloody.

By this time, Snout Nose and Hairy Ears had just regained their feet. Snout Nose, having just felt the power of the priest's hand around his throat, followed Bat Face's example and took off running – albeit without the accompanying shrieks of a girl in distress.

Hairy Ears took a little longer to convince. As he stood there, sword in hand, he watched in nervous anticipation as Sohar produced his unusual, double barrelled flintlock pistol. All Sohar had to do was point the weapon in the direction of Hairy Ears and he, too, took off in a dead sprint.

Very pleased that he hadn't been forced into killing anyone this time – assuming, of course, that the man he had struck was only unconscious, and not dead – Sohar grunted in satisfaction. Then, realising that Stephen was still standing there, he turned slowly and looked in his direction. When he was confident that Stephen had no intention of engaging him, Father Sohar simply nodded as if to say *You're welcome.*

Then, as the mammoth priest remounted his horse and rode into *Leutkirch im Allgäu,* Stephen and Kimber looked at each other, and both exhaled for the first time in several minutes.

The "victory" over the Catholics at *Pilsen* meant that the Protestants were winning the war, at least for now; however, the true outcome of this "victory" had not yet been determined. While Bohemia had been temporarily saved from destruction at the hands of the Hapsburgs, it was now subjected to the competing whims of at least four self-professed leaders of the cause, meaning that the Stormsong plan to exploit the jealousies of these petty and power hungry men was working. And if either von Thurn or von Mansfeld hoped to be commended for this victory, they were both gravely disillusioned – for Christian I, the Prince of Anhalt-Bernburg and Friedrich V, the Elector of the Palatinate and the unofficial king of Bohemia, had very different ideas.

Christian I wanted to reward his sole surviving son – the nineteen year old Christian II – for his "excellent work" at *Kostel svatého Ducha*, by giving him command over at least part of the Protestant army. Additionally, he and his son both wanted to see Friedrich V, the Elector of the Palatinate and the unofficial *Winterkönig* (Winter King) of Bohemia, fully recognized as Bohemia's official king and given ultimate command over all Bohemian troops.

The fifty year old Christian I was an avowed enemy of the Hapsburgs, a prominent Protestant, and a diplomat of unrivalled ability who used his skills to curry favour with King Henry IV of France and with leading Huguenots, all in an attempt to fracture the Holy Roman Empire. He was also one of the earliest supporters of the young Friedrich V's candidacy for the Bohemian throne. However, he was as unsuccessful when it came to military acumen as he was successful in the field of diplomacy. Specifically, in the best of times he was a battle-field commander of dubious aptitude, and in the worst of times he was known to feign bouts of everything from syphilis to haemorrhoids in order to absent himself from the battlefield.

After *Pilsen* fell, Mansfeld made it his primary base. Meanwhile, as Bucquoy and Dampierre fled southeast to *Budweis*, losing half of their men to disease, exposure, and desertion in the process, von Thurn recklessly pursued them.

Christian I had requested (demanded might be the more apt term) that one third of the army be placed in the hands of his son, Christian II, so that he could pursue Bucquoy and Dampierre. But because Christian I was not well-respected by either von Thurn or von Mansfeld (in fact, they both loathed the man, and the feeling was reciprocal), the two counts had rejected the *request*. Instead, and to the great embarrassment of both Christian II and his father, that task was entrusted to Joachim Andreas von Schlick, *Graf von Passau und Weißkirchen.*

Meanwhile, just as Napoleon would some two-hundred-years later at Waterloo, von Thurn and von Mansfeld foolishly divided their forces. While von Schlick used his portion of the army to pursue Bucquoy and Dampierre, Count von Thurn kept the remainder of his troops under his direct command and marched on Vienna, maintaining the preposterous notion that the war could be won by Christmas. All the while, Count von Mansfeld decided to keep his troops in *Pilsen*, ostensibly to rebuild the city into a Protestant stronghold, when in reality it was his secret aim to convert the entire area into his own personal fiefdom.

In other words, the management of Bohemia's successful start to the war had, as Archduke von Stormsong had cleverly foreseen, already begun to divide into at least two, if not three, different camps.

"Is this really necessary?" Vanessa had asked before the bizarre ritual began.

"Necessary? Not really," one of the Peters had answered honestly. Vanessa had long since given up trying to figure out which one was which.

"But you can be sure it will be entertaining as hell," another Peter had added, prompting laughter among all of the Peters and Kateřina.

Mildly amused by the simplicity of the male brain, Vanessa smiled slightly and asked, "And what if I simply say no?"

All of the assembled Peters looked back and forth at each other in confusion. No one had ever really asked that question before.

"Then you can just stand there while I beat the shit out of you, you pompous little bitch!" Kateřina the massive had barked at her, cracking her knuckles in the process.

And so it began.

While Kateřina's moves were slow and ponderous, Vanessa moved like lightning itself, her movements impossibly quick, smooth, and steady. In fact, she had struck several blows (none of which seemed to faze the female goliath, however) before Kateřina made her first attack. When she did, she allowed Vanessa to come in close for an attempted strike to her rock hard abdomen; then, as she did so, she reached down, grabbing Vanessa by her hair, and pulled her backwards, slamming her to the ground with more force than Vanessa thought was humanly possible. Even dazed, and with the wind knocked clear out of her, Vanessa was able to roll aside before the woman's monstrous foot came crashing down where her head had just been seconds earlier.

But as she attempted to regain her feet, it started all over again.

The light sensitivity, cloudiness in her vision, and nausea that had struck Vanessa so suddenly just outside of *Český Krumlov* had all returned, only much stronger than before. All of those, however, could easily be attributed to the fact that she had just been slammed to the ground with more force than she had ever experienced before.

But the voices were back, too.

And those could not be attributed to….well, anything.

Slow and ponderous as she was, Kateřina had ample time to approach Vanessa, who appeared to be so stunned by the first blow that she was hallucinating, and land an uppercut straight to her chin that simultaneously sent Vanessa sprawling flat on her back and sent the assembled crowd into a chorus of chants, cheers, and a few sympathetic groans. Several of the other Kateřinas, and even a few of the Peters, had been on the receiving end of a strike by Kateřina's massive fists, and no one present had ever seen anyone take one of those blows and stand back up – at least not for several minutes anyway. So it was no surprise when the crowd assumed that the fight – all three minutes of it – was over.

But something drove Vanessa to get back up.

It wasn't stubborn pride, nor a spirit of competition.

It was the voices.

The voices in her head, louder and more familiar than before, were laughing at her. Judging her. Telling her that she wasn't good enough. That a female Stormsong was as useless as tits on a bull. That *the other* might have amounted to something, but it could never be known....now.

Angry at those voices, and determined to prove them wrong, Vanessa staggered slowly to her feet – to the shock and amusement of everyone there.

Everyone but one.

Kateřina was shocked, but not amused. Shaking her head in disbelief, she approached a still wobbly Vanessa and asked, "In addition to being a spoiled, rich little princess, are you also too stupid to know when you've been beaten?" But before Vanessa could answer, Kateřina landed a savage roundhouse kick to Vanessa's left temple, sending her face down in the dirt.

This time, the groans from the crowd were mixed with a few well-intentioned exhortations for Vanessa to stay down. But Vanessa couldn't hear those voices. She could only hear the ones in her head that were telling her what a disappointment it was that she hadn't been born a boy. As if having a penis meant anything more than being able to pee standing up rather than sitting down. *Why did it matter so much?* she asked herself.

As she was trying to suss out the answer, Vanessa reflexively, mechanically pushed herself back up onto her hands and knees. Fighting two equally dangerous battles, one in her head and one on the ground, Vanessa was barely aware that she had stood up again. It wasn't until Kateřina snatched her up into a violent bearhug and started squeezing the air from her lungs that she even realised she was still conscious.

But as arms as thick and powerful as her thighs began to exert tremendous pressure on her back and sternum, forcing the air from her lungs and making it feel as if her back bones were splitting into pieces, Vanessa suddenly became very aware....violenty aware of what was happening. Certain that at least one of her ribs had already broken, perhaps puncturing some vital organ, Vanessa felt a searing, white hot pain burn through her – almost as if lightning itself were running up and down her spine.

But it wasn't the pain. It wasn't even the fact that Kateřina was laughing while she squeezed the very life from Vanessa's body.

It was the voices. Voices that had, at first, seemed insignificant, like the sound of a swarm of bees in the distance, but which had grown louder, more distinct, and more familiar.

It wasn't Kateřina's impossibly strong grip that was making her feel as if her flesh was being slowly torn away from her bones. It wasn't the pain that made her feel as if her very soul was being stripped away from her body. It was those damned voices.

Judging her.

Laughing at her.

As more and more of the onlookers called out to Kateřina to release her, Vanessa began to scream a painful and tortured scream. It was silent at first, but then it suddenly exploded out of her. Her tongue felt like it was going to swell and burst. Her eyes like they would rupture and her very flesh felt as if it was erupting with fire.

As she screamed, the air suddenly became heavy and bitter and the raucous crowd stopped cheering and chanting. In fact, they stopped making any noise at all, for something was happening. Those closest to Vanessa could no longer just see and hear her, but as she continued her caterwauling, they could actually *feel* her presence all around them. It was as if Vanessa's primal screams had become a part of each of them, and each of them a part of her, and all of them a part of the air itself – which grew heavier and harsher by the second.

And then Vanessa screamed something in Latin. *"Quid gloriaris in malicia qui potens est in iniquitate?"* But none of the assembled Peters or Kateřina's knew what that meant, nor did they know to whom she was shouting, for it seemed like the question, screamed out like a curse, was intended for someone other than those present.

As her screams grew louder and sharper, and as the sky grew darker and heavier, Vanessa appeared to those assembled both wild and controlled. She was unimaginably beautiful….almost majestic, and yet primal….almost feral at the same time.

And then, as her screams reached a tortured crescendo, some-thing….just…. split. Those who witnessed it would later be unable to describe it any other way. Something had just split. It was as if the air itself had broken into two pieces.

And when it did, Vanessa was left alone. Having been dropped by Kateřina, Vanessa simply fell to her knees and toppled over.

But Kateřina….

Kateřina was gone.

All that was left of her was mist and memory.

Chapter Fifty Eight

———— ❧ ———— ≈≈ ————

Ferdinand of Styria was a tall, pleasant looking man who, in the presence of others, appeared to be both kind and generous. Having enjoyed a prestigious education at *die Jesuitenkolleg Ingolstadt* in Bavaria, where he studied science, theology, law, medicine, and the humanities, Ferdinand was bright, friendly, and cheerful – always exhibiting courteous manners and finely cultivated skills of conversation.

In matters of faith, however, he was neither kind nor generous, neither friendly nor cheerful. On the contrary, where his Catholicism was concerned, he was absolutely uncompromising and intolerant, spending most of his day either in prayer or at mass. While his religious fervour did not prevent him from devoting time to his two great hobbies, music and his horses, he often felt, and publicly stated that, the current emperor was weak and needed to be more resolute and vigorous in his persecution of Protestants and eradication of the so-called reformed religion.

With his fair skin, thin frame, auburn hair, and long nose, this forty-year-old father of seven could not have cut a more contrasting figure with the short, bald, and rotund Bishop Riphaen who stood at his right hand. Standing at his left was Lord Ernst Gundrham and his bastard son Rowland, and together these four stood as the only barrier between Gottfried Heinrich von Pappenheim's regiment of five-hundred cuirassiers and the main gates of *Schloß Stormsong*.

"What is this?" von Pappenheim asked of his second in command, Friedrich Georg Nehring.

"I'm afraid I don't know, my Lord," Nehring answered honestly. "The archduke should not have known of our coming. Certainly not enough to have sent someone to meet us upon our arrival."

Immediately suspicious, von Pappenheim jogged his horse out from the rest of his troops and took up a position of authority in front of them. *"Ich bin der Graf von Pappenheim*, and I have been sent here by...."

"We all know who you are, Count von Pappenheim," Ferdinand interrupted, but choosing to refer to the Count with proper title and respect. "And we all know why you are here."

Feeling very unsure of himself, von Pappenheim turned back around to face his men, hoping that someone....Nehring or anyone else, for that matter....could suggest what was to come next. But before he received any counsel from his men, Ferdinand spoke again.

"What's more, I know who has sent you. That is why Bishop Riphaen, Lord Gundrham, and Captain Gundrham have joined me in meeting you here. I was told that you are all men of faith, serious and sincere, and thus have I chosen to treat you as such."

Von Pappenheim, clearly unhappy at having been interrupted by someone who was professing how much respect he had for him and his men, turned back to look at Nehring a second time, but his lieutenant, equally confused, just shrugged his shoulders.

When von Pappenheim turned back around, Ferdinand had stepped out from the group of four and began speaking directly to the assembly of cuirassiers. "I am Ferdinand of Styria, King of Bohemia and Hungary, and I commend you men for your steadfast service to *your* emperor."

Von Pappenheim and Nehring couldn't help but notice that Ferdinand had said *your* emperor rather than our emperor, but neither felt confident enough to interrupt him.

"However, much has happened since you first left Vienna," he continued. "And you deserve to know the truth before you take your next action."

Ferdinand then paused dramatically, and as Bishop Riphaen nodded in support of what had just been said, von Pappenheim and Nehring both shifted uncomfortably in their saddles.

"Not two days ago, as a result of his woeful neglect of his realm and for his criminal negligence in dealing with the base and ignoble forces of heresy within his own kingdom, our emperor.... *your* emperor....was declared excommunicate and anathema by His Holiness Pope Paul V." Ferdinand was lying, of course, but because he had told the lie with such sincerity and certitude, and because the three men behind him had made no move to contradict him, he had managed to do so quite persuasively.

"Having justly received the reproach of our Lord and Saviour, Jesus Christ, Matthias then did the one honourable thing he has done during his entire six and a half year reign....he died."

An audible gasp rippled through the crowd of five-hundred men.

"Sadly, it is true," Bishop Riphaen confirmed falsely. "His Imperial Highness, Emperor Matthias....is dead."

Ferdinand allowed some time for a second wave of murmuring to subside before he resumed. "As you know....sadly, as we all know far too well....the emperor was unable to consummate his marriage with Empress Anna. And she, too, has passed within the past fortnight."

A third round of concerned whispers and murmurs.

"Therefore, there is no heir apparent for the throne. And while I have never aspired to hold the crown myself," Ferdinand lied, "I have been approached by His Holiness, Pope Paul V, and by Archduke von Stormsong to pick up the mantle of leadership."

Another long pause as the assembled men continued an indistinct buzzing.

"And I have accepted."

Total silence now.

"As many of you are aware, before I left I my hometown of Graz to pursue my education, I adopted as my personal motto those words of the Apostle Paul in his second epistle to Timothy: *Zu denen, die gerecht kämpfen, geht die Krone* (To those who fight justly goes the crown). Now, twenty-eight years later, I stand before you....no longer just Ferdinand of Styria, King of Bohemia and Hungary.... but as Ferdinand II, Holy Roman Emperor. And I intend to make those words of Paul's my official royal policy. I shall do what our previous emperor could not or would not do. I shall fight. I shall fight justly, of course, but I shall zealously take the fight to the enemies of our true Lord, and I will restore the Catholic Church as the only religion in the empire, and I will wipe out any form of religious dissent!"

The word *any* hung heavily and ominously over the assembled men.

"So, as you prepare to enter *Schloß Stormsong*, eager to fulfil your solemn pledge to a dead, excommunicated, *former* emperor, I pray you consider whether you enter as a friend of the Archduke, as a loyal subject of the new emperor, and as a follower of our Lord Jesus Christ....."

From several hundred feet above, the archduke looked down on his hand chosen successor to the throne and smiled. *Wait one beat*, he thought to himself.

"Or do you enter....as a foe? A foe to the crown. A foe to the Holy See. And a foe to the Lord our God?"

Perfect, von Stormsong thought to himself. *Just perfect. I've chosen the next emperor quite well.*

As if he could read the Archduke's thoughts, Pappenheim's second in command, Friedrich Georg Nehring, dismounted, knelt, raised his sword, and yelled, *"Alle hagel den Kaiser!"*

As the archduke looked down, contemplating how best to use his newly acquired regiment of cuirassiers, he smiled, for five-hundred other men had chosen to do the same as Nehring. As one, each had dismounted, taken a knee, and lifted their swords chanting *"Alle hagel den Kaiser!"*

And while von Pappenheim was slow to do so, eventually he, too, took a knee before the man he falsely believed to be his new emperor.

442

Šarlatová did not know that Empress Anna was near death. Nor did she know that Emperor Matthias, who had himself taken permanently to bed, had just been supplanted by his own cousin. Nor did she know that Archduke von Stormsong was no longer in Vienna, having returned to Prague some weeks earlier.

She didn't know. And, frankly, she wouldn't have cared anyway.

But she did know that the demented battle cries of soldiers and civilians, combined with the agonised screams of horses, women, and children, dying with their limbs severed or intestines spilled had made the battlefield at *Pilsen* sound like Dante's seventh circle of hell.

And she knew that the killing she had witnessed there was so casual, the atrocities so utterly unspeakable, that it was difficult to believe such human cruelty was possible.

She knew that the land in and around Pilsen had been littered with the dead and dying. And she knew that, so long as men like the Emperor Matthias and Archduke von Stormsong and Count von Thurn and Friedrich V still lived, nothing would ever change.

But she had been blessed, or cursed, with the ability to do something about it.

She could make it stop.

She could, almost single-handedly, bring peace to the empire.

And if she really could do these amazing things, then didn't she have a responsibility....a moral obligation....to do so?

And so it was with steadfast resolve that she led her three companions on a slow march to Vienna, with the intention of finding some of these men – men on both sides of the war who cared nothing about anyone or anything other than themselves. And upon finding them, she would end them.

As the foursome camped each night on the long road from *Pilsen* to Vienna, Šarlatová would eat in silence with the others, but then move away from the rest of the group before laying her head down for a few hours of fitful sleep.

Most nights, the others chose to leave her alone. They could all sense that something had changed, that this once lively and carefree girl had been transformed by what they had all seen in *Pilsen*. Occasionally, however, either Roan or Zahara would try to approach her after the others had fallen asleep, but Šarlatová could always hear them coming and feigned sleep until they went away.

Tonight, however, was different. Something was buzzing around in Šarlatová's head that wouldn't allow her even the cursory night-time naps to which she had grown accustomed. So she was wide awake and sitting up when Zahara silently approached.

For several long minutes, the two sat silently side by side. Neither spoke, but they held hands as they faced west, watching the last pink and gold rays of the dying sun slip below the horizon. Then, apropos of nothing, Zahara said, "Allah has given you a great gift, Šarlatová. Do you intend to use it now for murder?"

Šarlatová didn't say anything for several long seconds. When she did, it sounded much more confident and certain than she actually felt. "God has given me many things, Zahara. But I'm not sure that my….*gift* comes from Him. Nothing that dark could come from Him."

Zahara attempted to respond, but Šarlatová cut her off before she could. "And one thing he hasn't given me, is a spirit of fear. I know now what must be done, and I am not afraid."

"No one is questioning your courage, *Sadika*. But the things you intend to do…."

"Zahara….you know as well as I do that this world is not what He intended. The things that go on in this broken world….are simply not of Him."

Zahara hesitated a moment before responding; however, before she could, Šarlatová once again interrupted. "Do you know what *marriage by force* is? That's what they call it. *Marriage by force.*

I was *married by force* the first time at the age of twelve. Twelve. When I should have still been home playing with dolls, I was...."

Šarlatová's voice caught in her throat, and Zahara moved to place her arms around her, but she was cut off once more.

"And afterwards, I was so terrified that I might be pregnant. That I might be forced to bring some monster's....spawn into this world." Šarlatová paused just long enough to wipe a solitary tear from her cheek before turning to face her friend. "And the irony of it is, now that I am old enough....I can't. I can't ever have children, Zahara. I have been violated so often, by so many men....men of power....righteous holy men....that I can no longer have children myself."

"How do you know that?" Zahara asked. But Šarlatová simply responded with a look of desolation that seemed to say, *I know.*

Zahara squeezed Šarlatová's hand just a little tighter, expressing without words exactly what she needed to hear.

"But if I could have children....if I could have a little boy or girl all my own....this is not the world I would want him....or her.... to live in. There is nothing clean, or just, or whole, or pure in this world. There's no fairness, no balance. But I have been given the power to do something about that, and if I can bring just a hint of God's divine justice to this fallen, broken world...."

This time it was Zahara who interrupted Šarlatová. "How can murder ever be called justice? What could possibly be considered fair or just with regard to....killing the killers?"

Šarlatová shrugged her shoulders and turned away from her friend. "It's not my justice. It's God's."

"Oh....well, then, if it is God's justice, then let God tend to it. He's certainly a more than capable assassin."

Šarlatová laughed lightly. "Be careful, Zahara. That's blasphemy!" she joked.

Zahara grabbed Šarlatová's shoulders and physically turned her so that the two were facing each other again. "I'm not joking! And it's not blasphemy; it's history. You claim to love the Bible of your

Lord so much. Perhaps you should actually read it once in a while, *Sadika*. The Quran....the Bible....the Torah....they all say the same thing. Vengeance belongs only to Allah....only to God. It is up to Him, not to us, to deliver divine justice."

Šarlatová looked ready to interrupt again, but Zahara held up a finger indicating that she was to be silent. "I am not finished. No matter how deeply we desire to witness the sufferings of our enemies, we simply do not get to do so. Chapter forty-two, verse forty of the Quran says: *And the recompense of evil is punishment like it, but whoever forgives and amends, he shall have his reward from Allah; for surely Allah does not love the unjust.* I know that you know that, Šarlatová. That's what you learned at *Pilsen*. That's why you're on this....this crusade in the first place. You saw what was done to your enemies, and something in you broke, *Sadika*. So now, to make that part of you whole again, you would do what? Murder both your friends and your enemies?"

Šarlatová was furious. "So....what....I'm supposed to pardon and seek to reconcile with my enemies? Is that what you're telling me?"

"Yes, *Sadika*!" Zahara practically shouted. "Colossians, chapter three, verse thirteen says, *As the Lord has forgiven you, so you must also forgive.* Ephesians, chapter four, verse thirty-two says, *Be kind to one another, tenderhearted, forgiving one another, as God in Christ forgave you.* Shall I go on?"

"Can you?" Šarlatová asked defensively, her stubborn pride affronted by the fact that Zahara, an African Muslim, knew the Bible better than she did. *And just how does a slave become so wise and learned about Holy Scripture anyway?* she thought to herself.

Zahara paused and lowered her voice to barely a whisper. "Yes, I can, *Sadika*. What's more, you know that I can. I haven't told you anything that you didn't already know, my friend. You are the noblest person I have ever met. That is why I call you *Sadika*. It is a name in my country that means honest and sincere. But if you do this.... If you kill these men.... Then I'm afraid of what will become of you. In a million lifetimes you will not be able to undo what it is that you intend to do to these men."

Šarlatová was beaten. She knew that Zahara's arguments were correct....legally, morally, liturgically, ethically....even logically. But she just didn't care. On some deep-seated, visceral level, none of that mattered anymore. Legality, morality, Scripture, ethics, logic. All of that failed in light of what had been done to her as a child, and what had been taken away from her. And none of that squared with the horrors she had seen at Torben's Tree and most recently at *Pilsen*. Some part of her had been seriously damaged by those experiences, and she knew that that part of her would remain broken until she at least tried to restore some balance to the world.

But knowing now that her plan couldn't play out so long as she was watched over by Roan and Zahara....and, to a lesser extent, even Franz, she came to the realisation that she was going to have to take the rest of this journey on her own.

Expertly feigning acquiescence, as only a skilled and practised thief could, Šarlatová smiled at Zahara and hugged her tightly. "Yes....of course, you're right. And thank you. But I think I need some time alone now....time to pray, if you don't mind."

In return, Zahara smiled knowingly and hugged her back in a way that communicated that, at least on some level, she knew precisely what Šarlatová was thinking. *"Allah yuftah alaik,"* she said and kissed her lightly on each cheek, in a way that was both far more and far less than what Šarlatová wanted from her at that moment. With that, Zahara took her leave of Šarlatová, sensing that she would be very unlikely to see this remarkable woman ever again.

True to her word, Šarlatová did, in fact, pray. But rather than speaking to God directly, as was her custom, she instead closed her eyes and tried to visualise the words from chapter three of the book of Micah. Reciting four verses from memory, at least as best as she could recall them, she prayed, *"O ye princes, is it not for you to know judgement? Ye who hate the good, and love the evil; who pluck off their skin from them, and their flesh from off their bones; ye who also eat the flesh of His people, and flay their skin from off of them; and they who break their bones, and chop them in pieces, as for the pot, and as flesh within the cauldron. They shall cry unto the Lord, but He will not hear them; He will even hide His face from them at that time, as they have behaved themselves ill in their doings."*

Then she opened her eyes. "Heavenly Father, that time has come. I pray now that You hide Your face from these evil men, and that You fill me with Your power and Your spirit so that I might bring Your judgement to these wicked men."

Finally, hanging her head in a combination of resignation and penitence for what she was about to do, she thought to herself, *You've warned them so many times, Lord. And they've never listened. Well the time for listening is over. And I'm coming for them now, Lord. I'm coming for them all!*

Chapter Fifty Nine

Stephen knew that it was time to go, and this time he had no intention of stopping.

Not for anyone, nor for anything.

The unfortunate incident at *Leutkirch im Allgäu* had reinstilled a sense of haste within him, and neither he nor Kimber concerned themselves any longer with who or what might be behind them. All that mattered now was the road ahead, the road to Prague. However, after having traversed another thirty-five miles after having left *Leutkirch im Allgäu*, even the born-again- swift Kimber needed to rest.

So Stephen decided to stop for a few hours at *Mindelheim*, a Swabian town on *der Fluss Mindel* (the Mindel river) about fifty-five miles west of Munich. While no one was certain when *Mindelheim* had first been founded, it had been elevated to the status of Stadt (town) in the middle of the thirteenth century; however, as an unfortunate byproduct of Europe's on-going "Wars of Religion," it had been occupied militarily by Maximilian I (the Duke of Bavaria and the founder of the Catholic League) just two years ago.

The most renowned building in *Mindelheim* was *die Kirche Maria Verkündigung* (St. Mary's Church of the Annunciation). Famous because the Mindel river ran directly beneath the church's sacristy and chancel, the Gothic structure stood at the western end of *Mindelheim*, just in front of the town's *Unter Tor* (lower gate).

The church, which Martin Luther is said to have visited and preached from in 1518, had been founded as an Augustinian monastery in the middle of the thirteenth century, and remained one until the sixteenth century, when the Augustinian monks living there began to convert to Lutheranism. As punishment for this theological treachery, *die Kirche Maria Verkündigung* lost its status as a monastery in 1526, and had lain empty ever since. But in June of 1618, Duke Maximilian I had handed the vacant and dilapidated building over to the Jesuits, and ever since, a vigorous renovation program, which was expected to be completed by the end of the following year, had seen the west and north walls of the nave demolished and rebuilt, the six choir windows enlarged, and the stuccoed vaults and walls repaired.

Seventeenth century church renovations were usually raucous and dirty occasions, and the restoration of d*ie Kirche Maria Verkündigung* was no exception, offering passersby a veritable cacophony of construction clatter and dust clouds. Attracted by the loud and busy work on the south wall and nave roof truss, Stephen directed Kimber over towards the decrepit front entrance of the church to better survey the scene. Amidst the various roofers, stone masons, and other skilled labourers working on the reconstruction was a relatively young and unusual looking worker who appeared to be sitting all by himself.

He was a slender but sinewy man with extremely dark brown hair and long limbs. He looked to be only a few years older than Stephen and had swarthy, weatherbeaten features that probably came from a lifetime of working outdoors. He had been somewhat stooped over, seeming to be scratching at the dirt with hands that seemed somewhat too delicate for a carpenter or a mason. But when Stephen dismounted Kimber, the man looked up from whatever it was that he had been drawing in the dirt and waved at him, almost as if he had been expecting Stephen all day.

As Stephen drew closer, the man looked up and greeted him with a smile. "Could you please help me with something?" he asked, his blue-grey eyes catching and reflecting the golden rays of the early evening sun.

"Yes, of course," Stephen answered politely. "If I can. What is it?"

"Well," the anonymous worker said, standing and stretching his long and lean frame. "I find myself in the middle of an argument with one of the stonemasons here, and I was wondering if you might help me with it."

"Yes, of course," Stephen said again. "If I can be of any assistance. With which stonemason are you disagreeing?"

"I'm sure you don't know him," the exceedingly pleasant man responded. "And it doesn't matter anyway, because I'm quite sure he's wrong."

Stephen smiled somewhat uncomfortably and waited for more from the man.

"So, we've been hard at work rebuilding this church, and this stonemason and I got into.... well, a bit of a contest."

"What sort of contest?" Stephen inquired.

"A contest of biblical proportions," the man said, laughing at his own joke. Only when it was clear that Stephen didn't comprehend his meaning did the man continue. "So, this man claims that he has committed the entire book of Jeremiah to memory, and I challenged him on that. Well, it appears that he's actually quite close to being correct. However, I am fairly certain that he misquoted part of it, and....since a lunch of lamb and mutton *Sauerbraten* hangs in the balance....."

"Say no more," Stephen said politely. "I just happen to carry a copy of the Bible with me wherever I go, so we can simply check to see if he is right or wrong as to the verse in question."

"Ausgezeichnet!" the man said, clapping Stephen on the back. "How opportune is it that the first person I approach happens to be carrying a Bible with him? God has really smiled on me today. I should seriously think about doing that myself. How long have you been doing it?"

Growing just a little uneasy with how curious the man had suddenly become, and further unnerved by his unusually penetrating gaze, Stephen simply produced the Bible from Kimber's saddlebags and asked, "Which is the passage from Jeremiah in question?"

In a silvery voice, the man said, "Chapter forty-two, verse three."

"Oh – well....that's easy. We don't need a Bible for that," Stephen said proudly. "That's one of my favourite verses. It reads, *That the Lord thy God may show us the way wherein we may walk, and the thing that we may do.* In other words, it's directing us to pray to God who will tell us where we should go and what we should do."

The man smiled. "No, I'm afraid that's Psalm twenty-five, verse four."

Now it was Stephen who smiled. "No....and now I'm afraid that you're going to lose this contest. Verse four of Psalm twenty-five says, *Show me thy ways, O Lord; teach me thy paths.* Which means...."

"Show me the right path, God. Point out the road for me to fol-low," the man interrupted. "Yes, I think you're right. Well, you had the look of an educated man, so I had a feeling you'd be familiar with the New Testament."

"But Psalms, like the book of Jeremiah, is a book from the Old Testament," Stephen said, correcting the pleasant man.

"Of course. Yes....they are. Once again you're quite correct. Thank you so much, my new friend, you have been most helpful."

Feeling somewhat disquieted by this bizarre conversation with this unusual man, Stephen turned away and started back towards Kimber when the man said, "Oh – just one more thing, Stephen. Have you ever noticed how many passages in the Bible talk about God showing us the right path, or leading us the right way? I've always felt very comforted by that. No matter where we are or what we're doing, like a patient father, he's always there to guide us. That's sort of reassuring, don't you think?"

Stephen just nodded and smiled, took Kimber by her lead rope and started walking her in the other direction. They had only gone a few steps when Stephen suddenly realised that he hadn't introduced himself to the polite man who had somehow known his name. Turning abruptly, Stephen asked, "How did you….."

But there was simply no one there.

Vanessa knew that it was time to go.

Even before *der Orden der fünf-blutige Rose* had demanded that she leave, she was prepared to go. She was so shocked by what she had wrought, that she was incapable of words. What she had done to Kateřina was….was simply indescribable. Nothing she had ever done….in fact, nothing that had ever been done to her could compare to….whatever it was that she had done.

From where had all of that power come? she wondered. *Was it hate? Rage? And if so, why had it….whatever it was….never happened before?*

With all that she had been forced to do by her father, and with all that he had allowed Monsignor Mučitel to do to her, she had never experienced anything like that before. In fact, the only time she'd seen anything that powerful or that dark before had been when….

That's it! she thought suddenly. *The red witch. What she had done at Torben's Tree had looked and felt just like that. It had defied all belief and description, and the execution scaffold had been reduced to a smouldering pile of rubble just as Kateřina….*

No, she thought to herself. *Don't complete that thought. It's too terrible.*

But the power that the red witch had shown was….overwhelming, Vanessa thought. *And if she was capable of that, then she was certainly capable of casting some sort of spell over Vanessa, meaning that she might be responsible for the voices in her head. That was it. It made perfect sense. In fact, it was the only possible explanation – for everything. It was the red witch.*

That's why I've had such a nagging sense of familiarity with her, Vanessa realised. *It must be a result of her having charmed me or* bewitched me in some way. Perhaps she'd done it as a response to my having wounded her at the battle on the shores of the Danube.

A dizzying cocktail of realisation, anger, and vengeance coursed through Vanessa's veins. But now was not the time to resume her search for that sorceress. At least for the moment, her thirst for answers and explanations would have to remain secondary to the plight of the poor people in *Josefov* and *Rosenberg an der Moldau*. For now, in order to fulfil her promises to Rabbi ben Mordecai and to all of the remaining Rosenberg loyalists, she had to complete the remainder of her journey.

For now, she had to reach Vienna.

Šarlatová knew that it was time to go.

Placing her faith in her own resourcefulness, she wrapped herself in the white *Jump Mieder* that she had taken from the ruins at *Pilsen* and slipped silently away from her friends in the dead of night.

That bodice, a sad reminder of the tragedy she had witnessed at *Pilsen*, cast nicely against the light snow that had begun that night and gave her ample camouflage as she resumed her journey towards Vienna. Provided, of course, that neither the blood stains at the bottom of the garment nor the crunch of her boots in the new fallen snow announced her presence to anyone who might be looking for her, she should be able to remain undiscovered the rest of the way.

She was only days away from Vienna, and death was on her mind.

When she slept, she alternated (depending on whether or not it was snowing) between the white bodice and her dark green cloak to provide her with cover and camouflage. During the day, she picked her way slowly through the steep countryside, often cloaked in white, repeating to herself again and again part of a verse from the Book of Revelation: *The one who is victorious will, like them, be dressed in white.*

While she suffered no illusions about being sent by God to fore-warn the pagan people of the some ancient Persian city about the second coming of the Lord, Šarlatová did feel very much like a white-clad avenging angel, and she kept reciting to herself another passage from Revelation: *And I looked, and before me was a pale horse, and his name that sat on him was Death, and Hell was follow-ing with him. And power was given unto them over the fourth part of the earth, to kill with sword....*

But that was as far into the verse as she ever got. She always stopped at that point thinking to herself, *I have the sword, I'm dressed in white, and I'm bringing Hell and Death with me.... but what I wouldn't give for a pale horse right now.*

Then, as if God had heard her prayer, she came upon a small fishing village on the outskirts of *Vodňany*, which was known as *Wodnian* to the local Germans, many of whom made their living fishing for the variety of carp found in the ponds in and around the small Bohemian town.

Residents from a small cluster of five houses on the western edge of *Záhorský Rybník* (Záhorský Pond) were gathered around what appeared to be an Imperial tax-collector, arguing about how much was due this week.

Standing next to a Bohemian royal oak tree, but not properly tied off, was a pale grey Lippizaner that, based on the Hapsburg brand on its hindquarters, almost certainly belonged to the Imperial tax-collector. The powerful horse stood around fifteen hands high and had a sturdy yet arched neck and a long head with a straight profile. The beautiful animal had a deep jaw, small ears, and a wide, deep chest. Its broad croup sported a well-set, white tail, and its well- muscled and strong legs ended with small but tough feet. Displaying a sense of boredom with the escalating conflict over money, the horse began to wander away from the dispute, but when its expressive and intel-ligent blue eyes met Šarlatová's, the horse was enthralled.

The Lippizaner cantered quietly and elegantly towards Šarlatová who could not believe her luck. Keeping a careful eye on the fishermen as they argued with the tax-collector, she leaned into the horse and very softly sang into its small left ear, *"καὶ σὺ λέγεις πρὸς μέ κτῆσαι σεαυτῷ τὸν ἀγρὸν ἀργυρίου· καὶ ἔγραψα βιβλίον καὶ ἐσφραγισάμην, καὶ ἐπεμαρτυράμην μάρτυρας, καὶ ἡ πόλις ἐδόθη εἰς χεῖρας χαλδαίων."* And just like that, the powerful and well-balanced horse was hers.

After calmly and quietly mounting the Lippizaner, Šarlatová directed it away from the edge of the pond and started southeast. By the time the tax-collector realised that he had been robbed, Šarlatová was five miles closer to Vienna.

Rattled by the sudden disappearance of the kind man with whom he'd been speaking just a moment ago, Stephen returned to *die Kirche Maria Verkündigung* and looked around. Unable to find the man, he looked at Kimber who stared back with an expression that seemed to say, *Don't ask me. I don't know what happened to him either.*

Stephen then proceeded to call out to the masons working on the south wall. One of them, a wispy, dour little man with a manner so phlegmatic that Stephen wondered if he was more stone than stonemason, patiently put down his tools and slowly approached.

"Yes, my lord. How can I be of service to you?" he asked placidly.

"I was just speaking with a man....maybe a carpenter....at least I think he was a carpenter. Anyway, I was speaking with him....I don't know his name, however. We were speaking about the Bible....the book of Jeremiah, specifically...

The mason looked at Stephen as if he had two heads. "My lord? You were speaking to a *maybe carpenter*, whose name you don't know, and you were talking about the Bible?" he said calmly. "Are you okay, my lord? Have you been in your cups a little? Or are you just having a bit of fun with me, because I actually have quite a lot of work to get to."

"No….I'm fine. I'm just….well, he was right here a second ago and…."

"But there's no one here now though. Can I be of some service to you, my lord?"

"No…it's just that…no, I suppose not. It's fine. Thank you."

The still unruffled mason simply shrugged his shoulders and turned and started to go back to work. But even though he was a complete stranger, one he would probably never see again, Stephen didn't want the man to simply walk away with the impression that he was a complete idiot, so he tried again.

"It's just that we were talking about paths," he called out, causing the equable man to turn back around. "Paths that the Lord…. never mind. It's unimportant."

Feeling somewhat bad for the obviously troubled knight, the mason decided to play along. "Paths, you say? Well….I'll tell you a path, my lord. *Der Fluss Mindel* runs right beneath this very church. That's right. Starts down in *Kaufbeuren*, that's my home town, just a few miles south of here, my Lord. Then it flows north until it runs into the Danube. From there, it makes its way southeast all the way to Vienna. Actually goes much further than that I think, but that's a path for you. From right where you're standing now, all the way to Vienna."

"But I'm not heading to Vienna," Stephen offered, somewhat confused. "I'm trying to reach *Schloß Stormsong,* in Prague."

"Not anymore," the mason said. Later on, Stephen wouldn't be as certain, but at least for the moment, he was sure that both the timbre and tone of the man's voice changed dramatically when he said, "May God bless you on the road to Vienna, *Stephen*." Then, just like that, the impassive mason nonchalantly turned around and went straight back to work, leaving Sir Stephen and Kimber to stare at each other once again.

"That's good enough for me," Stephen said, knowing that they would no longer be travelling hundreds of miles northeast to *Schloß Stormsong*, but would be travelling due east to Vienna, instead. He immediately remounted Kimber and set her off to a full gallop, offering a brief prayer from chapter three of the book of Proverbs: *Trust in the Lord with all thine heart, and lean not unto thine own understanding. In all thy ways acknowledge Him, and He shall direct thy paths.*

Very well, Lord, I'm leaning into You right now, Stephen thought. *Show me the path.*

And just like that, they were on the road to Vienna.

Chapter Sixty

Stephen was exhausted.

But Kimber was possessed.

No matter how much he exhorted her to stop, or at least to slow down, Stephen could not get Kimber to ease up. In a complete reversal of her earlier sloth-like approach to getting to *Lindau*, Kimber now ran as if the devil himself was right behind her. Whereas it was once all he could do to get her to trot, now it was all he could do to slow her from a full on gallop. And when Stephen did, finally, get Kimber to pause long enough to eat and drink, she seemed to be chomping at the bit again within a matter of minutes.

"You really are an incorrigible bitch, aren't you?" Stephen asked. "What happened to the stubbornly lazy horse that brought me here? Now you're going to end up killing yourself, or killing me, in your haste to get to Vienna. Why can't you just settle on a nice and steady canter?"

Stephen was certain that the look the horse gave him was meant to communicate something like, *Are you done whining now? Because I'm ready to go.*

"Okay, fine. Have it your way," Stephen said after watering her for just a few minutes. "But at this rate, the next two days will either find us in Vienna....or in our graves."

Joachim Andreas von Schlick, *Graf von Passau und Weißkirchen*, was a wealthy and well- credentialed man who came from a rich and noble family. He had studied at *die Universität Jena* and had fought for Emperor Rudolph II during the *Bocskai* rebellion in Hungary in 1605. Later, he served in the army of the Spanish Hapsburgs in both Flanders and Milan and displayed his skills as a talented diplomat while serving at the Saxon Court in Dresden, where he was responsible for educating princes like the young John George I (who would go on to become the Elector of Saxony).

Even as a child himself, he had displayed a serious countenance and a voracious appetite for education and, as an adult, became a consummate negotiator with a tendency to moderate solutions to both political and religious problems, as demonstrated by his role in helping to craft Emperor Rudolph's *Majestätsbrief* (Letter of Majesty). However, as both a Lutheran and a quiet supporter of Bohemian autonomy, he had sided with the Protestants when civil war had broken out after the third Defenestration of Prague, an event for which he had personally been a witness.

Counts von Schlick and von Thurn were rivals and polar opposites. Von Schlick was known to be an honourable, diplomatic, and peace-loving gentleman. But despite being intelligent, brave, and conscientious, he was no military leader. Von Thurn, on the other hand, while not nearly as well-educated as von Schlick, was single-minded, quick in making decisions, and unscrupulous in both thought and action; in short, he was a soldier, not a diplomat. While von Thurn lacked the good will and good humour to be more than a military man, von Schlick lacked the confidence and bravado to be an effective battlefield commander, and while they both fancied themselves the face of the rebellion, neither was immune from criticism.

Many Bohemian nobles viewed von Thurn not as valorous, but as overly ambitious and reckless, while von Schlick's detractors saw him not as being skillfully shrewd so much as they viewed him as weak and indecisive. Unsurprisingly the two clashed numerous times, but despite their equally strong characters, they were astute enough to understand that, at least for the time being, their fortunes were tied together.

Therefore, as von Schlick continued to pursue and harass Marshal Bucquoy, and while von Thurn marched unabated towards Vienna, the two would-be-leaders of the Bohemian rebellion behaved diplomatically enough to ensure that their relationship never spilled over into any sort of counterproductive hostility.

Von Schlick's relentless pursuit of Bucquoy had begun at *Pilsen*. After having captured that vital Catholic city, the Protestant Bohemians had chased the routed imperial army some eighty miles southeast to *Budweis*, a city that had been made wealthy in the sixteenth century by its many silver mines and extremely profitable fish and salt markets. But Budweis had been a repeat, albeit a faster one, of what had happened at *Pilsen*.

Marshal Bucquoy, still operating under the orders of Emperor Matthias, had allowed himself to become trapped there. As at *Pilsen*, the people of *Budweis* had suffered greatly and, by the time Bucquoy had fled another sixty miles southeast to *Krems*, there was scarcely a crust of bread left to eat in the once thriving silver town.

Krems an der Donau, situated at the confluence of two rivers at the picturesque eastern end of *das Wachau Tal* (the Wachau valley), was one of the largest cities in Lower Austria. During the eleventh and twelfth centuries, *Krems an der Donau* (or *Chremis*, as it was called then) was almost as large as Vienna, a city which lay less than fifty miles to the southeast. Perhaps best known for producing *Marillenschnaps* (a popular alcoholic beverage made from apricots), *Krems* was the last major city standing between Vienna and the hard-charging armies of Counts von Thurn and von Schlick.

Whether *Krems* would meet the same wretched fate as both *Pilsen* and *Budweis* would likely be determined within the next few days; however, at least so far, the only thing that had slowed the Protestant advance was the onset of an early and harsh winter. Von Schlick's men, now numbering just under four-thousand, were not properly outfitted for a winter siege; consequently, he aimed to take Krems as quickly as possible. However, just as his troops tightened their grip on the city, so, too, did winter's pale death tighten its grip on them.

As Vanessa reached the outskirts of *Krems*, she saw a number of black shapes on the horizon, swirling back and forth around each other and sweeping, in irregular patterns, up and down the lightly snow-covered hills around the embattled town. At first they had looked insignificant to her, like swarms of black insects drifting across the hills. But as she drew closer to the city, it became clear that they were cavalrymen.

Apparently Bohemian forces had already begun their assault on the city, making for a grisly and awful scene. The cold air around *Krems* was filled with the deafening clang of metal on metal, the sickening crack of metal striking bone, and the appalling sound of blades plunging into the flesh of both men and horses. The fighting, which was rampant both in and around the city, had already left the snowy streets of *Krems*, like the hills surrounding the city, stained by bloody human and animal entrails.

Vanessa sat at a crossroads – both literally and figuratively. On the one hand, she was now less than fifty miles from Vienna. In just one more day, she could reach Emperor Matthias and entreat him to do something about the impoverished peoples she had encountered of late. On the other hand, the flames of the war her father had helped to stoke were burning brightly right in front of her. How could she, in good conscience, simply turn her back on the tragedy playing out in *Krems*? Was it not her obligation as the sole heir to the Stormsong name to help lead the valiant armies of her pope and emperor against these marauding Protestant hordes? Especially when the city's defenders – dirty, freezing, and starving – appeared to be on the verge of defeat or surrender.

In making this decision, her physical health was no longer one of her considerations. As had so often happened in the past, the wounds she had suffered in *Rosenberg an der Moldau* had almost completely healed already. And the voices that had so recently paralysed her had, at least for the moment, gone silent. However, as she observed the brave but badly outnumbered and disorganised defenders of *Krems*, and listened in horror to their blood curdling screams, masculine grunts of effort, and wet, gurgling gasps, she feared that the voices might return, rendering her incapable of providing aid to the besieged Catholics.

Exhaling in resignation, Vanessa drew her sword, offered a silent prayer for *Starke's* safety, and uttered *"Christus vincit, Christus regnat, Christus imperat."*

Then, reluctantly, she urged *Starke* forward.

Less than two hours after Vanessa had joined the battle being waged for control of *Krems*, Šarlatová arrived on the outskirts of the city. She was just as shocked by the brutality of the scene as Vanessa had been, and equally conflicted as to what she should do about it.

There was nothing here that resembled the majesty of the Athurian legends, or the heroic chivalry of fabled outlaws like Robin Hood. Even the exaggerated romance of the Hundred Years' War and the legends surrounding Joan of Arc's legendary exploits during the siege of Orléans failed to capture the grisly picture of real war. There was no chivalry here. No knights in shining armour. No romance or beautiful damsels-in-distress. This was war, and there was nothing *civil* about it.

It was savage and cruel.

And for the second time in as many weeks, Šarlatová was a reluctant and horrified witness to its brutality.

So common sense and all practical considerations seemed to dictate to Šarlatová that she simply ride south around the city, avoid the battle altogether, and travel on to Vienna so that she could proceed with her plan to eliminate the leadership on the Catholic side of this idiotic conflcit. But something deep within her screamed out that she had a responsibility to inject herself into the proceedings here at *Krems*. After all, what was the sense in bypassing the very war to which she was trying to bring an end? Additionally, who knew which of the Catholic imperial leaders were down there directing the defences of the city?

Could Archduke von Stormsong or even the emperor himself be in Krems? she wondered.

Probably not, she surmised. *But it was possible that Count von Thurn or one of the other so- called leaders of this rebellion was down there personally directing the assault.*

Either way, she thought, *It is possible that my best chance to bring an end to the senseless violence of the past year is right here in front of me, rather than in Vienna.*

Ultimately, however, assuming correctly that men like von Thurn or von Stormsong would, like the pope or the emperor, keep themselves as far from the front lines of battle as possible, Šarlatová made the painful decision to bypass the battle for *Krems*. So she directed her stolen Lippizaner, who was clearly skittish from the harsh and discordant mixture of sounds coming from the city and very eager to leave, to canter around towards the southeast. But she had gone no more than a mile when she saw a dozen cuirassiers, bearing the distinctive red and white colours of Bohemia, riding out from the city.

The dragoons had not seen her, but she saw them.

And she saw their intended targets.

A small group of women and children, being led on foot by a plump, bald priest with fleshy jowls and a rumpled cossack, were attempting to slip away from the city unnoticed. However, the slow place that the cold and snow dictated, combined with the fact that the children were very young and moving very slowly, left them ex-posed for far longer than the priest had hoped. Long enough for the detachment of cavalrymen to spot them.

Šarlatová didn't even have time to scream out a warning be-fore the cuirassiers descended violently upon the small band of would-be-escapees.

So stunned was she by how quickly and savagely the cuirassiers had cut through the small band of runaways that Šarlatová didn't notice that two of them had peeled off and had started riding in her direction. Physically ill at the sight of innocent women and children being hacked to pieces, staining the new fallen snow with blood and severed limbs, Šarlatová leaned over the side of her mount and vomited into the snow. While she was getting sick, she was spared from witnessing the butchery of the brave priest who had tried to use his body to shield one of the children from the massacre, but she looked back up just in time to see one of the cuirassiers produce a long-barrelled wheel-lock pistol and aim it in the direction of the small child who was now weeping and laying over the mangled body of the priest who had tried to save him.

The wave of shock and rage that swept over Šarlatová was so strong that she wasn't even consciously aware of the fact that she had opened her mouth to sing. A sharp rush of cold air filled her lungs, and her voice came out as a thin piping sound, significantly outdone by the din of the battle around her. But before her voice could rise in either power or pitch, a pair of lead balls, fired from the weapons of the two cuirassiers who had been riding down on her unnoticed, tore into her mount. The Lippizaner took one shot in his left flank and the other in the pastern of his front right leg, shattering bone and sending the heavy animal straight to the ground.

Miraculously, Šarlatová somehow managed to roll away from the horse as he fell and just barely avoided being pinned underneath him. But she was still dazed and lying breathless on her side when the two cuirassiers who had just shot her horse pulled up. Only because she was so stunned by what had just transpired were the two men able to approach her without being cut down by either her bow or her blade. Under normal circumstances, they would have died while still in their saddles.

But these were not normal circumstances, and the first soldier to dismount struck her so hard across one cheek that, as she fell back down to the ground, she was certain the entire left side of her face had just exploded. Still reeling from this sudden and unprovoked onslaught, Šarlatová struggled to make it back up to one knee when she saw the second cuirassier dismount. He immediately started to undo the flaps of his riding breeches, and the lecherous look on his face, as well as the way he licked his lips in eager anticipation of what was about to happen, told her everything she needed to know.

Just then, her power swelled inside of her.

The very power she had been ashamed of and had tried to repress.

The same power she both loathed and coveted more than anything in the world.

Loathed because of what she knew it could do to her.

Coveted because she knew what she could do with it.

And as that power rose within her, it blazed like a fire, surging through her like hot needles piercing every muscle in her body. As it did, the ghastly images from Torben's tree and *Pilsen* co-mingled with what she had just witnessed and what she had experienced as a child.

And she snapped.

The last thing she remembered before fire and death blazed out from her in all directions, was that she was no longer attempting to sing.

This time was different.

This time….she started to scream.

Having battled for the better part of two hours, Vanessa was completely exhausted. Her back felt like a bag of broken glass and her shoulders burned from the multiple swings of her blade. She had lost count of how many lives she had taken, but she knew precisely how many wounds she had suffered. The stab wound to her sinewy left thigh, the piece of debris sent flying by an artillery explosion that was embedded in her right shoulder, and the broken rib from a savage punch to her midsection had not slowed her down. But now, as mental and physical exhaustion began to set in, the accursed voices returned.

This time, however, the judgmental and stentorian male voices were joined by a girl's....no, a woman's.

But she wasn't just speaking. She was screaming. And as she screamed....

The fiery blast could be seen and heard for miles, and it rocked the entire city of *Krems*. No artillery blast could have made such a rending but organic sound. So unusual and deafening was the blast, and so unsettling was the accompanying electric current that rippled through everyone in or around *Krems*, that the battle literally stopped.

Uncertain as to whether it was an earthquake, some other natural disaster, or perhaps even the hand of God Himself that had just struck *Krems*, combatants on both sides of the skirmish re- treated towards the relative safety of their groups. Von Schlick's invaders, like dogs with their proverbial tails tucked up underneath them, fled the city and retreated back into the surrounding hills. Likewise, the beleaguered Catholic defenders shrank from duty and huddled together in a series of frightened clusters deep within the city's interior.

Only Vanessa stood her ground. With the screaming voice in her head now gone, she looked towards the horizon where a ghastly column of smoke and red mist was rising into the air.

It's her. The red witch is here, she concluded before racing to find *Starke*. Once she had mounted her trusted companion, she rode straight out through the city's shattered gates and sped hard in the direction of the explosion.

She rode undaunted and determined, but knowing full well that her odds of finding answers today were about even with her odds of finding death.

Stephen was still more than twenty miles west of *Krems*, but he heard and felt the blast too. Kimber, earlier so obsessed with getting him to Vienna, pulled up instantly and would simply go no further.

Whatever it was that had just happened had terrified her to the point of paralysis. As far as she was concerned, the road to Vienna would no longer go through *Krems*.

Because they had been attempting to follow Šarlatová on foot, Roan, Franz, and Zahara were still much too far away from *Krems* to either see or hear the massive and frightening explosion.

But Zahara felt it.

A cold and electric shiver coursed through her, causing her to come to a sudden stop. "I've found her, Roan. But I fear we may be too late."

It wasn't very hard for Vanessa to find her.

The stunning red-head was on her knees with her hands folded in her lap as if in prayer, but radiating out from her was a circle of devastation unlike anything Vanessa had ever seen. Even the carnage she had witnessed at Torben's tree, even what she had done herself at *Rosenberg an der Moldau*, paled in comparison to the eerie portrait of devastation in front of her now.

Literally nothing was left but scorched earth. Not a person, not an animal, not even a plant or tree existed anywhere within the burnt circle. Even the snow had been blasted away, leaving the ground flickering in an odd, crimson colour – and at the centre of it all, in an almost ghoulishly serene trance, knelt the red witch.

Vanessa couldn't tell whether the woman was in a trance, or praying to some pagan spirit, or just recovering from whatever it was that she had just done. *Or, perhaps, she's preparing to cast another spell,* Vanessa thought. Not one to take any chances, she dismounted *Starke*, entered the circle of devastation and cautiously approached the witch, unsheathing her blade as she did.

Roused from her stupor by the metallic scraping sound of Vanessa's blade emerging from its sheath, Šarlatová slowly opened her eyes – both of which were completely coated in some kind of pale, milky liquid that ran down her cheeks like tears – and said "Not today, 'Nessa."

"What did you just call me?" Vanessa shouted in an almost child-like rage. As she did, something familiar to Šarlatová, something akin to lightning flashed in Vanessa's gorgeous blue eyes.

And that's when Šarlatová knew for sure that she was right.

From the colour of their hair to the colour of their complexion, these two women bore almost nothing in common in terms of their physical appearance. Both strikingly beautiful in their own way, they could not look less alike.

One was pale, raven-haired and blue-eyed.

The other was dark-skinned, red-haired, and green-eyed.

But none of that mattered right now. Despite the discoloration in her own eyes, Šarlatová could still clearly see Vanessa's. And in those sparkling blue eyes, Šarlatová saw a familiar fierceness. It had been eighteen years since she had last seen those beautiful blue eyes, but as she looked at them now, a flood of memories crashed over her like a tidal wave.

Unsettled by the strange way the witch was staring at her, almost as if she was looking right through her, the only thing Vanessa could think to do was to tighten her grip on her sword. "You put some kind of curse on me," she spat. Then, as she watched the faintest hint of colour return to the red witch's eyes, Vanessa added, "And you will have to pay for that!"

But, as she said it, Vanessa felt a sudden and strange urge to call this woman Marina.

"I've done some truly horrible things in my life, 'Nessa, but I've never done any harm to you," the red witch said calmly.

"Why do you keep saying that?" Vanessa demanded.

"Oh….that's right. I'd forgotten. You always hated that, didn't you? I guess that's why I always did it….just to irritate you, I suppose."

Vanessa just stared back at the mad woman, completely dumbfounded.

"It's been eighteen years, 'Nessa, but those eyes of yours haven't changed one bit."

"What….what are you talking about?" Vanessa asked, her voice breaking.

"You haven't figured it out yet, have you? That's okay, 'Nessa. Neither did I. Not until today. Really not until this very moment. Not until I…."

The strange-eyed woman trailed off for a moment, but before Vanessa could respond to her crazed ramblings, she added, "I should have, but I didn't. Well…."

She trailed off again, and Vanessa was now completely certain that the woman was either demented or preparing to cast yet another spell on her. As Vanessa raised her sword, prepared to strike a killing blow, the woman then asked, "Have you learned to sing yet?"

Her hand stayed, at least for the moment, by such a strange question from an even stranger woman, Vanessa took a step backwards. A million questions came to mind, but none of the words needed to formulate them accompanied the questions.

"I wish it was under different circumstances, 'Nessa. I really do," Šarlatová said. "But even under such odd circumstances as these, it does my heart much good to see you again….*sister*."

Vanessa and Šarlatová will return in….

Storm Surge

Book Two of the *Stormsong* Trilogy

A Final Note From the Author

Despite the tantalising teaser I offered at the beginning of this book (at least, I think it was tantalising; it did get you to read this book, after all), much of what I have written here is not historical fact. In fact, I would hesitate to even call this historical fiction. It's more historical fantasy than anything else.

I had a certain time period about which I wanted to write. I had certain characters in mind whom I wanted to create and develop. And I had a particular story that I wanted to tell. In order to accomplish all of that, I have played it somewhat fast and loose with little details like dates and locations. I have also had characters (many of whom were actual players in the real Thirty Years War) do things, say things, and even live or die all in service to the story I wanted to tell.

Having said that, there is much in this work that is, in fact, well….fact. But please don't put this book down (or pick up the next two parts of the trilogy) thinking that you have an accurate understanding of the intricacies and complexities of the Thirty Years War. Providing you with one was not my goal.

However, if you found this story compelling (and I hope you did), and if you would like to know more about what really happened in the Holy Roman Empire between 1618 and 1648, I strongly recommend *The Thirty Years War* by C.V. Wedgwood and *The Thirty Years War: Europe's Tragedy* by Peter H. Wilson. These two works are serious pieces of scholarship by two brilliant historians, both of whom I admire and respect.

But if reading six- to nine-hundred page history books is not your cup of tea, I hope you will at least consider coming back to the *Stormsong Trilogy* for book two (*Storm Surge*) and book three (as yet untitled).

CPSIA information can be obtained
at www.ICGtesting.com
Printed in the USA
BVHW090801071222
653536BV00002B/10